CASHMERE CRUELTY

GROZA BRATVA
BOOK 1

NICOLE FOX

CASHMERE CRUELTY

GROZA BRATVA DUET BOOK 1

When is the worst time to tell someone he's going to be a father?

Probably the day of the wedding...

When he is getting married to someone else.

Well, that is exactly what I did.

But my hands were tied.

Literally.

Matvey Groza is a dangerous man.

And nine months ago, he strolled into my shop looking for a custom suit.

But when I accidentally walked in on him in the changing room,

I was the one that ended up needing a new set of clothes.

It was a one-time mistake.

After that… good riddance.

But the **pregnancy test** I took a month later had other plans.

I kept it a secret from everyone.

Or so I thought.

But when Matvey's enemies learned that I was pregnant with his child,

They kidnapped me and held me hostage.

Until I broke free and ran as fast as I could.

And I had no one else to turn to but the devil himself.

What better time for me to enter the church…

… than as the pastor says, "Speak now or forever hold your peace"?

CASHMERE CRUELTY is Book 1 of the Groza Bratva Duet. The story continues in Book 2, *CASHMERE RUIN.*

PROLOGUE: APRIL

I burst into the wedding I'm not supposed to be at with my hands still cuffed tight. I sprint halfway up the aisle, look the groom dead in the eye, and blurt out the truth behind this entire nightmare: "I'm pregnant. And it's yours."

The groom doesn't speak.

For one endless moment, no one does.

And, honestly, I can't blame them. I can only imagine what this must look like. What *I* must look like. Between getting kidnapped, escaping by the skin of my teeth, hailing a cab in the thick of Manhattan traffic, and stalking the man in front of me on all social media platforms until I could figure out who and where the hell he was, I didn't exactly get a chance to look in the mirror.

My hair must be a mess. Nothing like the braided work of art sitting on the bride's tilted head.

The rest of me isn't much better. Instead of a delicate gold ring around my finger, I'm sporting a gleaming pair of handcuffs. I've sweated through every piece of clothing currently touching my skin and then some. My voice is breathless and strained, though in my defense, it's been a good few months since I last hit the gym.

Nine months, to be exact.

Which leads me to the most glaringly wrong aspect of my appearance: a humongous, pregnant belly, jutting under my ruined maternity dress like it's trying to make contact with the man responsible for it.

The man who's now staring at me like I just ruined the biggest day of his life.

Which, to be fair, I did.

The silence breaks. The guests start whispering to each other. The whispers quickly grow into a tidal wave of confused static, louder and louder, worse and worse.

I force myself not to glance around the room. Why bother? I saw enough the second I entered. Tall, broad men in black suits and mysterious, gun-shaped bulges under their jackets that tell me how *un*happy they are to see me. Hostile-looking women in cocktail dresses that could easily hide a knife sheath.

I keep my eyes fixed on the groom. It's my one lifeline, my one hope—getting this man to listen. This dark, dangerous man who's looking like he wants nothing more than to summon lightning out of the sky and smite me into a plume of smoke.

But I don't have a choice.

I'm aware I just pulled the trigger on a suicide mission.

Something I can never come back from. But this desperate move, this Hail Mary of mine, is the last play I've got left.

If I'd known, all those months ago, that giving in to temptation with this man would paint a target on my back for the rest of my life, I'd have thought twice.

Maybe.

Or at least, I hope I would have. That those magnetic cerulean eyes wouldn't have made me sign my own death warrant willingly.

I can't know that now, but I know one thing: I never intended for him to find out about this baby.

For nine months, I kept it a secret. Hid it from everyone but my closest friends. Because a part of me knew, *must* have known, that Matvey Groza was not a good man. Not the kind of man you'd tie yourself to for the rest of your life. Certainly not the kind that you'd tie *your child's life* to.

But now, with this man's enemies after me and the precious cargo I'm carrying, my hands are tied.

Literally.

"I'm pregnant," I repeat, "and it's yours."

As I speak, only that one thought presses against the walls of my skull, begging to be let out like a scream. As chaos begins to erupt around me, the crowd's whispers rising to shouts, only one thought crosses my mind.

How the hell did I let this happen?

1

APRIL

NINE MONTHS EARLIER

"Third Chance Tailor Shop, how can I help you?"

Holding the phone between my cheek and shoulder, I sweep through the racks. It's taking me forever to tidy up the approximately one million items of clothing Mrs. Kurt left lying around during her fitting. She must have found them interesting—because she took great care to pull each one off its hanger—and then not so interesting—because she took way less care in leaving them heaped in ragged piles in every corner of the shop.

You can always tell when a customer's an artist. A con artist, in Mrs. Kurt's case, but an artist nonetheless. Being twice widowed and thrice married at the age of twenty-eight is nothing short of impressive, especially when your husbands are old enough to recognize your grandfather from the trenches.

"We absolutely do make custom wedding gowns," I say to the customer on the phone. "Did you have anything specific in mind?"

Trick question: brides-to-be always do. As the customer launches into a detailed explanation of the dress of her dreams—a natural white fishtail model with a pearl-studded Bardot neckline—I finish dismantling Mrs. Kurt's masterpieces, stash everything back where it belongs, and make for the back of the store.

I ask the bride-to-be about her veil. That'll buy me another five minutes to finish boxing up Mr. Boyd's suit for pickup.

I can recognize my boss Elias's handiwork in the stitching, the perfect details that sign a piece as his. At the age of "seventy plus a few," as he puts it, Elias Turner is still the most renowned tailor this side of the East River.

There's so much to do; I feel like my head might explode. I sigh and curse myself for my stubbornness. I could have really used an extra pair of hands around the shop, especially an expert pair like my boss's. But I can't exactly complain— I'm the one who sent him home.

I can handle it, I told him, like a big, lying liar. And Elias, bless his soul, eventually relented and took the afternoon off.

Leaving little old me in charge of the whole shebang, which is precisely what I wanted.

"Mhm. That sounds lovely." I take stock of the work I've got left before closing: patch up Mr. Connor's coat, alter the waistline on Ms. Forrest's skirt, sketch out a pantsuit for Dr. Brown's conference, count the change in the register, fix the lightbulb in the bathroom, and take out the trash before the raccoons wake up. All in an honest day's work.

Like I said: I can handle it.

The door chimes. "Be right with you!" I call out, covering the phone as Ms. Holland finishes explaining the concept behind the corset's elaborate decorations. I give her an appointment for a first fitting, jot down her details, and wish her a happy day.

By the time I make it out the back, the new customer's already tapping his shoe.

Very bad sign.

"About time," the customer growls, clicking his tongue in annoyance. "I was starting to wonder if I'd have to come fetch you myself."

Normally, I'd tell anyone who spoke to me that way to take that sass and stick it where it rhymes. However, in this case, there are two very good reasons why I can't.

The first is that I'm at work. And, in my line of work, you can't just ask the customer to kindly fuck off. You can think it—very hard—but you have to do it with a smile.

So I smile. "My apologies," I say, keeping my middle fingers holstered for the time being. "Is there anything I can help you w…"

The second reason I don't tell him off is that, as soon as he turns, I can no longer form words.

Clear, piercing, cerulean eyes root me to the spot. I've never seen a color like that on a human being—like the surface of a frozen lake. Being on the receiving end of that stare, I feel like I'm standing right in the middle of one. One wrong step, and I'd be plunged into the icy depths below.

Those eyes are *dangerous.*

"With…?"

I shake my head. "Sorry, come again?"

The customer walks up to me. Slowly, like a panther on the prowl. "'With.' Is that the word you were looking for?"

"I—Uh, yes. Sorry. I'm a bit out of sorts today."

"I noticed."

That snide comment immediately brings me back on solid ground. Just who the hell does this guy think he is?

"So what can I help you with?" I say instead, my best smile on display.

The man gives me a long once-over. It makes me feel exposed. Like I couldn't hide if I wanted to. "I need a suit."

I exhale quietly under my breath. Now, *this* I can work with. "What kind of suit did you have in mind?"

"Three pieces, made of fabric. You've heard of those, I assume?"

Deep breaths, April. You need this job. You want *this job.* "Why, yes, I have heard of those. Are we shopping for any occasion in particular?"

The man gives me an odd look. "None that you'd need to make it your business to know about, Ms.…." He tilts his head towards my name tag. "Ms. Flowers."

You need this job, I keep chanting in my head, like a mantra. *If you stab this customer, you'll lose this job. You can't lose this job, April.*

It's the only scrap of your dream you've got left.

"Just formal, then," I settle on, knuckles whitening behind my back. Then I dive into the racks.

Clothes are my kingdom. When my hands are buried in fabrics, I am in my element. I pick out three vintage jackets that look roughly the customer's size, eyeballing the measurements of his broad shoulders, and lay them on the table.

But there's one in particular that I want him to pick; one that I just know would go stunningly with those blue eyes, his black hair, his fair skin. He may be an asshole, but he isn't a bad-looking one. With that thought, I put my pick third.

Most customers will be drawn to the option in the middle. Put a cheap jacket first, a wildly expensive one third, and the costly but fairly-priced vintage one in the middle. Whenever I want to find an old-timey piece a good home, that's how I do it. Most of the time, it works like a charm.

Sometimes, however, a customer will walk in and just smell like money. While we were talking—correction: while he was insulting me and I was trying to remind myself of all the good reasons not to end up in jail at twenty-four—I sized him up just as much as he sized me up. I was just more discreet about it.

I know, for example, that his current suit is Tom Ford; that his watch is the brand-new Rolex they've been advertising nonstop in Times Square; and that his cologne is Dior Sauvage X.

A man like this would never settle for second-best.

The customer approaches the jackets. I begin to describe the first piece: "This is a 2009 Dolce & Gabbana. Midnight blue, stretch wool. Not a limited edition, but still extremely rare to find." He barely glances at it, moving on to the second before I've finished. I pick up the pace. "Versace, 1991. Embroidered black velvet, number 873 of only 1,000 pieces ever produced.

Extravagant, but tastefully so. I would recommend a dove gray shirt underneath—"

"This one."

Bingo. Never fails.

"Ah, yes, the Turner." I pick it up, smoothing out the fabric to show off the colors. "Embroidered silk, anthrax gray with Han blue reflections. A pioneer work: Vuitton would only get there in the late 2010s, with its Oriental collection, but in much brighter hues. However, this piece was hand-sewn in 1983, using antique Chinese textiles for the embroidery. The pigment is 100% original."

I take his hand and run it over the fabric, guiding his fingers over the floral pattern, barely distinguishable from a simple arabesque one. That's Elias's specialty: hiding secret messages in his work.

In this one—the only floral piece in his entire collection—he hid it in the petals: *forget-me-not.*

It was the piece that made me fall in love with this place.

The man's breath hitches. I realize I may have forgotten personal space entirely, taking his hand like that, but what comes out of his mouth is not a reprimand. For once.

"Why would you keep this out here?" he murmurs, something close to awe in his voice. "Where everyone can touch it?"

"Pretty things are made to be touched." At some point—I don't know when or how—his hand took over. Now, it's guiding mine as it moves across the design. "To be used." His skin is warm; I don't know why that surprises me, but it does. I guess I thought that the man with icy eyes would be just as cool to the touch. "Nothing this beautiful should ever be left behind glass."

He looks at me. At my hand, still on his. Belatedly, I realize how wildly inappropriate the air feels suddenly. We're close —when did that happen?

"Would you, um…" I mumble something incoherent and pry my fingers gingerly from his grasp with sheer force of will. "Would you like to browse some mo—"

"I'll try it on."

I blink. "Pardon me?"

"I said I'll try it on." His gaze on me is even, steady, but there's an undercurrent of impatience in his voice that I don't want to test. "Lead the way."

And, God help me, I do.

2

APRIL

Update: the jacket looks *amazing*.

I watch it shine under the changing room's lights, the embroidery perfectly matched to the blue of my customer's eyes, and I feel a tingly burst of pride.

I'm this close to pumping my fist in the air, but I restrain myself. The man has a glare that could melt steel, and I'd love to not feel that heat again quite yet.

Instead, I keep it professional. "So, what do we think?"

"It's a bit loose," the man comments, scrunching up his face in distaste.

"That it is," I agree. "Luckily, it's an easy fix." I walk up to him with my trusty tape measure. "May I?"

He gives me a curt nod.

"Jacket off, please," I tell him, positioning myself behind his back. I help him out of the garment and hang it carefully inside the changing room. Then, tape measure in hand, I mount the stepstool.

But even when I'm elevated, I have to rise up on my tiptoes to reach him.

This man's built like a tree—strong, lean, tall. If I can just reach a little higher, though…

"Should I hunch?" the man drawls.

Dammit. I keep forgetting about the stupid mirror. Has he been watching me struggle all this time? "No need," I reply, still straining on my tiptoes like a ballerina.

I can feel the heat radiating off his body. It definitely isn't helping me sweat any less. Between the freckles and how red my face must be, I probably look like a strawberry right now.

"There," I say with relief. "Done."

"Where's the rest?"

The rest? It takes me a moment to grasp what he means. "Of the suit?"

"Yes," the man replies, that familiar impatience ringing out again. "Unless you were planning to send me out there in nothing but the jacket."

I hastily delete that particular mental image. Not because it's unpleasant—far from it, actually. That's the problem.

I won't be *that* tailor. I won't ogle my customers, no matter how handsome or ripped or—

"So?"

Right, the rest. "The jacket's a unique piece," I explain with a gulp. "We can have matching trousers and waistcoat made on a custom order. The jacket's our very own Mr. Turner's work, so the integration will be seamless." It's easy to lose myself in work. If nothing else, it's a welcome distraction from the man's gaze. "We'll take the rest of your measurements and schedule a fitting to make sure everything's the perfect size."

"Hm," the man says.

And, for a while, that's *all* he says.

It strikes me suddenly how alone we are. The building is hushed like only quiet tailor shops can be. The windows are far on the other side of the room. There'd be no one here to watch if I knelt down from the stepstool and...

"Well then?" he demands eventually, making me blink in confusion.

"Pardon me?"

He doesn't even try to hide the eye roll. *Asshole.* "Aren't you going to measure me?"

"Oh, that's—" I swallow hard. "We can put you on the calendar, for sure. It's just that Mr. Turner has already gone home for the day, so—"

"You do it."

I'd really, really rather not. "I, um..."

Wrong answer. "I'm a busy man, Ms. Flowers," the man snaps, not bothering to disguise his annoyance. "Either we get this done quickly, or we won't be getting it done at all. Am I making myself clear?"

For one moment, I reconsider prison.

Then I reconsider it again. I put my best smile back on and stuff my hands in my pockets. "Certainly, sir. Let me just get my notebook."

I hurry out of the changing room, counting down from ten in the process. *What a huge, insufferable, selfish—*

"Should I undress?" the man calls out from the changing room.

"No!" I squeal, perhaps a bit too loudly. "I mean, uh, no. There's no need." And then, because there's no blood left for my brain, apparently, I add, "Thank you, though."

Silence.

I bury my face in my hands. "What the fuck?" I mutter to myself, burning to the tips of my ears.

Then I yank my godforsaken notebook and pen out from under a mountain of tags and tickets and make my way back into the devil's den.

Thus begin the most painfully awkward ten minutes of my life.

Get it over with, I coach myself again and again. *Just get it over with. This'll all be over soon.* I take mystery man's measurements from head to toe—literally. He's gonna need shoes, too, so that's important.

Most of all, though, he's gonna need pants.

When I kneel in front of him, touching my tape measure to his belt and looping it all the way around his groin, I wish for instant, sudden death. Is it possible to die from mortification?

No, clearly not. Otherwise, June would be writing my obituary right now. *April Flowers, Diligent Employee, Died in the Line of Duty. Leaves Behind a Bereaved Best Friend, a Half-*

Blind Cat, and a Sexual Harassment Lawsuit.

Normally, I'd be making small talk to break the tension. Cracking jokes, even. But this guy's like a statue: unmoving, unspeaking, unblinking.

That last part especially is messing with my head. Whenever I find myself glancing up, there he is, blue eyes burning a hole in me from above. Looking *down* on me.

How easily I can picture his big hand sliding into the roots of my hair, my hands sliding up his—

"All done!" I blurt out, jumping to my feet. "Will you, uhh— will you be needing a shirt as well?"

The usual glare ensues. "Unless you—"

"Figured," I cut in with a nervous chuckle. "I'll go grab it for you. I have just the thing."

I disappear as quickly as my feet can carry me.

In the shop, I take a few seconds more than my task would warrant to catch my breath. My head's spinning, and I'm afraid low blood pressure has nothing to do with it. God, this is all June's fault. My best friend is always saying I need to "get out there," need to get myself on Tinder, need to get myself some *that.* No wonder my mind's in the gutter.

"Ms. Flowers?" an irritated voice calls from the changing room. "Are you sewing my shirt from scratch?"

"Coming!" I call back, instantly cringing from the word choice.

"In the gutter" might be a step up from where my brain currently is, actually.

I bring him a sleek gray shirt. "It might seem counterintuitive, to wear something this dark underneath," I explain, holding out the piece to him. "But trust me. You'll thank me later."

The man frowns. After a beat, however, he takes the shirt. "I guess we'll see."

I leave the changing room, giving him privacy and giving me permission to breathe again. As soon as I'm out, I loose a big exhale, letting my shoulders slump.

"What a day," I croak, walking around the shop to gather myself.

That's when I see it. In the accessories section, rolled up neatly in its display case: a tie. Cornflower blue with indigo details.

It's a perfect match.

I run excitedly back into the changing room, forgetting everything. When clothes are involved, I tend to forget about the world. "Sir, I think this would look great…"

I did say forgetting *everything*, right? Including the purpose of changing rooms.

I don't knock. That's my first mistake. I just swing the door wide open, picturing that beautiful tie framed by the lapels of Elias's masterpiece—

"… on you."

And my half-naked customer glares at me.

3

APRIL

That's when I make my second mistake: *ogling*.

I can't help it. All my Good Girl™ resolutions crumble into a pathetic heap once my gaze falls over the stranger's eight-pack. And I do mean eight-pack. Two, four, six, *eight*. Taut skin over bulging pecs, a sculpted V-cut barely concealed by his unbuttoned pants, and a washboard I could see myself switching careers for.

I must be sweating away every drop of self-respect, because suddenly, I'm wondering if this guy's in the market for a laundry maid. Uniform up for negotiation.

Get it together, girl. Get it—

"Should I get you a picture?"

I snap back to reality. *God, can this day get any more embarrassing?* "I am *so* sorry, sir." Covering my face with both hands, I make a belated attempt at respecting my customer's privacy.

Which would probably go over better if I hadn't just gotten a full frontal of his happy trail.

"That was inexcusable. I wasn't thinking."

"You were thinking of something, alright."

I grit my teeth. "I promise I wasn't." *Grovel, April. Just grovel.* "I just... I saw this tie outside and I..."

Suddenly, the tie slips from my grasp. I panic, thinking I must've let it fall. So I open my eyes again—

"Pretty little thing."

And he's right in front of me.

I swallow. I know he's talking about the tie, but the way his ice-blue eyes trail over my frame makes it difficult to remember that. "Smooth," he adds, thumb drawing circles into the fabric, his gaze still fixed on me. "Silk?"

Close. When did he get so close? "Uhh—yes. Mulberry."

"Finest there is."

I nod frantically. Maybe I can still salvage this. "The hue is very similar to the embroidery on the jacket. It would also, uhh..." *Bring out your criminally blue eyes.* "Compliment your skin color."

The man hums. I start to sigh with relief: shop talk has never failed to save my ass...

"And yours, I'd say."

... until now.

His hand circles my wrist. Trapped in that wide palm, my arm looks like a chopstick. It occurs to me that he could snap me like a twig if he wanted to. It occurs to me a moment later that some part of me very much likes that concept.

He lifts my wrist up and holds the tie against it. "Mhmm. Perfection."

I feel my face go very, very red. "Oh, well, you should really... try it on yourself," I stammer, trying to draw back. "Skin tones can be... deceptive. I'll leave you to it—"

"Not a chance, Ms. Flowers."

He grabs my other arm, lightning-quick. How in the hell is he so fast? That's not the kind of speed that goes with that amount of muscle. Sure, he isn't steroid-ripped, but still...

Before I can shake myself out of my reverie, the stranger's got both my wrists bound.

That's what snaps me back to reality. Customers with a poor sense of personal space? I've had those. Customers who speak like a phone sex hotline? Rare, but also not unheard of. In my line of work, there's no such thing as too weird. Whatever the client wants, you go along with it, and you do it with a smile.

But no client's ever *tied me up* before.

"What are you doing?" I squeak, doing my best not to let my voice crack. I test my bindings: the tie's not looped too tight. I could break out of it, if I wanted to.

"I should be the one asking that," the man rumbles, pressing me up against the changing room wall. I take a step back, but that's all I'm allowed. Soon, there is nowhere left to go. "What are *you* doing?"

I'm suddenly very aware of how charged the air feels. How in the hell did I miss it until now? Am I so used to indulging my customers' every whim that I couldn't tell I was being cornered in my own place of work while someone cranked the sexual tension to an eleven out of ten and broke off the knob?

Apparently, yes.

"I'm... helping you?" I venture.

"Wrong." The man's breath is on my cheek now, his cologne overpowering in the small space. He smells like pine and ozone—the darkening sky before a thunderstorm. "You're denying yourself."

"Pardon me?"

"You've wanted me ever since I stepped foot in here," he states, matter-of-factly. "That's why you 'accidentally' walked in on me, right?"

"Listen up, James Bondage," I snap, feeling my hackles raising. *So much for being polite no matter what.* "I don't know what you're insinuating, but—"

"Oh, you know exactly what I'm insinuating." He sinks his face into my neck and breathes, long and deep. "Are you really trying to tell me you weren't looking earlier, Ms. Flowers? *Gawking?*"

I squirm, but it's not out of fear. More like shame: what must I smell like after such a long, hard day of work? My own perfume's bound to have evaporated by now. No dollar store mix lasts that long.

But that's not even in the top fifty of things I should be worrying about. What with the huge, half-naked stranger looming over me and all. "I was just... surprised," I croak out.

"You saw something you liked. You took it."

"I didn't take anything."

"Not yet," the stranger concedes. "But things are made to be touched. Aren't they? Isn't that what you said?"

"That's not what I meant!"

"You want me." He runs his free hand down my neck. *Touching* me. As if I'm made to be... "And that's a good thing. Because, you see, Ms. Flowers..."

His blue eyes meet mine.

"I want you, too."

The revelation shouldn't shock me, but it does. Because, out of all the boyfriends I've ever had; all the strangers I gave a chance to in the dark, long before I decided it wasn't worth the trouble—

No one has ever said those words to me.

And then, as if wanting to prove it, the stranger closes the last of the space between us.

I gasp. There's no mistaking the hardness pressing against my thigh, just like there's no mistaking how badly it's affecting me. Through my thin satin blouse and lace bra, my nipples are visibly standing to attention.

I pray he hasn't noticed the state of me, but it's a short-lived hope. I can see him looking, licking his lips like a wolf cornering its prey.

"That's right," he rumbles, low and dark. "It appears you've managed to bring me something to my liking after all. And I never leave something I like on display."

"I'm not for sale," I say through gritted teeth.

"And I'm not offering to pay." He brings his face even closer to mine. One miscalculation, one little twitch, and our lips would meet. "Are you going to leave what you want on display?"

He waits.

He waits.

I don't say no.

So he takes that for exactly the answer it is: *Claim me.*

I kiss him.

That's my third and final mistake. I surge forward and claim his lips with mine, dragging him the rest of the way down. I use my teeth; I'm not afraid. I *want* this. And wasn't he the one going on and on about taking the things you want?

For once, I'm apparently right.

It's a kiss unlike any I've ever had before. It's not particularly nice, to be honest, or kind, or tender, or gentle.

Actually, it's fucking *savage*.

He pries my lips apart and licks into my mouth, hot and hard and *deep*. If there was any doubt left on whether this man was truly made of ice, this kiss melts it all the way away.

Under the surface, fire smolders.

His hands are on me in seconds. I can feel his rough palms mapping out my body, the curves and dips of my breasts, of my hips. My buttons don't stand a chance: they go flying everywhere.

"You're lucky," I blurt between kisses, "that I have a spare set of clothes."

In response, the man chuckles in that dark way of his.

Then he yanks my head back and turns my neck into a battleground.

My hands itch to touch back. To give just as good as I'm getting. But, as if reading my mind, the man yanks on the tie, securing the knot all the way.

"Not so fast, *kalina.*" He loops the tie's tail to the free coat hook above my head, pulling twice to ensure it won't come loose. "I'm not done with my purchase yet."

God help me, I moan.

I'm so used to being the one in control—the one who *has* to be in control. If I'm not on top of every little thing, I feel like my life will just spiral out of my grasp.

Like it used to be.

So, *this?* Being stripped of all say? I'm not gonna lie: it's doing it for me.

I feel my thighs being pried apart. I don't resist: I could never. I'm so wet I can't breathe.

He notices it, too. "*Blyat',*" he growls, pushing my skirt up and my panties aside. I have no idea what that word means, but right now, I can't say I care. All I care about is his fingers, rough and wonderful, pushing up *just right*—

"Oh, God."

He starts with one. It's not enough. "More," I whine, squirming against the restraints, trying to hook my leg around his half-naked hip, because if I don't get more skin-on-skin contact *rightthisfuckingsecond*, I think I might die.

In the crook of my neck, the stranger groans. "Fucking hell, *kalina*. You want me that bad?"

"Yes," I breathe. I'm too far gone for lies. It's so hot to say it— to admit it out loud. No one's ever asked me what I wanted before. I don't know if that makes me pathetic or unlucky, but either way, I couldn't care less.

Right now, I make my own luck.

Another curse, this time just shy of my ear. "Damn." Two fingers are pumping in and out of me now. It's still nowhere near enough. "Like me that much, huh?"

"Fuck no," I moan. "I *hate* you."

"Yeah?"

"Yeah. You're the worst customer I've ever had."

That makes him laugh. "Well, then, I'd better fix that."

The second I hear his fly being unzipped, my eyes dart downwards. For one moment, I wonder if I'm seeing things. Because there's no way, right?

There's no way anyone can be this big.

"Having second thoughts?" he taunts.

I glare at him and jut out my chin proudly. "Never."

With a single drive of my hips, I wrap my legs fully around him. I revel in the shocked look on his face—but it's his own damn fault. If he didn't want me to move, he should've bound my ankles, too.

"How about you?" I breathe, pulling him closer. "'Cause, if you're too chicken, door's right there."

His face splits into a rare grin. "You asked for this, Ms. Flowers. Don't go sending me a complaint in the morning."

"That depends entirely on you."

I can see the spark of a challenge in his eyes. The second he takes it, I know. "So be it."

True to his word, he doesn't give me another minute. Before I can take a single breath, he's spreading my thighs wide, holding me up by the back of my knees. I cling to his waist with my lower body, suddenly terrified I might fall.

But he doesn't let me fall.

He doesn't let me do anything at all.

He grabs, and he pushes, and in one smooth thrust, he's inside me.

I can feel him. I can feel every inch of him, driving into me with torturous slowness. He can't afford anything less: one wrong move, and he might literally split me in half.

The thought turns me on in all the wrong ways.

"Harder," I beg, canting my hips against his.

"*Blyat'*," he groans again, that word that might mean *Fuck you* or *Fuck me*. Maybe just the first half of both. "So fucking tight."

He starts thrusting inside me. Pulling out all the way before grinding back in, setting all my nerve endings on fire. His spare hand is playing with my clit, sending sparks skittering down my back with every touch.

I can't find the voice to moan—it all feels too goddamn good. The stretch, the burn, everything. "Harder."

"Careful, *kalina*."

"I said fuck me harder!" I cry out, inhibitions forgotten.

With a savage drive of his hips, the stranger pins me to the wall—and stays there. *Goddamn him.* I cry out: I don't know what secret button inside of me he hit, but I need him to do it again. Immediately. Repeatedly.

But he stays, ground to a complete halt.

"You don't make the rules here, little flower," the man growls. "*I* do. So from now on, if you want something, you'll learn to ask nicely."

I could sob right now. What kind of monster could give someone all that pleasure, only to take it away?

"Please."

"I said *nicely*."

I arch off the wall. "Please, sir," I babble incoherently, glistening with effort, my breasts falling out what little's left of my blouse. "Please, please, fuck me, *please—*"

He kisses me silent.

And then, finally, *finally*, he gives me what I need.

There is no restraint this time. No lingering concerns. There is only want, and heat, and waves of pleasure rolling over me. Threatening to pull me under.

I hope to God they do.

Because I can feel my orgasm building inside me. Higher, higher, tighter, tighter. "Please," I moan, no longer knowing what I'm asking for. Only that I need it more than I've ever needed anything in my whole damn life. "Please, sir—"

A bite on my breast. My skin tingles with pain, then pleasure. I can feel him sucking, ready to devour me.

I wish he would.

"What do you want, *kalina*?" he asks then, nearly sweet.

"I want you," I keen, desperation in my voice. "I want to come, want you to make me, want you to come inside me—"

"You want me to breed you?" he groans, lips back on my throat.

Fuck no, the rational part of me says. *That sounds like a nightmare.*

Unfortunately, it's not the part that's calling the shots right now.

"Yes!" I cry out. Even though I know it's just dirty talk, it feels insanely hot to think it. That this stranger might mark me in such a permanent way; own me. "Yes, fuck, breed me, make me yours—!"

I come so hard I nearly black out.

My body shudders, suspended in the air, held up by nothing but the blue tie and him. And then I feel him shudder, too, fucking into me harder, harder, until—

I come again. I don't know how that's possible; I still haven't stopped coming from before. But as soon as I feel him spill inside me, that spark flares anew, making me arch all the way off the wall.

I nearly rip the tie off the hanger in the process. In any other context, it would be unforgivable.

Right now, I don't care.

But that's part of what sobers me up in the end. I'm still catching my breath against this man—this man I don't even know the name of—when, terrifyingly, something else happens.

The door chimes.

"Oh, *fuck*," I curse, scrambling to get my feet back on solid ground.

"Let them leave," the man murmurs into the crook of my neck.

"Hello?" calls the voice I instantly recognize as Mr. Boyd's. "April, are you there?"

"Please untie me," I squeak as quietly as I can.

"Why? I'm not done with you yet."

"I'm definitely done with *you*," I hiss, trying to magic my way out of my bonds like a sartorial Houdini.

"Yeah, see, I don't buy that."

The tie tears.

Fuck.

I cling to the only thing I can: the man who's currently still inside me. "I can order a new one of those," I squeak, slipping back into customer service mode.

"You'd better. I quite liked it."

Then, out of the blue, I feel his fingers pulling something out of my hair.

My ponytail comes loose, curls all over the place.

Great.

"In the meantime, I think I'll take this," he says, dangling my hair ribbon in front of me. Cornflower blue, just like the ruined tie. "As insurance."

"April? Elias? Anyone?"

I start squirming and thrashing and whimpering and finally, the man takes the hint, letting me down with a grimace. "Fine. Be that way if you choose."

"I absolutely will be that way," I growl back, rushing to put myself back together. My blouse is unsalvageable, but maybe—

"I thought that was *my* shirt," the man frowns, watching me steal the dark gray shirt I gave him to try on earlier.

"It will be. In ten to fifteen business days," I tell him curtly, rolling up the sleeves. "If you decide to purchase."

"Well, now, I'm not so sure."

I give him my worst glare. But I can't waste time trading evil looks with this arrogant, beautiful asshole, because Mr. Boyd is still thumping around in the shop impatiently.

I compose myself as best as I can, watching him do the same in the mirror. There's a ripple of muscle across his chest, his arms, as he briskly slips on the clothes he came in with.

I force myself to tear my gaze away.

Then, without turning back, I start to head out.

Somehow, he beats me to the door. "Here." He hands me a business card. "Contact info's on the back. Address, too, for delivery."

Frowning, I read over the card.

Matvey Groza, CEO.

"See you at the final fitting," Mr. Groza drawls, pocketing my hair ribbon. Then, unexpectedly, he picks up my hand and kisses it. "… Ms. Flowers."

And then, as if nothing happened, he walks.

I hear Mr. Boyd outside going "Oh!", probably expecting Elias and then noticing at the last second the man in front of him is much paler and much taller and much, much scarier.

The door chimes.

And just like that, he's gone.

With one last look in the mirror, I head out, calling out a thank you to Mr. Boyd for his patience.

Matvey Groza. Whoever he is, I can tell he's trouble. It's better this way, really: I've got no desire to ever see him again.

Or at least that's what I tell myself.

And then, one month later, the universe holds up both middle fingers to me…

In the form of two pink lines on a pregnancy test.

4

APRIL

"Well," the doctor says, taking off the stethoscope, "everything seems to be in order. Baby's still oblique, but close enough to cephalic that we can expect it to turn. No signs of fetal distress, either."

I let out a breath I didn't know I was holding. "Everything's fine, then?" I ask, feeling stupid for not speaking Doctorese. Are there such things as stupid questions when you're pregnant?

Luckily, Dr. Allan doesn't seem to think so. "Yes," she replies, a small smile on her face. "Almost too fine, to be honest." For the first time, her smile falters into an equally small frown.

And just like that, my anxiety rushes back tenfold. "And, uhh… why's that?"

"You're in your thirty-ninth week," she says, like it explains everything.

I nod along, pretending I'm not about to have a panic attack while half-naked with my bits out in my OBGYN's studio.

Dr. Cecilia Allan has many great qualities, but tact is definitely not one of them.

"In normal circumstances," she continues, "your baby would have kicked its way out already."

What a reassuring mental image. "Well, a due date's just a guess, right?" I ask with a nervous chuckle.

"That certainly seems to be the case with your family history," the doctor muses, pulling out a file. I can tell it's mine by how thick it is. Ever since my baby decided to sleep through its own birth, we've been meeting weekly for ultrasounds and check-ups. One more week, and it's gonna start looking like *War and Peace.* "You mentioned your mother's pregnancy with you ran forty-three weeks?"

"Forty-four," I correct. "And forty-six with my little brother."

"She didn't consider an induction?"

"With Charlie, yes. But it was…" I struggle to find the right words. I have a feeling *"bloodbath"* isn't a term to be throwing out inside a doctor's office. "Difficult," I settle on. "If possible, I'd like to avoid that."

"Yes, you've said," Dr. Allan muses, turning a page. "Well, for now, the baby's health looks good. The heartbeat's strong. No signs of fetal macrosomia, either." Then, snapping the folder shut, she turns to me. "But I really can't recommend letting this go on too long. As your physician, it's my job to look after your baby's health. And yours, too," she adds, squeezing my shoulder warmly.

"I know." It gives me a pang of guilt—the implication that I'm not thinking of what's best for my baby. But I know Dr. Allan didn't mean it like that. For better or worse, she's been my rock these past nine months. "Thank you, Dr. Allan. I promise I'll consider it."

She smiles. "I know you will. Oh, and by the way," she adds, rotating in her revolving chair, "here's your test results."

I take the envelope with trembling hands. "Thank you."

"Sure you don't want to know the sex?" Dr. Allan jokes, typing something on her computer. That's usually my cue to get my clothes back on.

"Nah," I tell her as I pop up and get dressed. "I want it to be a surprise."

It's more than that, really. But I don't see a point in burdening Dr. Allan with my existential musings, so I don't bother elaborating.

"Alright. I blacked it out in there, like you asked. But feel free to call anytime if you change your mind."

"Will do," I promise, rising to my feet. "Thank you again."

"See you in a week!" Dr. Allan calls after me, her eyes already on the next patient's file, and I give her a quick nod.

On my way out, I pass by couples holding hands in the waiting room. Partners supporting partners, come what may.

I squeeze the envelope between my hands, walking out alone.

Once outside, I take a deep breath. "Looks like you're pretty comfortable in there, huh, Nugget?" I run my hand over my watermelon-sized belly. One wrong wardrobe choice, and I'd have people knocking on it at the grocery store to check for ripeness.

Nugget doesn't reply. It rarely ever does. Even then, it's mostly in Morse code.

"Don't worry. I won't force you to come out here. Not until you're ready."

Guilt pricks at me again. I know why I'm doing this, but it doesn't help one bit. When the second-guessing marathons start, I'm the undefeated champion.

To distract myself, I rip the envelope open. I'm pretty much trading guilt with guilt, but who's keeping score?

I take the papers out. The amniocentesis sheet's got all kinds of data on it—numbers Dr. Allen already explained to me over the phone. No chromosomal anomalies, no illnesses. In short, nothing to worry about.

The second sheet, however, is different. I asked to see these results on my own; I wanted to be prepared. Of course, I'm realizing now that no number of pep talks in the mirror is going to make this easier.

Paternity tests aren't supposed to be taken behind the father's back, after all.

In my defense, I didn't have much of a choice. It was either "swipe the guy's hair from the jacket he tried on once and forge his signature on the consent form" or "call him and tell him you're pregnant," and I sure as hell wasn't going to pick the option behind Door #2. Not unless someone held me at gunpoint.

Because if the Internet rumors are true, Matvey Groza is *not* the kind of man you'd want for a baby daddy.

"Alright, Nugget," I say out loud, trying to calm my hands from shaking. "Moment of truth."

I unfold the sheet. The words **DNA Paternity Report** stare judgmentally up at me. I glance over the columns in the first page—more numbers. I don't care about these ones. The only number I care about is at the end of the second page.

The number that will spell out my doom.

Based on the analysis of the STR loci listed above, the probability of paternity is...

"Ninety-nine percent," I mutter to myself. "Of course. Figures."

I can't say I'm surprised. Honestly, it was either him or Jesus. But I guess a part of me was hoping for a miracle.

"Well," I sigh, giving Nugget a small pat over my belly, "you might not be the Second Coming, but you're still my special little guy. Or girl."

I start making my way back to my car. Well, mine and June's. People argue there's little point owning a car in New York City, but they clearly haven't tried taking the subway while a bazillion months pregnant. If the elbows and mariachi bands don't get you, the rats will.

I reach the parking lot. My little Honda Civic is still where I left it—never something to take for granted—but significantly snugger, I note.

Courtesy of the big black van parked right next to it.

"You've got to be kidding me." I squeeze myself into the narrow passage, trying to suck in my belly and failing. Because—newsflash—you can't suck in your uterus.

I've got half a mind to key the fucker. I'm debating whether I should actually go through with it when, all of a sudden, the van door slides open.

"Oh, thank God," I sigh, turning in the newly-freed pocket of space. "Look, I've gotta get out of here. Would you mind—"

They say hindsight is 20/20. For example, I know *now* that I shouldn't have squeezed myself between my car and an unknown van.

I know *now* I shouldn't have forgotten Girl Safety 101: never be alone in a parking lot.

But knowing *now* is pretty fucking useless.

Because, as soon as the guy grabs me, I'm already done for.

5

APRIL

One thing to be said for the dumb girl who just got herself kidnapped: I don't go down without a fight.

I scream.

I kick.

I scratch.

I *bite.*

That last part makes my captor scream, which is strangely satisfying. By the time I've got a black bag over my head and cuffs around my wrists, I'm pretty sure I've done more damage to him than he's done to me.

And then I hear him curse.

"*Blyat'*," he spits, manhandling me into a corner of the van.

My blood turns to ice.

"*Stai bene?*" another voice calls from the driver's seat. I'm no linguist, but I'm fairly certain that's an entirely different language than the one my first kidnapper just spoke.

He must realize it a split second after I do, because he quickly corrects himself. "You okay?"

English. That, I can work with. "The bitch just bit me," Shithead #1 growls.

"Hey!" I snap. "Language, asshole."

Not the smartest thing to say. Again: hindsight. Mine is sorely lacking.

Pain sparks across my cheek. A loud *crack!* echoes through the moving van. "Shut the fuck up, *curva.*"

For Nugget's sake, I do. Then the man snatches something from my hands.

The paternity test. I didn't realize I was still holding it. I must've done it subconsciously when he grabbed me.

"Like your boss said," Shithead #1 gloats, "it's a match. This is Matvey Groza's kid."

Fuck. I try to calm myself. *Deep breaths, April. So this is a mob hit. So what? You've handled worse. Remember Carolina Torres's quinceañera? You saw that cake topple. You can handle this.*

"Of course it's a match," Shithead #2 bristles. "*My* boss doesn't make mistakes. We put a tracker on Groza's records as soon as he crossed the ocean. Your boss could learn a thing or two."

The air is tense. I can tell. Whoever these two are, something tells me they're not from the same circles. That they haven't been working together for long.

Good. I can use that.

For a while, I remain silent. I listen to the sound of asphalt under the wheels: a bump, then two. We're exiting the hospital compound. Any moment now, we'll have to make a turn.

Left, I pray to whoever's listening. *Make a left. Take the Expressway. Then, once you're stuck in traffic—*

They go right.

Sonofabitch.

I slump against my corner. Of course my rotten luck would make an appearance now. Back in school, I used to get teased about it all the time. *April Flowers brings May showers*, the kids would chant, running around me in a circle under the rain.

Because it would rain, without fail, every time I decided to come on a field trip.

I learned to stay home quickly after that.

But now, I don't have that option. Now, if I ever want to see home again, I need to make my own luck.

I keep track of the route. I've driven to this hospital and back for months: I know every shortcut, every road, every crossing. It doesn't take long before I recognize the bustle of Times Square.

The traffic packs us in. The driver curses. Horns blare all around me, in full NYC rush style.

Now or never, April.

I cough once, twice. Then I cough some more. "Hey," I call, meeker this time. Inoffensive. "Could I have some water?"

"You'll get it once we're there."

"I can't—" I wheeze a bit, just for good measure. "I can't breathe."

For a moment, I'm terrified Shithead #1 simply won't care. He's already slapped me once: how hard can it be to ignore me, too?

But then I hear another voice. *The driver.* "Just give her a sip, dude. She's pregnant."

"I don't give a fuck what she is."

"The boss needs her whole. Give her some goddamn water."

With a click of his tongue, Shithead #1 relents. "Here," he grumbles, all but shoving me a plastic bottle. "Don't try anything funny."

What am I gonna do, belly bump you like a sumo wrestler? "Thank you," I croak instead, taking the bottle with my cuffed hands.

It takes a couple of tries to get it open. Shithead #1 certainly isn't rushing to help me. *Asshole.*

If only this bottle were glass.

"Could you...?" I ask, gesturing to the hood over my head. With a sigh, my kidnapper complies.

"Fuck you," I murmur sweetly.

"What's that?"

"Thank you."

He scoffs. "Just be quick about it."

I take slow, deliberate sips. Now that I can finally see him, I realize my captor is nearly as tall as Matvey was. He has to hunch over to avoid bumping his head on the roof with every pothole.

Perfect.

The second he turns, I spill some water between my crossed legs. Discreetly, though. Then, as if nothing happened, I drink the rest of the bottle and crumple it.

"Thanks," I say again, offering it to him. "Sorry, did you want some?"

"It's fine," the man grits, clearly irritated. He moves to take the crumpled bottle from my hands.

That's when I act.

"Ah!" I cry out suddenly, folding on myself. I let the bottle fall, then hunch some more. "God, it hurts!"

"What's happening?" the driver calls, concern in his voice.

"I don't know, man." Shithead #1 is panicking now. "She just started fuckin' screaming!"

"Well, ask her then, dumbass!"

"Oh, God," I sob, making a show of feeling the floor between my legs. "I think—my water's..."

"You piss yourself?" the man frowns, taking a step back in disgust.

"No," I say. "My water broke. I think... I think the baby's coming."

The van screeches to a halt.

Bingo.

"The fuck you doing, man?!" Shithead #1 yells.

"Are you fuckin' serious right now?" Slightly Less Shithead #2 shouts back. "She's about to give birth, dude. We need to turn back!"

"It could be a trick!"

"Please," I babble, wishing I could send footage of this to the Academy. I deserve gold statuettes for the show I'm putting on here. "Is there blood? I can't tell…"

"I don't know," stammers Shithead #1. "It's too dark—"

"Check," I plead, my final gamble. "Please, check with your hand, I can't do it with the cuffs, I can't—"

"She's right," the driver calls, seemingly oblivious to the horns blaring all around us. "You need to check for blood. The child could be in danger."

"No way," my kidnapper balks. "No way in hell am I sticking my hand in there!"

"Then let me!" I beg, inwardly cheering.

"*Blyat'*," he spits again, fumbling with a set of keys. It's weird, how different it sounds in this context. So unlike the way *he'd* said it.

The second he leans over to unlock my cuffs, I act.

Pretending to spread my legs in a panic, I kick out. My kitten heel connects with the man's ankle. Hunched over like he is, he goes tumbling down like a tripped giraffe.

"Oh, no!" I yell for the driver's benefit, kicking my kidnapper's fallen gun within my reach. "Are you okay?"

Then, without a moment's hesitation, I slam it into the back of his head.

"What's happening?!"

"Help! I think he hit his head!"

And the Oscar goes to...

"*Porca puttana.*" With a yank on the hand-brake, the driver gets out of his seat. "Hold on, I'm coming over—"

I don't hear whatever he says next. By the time he walks around the van, I'm already out.

With my cuffed hands, I rip a cab door open and slip inside.

"Hey!" the passenger calls. "You can't just—"

"Drive!" I scream—and thank God, the cabbie does.

It takes me a full minute of catching my breath to realize why they'd been so quick to obey. "Oh!" I blink at the gun in my hand. "This—I'm so sorry. It's not mine. I wasn't—"

"Whatever you say, Miss," the cab driver says, his voice reduced to a squeak.

The man in the backseat next to me is positively pale. "Please, let me go," he stammers. "I have a family."

"I, uhh... Sure."

He flies out of the still-moving car. It's lucky we're driving so slowly—my kidnappers have all but halted traffic in the crossing.

Quickly, I toss the gun out the window.

"I need to go somewhere," I tell the cab driver, who's still staring at me like I've got two heads. Which, I suppose, if you're counting Nugget's—

"Anywhere," he breathes.

I pull my phone out of my coat pocket. Then I fish something out of the case: a business card.

His business card.

I type his name into my browser. After that wretched afternoon, we haven't had any more contact. I made sure to call in sick at that final fitting. I had no desire to ever see him again.

I can't say I want to now.

But I also don't have a choice.

The man is a social media ghost. For a moment, despair takes hold of me. Maybe I could have the cab drive to the address on the back of the card. Maybe—

Then I find it: a single picture, posted by the account of the most beautiful woman I've ever seen. Her blond hair is made up in a long tress, her clothes impeccable. Next to her, Matvey Groza stares impassively at the camera, looking as if he just ate a lemon.

And then, on the woman's finger…

A diamond ring.

Caption: *I said yes! Save the date: January 15th, Jupiter Hotel in Manhattan. Ceremony on the terrace at 12:00.*

I check the time: 11:48.

"Here," I tell the cab driver, giving him my phone. "Please take me here. Fast."

As the driver takes my word for it, speeding through traffic like I still hold a gun to his head—again, my bad—only one thought haunts my mind.

I'm about to crash a mob wedding.

6

MATVEY

The suit's a perfect fit.

Of course, I knew that already. I made the trek back to that little shop specifically to make sure of it.

But *she* wasn't there.

I adjust my tie in the mirror. The sensation of silk on my fingertips brings back memories. It's been nearly a year, but my mind still likes to go there sometimes. That changing room. That scent.

Her.

I pull something out of my pocket: a ribbon, long and sleek, the same color as my tie. A little souvenir I've kept with me since then. If I hold it close, I can still smell her perfume.

I shake my head and huff. Is this what Grisha was warning me about? Pre-wedding jitters?

Nonsense. I'm Matvey Groza. The head of the most powerful Bratva in New York City. I don't get nervous.

Especially when it comes to politics. And make no mistake, that's all this is.

A knock sounds on the door. I turn my head and call, "Come in."

A whistle follows in lieu of a greeting. "Wow. Look at *that*. Trying to upstage the bride?"

I roll my eyes at her. "If you were afraid of that, you should've picked a better tailor. I can introduce you, if you'd like." It's my best attempt at a joke, even though the mere thought of *sharing* makes blood rise to my head. "What are you doing here? Don't you know it's bad luck for the groom to see the bride before the wedding?"

My blushing bride doesn't blink, nor does she blush. The day Petra Solovyova gets flustered because of a man, hell will freeze twice over.

She glides to me instead, dressed in white from head to toe. Her fairy tale gown shimmers with every step, catching the light like the diamond-studded hilt of a dagger. Regardless of her jokes, I don't think anybody could upstage her today.

Not that they'd be dumb enough to try.

"Luck doesn't concern us anymore," Petra declares, wrapping her arms around me from behind.

I try not to flinch at the contact. If we're going to sell this, we both need to look like we can stand each other's presence.

Her gray eyes meet mine in the mirror. "Starting today, nothing will stand in our way. Not luck, not fate. Not anyone." She fixes my tie as she talks, and it takes every ounce of my willpower to stop from slapping her hands away.

Don't touch what she *touched. It's not meant for you.*

Her diamond ring glitters on her hand. Somehow, she makes that look like a weapon, too.

I finally shake her off. "You sound awfully confident."

"As should you," Petra shrugs. "We're here, Matvey. We made it. You don't have to keep waiting for the other shoe to drop."

She's right, in theory. But old habits are hard to break. Until we say, "I do," I'm not leaving anything to chance.

"Soon," she murmurs, drawing close again, "all of our dreams will come true. You'll be *pakhan* of the strongest Bratva on the East Coast, the combined power of the Groza and Solovyov families at your beck and call. And I…"

"And you'll be *vor*," I complete for her. "Just like your daddy never wanted."

A feral grin splits her face in the mirror.

Petra. Ever since we crossed paths two years ago, I knew right away I'd finally met my match. Not in strength or cunning, but *hunger.* That's what being Bratva is all about: not how much money you can be buried with, or how many cops you've got in your pocket, or how many skyscrapers you can slap your name on.

That's the American dream—it was never ours.

A Bratva is made for one thing: to *rule.*

Coming here makes it easy to forget that simple truth. I never did, though. Even as my *vory*, my generals, let themselves grow complacent in the lap of luxury, I kept striving for more.

To accomplish that, I need numbers. Numbers that Petra can provide.

Numbers *her father* can provide, to be more specific.

Vladimir may have crossed an ocean to make his fortune here, but his heart never left the old Russia. He wanted a husband for his daughter; I wanted the soldiers he'd offer up as dowry.

And Petra? Petra had goals of her own. She wanted more than to be a pretty thing on someone's arm. I was happy to indulge her.

I'm not Vladimir, after all—I don't give a shit what's between someone's legs. I care only how they can contribute to my cause. And if someone brings me an army, man or woman, they have earned a place in my ranks.

Now, if only she would quit *touching me.*

"Won't you let me kiss you?" she blurts suddenly. Her fingers stroke the line of my jaw.

I push her hand aside. "You can kiss me at the altar."

"And after?" she presses, all but hanging on my tie.

I do my best to smother my irritation. The worst thing I can do is give Petra the satisfaction of seeing me snap. That's what she lives for—getting a rise out of people.

"I don't get it, you know," she muses when I don't answer. "It's not like I'm ugly. Aren't you curious what it would be like? Just once?"

I've wondered the same thing. By all accounts, I should find Petra beautiful. In an objective way, I guess I do. She looks like a statue: sculpted out of marble, perfect in every proportion.

And just as cold and sharp.

"Why are you even asking?" I counter. "We both know you don't like me, either."

Her face tells me I'm right on the money.

Maybe the same reason goes for both of us: we're too alike. Two alphas, gunning for the top. She'd never yield to anybody—and as for me? I prefer women who *will* yield. Warm, pliable, mine for the taking.

Just like—

"Fine," she pouts, whirling away. "You're no fun to play with anyway."

"I'm not made to be played with," I snarl with a sudden lash of violence that takes even me by surprise. "So don't try."

Then my gaze falls to my watch.

"You should get back to your suite," I advise. "We wouldn't want your father thinking you're up to something improper."

"Yes, yes, *moy pakhan*," Petra teases, hands up in a mocking gesture of innocence. "God forbid, right?"

I watch her retreating back in the mirror. Her hips, swaying with every step. Alpha or not, I should at least be tempted.

So why aren't I?

Without thinking, my hand goes back to my pocket, where the ribbon rests. I blame the fabric: smooth, soft to the touch. Ideal for discharging my kinetic energy. With my mind always running calculations a mile a minute, it's a welcome reprieve. A purely physical thing.

It has nothing to do with the woman who wore it.

"There you are." I turn to the door, following the sound of Grisha's voice. "I was starting to think we had a runaway bride on our hands."

Petra answers with a coquettish laugh. "Oh, I would never. Just making sure my husband doesn't get cold feet."

"I'm not your husband yet."

"See?" she jokes to Grisha. "Can't leave this one alone, I'm telling you."

"I'll make sure he's well looked after," Grisha replies good-humoredly, holding out a hand. "Now come, *moya printsessa.*"

Petra lets herself be led out. My ever-gallant subordinate throws me a wink over his shoulder.

I roll my eyes.

"Bit insulting, don't you think?" another voice comments snidely from the doorway. *Yuri.* "Petra's a trusted ally. She wouldn't betray us."

"I know that, Yurochka," Grisha replies amiably. "Just like I know you wouldn't recognize a joke if it bit that dainty little nose of yours."

"Get your hands *off—*" my brother starts, voice turning nasal mid-sentence.

"Boys," I bark, my patience running thin. "Quit stealing each other's noses and get the fuck to work. Otherwise, I'll shoot them both off."

My second- and third-in-command obediently break it up.

"Unbelievable," Yuri mutters under his breath.

"Let it go," I warn him. "I swear, the second you're in a room together, you both revert to toddlers."

I can see an objection on Yuri's lips, but he seems to think better of it. *Good.* I'm not in the mood for games today.

"Are you ready?" he asks instead.

I throw one last glance in the mirror. The jacket looks as crisp as it did that day in the shop. Better, even. "As ready as I'll ever be," I sigh.

"And..." Yuri pauses, looking for the right words. "Are you sure about this, brother?"

Am I? "I have to be," I settle on. "We need the Solovyov numbers. Otherwise, it'll take years before we grow big enough to take on..."

I don't say the name. Yuri knows perfectly well who I'm referring to.

"I understand," he says finally. He still looks conflicted, but I choose to ignore it. Brides and grooms probably aren't the only ones who get nerves on days like these. "But..."

"Yura."

He stops.

The nickname always makes him listen. It reminds him of when we were kids—just two orphans stumbling in the snow, learning how to wield a gun to survive.

"It's just a wedding," I say, squeezing both his shoulders. He's so tall, it's hard to remember he's only twenty-two. I used to dwarf him by a whole head: now, it's mere inches. "It's not that big a sacrifice."

"But you don't love her."

"I was never planning to marry for love, brother."

"But—"

"*Blood*," I tell him, turning serious, "is the only tie I need. The only tie we can *trust*. Anything else is fleeting at best. And, at worst, a lie."

I see him swallow, then nod. "I know, *Motya*."

"I know you do." With one last pat, I let Yuri go. Then I cross the distance to the door. "Is it time yet?"

"Yeah," Yuri says, checking his watch. "It is."

I grin. One last effort, and everything I've ever wanted will be within my reach. Allies, power, means.

Best of all... *revenge.*

"Well then," I say with a grin, "lead the way, brother."

I walk up to the altar.

By my side, Yuri takes his spot as best man. I can see Grisha in the crowd, giving me a sneaky thumbs-up.

Then the march starts playing.

As the organ sings, Petra walks in on her father's arm. Decked out like this, in six-inch heels and a tiara that would put any *tsaritsa* to shame, she makes Vlad look like a garden gnome. Somehow, I get the feeling it's intentional.

With each step she takes, I can feel my dreams closing in. With each word out the priest's mouth, I can feel my ambitions settling in my grasp. With each respective "*I do*," I can sense the balance of the world shifting.

When the officiant says, "Speak now or forever hold your peace," I nearly laugh. Who in their right mind would cross us? Who in their right mind would oppose *this*?

And then, like lightning striking twice, April Flowers rushes in.

"I'm pregnant," she announces breathlessly, sporting the most gigantic belly I've ever seen. "And it's yours."

7

MATVEY

It happens in slow motion.

That's what it looks like to me, at least. After my wedding-crashing tailor drops her bomb, the terrace goes deadly quiet. For a second, the air is still, like the instant before a shootout.

And then it begins.

The first punch flies from the back rows. Of course it does—that's where the Groza and Solovyov men sit mixed with each other. It was Grisha's brilliant idea: a show of unity.

Right now, "unity" looks like a broken, bloodied nose.

"You!" the Solovyov grunt yells above the crowd. "How dare you insult our *printsessa* like that?"

"The fuck's wrong with you?!"

"Know your place, *salaga*. Did you forget who's your new *pakhan*?!"

Fists go flying.

So does the furniture.

… and Vlad's *very* expensive, imported ornaments.

A chair soars above the crowd, landing with a vicious crack on the back of one of my men. The Groza group responds by hurling the entire row back at the offending Solovyovs.

A wooden leg hits the latch on the birdcage. White doves are released, flocking at the wrong angle, diving straight into the brawling guests' faces. Cheeks get scratched; eyes get pecked; feathers scatter everywhere.

I duck under a Fabergé egg screaming toward me like a bullet. It misses my head by a hair and buries itself in the six-tier wedding cake resting at the center of the table.

I can hear Petra's horrified gasp as the cake begins to sway, threatening everyone in the vicinity with a Madagascar vanilla bath. Which is probably the finest thing most of these men have ever bathed with, but still—not exactly the use we had in mind.

Yuri rushes over to save it, but to no avail. The cake swallows him whole.

I turn my eyes to the cause of this whole nightmare as it explodes in every direction around me. There she is: April Flowers, dodging chairs and plucking feathers out of her hair.

"Congratulations, Miss!" one of my men has the gall to yell over the chaos, giving the woman a quick bow of respect as he kicks a Solovyov grunt in the knees.

"Oh, um. Thank you," Ms. Flowers replies, ever-so-politely.

I decide I've had enough of this farce.

I take out my gun and shoot.

As quickly and violently as it began, the brawl halts. The terrace falls silent. My gun, pointed straight at the sky, smokes. No one is looking anywhere else now—anywhere but me.

April Flowers included.

And then a dead dove falls on Petra's white shoes, and my bride screams. Chaos resumes quickly after that.

So much for crowd control. This situation is officially beyond saving.

"Boss," Grisha calls, rushing over to me, "we've got a problem."

"No shit."

"No," he insists, grabbing my elbow. "We've got a *problem*."

I follow Grisha's line of sight. On the other side of the altar, flanked by two bodyguards, Vlad the Garden Gnome is making his way to me.

And he doesn't look happy in the least.

"*Blyat'*," I curse, holstering my gun and jumping down the altar. On my way down the nave, I mutter to Grisha, "Get this under control."

"I'll do my best, boss."

"Don't do your anything. Just get it done."

Then I stride towards the source of "this," who is now back to dodging chairs and congratulations while skittering around dead birds on the grass.

I make up the ground between us in a few swift strides. When I'm close enough, I snarl, "You're coming with me."

I don't give her a chance to argue. I don't give her a chance to speak. I just grab her hand, hold tight, and run.

Her eyes are huge as she drinks me in. Her throat bobs with a swallow, and I almost bark out a laugh at the ridiculousness of that. She has no problem crashing a five-hundred-person wedding filled with killers and criminals, but she pales now that it's just her and me?

She opens her mouth to speak. I'm ready for anything—an apology, an explanation, an extortion demand. Instead, she mutters dreamily, "It really is a perfect fit…"

"Excuse me?"

"Nothing! It's just, um… the jacket. It suits you really well."

I glance back at the tailor in disbelief. "That's your concern?" I growl. "You just *crashed my wedding*, and you're wondering if my suit fits?"

I weave through the crowd, dragging her behind me. I can see my men forming a perimeter around us, watching both our backs. I didn't even have to say anything—they just fell in line with their *pakhan*, no questions asked.

By contrast, I can still hear Vlad barking orders to his disorderly troops at the altar.

"Should've added a pocket square, though," the woman next to me mumbles.

I'm going to kill her.

We get in the elevator. It's not a long ride to the penthouse. In fact, it would've been faster to take the stairs. But I wasn't certain she could do that, what with her—

Don't look at her belly.

But it's impossible. Every time my gaze darts towards her, that's where it goes. Not her warm, hazel eyes, as wide as a doe's. Not the spray of freckles on her cheeks, so far from innocent.

There.

This miniature hall of mirrors doesn't help. Wherever I turn, there she is: April Flowers, now sporting an enormous baby bump.

My baby.

If she's to be believed, that is.

As if reading my mind, she turns to me. "It *is* yours," she huffs. "I can prove it."

"Can you?"

It's ridiculous. I've seen pregnant women before. None of them looked like *this*. She's fucking glowing. Ethereal.

I tear my gaze away and step off the elevator. I don't let go of her hand, though. I doubt she could escape far, but I won't risk it. April Flowers owes me answers.

And, perhaps, something more.

"Of course I can," she snaps. "It's in my left pocket."

She tries to free her still-cuffed hand from my grasp, but I don't let her. Instead, I swipe my key card at the penthouse door, unceremoniously dragging her inside. Only with the door safely shut behind us do I finally let her go. "Speak, then."

She glares at me. "I'll trade you the proof for a pair of bolt cutters."

Un-fucking-believable. "Let me make something very clear, Ms. Flowers: you don't get to negotiate. You just crashed a very important event—"

"A mob wedding," she completes.

"—and half the people on that terrace want you dead right now. So I'd start talking if I were you."

For a long moment, April Flowers doesn't say anything. Neither do I.

Then, after what feels like an eternity, she holds out her wrists and repeats, "Bolt. Cutters. Then I'll talk."

Exhausted, I walk to the sink. I take out the toolkit and set it on the table. I make sure the bolt cutters are visible, but make no move to get them just yet. "Talk. Then I'll cut you loose."

My feisty tailor doesn't move. So I take out my gun and set that on the table as well.

That seems to get a reaction out of her. "Wow. Class act, aren't you?"

"Yes. And, if I decide to use this, it won't matter whether your hands are free or not. So talk. Now."

Trembling with rage, she stuffs both her cuffed hands into her pocket. Then she fishes out… *something.* "There. Asshole."

I take the crumpled paper from her. "What's this supposed to be?"

"You can read, can't you?"

I grit my teeth. In my entire life, no one has ever dared speak to me like this. Oddly, I don't hate it.

I scan the document. I quickly realize what it is: a paternity test. "How did you get this?" I ask in disbelief, skimming over the data-filled columns.

"Your jacket," she answers. "You left hair on it. It's inevitable, really. Happens to the best of us."

"And you... swiped it?"

"Yeah." She shrugs. "So, you know... It's either your kid or Mr. Buttons's."

"Who's that?"

"My cat."

I stare at her. "These tests require a consent form."

"Which I handed in."

"How?"

"Your receipt."

I keep staring.

"Don't look at me like that," my tailor-slash-forger says, cuffed hands raised in a show of innocence. "If you don't want your signature forged, next time, order on our website."

I ought to be mad. I ought to be fucking furious. I ought to put this defiant little seamstress in her place and show her what I am, what I've done, what I'm still capable of doing.

But in reality...

I'm *impressed.*

I keep reading the document. At the end of the second page, after endless gibberish, the only number I can understand stares at me in bold:

99%

I take a moment to collect myself. For a full minute, I do nothing but pore over the document again and again. Nothing but reread that number, as if its meaning could change with one more glance.

But it doesn't.

This child is mine.

"Look," she says, "I'm sorry I crashed your wedding. Believe it or not, I really am. And not just because your bride's family wants to kill me right now." She wrings her bound hands, gaze suddenly low and shy. "I just… didn't have a choice."

I have no reason to believe her. She could be a liar, a spy, both, something else entirely. And yet, for some reason, I do.

"I'm guessing those have something to do with it?" I say, glancing towards the cuffs.

She gives a stiff nod. "I was kidnapped today. One of the guys was Russian, I think. The other—I don't know. But they mentioned you by name."

Just like that, my blood begins to boil. I stride towards Ms. Flowers—*April.* The mother of my child. I see her flinch: does she think I'd hit her? That I'd *ever* hurt what's mine?

I bring the bolt cutters to her handcuffs and snip the chain in half. "Grisha will help you with those," I tell her, resisting the suddenly powerful urge to tuck away a stray curl behind her ear. "Later."

I'm furious. Of course I'm furious: April Flowers just single-handedly destroyed months of careful planning. My dreams, which were so close only minutes ago, are already slipping away from my grasp. If I don't handle this the right way, I will lose everything.

And yet, I'm not furious with her now.

I'm furious with whoever thought they could lay a hand on *my child* and live.

My child—and the mother who carries it.

"How far along are you?" I ask.

April blinks at me, like she wasn't expecting this question. "Thirty-nine weeks."

I frown. "You're due soon."

"Last week, actually," she mutters. "It's—a thing. My family does this. Our babies tend to run late."

Kidnapping a nine-month pregnant woman. When I find the pieces of shit who did this, there won't be a single bone left to bury.

"I swear I'm not making this up," April carries on, panicked. "You can check on the test; it's all in there—"

"I believe you."

It's the second time I've said that today. It's not a usual thing for me. But nothing about today is usual.

I finally let myself look at her belly. Full, swollen—with *my* child. *I'm going to be a father.*

"Matvey!"

Someone bursts in. I make a grab for my gun, pushing April behind my back, ready to defend her against the entire Solovyov Bratva if I have to—

—and then I see who it is.

I pinch the bridge of my nose. "I was about to shoot, you know."

Perhaps I should have. Instead, I'm treated to the sight of my second- and third-in-command elbowing each other to get to me. Yuri's still covered in cake frosting, while Grisha has a long, white feather sticking out of his hair like Yankee fucking Doodle.

"Are you okay, brother? What—"

"Is everything alright, boss? I thought—"

"Quiet."

At my command, they both settle down.

"Good," I tell them. "Ms. Flowers, these are Yuri and Grisha. Yuri's my brother. Grisha's my third." I point at each in turn, watching as they each give a stiff nod and stare at me like I've lost my last marble. "Sometimes, they both act like babies. I think they'll make excellent practice for parenthood, so feel free to use them as such."

Behind me, I hear April stifle a snort. She recovers quickly. "Pleasure to meet you," she greets, the picture of perfect courtesy.

Back in customer service mode, no doubt.

"Yuri, Grisha," I continue, "this is Ms. April Flowers. Tailor, signature forger, unrepentant wedding crasher—"

"Hey!"

"—and the mother of my baby."

Two pairs of eyes widen. I pretend I don't notice.

"Now," I say, cracking my knuckles, "which one of you is gonna give me a status update?"

8

MATVEY

"'Baby'?!"

"Wait, how are you supposed to know—"

"—something's not right here—"

"Motya, what the—"

I slam my palms on the table. "I asked for a status update, not a fucking press conference." I force myself to take a long, deep breath. It's either that or someone's going to eat lead before the day's done. "Grisha. You go first."

For once, Yuri doesn't argue.

Grisha clears his throat. "It's hell out there, boss. The only reason people aren't shooting is because Ms. Solovyova threatened to shove their guns up—"

"I can imagine," I cut in. "How is Petra?"

This time, it's Yuri who answers. "She's upset, brother. She stormed out of the terrace with her bodyguards a minute ago. Her father's still there, settling the men."

I have about as much faith in Vlad's ability to settle his men as I do in the damn Tooth Fairy. "Alright. Grisha, you go back up there. Get our men in line, then tell Vlad the wedding's postponed. The Solovyovs threw the first punch, so make it look like it's his fault we can't move forward today."

Grisha smirks under his mustache. "Will do, boss."

"Yuri," I say, turning to my brother, "you'll stay here."

"But—"

"Guard her with your life," I tell him, stressing how important this is. If that baby's truly mine, I can't entrust this to anybody else. "Got it?"

He swallows. "Got it."

"Good." I start heading towards the exit with Grisha. "I'll look for Petra. We meet back here in fifteen."

I spare April one last glance. Like this, with her hazel eyes staring at the floor and her whole body pressed against the arm of the couch, she doesn't look like the spitfire tailor I was sparring with only minutes ago. If anything, she looks like she's trying to make herself as small as possible. To *hide*.

But there's no hiding the obvious bump under her flowy maternity dress, nor the precious cargo it carries.

I don't want to leave. But I have to.

"Stick with Yuri," I tell her. "He'll keep you safe."

"I can keep myself safe!" she argues—but it's weak. Exhausted. Like it's taking all of her strength to just stay upright.

She was kidnapped. She escaped. She ran all the way here.

"You asked for my protection," I say, with a tone that brooks no argument. "So let me protect you."

This time, April doesn't say anything.

I force myself to tear my gaze away from her belly. Then, my mind bursting with everything I still need to do to salvage this shitshow, I finally stride out the door.

"Wait!"

"What, Yuri?"

I turn. My brother's there, halfway out the door, with a look in his eyes I know all too well. "I can help."

"Is this about your pissing contest with Grisha?" I sigh, starting to feel beyond irritated. "Because if that's the case—"

"It's about Petra."

I stop walking. "What about Petra?"

"She was upset, Motya." Yuri doesn't meet my gaze as he speaks. "Will she even talk to you?"

"Of course she will," I answer without missing a beat. "We were supposed to be married by now. If she won't talk to me, who else is left?"

"I…" Yuri hesitates. "I can help."

I massage the bridge of my nose, feeling a headache coming on. Good intentions, road to hell, et cetera. "You are helping, brother," I insist. "By staying here. Where I need you most."

"But—"

I walk up to him, squeezing his shoulders with both my hands. Grounding him. I don't know what's got him so out of sorts, but I need him to snap out of it, and fast.

If I can't rely on Yuri, I can't rely on anyone.

"You don't have to keep competing with Grisha for top spot, Yuri. You're my second." I stare him right in the eye, hoping my words will finally get through his thick, thick skull. "You're my blood. No one else can say that. No one in the whole world. Do you understand?"

No one, a voice inside me whispers, *except—*

"I understand," Yuri finally gives in. "But I can do more if you need me to. That's all."

An idea comes to mind then. If more responsibility's what Yuri wants, then I have just the task. "Tell you what," I say, pulling out the crumpled sheet of paper I was handed earlier. "If you want to help, you can help. With this."

He scans the document. "A paternity test?"

"I want a new one." Without hesitating, I yank a few strands of hair off my scalp. It doesn't even sting. After Siberia, anything short of a bullet feels like a hot stone massage. "Feel free to forge my signature on the consent form. Apparently, that's commonplace now."

Yuri frowns, but doesn't say anything. As my second, he's done far worse than commit some light forgery. "You think she's lying?"

"I think we have no reason to believe her," I answer coldly, ignoring how wrong the words feel in my mouth. "She's a stranger, after all."

Not a complete *stranger,* a part of me points out, reminding me of all the ways we got intimately acquainted with each other.

But that's neither here nor there.

"What about the baby's DNA to match against?" Yuri asks.

"The data's already in the system, so—"

That's when I realize something. Something I should have realized a conversation ago. The test, the kidnapping—what if it's all connected? What if this piece of paper is the key to all of it?

How could they *know about my baby, when even* I *didn't?*

"Actually, forget consent forms," I backtrack. "I want this done discreetly. Under the radar. Bribe someone at this hospital, get the records, match against that. Got it?"

After a moment of consideration, Yuri nods. "Got it."

I squeeze his shoulders harder. Not enough to hurt—but enough to make him understand. "This is important, Yuri. I can trust no one else to do it for me. Just like I can trust no one else to look after the woman in that room. Because if she really is carrying my child—"

"Then that's your blood, too," Yuri completes for me. "Don't worry; I get it."

Good man. "*Our* blood," I correct him with a smirk. "You'd be the youngest uncle in the family."

"I'd be the only uncle in the family, brother."

"Still."

If anybody else kept second-guessing me like this, my patience would've run out a long time ago. But Yuri's blood. And, aside from that, all he ever wants is to help. I can't punish him for that, can I?

"Matvey…"

"What now?"

He pauses. "Look in the kitchens. You know how Petra gets when she's nervous. She—"

"Stress-eats," I finish, realization dawning on me. "Thanks, *bratiška.*" I grin, patting him on the back. "See? You're plenty of help."

Yuri doesn't say anything to that. Whenever a compliment's thrown his way, he ducks it like a bullet. "Just hurry. The chef might still be alive."

I head to the elevator. The day's still a mess, but maybe I can salvage what matters.

And what matters right now is my alliance.

To Yuri's credit, I find Petra exactly where he said I would.

"Is there any left for me?" I ask, strolling in.

Petra's twin bodyguards, Julia and Lena, give me the evil eye as I pass by them, but I pay them no mind. With their own faces stuffed full of tarts, they don't look half as intimidating as their mistress.

Petra glares at me with bloodshot eyes. "Which do you prefer? Cyanide or arsenic?"

"I'm usually a fan of nightshade."

"I'll see what I can whip up."

I walk around the stainless steel counter. I glance around, realizing I haven't seen Rowan anywhere. "Did your bodyguards eat my chef?"

"You should be asking if *I* ate your chef."

"Fair." I drum my fingers on the counter. I'm not the type to grovel—that's never really been my style. But even I'm not cruel enough to deny what I just put Petra through. "Look, I… regret how things went down."

"That's not a '*sorry*,' asshole."

"I didn't know she was going to do that."

My bride barks out a laugh. "Oh, I believe you. You should have seen the look on your face." She strangles a salmon tart in her fist, nearly squeezing it back into an egg. "Like the Ghost of Christmas Future just showed up with your Nobel Peace Prize."

"Are you saying I'll never win a Nobel Peace Prize?"

"Maybe you will," she sniffles. "After today, you won't have an army anyway. Might as well think of a career change."

Her words sober me up. "It's not all lost, Petra. This is just a setback."

"'A setback'?" Petra laughs, bitter and cruel. "That's a *pregnant fucking woman* you've got in your penthouse, Matvey. And yes, I know where you're hiding her. We're not all idiots in here."

The implication makes my blood boil. "You won't touch her."

"*You* shouldn't have touched her!" Petra all but shouts. "We agreed to this, Matvey! Us!"

I grit my teeth. "A political agreement, I'm sure you'll remember."

"Well, how's this for politics?" my scorned bride-slash-business partner snarls. "My father—who's also the *pakhan* of the Bratva you're looking to take over, in case you forgot—is never going to let me marry a cheater!"

I pinch the bridge of my nose. I hate Petra's screaming tantrums, but I hate even more when they're justified.

Vlad's a man of tradition. To someone like him, honor matters more than anything. And nothing screams "*dishonor*" like an out-of-wedlock baby on the way.

"We have no choice," Petra says, pacing up and down in her gigantic skirts. "We have to handle this."

"Petra."

"Maybe it's not yours," she continues, a crazed look of hope in her eyes. "She could be a spy, right? She could be on our enemies' payroll—"

"*Petra.*"

My tone forces her to look at me. Like this, all dressed in white and with tear marks on her cheeks, she would make even the most stone-hearted man feel like the worst piece of shit to ever walk the Earth.

Luckily, that's not my case. A heart of stone is still a heart, after all, and I don't have that burden. "She had a paternity test. It's mine."

Petra slumps on the floor like a deflated soufflé. "Then we're done. It's over."

"It's not over." I crouch to her level, forcing her to look me in the eye. To listen, for fucking once. "No one knows about the test. Only me, Yuri, and now, you. And I'm having him run the DNA again to be certain."

"So it could be fake?" Petra blurts out, a glimmer of hope in her eyes.

"It could be... but I don't think it is."

The hope shatters.

"But," I add, offering Petra a handful of tissues, "taking the test will buy us time. Time to convince Vlad to let us move forward."

Petra blows into the tissues. "He'll never buy it."

"He will," I tell her confidently. "Because we'll sell it. We'll sell it like we sold him this," I say, gesturing between us. "And because his baby girl will be there, advocating for her fiancé's honor."

Petra pauses mid-sniffle. "You're dumping this on me, aren't you?"

"Never," I lie. "I'll talk to Vlad, too. I'll sing him your praises and say my hands are tied. Waiting for the test is the honorable thing to do. He won't like it, but he won't say no."

"But you still need me to sell it."

God help me, I do. I nod grimly. "It won't work unless it comes from you first."

Petra seems to mull it over. I can tell she's almost there: she just needs a little push.

"You can consider this your first mission as *vor* of the Groza Bratva," I add.

"Alright," Petra finally sighs. "I can tell you're fucking with me, but frankly, I don't care."

"Attagirl."

She rises to her feet unsteadily. "What about the pregnant elephant in the room?"

"Let me worry about her."

I start heading towards the door, but Petra's voice stops me. "Matvey."

I turn. "Yeah?"

Her gray gaze is unreadable. "Fatherhood really agrees with you."

"Why would you say that?"

"You're smiling."

I touch my lips. The unfamiliar shape catches me by surprise. Muscles I scarcely ever use are warming up. "That's your fault," I tell Petra. "You've got a cream cheese beard."

As I leave my bride-to-be furiously scrubbing at her chin, I keep checking the corners of my lips. Curved. Upturned.

I'm pregnant. And it's yours.

"A father," I murmur to myself, stepping back into the elevator. "I'm going to be a father."

9

APRIL

Crash a mob wedding: *check.*

Tell the baby daddy he's going to be a father in front of his bride: *check.*

Get executed Godfather-style: still working on it.

But, going by the way this guy's glaring at me, it might happen sooner than I'd like.

I should break the ice, I mull over. *I should say something, right? Something smooth. Something nonchalant. Something that will totally make this whole thing go—*

"I'm sorry I ruined your brother's wedding," I blurt out.

The guy only glares at me harder.

Great job, April. We'll make fish food out of you yet.

"You didn't ruin his wedding."

I blink. The guy's voice—Yuri, I recall—comes as a gruff but welcome surprise. *He's giving you a chance, April. Don't screw this up.*

"I mean…" I venture, trying to find the right words for the conversation. "You are still covered in cake."

Fuck my life. My mouth isn't big enough to fit all these feet in it.

"I didn't—" I curse my complete lack of a social filter. If this guy doesn't shoot me in the next five seconds, then surely it'll happen in the five seconds after that. "I just—"

"What you ruined was his business deal," Yuri explains, his expression cold. "His plans. His dreams."

I'm gonna die here. I'm gonna—

"But there was never a true wedding to ruin. Not really."

—what now?

With a sigh, Yuri slumps against the wall. "So, you know… feel bad, but not too bad."

I try to make sense of the words. I fail miserably. "Sorry, what does that mean?"

The tall Russian mobster rolls his eyes. He can't be that much younger than me, but his attitude screams "teenager." He reminds me of Charlie at thirteen, huffing and puffing like a chimney every time someone tried to speak to him. "I mean that the whole thing's a farce. An arrangement."

A lightbulb goes off in my head. "You mean, like a political marriage?"

"Precisely."

I feel my heart flutter. I don't know why this changes anything—why I'm suddenly feeling ten times lighter. I tell myself that it's just about the guilt: crashing a business deal isn't as bad as crashing another woman's dream wedding, right? I'm not a homewrecker after all. That must be it. The sweet relief of an innocent verdict.

Right?

He isn't with her, a treacherous part of me whispers from the half-closed lid of my heart. *He hasn't* been *with her. Not like he's* been *with you.*

I slap the lid shut. This is neither here nor there. I can't know that they haven't—and besides, what do I even care?

"Like I said," Yuri huffs, breaking into my thoughts, "a farce." He crosses his arms and turns away, glaring at the wall. Somehow, I get the feeling he wasn't thrilled about this whole deal to begin with. Who knows? Maybe I even did him a favor.

I try to imagine what it'd be like, knowing one of my siblings is marrying for interest. Power, maybe, or money. If it was Anne, I wouldn't bat an eye.

But if it was Charlie...

If it was Charlie, I'd try to talk him out of it until his last step towards the altar.

"You must really love your brother," I muse without thinking.

Yuri blinks at me in surprise. "Yeah," he admits after a beat. "I do. He's everything to me."

"That's nice." I smile. "Siblings should stick together. Who else are you going to complain about your parents to?"

"Our parents are dead."

Oh. I am overcome with the urge to kick myself. Is it socially acceptable for a pregnant woman to literally kick herself? Is that allowed?

"I'm sorry," I say, feeling mortified. "I didn't know."

To his credit, Yuri just shrugs. "You couldn't. You don't know Matvey."

The words sting like a slap.

I don't know why, but I feel anger mounting inside me. It's uncalled for—Yuri hasn't said anything wrong. To me, Matvey Groza is a stranger.

But you do *know him,* that voice inside of me insists, enraged. *You're carrying his child, aren't you?*

"Was it recent?" I ask, forcing myself back from the brink. This man's still a boy. He deserves my sympathy, not my anger.

"Nah." Yuri shrugs, like he's trying to tell himself it doesn't matter. Even speaking about something like this with me, a person he doesn't know from a hole in the wall—it shows how far he's willing to go. To tell himself it no longer hurts. I know a thing or two about that: telling myself stories to carry me through the day. "It happened back in Russia. His mom first, then mine. And our father—" Suddenly, he stops. Like he's said too much. "It doesn't matter," he repeats, that gruff edge back in his tone. "You don't need to know anyway."

Just then, the door swings open. Matvey Groza strides in like he owns the place. Which, considering he does, seems apt. "Any news from Grisha?"

"No," Yuri replies, as grumpy as ever. "He's taking forever."

"He's putting out fires. Let's give him the benefit of the doubt, shall we?"

Yuri doesn't seem thrilled about that, but he doesn't press. "How's Petra?" he asks instead.

His brother shrugs. "She's a big girl. She'll manage."

Then he turns to me, and that's when I realize...

He's *grinning.*

"Now, whatever shall I do with you, Ms. Flowers?"

Bad sign. Horrible, horrible sign. Remember the last time he grinned at you like that, April? You ended up buying maternity clothes.

"You could... let me go?" I venture.

"Sure. I'll see you at the next kidnapping, then."

Right. Somehow, I forgot why I even came here. Because Matvey Groza is dangerous, and he's just painted a target on my entire life. A target exactly as big as the baby in my belly.

"Yuri," he calls, "guard the corridor. I'll be there shortly."

Don't go, I want to tell that grumpy, overgrown teenager. *Don't leave me alone with him!*

No such luck. I watch him walk out the door. Then I watch his older brother walk around the couch. I feel like I'm being circled—a deer in a trap with vultures closing in.

But this man's no vulture. This man is a *wolf*, and there isn't enough wool in the world to hide that. I get the feeling he doesn't even try. The second he walked into my shop, I could smell the danger on him.

I still ended up with his tie around my wrists.

It dawns on me—yet again—how foolish I've been. From the start of this whole thing, I haven't made a single good choice.

And now, I'm fresh out of choices altogether.

"Let's hear it then," I sigh, trying to find my old, polite self and failing. "You've got something in mind, I assume."

"That's a bold assumption to make."

"I'll go out on a limb here. You're clearly a very resourceful man, Mr. Groza." I smile, putting my sweetest face forward. I have no doubt he can taste the venom in my words, but I don't care. I'm not liable for a customer's interpretation of what leaves my lips—a handy trick I learned early on. Granted, a man like Matvey Groza isn't likely to file a complaint, but still, I'll take what little satisfaction I can get. "So why don't you tell me what you're really thinking?"

It happens in a blink. One second, he's standing there with his hands in his pockets, the picture of a smug billionaire who's never gotten a slap he didn't earn—

And the next, he's kneeling in front of me.

"I'm thinking," he rumbles, bringing his big palm over my belly, "that you should call me Matvey."

I'm struck dumb. For a moment, I forget everything: how to think, how to speak. How to *breathe.*

"And why's that?" I exhale, voice trembling.

Mr. Groza—*Matvey*—smirks. "You're carrying my child. I think we can do away with the formalities, don't you, April?"

I reel from the way he says my name. *A-pril.* An open mouth, then a flash of teeth, sinking into the pulp of fresh fruit.

"I guess so," I force myself to answer, breaths coming in short. "Matvey."

A pleased hum. I can't imagine I've spoken half as seductively as he did, but I'll take what I can get.

"Good," he praises. "We'll be sharing a lot in the next few weeks. It wouldn't do to have you call me *'sir'* while living in my house." A beat. "Although I do like the sound of it…"

I feel my face go up in flames. "If you think I'll live with you—"

"Not *with* me," he corrects. "In my house. Here. I wouldn't make the mistake of laying a hand on you again, April. We both know how it ended last time."

I make a fist in a pillow, fighting the urge to throw it at his face. "Believe me, the feeling's more than mutual."

"That's a relief," he says sarcastically. "Now. You asked for protection, did you not?"

Fuck me, I did. "Is this the part where you tell me it'll cost me my soul? Because, fair warning, I've been working customer service for a while. I don't think there's much left."

Matvey gives me an amused smirk. For a brief second, I wonder if it'd be so bad to kiss it off his face. Just to see his flawless appearance ruffled, for once. I blame my hormones for that—always thinking of inopportune things, especially in this man's presence.

But then he lowers his eyes to my stomach, and suddenly, I can't look away, either.

I watch with rapt attention as he strokes my belly, his stormy gaze captivated by what's inside. His child.

Our child.

"This is my price," he declares.

Suddenly, my head goes light. "You want the baby?" I ask, filled with hurt.

"No, April. Believe it or not, I'm not a monster. I wouldn't take a baby away from their mother."

Relief washes over me, but only for a moment. "What, then?"

"I want to be a part of their life," Matvey states matter-of-factly. "As any father should."

"Oh." I frown. That's… surprisingly reasonable.

But part of me still rebels. Doing this… It would mean leaving my current life. My home, my family. To move in, however temporarily, in this man's space.

This man. The devil himself.

"In exchange for that," Matvey continues, offering me his hand like a businessman closing a deal, "I'll search for your kidnappers. I'll identify whoever wants to harm you and the child, take them out of the picture, and keep you safe. That's the deal."

I take a long, deep breath. This is exactly what I wanted to avoid, isn't it? Being involved with Matvey Groza. Being swallowed into his life, whatever that entails.

But I guess that ship has sailed.

I look at the broken handcuffs, still locked around my wrists. At Matvey's face, determined and quietly hopeful.

Then I look at my belly, with our child growing inside it.

And I realize that I don't have a choice.

"Okay," I exhale, shaking his hand and feeling like I just signed away my entire life. "Okay. But I have one condition."

He waits patiently, one eyebrow arched high on his head.

"I get to bring my cat."

10

APRIL

"What do you mean, he won't let you take Buttons?!"

I sigh. Of all things to be outraged about, I had a feeling June would pick this one. "The hotel has a no-pet policy. He said he can get it changed, but it'll take until the next board meeting."

"I don't get it," June harrumphs, crossing her arms. "I thought he owned the place. Can't he just do whatever he wants?"

Oh, he does. If the way he behaved in my shop is anything to go by, Matvey Groza is the kind of man who only learns the rules so he can better break them. But it didn't feel like a hill worth dying on—*sorry, Mr. Buttons*—so I didn't.

This is just for a few weeks, anyway.

"It's okay, June," I reassure my best friend as we pack up the last of my clothes. "Really."

"Doesn't feel okay to me," June grumbles. She drops cross-legged on the bed with Mr. Buttons in her lap. "None of this does."

I go sit near her. Like this, with her cheeks all puffed up, she looks like a very pouty hamster. "It'll be fine. I promise."

For a moment, June doesn't answer—just keeps tormenting Mr. Buttons's ears like they're made of playdough. Not that he minds.

"What if you didn't go?" she blurts out. "What if you stayed?"

I think back to yesterday. To the black van, the way its doors had swallowed me whole. To the men inside, both armed, both violent, both ready to do God only knows what to me.

"I can't, Jay. You know I can't."

"I'll get a gun!" June tries. "We both will. We'll splurge on a nice security system and—"

"And it won't matter one bit," I cut her off gently. "These aren't the kind of guys who'll let a locked door stop them. And I can't risk your life, too."

"I can protect myself," June objects. "I'll protect you, too. You and Nugget."

"From the actual *mob*?" I laugh, but not unkindly. The image of June Evans guarding the door with a Kalashnikov is certainly one I'd like to see.

"I don't care if Don fucking Corleone shows up—I can take him."

"I'm sure you could, babe." I pull her into a hug. June makes a noise like a kettle close to boiling, but doesn't resist. "Thanks, Jay. It means a lot to me."

"But you're still going."

I take a breath. "Yeah. Yeah, I am."

When I pull back, I can see that June's eyes are watery. Goddammit—she's gonna make me cry, too.

But then she rubs her face with her sleeve and says, like nothing happened, "Alright then. Let's go pack your books."

June Evans. Ever since first grade, she's been my rock. Whenever the other kids were picking on me, making fun of my name and my proverbial bad luck, June was the only one who stood up for me. She came swooping into the playground like a knight in shining armor, waving a stick like a battle ax and scattering my bullies as if they were just some squawking seagulls.

We became inseparable after that.

When the kids switched to making fun of both of us—the unfortunate combination of our names was just too tasty to resist—I felt so guilty. But June never held it against me.

And so, whenever a kid would swagger up to us, snickering the classroom-wide joke—"Hey, April and June! Where did you leave May?"—June would promptly answer, "Right here," raise a fist, and punch the little fucker's lights out.

I can't count the times that's gotten us into trouble. But we were never alone, and that was all that mattered.

"Where do you want this?" June calls to me from the kitchen island, holding up my Vivienne Westwood catwalk collection book. Third-hand, but worth every penny.

"Brown box," I answer distractedly, dusting a pile of old sewing books. Stitching, pattern techniques—you name it, it's there.

"Roger." In goes Vivienne, then Vuitton. "You're taking those, too?"

I falter. On one hand, I might not be at Matvey's that long. I could keep my treasures where I've always kept them: here, safely in June's care.

On the other hand…

"I think so," I mutter, brushing dust off the covers uncertainly. Ever since my belly grew the size of a basketball, I've neglected them: my *other* babies.

The books Grandma left me.

Wordlessly, June picks up another box. I keep staring at the covers. Some leatherbound, some not bound at all. Yellowed pages fraying at the edges. Books my grandma collected over the years, in a bunch of different languages, including her native French.

They're the only thing I have left of her.

I shake off the memories. It won't do me any good to think of the past now. My grandma's gone, and so is the home we shared.

And now, I'm going to have to say goodbye to another home.

Suddenly, there's a knock on the door. "Ms. Flowers?"

I recognize the voice. It's whatshisname—Sasha or Gasha or Misha or whatever. "Come in!"

Matvey's guy pokes his head in. "Apologies for the intrusion, ladies. Is there anything I can assist you with, Ms. Flowers?"

I blink. If I didn't know for dead-ass certain this guy was a mobster, I'd think my baby daddy sent over his prim and proper butler. "Oh, I, um—no. No, thank you, we're almost done."

"As you wish." Kosha-or-Whatever tilts his hat from the doorway, then takes it off before stepping in. Again: rather dapper for a hired gun. "And you must be Ms. Evans."

I never told him that. For June's sake, I pretend I didn't just realize the father of my child is apparently spying on us. *Great.*

Yasha-I-Think takes June's hand in his gloved one and honest-to-god *bows*. "My name is Grisha Aldonin, at your service."

Right, that's his name: Grisha.

June is rendered speechless. A hard feat to achieve, if I do say —wait, is she *blushing*? "June Evans. N-Nice to meet you."

"*Enchanté.*"

What are you, the French *mob now?* "Actually, Mr. Aldonin—"

"Please," the Moscow dandy interrupts. "Call me Grisha."

"Grisha," I amend. "Could I trouble you to bring down a couple of boxes? I can't really lift anything heavy."

"Nor should you," he promptly agrees. "Ilya. Anatoly."

With a single snap of his fingers, two burly bodyguards emerge at my door. Now, *I'm* speechless. Whoever this Grisha guy is, he's like the fairy godmother of mobsters. The fairy Godfather, if you will.

Without a word, the two henchmen begin to cart down my belongings: four boxes, three bags, two suitcases. All that's missing is the partridge in the pear tree.

Speaking of, I make my way over to Buttons. "Behave while I'm gone," I tell him sternly, looking him straight in his only remaining eye. "No more playing Tarzan with the curtains."

"Or my skirts," June adds.

"Or June's skirts."

Buttons doesn't give me any sign of life. Not that I expected differently: ever since he turned ten, he's become the laziest couch potato in history. He offers me a slow blink and curls back up on the cushions. Then, just in case he's gotten into trouble, he starts purring.

You big, fat ruffian. I'm gonna miss you, too.

"Thank you," I say, turning to June. "For looking after him."

June rolls her eyes, but there's a smile on her face. "What was I gonna do, feed him to the wolves?"

"To the subway rats, maybe."

"They've gotten bigger than him, haven't they?"

"Speaking of transportation," I whirl around, addressing Grisha this time. "Our car's still in the hospital parking lot. I don't suppose you could...?"

"I'll put my people on it," he assures me.

I try to give him the keys, but he's already gone.

"Relax," June says, picking up the keys from my palm. "I think the Bratva can handle recovering a Honda Civic."

"They're gonna hotwire it, aren't they?"

"You know they're gonna." I slump on the couch, sighing, as June adds, "Besides... that guy looks like he knows what he's doing." I catch her trying to ogle Grisha, who's making a call on the balcony.

"June. *June*, no. Absolutely not."

"What?" she says defensively. "He ain't bad to look at."

"That's what *I* said last time I met a Russian mobster!" I point out, flailing my arms. "Look where that got me!"

"It got you this Nugget right here," June coos, making kissy faces at my belly. "Didn't it?"

"Stop that."

"Who's a good Nugget?"

"That's for dogs, June."

She shrugs. Then, in a rare moment of seriousness, she asks, "You know you can come back anytime, right?"

I know why she's saying this. Why she's going through the trouble of spelling it out for me. For the longest time, I didn't have a home to return to. None that actually wanted me, anyway.

"I know," I murmur, feeling myself smile despite everything. It's June's superpower: making me forget that I'm in deep shit by jumping in right after me. "Thanks, Jay. I love you."

"Love you too, Apes."

We hug. It's pathetic—two grown women trying not to break down into ugly sobs.

"Hold on 'til May," she whispers into my hair. "Promise me."

It's our secret mantra. Since we're April and June, "May" is whenever we're together. It's family—and it's the family *we* chose. No one else.

"I promise," I croak.

"Good," June says briskly, freeing me from the hug and

scrambling for the kitchen. If she's trying to dry her eyes unseen, she's doing a poor job on the "unseen" part.

But fuck it, so am I.

Grisha appears from the balcony. "Everything's ready, Ms. Flowers," he declares. "After you."

I give Buttons one last kiss on the head. Then I give June's hand one last squeeze.

"'Tell Baby Daddy Dearest to sleep with one eye open," June warns, a bit to me and a bit, terrifyingly, to Grisha. "If he tries anything, I'll know."

"Please don't tell him that," I murmur to Grisha on our way down.

Grisha gives a hearty chuckle. "I don't think he'd mind, Ms. Flowers. The more people in your corner, the better. Right?"

"Right," I mutter, wondering about those words: *in my corner.*

Is Matvey in my corner? Or is the baby all he wants from me?

Believe it or not, I'm not a monster. That's what he told me. He meant it—I think. But I don't know if I believe him quite yet.

From the car, I turn to look one last time at the home I'm leaving behind. A temporary change, nothing more.

So why does it feel so damn permanent?

"Please," Grisha says, swiping the keycard to the penthouse and holding the door for me. "Make yourself at home."

"Thank you." I gulp.

I didn't truly get a chance to look around before. I do now, taking in what's going to be my new home for the next few... weeks? Months?

I don't dare think "years." I'm not sure my heart could take it.

The place is—well, it's a luxury hotel penthouse. That alone sets it apart from any apartment I've ever seen. When I first went house-hunting with June, two eighteen-year-old girls with pennies to our names, the nicest place we could afford was our current one-bedroom in Brooklyn—and even then, it took months (and the adoption of a one-eyed cat) to chase out the rats.

But *this* place?

The countertops are all marble. The furniture is a sleek, matte black. The couches—plural—are the highest-quality leather I've ever touched. Everything here screams *money*.

And nothing here screams *home*.

A knock on the door jolts me out of my thoughts. "Come in," I call, thinking it must be Grisha with a hot towel or a mint chocolate for my pillow or something.

But it isn't Grisha.

"Well, well," a petite blond woman croons from the doorway, "if it isn't Matvey's *koshka*. I trust you didn't have any trouble finding the place?"

I recognize her immediately. Even with her hair down, her clothes businesslike, there's no mistaking who this person is.

The bride whose wedding I ruined.

From the doorway, two more figures come in. Women, though at first glance you'd never know. Tall, burly, muscled, they look every bit the part of what I suspect they are: bodyguards.

And not of the law-abiding kind.

"It's Petra, right?" I ask, remembering Matvey's words from yesterday. "I'm—"

"April Flowers," Petra replies sweetly, taking hold of my hand. "My fiancé's tailor. And, well…" She looks down at my belly. "Something else, I'm certain."

I blink. Maybe I'm misinterpreting here, but—

Did this bitch just call me a bitch?

"Look," I start, not wanting to drag this on any longer, "I'm so sorry about yesterday. I didn't mean for things to happen the way they did, but—"

"But you just *happened* to stumble upon our wedding," she completes for me. "And you really couldn't wait any longer to break the news to my husband-to-be. Is that right?"

"That… Actually, yes," I mumble. "That sounds about right."

Petra smiles, all teeth. For a second, I'm reminded of a lioness —the pride's hunter, capable of slaughtering gazelles with a single bite.

And, for some reason, I feel an awful lot like a gazelle.

"Let's get one thing straight, *cvetoček*," Petra coos, sticky-sweet. "I don't know what tragic tale you spun for Matvey—"

"'I'm pregnant,'" I deadpan. "You know. You were there."

"—or whose little *ubljudok* you're carrying in that kangaroo pouch of yours," Petra continues, as if I hadn't spoken.

Should I have taken Russian in high school? I'm starting to think I should've taken Russian.

Not that I need a translator to understand what Petra's trying to say to me. The language of catfights is universal.

"I'm not lying, if that's what you're implying." I don't grit my teeth, nor do I yell—I don't want to give her the satisfaction. But I'm not going to take this lying down, either.

Insult *me*? Fine. Maybe I deserved it.

But insult *my baby*?

Not on my watch, *kalinka*.

"Maybe not," Petra concedes. "But the timing sure is interesting."

"I'm not—" I start, but my words are cut short.

Because suddenly, Petra's hand is twisting mine. Her handshake now feels like a vise—tighter, *tighter*.

I press my lips together, refusing to make a sound. *Hurt me all you want. I promise you one thing: I've felt worse.*

"All I care about," she enunciates, her face now uncomfortably close to mine, "is my dream. And if you ever get in the way again, I'll make sure your little *komuk* grows up calling every single nanny 'Mama.' Have I made myself clear?"

I've never wanted to hit someone this bad. Scratch that—I've never wanted to *kill* someone this bad.

One day into this nightmare and I'm already homicidal.

"Crystal," I grit out.

Only then does Petra finally let go.

"Splendid!" She claps, as if that settles that. "I'll leave you to unpack, then. Just don't throw out the boxes, 'mkay?" she winks. "You never know when you might need them again."

With that, she sashays out the door, her bodyguards trailing after her.

As soon as she's gone, I shake out my hand. "Ow," I mutter. "That *hurt*, bitch."

Alone, I look around the room again. The sealed boxes, the cold countertops, the emptiness. And, not for the first time, I wonder...

Just what the hell did I get myself into?

11

MATVEY

"Having fun?"

Petra turns to me with a surprised look. "My, my, if it isn't the runaway groom," she croons in Russian. The automatic doors of the Jupiter Hotel whirr shut behind her back. On each side of her, Petra's bodyguards glare at me in unison. "What brings you here, fiancé? Come to guard the princess's tower in person?"

I ball up my fists. "I'm not in the mood for your games. What the hell are you doing here?"

She gives me an enigmatic half-smile. Who does she think she is, the fucking *Mona Lisa*? "Just popped by to compliment the chef. Those salmon tarts? Delicious. Tried to bribe the recipe out of him, but he wouldn't stop shaking long enough to speak."

Note to self: give Rowan a raise.

"That's it?" I sigh. "Cut the shit, Petra. I know you were at the penthouse just now."

A light chuckle. "What, caught me on those pricey cameras of yours? Or did a little bird whose name rhymes with Trisha sing a pretty song in your ear?"

I step closer to her. Her bodyguards tense, but I don't give a shit. I'm a way faster draw than either of them. "If you harassed her in any way—"

"Oh, '*harass*' is such an ugly word." Petra scoffs theatrically. "Please. What's a little girl talk between friends?"

"She's not your 'friend.'"

"And she's not your anything," Petra retorts, her tone suddenly sharp. "So what's she doing here?"

I grit my teeth. "I don't have to justify myself to you."

"Tough shit," she hisses, taking a step forward. Despite her doll size, she's managed to get herself all up in my face, and I don't like that one bit. "Because I own your army, Matvey. *Me.* So yes, actually, you do owe me some sort of—"

"Let's get one thing straight here," I snarl, too far gone for games. "*You* don't own shit; your *father* does."

"Listen—"

"No, you listen." I force her to take a step back, pressing her up against Tweedledee or Tweedledum, I don't fucking care which. "I can get my alliance anywhere. There isn't a single Bratva in New York who'd turn down the Groza name, and you know it."

"And what would that cost you?" she spits, a snake reeling back to bite. "No *pakhan* worth their salt is going to give up their title to you."

"Maybe not," I concede. "But none of them is ever gonna make you *vor*, either."

I watch her swallow that hard truth. *Good.* Let her remember where she stands.

"Is this your word's worth?" she murmurs with venom. "A bastard child and a common whore?"

"My word," I growl, "is my bond. So I'll honor my end of the deal."

She exhales. "Good—"

"—unless you give me a reason not to."

I can see her lip quivering. Her face is a mask of fury, barely contained. Petra Solovyova was always too small for the storm raging inside her. I can respect that. Hell, I can even admire that.

But I won't tolerate her slights toward me or mine. And make no mistake: April Flowers is *mine* now.

So is the child growing inside her.

"What's that look like, then?" Petra asks in a bitter whisper.

There it is: surrender.

"Disrespecting my child, for one."

"And the mother, too?"

"And the mother, too." I raise my arm just enough to let my jacket lift over my gun. "And I'm sure I don't need to tell you what *harming* either of them would mean, do I?"

For a long moment, Petra's silent. She takes the hit with her usual grace—blinking away her frustrated tears like they were never there. Recomposing herself, her mask, one cracked piece at a time.

And then, finally, there she is again. Cold and smooth as ice. "Well, then," she says with a forced smile, "sleep easy. I won't get in the way of my own dreams."

"I had a feeling you'd say that."

"Mm," Petra hums, walking up to fix my tie. A peace offering —or a hidden knife. "Give your little flower my regards. After all, we're going to be family soon. As long as she behaves, I won't touch a petal on her pretty little head."

"And if she doesn't?"

"Then there won't be a stem left to find."

I'm about to yank her wrist right off when she lets go herself, chuckling amiably. "Relax, Matvey. I'm just pulling your leg. I agreed, remember? No disrespect. No harm." She starts to walk around me, dragging her manicured nails lightly along my sleeve as she passes. "Just a little condition of my own. After all, we're partners. Right?"

"I don't enjoy being threatened, Petra."

"'Threatened'? What threat?" she asks innocently, blinking up at me from afar. "For goodness's sake, you're Matvey Groza. Surely you can keep your house in order…?"

She starts sashaying away with her bodyguards in tow. I debate pulling out my gun and dropping a body right here, right now, in the middle of the street. Teach Petra Solovyova what it means to truly cross me.

But, before I can make up my mind, she calls over her shoulder, "Oh, by the way. I talked to my father. For the sake of his little girl, he'll allow this farce to continue." She throws a smile from behind her shoulder, all teeth. "But you should probably talk to him soon, too. Vladimir Solovyov isn't a patient man, after all."

Vladimir Solovyov is a has-been, I want to spit in her face. *He's a septuagenarian with a dying Bratva and no heir to take over. He'll be patient if he knows what's good for him.*

Before I can indulge the urge, Yuri appears at my side.

"*Dasvidaniya!*" Petra waves, blowing us a kiss and climbing into Vlad's limo, her twin hounds in tow.

I itch to grab my gun. But Yuri places his hand firmly on my shoulder and whispers, "Don't. We need her."

I shake him off, cursing up a storm. "Fucking insufferable."

"She can be, yeah."

"I'd rather marry her goddamn father."

"I don't think you'd look that good in a white dress."

I glare at Yuri. "Is there a reason you're here, or did you just want to finish what Petra started?"

Yuri clears his throat, stepping back. "My bad. I just wanted to tell you it's done."

I frown. "You have the test?"

He shakes his head. "That's... still underway," he says, sounding weirdly uncertain. I'm about to pry into what exactly's got him acting so strange, when he adds, "I meant the other thing."

I massage my temples. If this day goes on any longer, the migraine I'm brewing might be the death of me. "Quit speaking in riddles, brother. What thing?"

"The kidnappers. We have them."

That jolts me to attention. "Where are they?"

"In the warehouse, with our men keeping watch. I'm heading there now."

I give a quick nod. "Good. Do that. April mentioned one of them was Russian. He could be one of ours."

Yuri frowns. "You think our men got turned?"

"I don't know, but I'll need you there until I find out. If there's a traitor in our ranks, they might not be working alone."

"Understood," Yuri answers, straightening where he stands. If he were to salute me right now, I wouldn't even blink. Nothing whips Yuri into shape like an important task to oversee. "Will you be coming along for the fun?"

"No." I shake my head. "I'll meet you there later. Start without me. Make those lowlifes understand what it means to mess with one of us."

For a moment, there's only silence. Then: "That was quick," I hear Yuri half-joke, half-sulk.

I whirl around. "What's that supposed to mean?"

"Nothing," he backtracks. "Just…" A pause. I can see his eyes grow uncertain again as he gathers up the courage to ask the question burning up inside of him. "Is that what she is now? 'One of us'?"

I roll my eyes all the way to the back of my skull. "Not you, too."

"I'm just saying," he mutters. "We don't know if she can be trusted yet. What if the kid isn't yours?"

"She *can't* be trusted," I tell him flatly. "She's not blood. And if the kid's not blood, either, then they can both go fend for themselves."

Out of the corner of my eye, I see Yuri flinch. Does he think I'm being too harsh? Maybe. Yuri always had a kinder heart than me.

Luckily, I don't have a heart at all. That's what I tell myself, even as images of April on the run start crowding my head.

April, with a bundle in her arms.

April, running for her life.

April, staring down the barrel of a gun...

No, I tell myself resolutely. *That won't happen. If the child's mine, then they will have the full force of the Groza Bratva to protect them.*

And if it isn't...

"If it's not mine," I say out loud, "whoever's after her will soon realize their mistake, too. So don't worry, Yura: no one's going to get hurt here. Do you understand?"

No one that doesn't deserve it, I add with a rush of bloodlust, picturing April's kidnappers with a missing row of teeth.

Yuri nods. "I understand, Motya."

"In the meantime," I say, "put a rush on that paternity test. The sooner we know, the better."

"Yes, *moy pakhan.*"

I ruffle his hair. "What's with the formalities now? You're so weird tonight. Anyway, go. I'll catch up."

"Where will you go?"

I glance up at the hotel. At the balcony above all balconies, up on the penthouse floor. The one I know is mine.

The one that's now April's, too.

"I think," I answer, feeling an uncharacteristic grin pulling at my lips for the second time in as many days, "I'll go have dinner."

12

APRIL

I'm almost done hanging my clothes when the doorbell rings.

I rush to the door, trying to fix the mess on my head in the process. After hours spent ducked between bookshelves and riffling through a closet bigger than my entire apartment, it's safe to say I don't look my best.

Or so I assume. I haven't had a chance to look in the mirror yet.

It's so weird—answering the door here. Like this place belongs to me. Even if this temporary arrangement gives me full run of the joint, I can't help feeling like a guest. An intruder.

I crack open the chained door, once again expecting Grisha…

And it's not.

Instead, it's *him.*

"Oh," I blurt out stupidly. "Hi."

Matvey inclines his head. "April," he greets back flatly.

Every time I see this man, he's looking his best self. Composed, put-together, all smooth fabrics and artful scruff and expensive cologne. By contrast, I feel like I just crawled out of a hole.

An *ass*hole, to be specific.

"Gonna let me in at some point?" Matvey asks, that pinprick of impatience clear in his voice.

"I—Yes. Of course. Just a second…"

I unlock the chain at the door. It takes me an embarrassing amount of tries—damned butterfingers. But in the end, I manage, and the sight that greets me is…

Unexpected.

Because there Matvey is, tapping his foot with mounting irritation, towering over me in all his mob bossy glory—

—and pushing a *food cart.*

I step aside to let him through. If he taps his foot any harder, I'm afraid there might be victims. "Come on in."

Matvey rolls the cart forward. Somehow, he manages to do even that in an intimidating way. I'm suddenly feeling sorry for his secretaries.

"What, uh…?" I babble, racking my brain for a conversation topic. Anything to dispel this awkward silence, really. "What brings you by?"

I cringe. I sound like the corny neighbor on an 80s sitcom that didn't get renewed for a second season.

"Do I need a reason to come to my own penthouse?" Matvey ponders without looking up from the trays he's setting on the table.

I want to smack myself. At the same time, I want to smack him. Who even has that kind of attitude?

I'm debating whether to give him a piece of my mind when—

"Evening, boss," Grisha calls from the doorway. "I trust everything's up to standard?"

Aaand they're speaking in code again.

"Everything's fine," Matvey says, which tells me absolutely nothing. I'd try reading his expression, but I'd have more luck with the Easter Island statues. "You can go, Grisha. I'll take it from here."

Grisha gives a small bow. "I'll be on standby downstairs. Ms. Flowers," he adds courteously, taking his leave from me as well.

I feel my hands twitch as the door closes behind his back. *Don't go!* I want to whine like a goddamn toddler. *Don't leave me alone with the scary hot man!*

Despite myself, I was starting to feel at ease around Grisha. At the very least, he was someone I could read. Calm, approachable, always with a joke on his lips.

But Matvey?

He remains a mystery wrapped in Tom Ford.

"Should I bring you a chair over there?" Matvey asks sarcastically.

I shake myself back to reality. In my stupor, I completely

forgot about the covered trays he just carted in. He uncovers one now, and the smell is...

Well, the smell is heavenly.

My belly gives a loud rumble. I pray he didn't hear it, but as soon as I look up, I can see the ghost of a smirk playing on his irritatingly handsome face.

Oh, whatever. I'm pregnant. I get to be twice as hungry as everyone else.

I slide into the seat in front of him. "Thank you," I murmur, staring at the feast in front of me.

"Here," Matvey says in a clipped tone, handing me a single-sheet menu. "I instructed the chef to avoid anything unsafe for pregnancy, as well as mustard and celery. But you should check just in case."

I accept the menu with unsteady hands, my mind reeling. It must have taken a lot of work to do something like this. Above all else, that's what strikes me first: a tremendous amount of care.

My second thought is that I never told him about my allergies.

Deep breaths, April. So the scary mobster's got his hands on your medical records. So what? He isn't using them to kill you.

... yet.

"Thank you," I say uncertainly, still not sure if I'm about to suffer death by Dijon.

Then we eat.

According to the menu, the dish that made me dizzy with its heavenly scent is something called *tomato consommé with smoked ricotta tortelli.* The taste is delicate and delicious, unlike anything I've ever eaten. Is this what it feels like to be rich?

"Is the food to your liking?" Matvey asks in his deep, rumbling voice.

Is rain wet and the Earth round? "It's amazing," I answer sincerely. "My go-to dinner is usually boxed mac-and-cheese, so this is definitely new."

Matvey looks at me with pity. "You... cook, then?"

"Store-bought," I clarify.

He cringes.

For some reason, that's ridiculously funny to me: Matvey Groza, scandalized by the eating habits of the common folk. Without realizing it, I let out a laugh. "I know, I know. Not exactly worthy of a Michelin star, am I?"

Matvey shrugs. "Everyone's got their talents. You're a decent tailor, at least."

"Just 'decent'?"

"Your professionalism leaves something to be desired."

"Hey!" *The nerve of this guy!* "It's not like I'm used to customers wanting to tie me up," I mumble, feeling the urge to sink into the floor.

"I find that very hard to believe."

Forget the floor. I'd like to sink into the core of the Earth, pretty please.

The second course—because this meal has actual *courses*, apparently, as opposed to me just refilling my bowl with some more cheesy Kraft goodness—is duck confit. I eye the side of crispy potatoes and cauliflower gratin, and my mouth starts watering.

"So," I say, trying to at least pretend this fancy food hasn't hypnotized me completely, "what's your talent, then?"

Matvey takes a sip of his wine. I'm almost jealous—that must go spectacularly with the meat. "I'm a man of many talents, April."

"First of all, *vomit*. Secondly, that's cheating. Answer the question."

The corner of his lip twitches. Wait, am I making the ice man laugh? Someone give me a Nobel Prize. "Should I just pick one, then?"

"Yes. And being good at mafia-whatever doesn't count."

"*Bratva*," Matvey corrects. "And if that doesn't count, then…"

He looks at me intensely. I can feel heat rising to my cheeks. Then his gaze moves to my belly, and my face catches fire. He's not implying what I think he is, right? He's not saying his talent is—

"I guess I consider myself a family man."

Thank God.

"Is that so?" I mumble around a forkful of duck. If stuffing my face ungracefully is what it takes to keep my stupid mouth from voicing my embarrassing thoughts, then so be it. I'll make the sacrifice.

"Mm," he hums in response. "'*Bratva*' means 'brotherhood.' It's not a family, not by any means—but it's the closest thing you can get without blood in the mix."

"So like a found family?" I perk up. Finally, a topic I can relate to.

"There's no such thing."

My enthusiasm shatters. "Pardon?"

Matvey sets down his fork and knife. "There's no such thing as family without blood ties," he repeats darkly, staring at me with those stormy eyes of his. "The concept alone is ridiculous."

Whatever warmth I'd felt instantly plummets. "Is that so?" I squeak.

"Of course," Matvey asserts. "Family means trust. And you can't trust anyone who isn't blood. You'd be a fool to ever try."

I think of June, holding back tears in our apartment. Of Elias, who's been more of a father to me than my own ever was.

Of...

"What about Petra?" I ask, not a trace of warmth left in my voice.

Matvey sneers. "Petra's an ally. She'll never be family."

"You were supposed to get married."

"A mutually beneficial arrangement," he concedes. "Nothing more."

"*Nothing*?" I press in disbelief. This whole tirade—it's just about the saddest thing I've ever heard. Trusting no one? Treating your friends like pieces on a chessboard? What stone-cold way to live is that?

It must show on my face, because a mocking smirk suddenly blooms on Matvey's lips. "Nothing worth mentioning, anyway."

I fist my dress. So it wasn't *all* business after all.

I force myself to take a breath. *There's no reason to get worked up over this*, I tell myself sternly. Either Matvey's messing with me—in which case, I won't give him the satisfaction of taking the bait—or his "arrangement" with Petra is slightly more than what Yuri made it out to be.

And if it is, so what? What's it to me if Matvey Groza's having fun with his bride-to-be?

"I see," I answer coldly.

Honestly, it makes sense. It was silly of me to think he'd leave a woman like Petra untouched in the first place. He didn't hold back with plain old me; why should he have held back with someone who so clearly belongs on the cover of *Vogue*?

I get that.

I do, truly.

What I don't get is why this bothers me so goddamn much.

"I hear you two met," Matvey mentions casually. Like he's talking about the weather or something. "I trust she behaved."

I could tell him my hand still hurts. That I've actually had to ice it after that harpy was done with it.

Instead, I tuck it in. I may be new to this Bratva thing, but I know how the mob feels about snitches. And say what you want about me, but I've never been a snitch.

"Charming," I reply with my fakest smile.

"Good. I've already made myself very clear with her anyway."

"What about?"

Matvey's eyes pry into me from the other side of the table. Once again, I feel incredibly small. A rabbit in the clutches of a wolf. "You're carrying my child, April. My blood. And as long as that's true, no one will be allowed to hurt you."

It would almost be romantic. It would almost make me feel warm again. Instead, all I can think of is that teensy little disclaimer in the middle of his promise: *As long as that's true.*

"And after?"

Matvey remains unfazed. "After," he answers, clearing away our plates, "you'll be the mother."

He makes it sound so simple. So *easy*. None of this is easy to me, though.

"And what does that mean to you?" I force myself to ask. If I have to spend my time here wondering whether Matvey Groza's gonna get rid of me once I've served my purpose, I'm going to drive myself crazy.

"Everything."

I blink. Matvey's standing now, looking for all intents and purposes like a predator ready to jump.

But he doesn't. He just walks to the fridge and plucks two small trays. Then he continues, "Blood is everything to me, April. That's why I'm here tonight—why I'm planning to be here *every* night. I want my child to grow up with a family." He pauses to place the trays on the table. "And that starts with this."

"Dinner?" I blurt out.

"*Family* dinner."

He sits back down. For a moment, I retreat inside my thoughts. "That's a tradition of yours, I take it?"

"The opposite," Matvey clarifies. "I never had the chance."

That takes me by surprise. I can't understand this man at all —his motives, his reasoning. And yet, I can understand this: wanting to be different from the people who raised you.

Maybe, in a way, we're alike after all.

"So I'll expect you to be there, too," he says then, jolting me out of my thoughts. "Every night. Before the baby's born, and after."

It sounds like a line straight out of *Beauty and the Beast*. That doesn't reassure me one bit. Belle might have gotten her happily ever after, but I seem to remember the Beast being a controlling asshole for roughly half the movie. And I doubt Matvey's got a magic rose stashed in his holster.

I end up picking at my dessert: a slice of black forest cake that should make my mouth water. But, for some reason, I'm not that hungry anymore. Leave it to Matvey Groza to make a pregnant woman lose her appetite.

But that's just it. I'm *pregnant*. I can't afford to make a scene or lose my head. So I swallow my anger and choose strategy.

"So that's it?" I ask finally. "Stepping up for the child—that's what you're doing?"

"That's what *any* parent should do," Matvey answers without missing a beat. "Anything less is a blood betrayal."

There he goes again—*blood*. "And I'm the child's blood."

"You are."

"But I'm not yours."

A beat. "You are not," he confirms eventually.

I decide I've just about had enough. "That's cool and all," I say, pushing away my plate, "but I've got conditions, too."

He arches an eyebrow. "'Conditions'?"

"Yes," I declare, "conditions. You want family dinner every night? That's fine by me. But I want something in return."

Something flashes over Matvey's face. I can't tell what it is—irritation, stupor—because, just as quickly, it's gone.

"Very well," he says, steepling his fingers, his expression carefully neutral. "What is it you want, then, Ms. Flowers?"

What do you want, kalina?

I shake off the memory. "First, I want to see my friends."

"I think that's unnecessary."

"Well, think again," I press. "'Cause you may not believe in found family, but that's the only kind I've got. Frankly, if I had to rely on blood, I'd have been dead ten times over." I don't bother to sugarcoat it. Matvey Groza's got his opinions —I've got mine. "So I get to see them."

For a moment, Matvey's silent. I'm wondering if I didn't push too hard—if this isn't the moment I discover just how unpleasant this man can make it for me here—when, to my surprise, he nods. "Fair enough. Supervised visits, in the lobby. Planned in advance."

Just like prison. Joy.

"Alright."

"And everyone gets vetted."

Is that Bratva code for 'stalked and interrogated'? I decide not to press. I don't think June will mind if the mob unearths her parking tickets. "Okay. Second, I get to keep working."

"Absolutely not," Matvey growls.

I hold up a hand. "I don't need to go to the shop," I tell him. "I can work from here. But I'll need Elias to bring work to me."

He pauses. "That's your boss from the shop?"

"That's him. I believe he did your final fitting for you."

I can see his teeth gritting. He isn't liking this one bit, is he? "Fine. But only part-time."

"Part-time's good," I agree. "One last thing, then."

Forget seeing: I can *hear* his teeth gritting this time. "What else could you possibly want?" Matvey all but snarls.

"You."

For the first time in the whole evening, I'm treated to the sight of a speechless Matvey Groza. "Come again?"

"I'll be here twenty-four-seven," I state, matter-of-factly. "Endlessly available to you." I push my phone across the table. "So I'll expect you to be available to me, too."

He stares at my phone. Then, suddenly, he grins. "If you wanted my number, Ms. Flowers, all you had to do was ask."

Don't slap the father of your child, April. He's stronger than you and he's got guns.

Then Matvey plucks something from his pocket and slides it across in return. I take it.

"A burner phone?" I blink.

Matvey nods, that shit-eating grin still firmly planted on his face. "I wasn't going to leave you without a way to reach me, April. Though I did enjoy how forward you were just now."

Don't hit the mobster, April. Do not—

He rises before I do something regrettable. I do the same. It seems that family dinner's come to an end.

And not a moment too soon.

"Well then," he says, taking my hand. "I'll see you tomorrow night."

Then, out of the blue, he *kisses it.*

I can't move. I can't think. I can't *breathe.* My face turns into a hot plate. You could cook an egg on it: that's how searing it feels.

"Goodnight," Matvey croons, still grinning like a wolf.

I force myself to inhale. "Goodnight," I echo in a whisper, trying not to sway from how lightheaded I'm feeling.

Then he's out.

As soon as I hear his steps fading in the corridor, I slump against the door, cradling my face in my hands. My *hands.* One of which he *kissed.*

What the hell, I wonder helplessly for the second time today, *have I gotten myself into?*

13

MATVEY

I can't stop feeling her.

The whole car ride to the warehouse, I keep touching my lips as if I'll find her there. Where her warmth lingers like a spell.

April Flowers, what kind of witch are you?

What if I'd kept kissing a little higher? All the way up the smooth skin of her inner arm, and then higher still?

Her neck, long and velvety. Her cheeks, so deliciously flushed.

Her lips.

Get it together, I growl to myself. The last thing I need is to get rock-hard in the backseat of my own limo. *You don't get to touch her like that anymore.*

A part of me rebels at the thought.

I know it would be the stupidest possible thing to do—falling back into April's arms. With a child on the way, I can't afford to muddy the waters. I can't afford to let April think we'll ever be more than a one-time fling with consequences.

Co-parents. That's all we'll ever be.

So why can't I stop thinking about her?

Yuri meets me outside. He's wearing his usual scowl—nothing strange there—and holding an unusual envelope. Without a word, he hands it over to me.

"An early birthday card?" I joke. "Brother, you shouldn't have."

Yuri's scowl, if possible, deepens. "The DNA test came back. It's a match."

Fuck. *Well, that settles that.* I open the envelope and run a cursory glance over the information there. Alleles, Doctorese, yada yada—ah, there it is.

99%

Un-fucking-deniable.

"It was a long shot." I shrug, unbothered by the revelation. Probably because it wasn't a revelation at all. Because a part of me knew, deep down…

That child is mine.

Could I feel the unbreakable bond that ran through our veins? Blood is mysterious like that. It was the same with Yuri, all those years ago: the second I met him, I *knew.*

"Are you disappointed?" Yuri asks me, voice low.

I think it over. "No," I answer truthfully. "I expected this. One more mouth to feed is nothing."

It's not just that. I know it's not. Some primal part of me is already laying claim on that child: wanting to protect, wanting to mold. *Mine.*

It's not "nothing." Not by a long shot.

"If…" Yuri hesitates. "Did you mean what you said? That if the child hadn't been yours…"

"Of course," I say without missing a beat, even as a part of me despises what I'm saying. *Casting out the child. Casting out the mother. Turning my back on the two of them.* "Who in their right mind would keep around someone who's nobody to them?"

Yuri flinches at my words, but I don't have time to worry about his delicate disposition. Not when the claim inside me is already extending to the mother of my child. If I want to avoid disaster, I need to nip this in the bud, no matter what.

"Bury this," I order, handing the envelope back to him. "Make sure Vlad doesn't find out. If he asks, the test is still underway."

Yuri nods. "Got it."

I force myself to snap out of it. Thoughts of April's warm body will do me no good right now. No, what I need is a distraction.

Which is why I came here in the first place.

Yuri opens the door to the warehouse. I follow. Already from the stairs, I can smell the stench of blood and human misery.

I walk into a wide, bare room. When I acquired this building, I didn't bother with renovations. For the kind of guests I had in mind, four walls and a roof were more than enough. All they had to do was drown out the screams.

A few men nod with respect as I pass them by. I recognize their faces: Yuri's most trusted, his most loyal.

Good. We can never be too careful.

"Where are they?" I ask, the sound of my steps echoing off the walls.

"We separated them," Yuri informs me. "One in Room A, the other in Room B."

"Prisoner's dilemma," I commend. "Nice work."

Yuri shrugs. "Hasn't yielded results thus far, though. Hopefully, seeing you will scare the truth out of them."

The truth. What a volatile concept. "I'll do my worst."

I fully intend to. With April wreaking havoc on my mind, I need to lose myself in something. Work—but not the sanitized kind. Not the kind you can do behind an expensive desk, earning praise from board members who don't know what their shares are really being used for.

No. I need the kind you do with your own two hands.

I walk into Room A first. One kidnapper is tied to a chair, soaking in a pool of his own blood and fitfully asleep. On a tray nearby, I spy the tools of the trade, still coated in red. Yuri's handiwork, no doubt.

I kick the chair. The guy jolts upright, yanking on his restraints.

And then he sees me. *"Blyat',"* he curses, spitting blood on the floor.

One of them was Russian, April's voice murmurs in my memories.

"Brother," I call him spitefully in his own language, tilting his chin up to see him. "Enjoyed the hospitality?"

This—now, *this* is my scene. Forget sexy baby mamas; this is what I was born to do. Lust is great and all, but it'll never hold a candle to *blood*lust.

Not for me.

Despite the gore and grime covering his entire face, I could swear I recognize him. I can't remember his name—which is odd; I make it my business to know all my men—but I remember his features. I can tell, without a doubt, that I've seen him before.

If only I could remember where.

The man stares at me like he's just seen the angel of death— which, to be fair, is mostly accurate. His entire body begins to shake. A pungent smell reaches my nose and I look down, realizing he's pissing himself.

If he was ever one of mine, I'm glad he no longer is.

I strike him across the face, hard. Something goes *crack* with the motion; seconds later, the man spits a tooth at my feet. "Please," he croaks. "You have to protect me! I'll tell you everything, but you have to—"

I could promise him that. I could pretend I'll ever consider letting him go. With how desperate he is, he'd believe me.

"No," I tell him instead.

This *mudak* kidnapped my child. He kidnapped *April.*

He doesn't get to beg for mercy anymore.

I crouch to his level. Like this, his beady eyes are mere inches from mine. "You have two choices. One, you can tell me what

I want to know. If it checks out, I'll have my best man put a bullet in your skull. Quick and painless."

He starts to shake his head frantically. "No, no, please—"

"*Two*," I cut him off, "I can pick up those pliers. You've got no nails left, but I can still see a good number of teeth ripe for the plucking." For good measure, I run my thumb along his jawline, feeling the ridge of each remaining tooth through his sunken cheek. "You have three seconds to decide, or I'll do it for you."

One.

"Please, don't."

"Then *talk*."

"I can't!" *Two.* "I can't, please, you have no idea—"

Three.

I wrinkle my nose. I was looking forward to doing this myself, but the smell has just gotten unbearable. "Yuri," I call from the doorway. "Take care of our patient here."

I hand him the pliers. "Gladly," he hisses, staring at the guy like he's nothing but a shit stain on the sidewalk. Which, considering the stench, might not be far from the truth.

I leave them behind and close the door.

Then I head to Room B.

The setup is the same. Tool cart, blood, restraints. Only this time, the guy isn't asleep.

"Matvey Groza," he spits with an accent I immediately place. "My boss sends his regards."

I don't need to ask any more questions. If I wanted to, I could pick up my gun and paint the walls with this man's brains. *This man*—the second motherfucker who dared lay his filthy hands on the mother of my child.

Instead, I pick up the pliers. "Really?" I drawl, feeling my face split into a grin. The grin of a wolf cornering its prey. "Then I'll have to send him something back."

I don't think of April again all night.

14

APRIL

When the doorbell rings that morning, I practically skip to answer it. I already know who it's gonna be. For once, no surprises: no scorned brides, no brooding billionaires, no Grisha with a tea tray.

"There she is!" Elias booms, pulling me into a bear hug. "My favorite employee."

I feel my spine creak slightly, but I let it happen. Honestly, it's a small price to pay. What's a few broken ribs to finally see a friendly face?

"I thought I was your *only* employee?"

"Details, details." Elias waves me off.

I usher him in, past the armed gorillas at the door. He glances back with good-humored suspicion. "Alright, where's Ms. Swift hiding?"

"Oh, you know." I shrug, helping Elias with the two giant suitcases he's carrying. "Some blank space or other."

Predictably, Elias doesn't let me touch his bags. "And how's my little Nugget been?" he asks, grinning at my belly.

"Comfortable." If nothing else, it's true. All throughout the kidnapping, the wedding crashing, *and* moving day, Mr. or Ms. Chicken Nug didn't bat an eye. Either I'm too tired to feel it kicking, or I'm carrying the next Buddha. "How about you?"

"Busy," he admits, though still grinning. "But nothing I can't handle."

I feel a pang of guilt. "I'm really sorry for dropping off the face of the Earth like that," I say. "It's just been crazy these past few days."

Elias tuts. "I've been trying to get you to go on maternity leave for months, missy. Now that you've finally listened, I'll be thanking my lucky stars."

"I still don't like it." I grimace. "There's so much to do lately. I don't want you to have to shoulder it alone."

Elias gives me a benevolent smile. "My darling girl," he says, squeezing my shoulders, "you're gonna be a mother soon. You can't keep worrying about everybody else—especially little ol' me. You feel me?"

I sigh. Of course Elias would say that. Eighty years old, and still nowhere near planning retirement. I was hoping, with my help around the shop, that day would come sooner rather than later. I was almost there, too, I think—I could see his resistance slowly giving in, the Bahamas pamphlets sticking out of his coat pockets, thoughts of white sand beaches and all-you-can-eat seafood buffets calling his name.

Then I went and got myself pregnant.

"Yeah," I concede. "But I can still offer you tea, right?"

"The day I say no to that is a very sad day indeed, Ms. Flowers. Pour away."

I busy myself in the kitchen, boiling water and plucking jars with all types of rare teas. What the hell's a Matcha Iri Genmaicha? Just reading that is giving me a headache.

I pour, dumping in a few Jasmine Pearls for good measure. If I'm gonna be a prisoner here for the foreseeable future, I should at least enjoy the benefits. Somehow, I don't think Matvey will mind that I'm raiding his pantry.

And if he does? All the better.

I offer Elias his cup. "Thanks for bringing everything here," I say, sitting down across from him. "God knows I need the distraction."

"And I'm happy to provide," Elias replies. "If that's *all* it is. If I find out you've been overworking yourself, I'll teach li'l Nugget in there the Lindy Hop."

"I'm frankly terrified."

God, I missed this. I didn't even realize how much. Elias's jokes, his New Orleans accent—all of it puts me at ease like nothing else. There isn't another boss in the world like Elias Turner, nor another mentor.

After Grandma died, he was the one who saved me.

"So," Elias says, snapping me out of my reverie, "those gorillas out there…"

I wave my hand. "Pretend they're furniture."

"Think they'll volunteer as mannequins?"

"You know, that's actually not a bad idea. They're always standing still anyway. I bet I could sew a whole jacket on each before they'd notice."

Elias's eyes crinkle. "And their boss?" he asks, his smile dimming somewhat. "He treating you alright?"

I cradle my cup in my hands. "He…" *He buys me dinner. He kisses my hand. He hates my guts.* "Yeah," I settle on. "Yeah, he is."

Elias squints. He doesn't miss anything, does he? I can't lie to this man. Is this how it feels to tell your dad you're going to have a sleepover at your friend Janice's and then sneak into a boy's car?

I wouldn't know. My dad never cared enough to ask.

But Elias is the closest thing I have to that: a father. And now, as he looks me up and down with that all-seeing, all-knowing gaze of his, I'm starting to learn what leaving for prom feels like.

Specifically, the *"Isn't that dress a bit short?"* part.

In the end, Elias doesn't call me out. All he asks is, suddenly serious, "Are you safe here, April?"

I think back to the wedding. To Matvey's strong hand dragging me away. I think back to his words last night: *No one will be allowed to hurt you.*

"Yes," I answer, more certain this time. I don't know how I know: after all, who's more unpredictable than my baby daddy, the mob boss extraordinaire? And yet… "I am. He'll keep me safe."

That clears Elias's face of all clouds. "Good." He wags a stern, wrinkled finger in my face. "He'd better."

We sip our tea in comfortable silence. At some point, Elias sighs. "It feels like yesterday that you came to me. A scrawny, scrappy thing with a binder under her arm."

"You asked for my ID," I laugh, reminiscing. "You couldn't believe I was eighteen."

"Darling, you were skin and bone," he points out.

Which—fair, I was. *Girls who misbehave don't get to eat dinner,* a cruel voice drawls from my memories. *They only get to clean it up.*

I shake it off. "I didn't think you'd recognize me, but you did."

"Child," Elias laughs, all booming and affectionate, "I'm ashamed it took reading your ID to jog this old man's memory. You're the spitting image of her."

I twist my fingers against the cup. "I doubt it. After all, we weren't…"

Blood, Matvey's voice echoes in my thoughts.

But Elias just shakes his head. "Blood isn't the only thing that binds us," he says, as if reading my mind. "I can see Maia in everything you do: the way you hold a needle, the Band-Aids on every other finger." He leans in, whispering mischievously, "The way you scrunch up your face like a li'l bunny when something doesn't match the idea in your head." He taps my nose gently as he says this last part, causing the exact scrunched-up face in question. "She might not have been your father's mother, but she was your grandma in all the ways that counted. And you're her granddaughter. You're hers, alright. You're Maia through and through."

I force myself to blink away the tears. *Goddammit, Elias.* Even after all these years…

Even after all these years, he still loves her.

I don't know the details of their story. Elias never shared the painful bits, and my grandma always got this bittersweet, far-off look in her eye whenever the topic came up. All I have is guesses: wrong place, wrong time, wrong family.

In the end, Maia Toussaint didn't marry Elias Turner. She married Augustus Flowers, gaining another woman's son in the process.

And then, eventually, me.

"I don't know what I would have done without you," I say. "I mean that. After she died…"

After she died, I was alone. My parents had new families, and I didn't fit into either one. If you hadn't been there…

I feel a gentle touch on my hand and I look up. Elias is there, smiling at me like the father I never had—the father I wish I'd had.

But, in a way, I guess I did.

Eventually.

"Maia was the light of my world," Elias says, his voice just on the wrong side of steady. "And you were the light of *her* world. Now…"

We both glance at my belly.

"Now," he concludes with a watery smile, "you're going to meet the light of your world, too."

We hug goodbye. I'm still fighting the urge not to bawl like a child by the time Elias says, with one foot out the door, "You let me know if you need anything, you hear?" He side-eyes the bodyguards as he says it, which makes me suppress a snort. Eighty-year-old tailor Elias Turner, threatening the Russian mob with a distinct lack of subtlety. "I'll be here lickety-split."

I nod, smiling. "Thank you, Elias. Truly."

I watch his back grow smaller in the corridor. Matvey's words come back to me: *There's no such thing as family without blood ties.*

That may be true for him. But for me, *blood* has never once meant *family.* To me, family is the people I chose. The people who chose *me.*

Now, I sigh to myself, retreating inside, *where do you fit in all that, Matvey Groza?*

15

APRIL

By the time family dinner comes around, I still haven't found my answer.

"Evening," Matvey greets, the picture of perfect courtesy. He's wearing a tailored anthrax gray jacket and a crisp burgundy shirt. His cologne wafts through the air with every step, nearly overpowering the delicacies on the tray.

God in Heaven above, one question for ya: why did You make Your biggest asshole so fucking hot?

I shake myself. This is not the time to be ogling the enemy. "Hi," I offer back, polite but distant.

Matvey arches an eyebrow at me. Then he motions for whatever poor waiter he plucked from his shift downstairs to push the cart inside. The victim in question isn't quite shaking, but I have a feeling I'll hear the cutlery rattle soon enough.

"Thank you," I say, hurrying to commandeer the cart. "I can take it from here."

The waiter shoots me a grateful look. Then, once Matvey finally nods, he can't duck out fast enough.

"You don't have to do that." Matvey frowns. "It's his job. He's paid to do it."

"And I'm paid to take measurements and make suits," I counter, gliding by with our trays. "But I think we both know customers can overstep."

Matvey stops just shy of a *Touché*. There's an amused glint in his eyes, but I force myself to pay it no mind. If I start appreciating all the little ways he's secretly charming, I won't survive the night.

Then he pulls out my chair. I die a little inside.

"How was your day?" he asks, settling across from me. To think that, just hours ago, it was me and Elias here, having tea and pouring our hearts out...

Fat chance of that happening. If Matvey has a heart at all, he has yet to show the symptoms.

"Good," I say, spying the menu for the night. I'm a girl of simple needs... and, apparently, a way finer palate than I imagined. I can't bring myself to splurge on anything fancy for lunch—though the salads here will make you cry for the opposite reason than most salads do—but part of me was already looking forward to this.

For the food, of course.

Certainly not for the company.

"How was yours?" I ask before digging into my smoked salmon risotto with asparagus cream. The lemon zest on top practically melts in my mouth. I swear, I've never had to try this hard not to moan.

Well. *Almost* never.

"Good," Matvey echoes.

I wait for him to say something else, but he doesn't. It's not fair of me to expect it—I was the first to choose the hermit life—but man... if this is gonna be the level of conversation, this family dinner thing is gonna be even more awkward than I feared.

"I never had family dinner before," I find myself blurting out. "Or, well, not at the table."

Matvey's eyebrow shoots up. "How's that?"

Great job, April. Way to trauma dump. "We weren't really... traditional." It's not completely true: at least one half of my family is traditional to a fault. So traditional, in fact, they used to send the bastard daughter to cook with the help.

It's why I don't do this anymore—it just brings up shit I'd sooner forget.

But I'm not about to tell a stranger that. Because that's what Matvey and I are: strangers.

Who just happen to share 50% of our genes with the same baby.

Instead, I pick the least traumatic of the two halves of my family history. Which is saying a lot, all things considered. "My stepdad usually ate on the couch. You know, like the Romans," I add, attempting to lighten the mood.

Matvey frowns harder. *Attempt failed.* "And your mother?"

"She preferred... the liquid variety," I say vaguely. If there's anything Eleanor actually likes in this world besides Charlie, it's things that come in dark, corked bottles. But again—not gonna tell him that.

"I see."

If he didn't think you were trailer trash before, he certainly does now. "What about you?" I ask before I can connect my brain-to-mouth filter. "Did you have family dinner a lot with your mom?"

It's only then that I remember two things. First: Matvey, last night, saying he "never got the privilege" of family dinner at all.

And, secondly, Yuri's words: *Our parents are dead.*

Fuck. Fuckity fuck fuck—

"I did."

My head shoots up. Matvey's watching me carefully, as if trying to gauge my motives. It feels a wee bit excessive, but then again, I did just put both feet in my mouth. Maybe he's just curious how that works.

"It wasn't all three of us together," he mentions off-handedly, switching our empty plates for full ones. "And it certainly wasn't as fancy as this. But I have... good memories of that. Me, my mom, and the dinner table."

Well, fuck me sideways with an Olive Garden breadstick. Is Matvey Groza... *sharing*?

"That must've been nice," I say sincerely. "Is that why you want to keep the routine alive for...?"

For our baby. The words stick in my throat. It still feels so weird—having a baby with someone I barely know. Having something to call *ours*. If I think about it any harder, I'm gonna give myself an aneurysm.

Instead, I focus on the mouthwatering contents of my plate. Right now, that involves quail legs with tamarind glaze and fig chutney. There are about three things I'm itching to Google in that name alone, but I don't think Mr. Family Dinner here would take kindly to that. I can almost hear it: *No phones at the dinner table, Ms. Flowers.*

Is it bad that the idea of him scolding me kinda hot?

No! Bad April. Bad, bad hormones.

Matvey hums in the affirmative. I have to track back two separate freakouts to even remember what my question was.

Then I can hear the silence stretching again between us.

Quick, ask something. Anything. "What about your dad?"

It's like the air freezes around us. Like in those ghost movies, where the windows start icing over and people's breaths begin to puff.

Shit. I fucked up, didn't I?

"My father was a traitor."

I look up from my plate. Matvey's face is a mask of tension, cold radiating from his arctic eyes. Every muscle has gone rigid, starting from the thin line of his mouth. If I think of last night—that sly grin painted over carmine lips—it feels like a fever dream. To think that face could smile at all.

I should take the hint. I should bring up the weather. Politics. The local sportsball team. Anything, really, to change the subject.

But I don't.

Bad April.

"What do you mean?" I ask instead, feeling a strange pull towards that topic. *Wanting* to know.

"Precisely what I said," Matvey replies curtly. "He betrayed us."

"But I thought you said blood—"

"I did," he cuts me off. "And I meant it. You can't trust anybody in this life, April. Only blood. So let me ask you this: what's the worst crime you could possibly commit?"

I don't want to play along with this. I want to go back to talking about nothing—about dinners and creating good memories.

But then I think of Eleanor's ever-present bottle. Of Dominic's new home, without a seat for me at the table.

"Betraying your blood," I croak.

"Exactly." Matvey pushes away his plate. He's barely touched it, but I can relate. I also seem to have lost my appetite. "No one's worse than a blood traitor. No one. Only death can wash out that stain."

He rises. So do I. Our mascarpone and blackberry tarts lie untouched on their trays, so I quietly stash them in the fridge. Maybe I'll share with Grisha in the morning.

And then, because I haven't learned my lesson yet, I speak up. "I don't disagree with that," I tell Matvey, trying to keep the tremor out of my voice. "Betraying your family is horrible. But I still don't think blood's the only way to make a family."

"Is that so?" Matvey comments noncommittally. "Well, we've have to agree to disagree."

When he takes his leave, he kisses my hand again. But this time, for whatever reason, his lips don't feel half as warm as last night.

Instead, they feel cold as ice.

16

MATVEY

I'm woken up by my curtains being wrenched open.

Forcefully.

"Rise and shine, sweetheart!" Petra's nightmarish voice screeches. Am I still dreaming? Somebody tell me I'm still dreaming.

Normally, I don't do slaughter before 9:00 A.M. I might make an exception today.

Sighing, I try to pinch myself awake and fail miserably. "You have five seconds to tell me what the everlasting *fuck* you're doing in my apartment."

Apparently, my bride only needs three. "We need to talk about Vlad."

I groan. The last thing I want to do is talk about a wrinkly old man who spits when he talks. Especially when I was just in the middle of dreaming up a certain tailor in handcuffs and nothing else.

"Is he dead?"

"No."

"Then someone's gonna be."

Petra scoffs—actually *scoffs*. "He's getting restless. I can't keep him under control anymore."

"God forbid you keep anything under control."

"I'm sorry—what was that, Mr. Unplanned Parenthood?"

The lion, the witch, and the audacity of this—

Something whistles from the kitchen. I jump upright, snatching my gun from under my pillow.

"Oh!" Petra goes, trotting to the stove. "Kettle's boiled."

Clearly, I have to rethink my *no-slaughter-before-nine* policy. Homicide doesn't keep office hours, apparently. "How did you even get in? I don't remember giving you a key."

Petra simply laughs. "God, you're hilarious."

I make myself count down from ten. *You can't kill her, Matvey. You can't marry a corpse, Matvey. Think of the mess on the carpets, Matvey.* "Tell me you made coffee and I'll consider sparing you."

"Strong as hell, just how you like it." Petra dangles a full pot. "Do I get to live another day, *moy pakhan?*"

"Hmph. For now."

I drag myself out of bed. I'm wearing nothing but a pair of sweats, but I doubt Petra's the modest type. If she were, she would've called ahead. Or, at the very least, she would've fucking knocked.

"What's got Vlad's panties in a twist?"

We both cringe at my word choice. "Okay, first: *ew*. Second: your little *komuk*, what else? He wants to know if the runt is yours or not."

I pour myself a generous mug. I'm gonna need a lot of caffeine for this particular conversation. Maybe something stronger mixed in, too.

"It's mine," I confirm.

"*Blyat',*" Petra curses under her breath. "You're positive?"

"The paternity tests are," I answer after taking a long, scalding sip that burns every inch of me on its way down. *Just what the doctor ordered.* The pain centers me. "Both of them."

"Okay," Petra exhales, pacing up and down the loft. "Okay. Fine. We're screwed, but fine."

"We're not," I yawn from the kitchen table. "As far as Vlad is concerned, the test is still in the works. If push comes to shove, we'll tell him it came up inconclusive. That'll buy us time until the birth."

"Oh, that's great," Petra bites out sarcastically. "And then what?"

"Then," I growl back, impatience pounding at my temples, "the waters will have calmed. Vlad will have come to his senses. He'll realize there's no point in blowing up a profitable business deal over an extra mouth to feed. The end."

"*The end,*" Petra mocks. "Sure. And maybe pigs will fly and hell will freeze over and my father will conveniently forget all about the woman who pushed out that extra mouth to feed."

"Yes, as a matter of fact, he will." I rise to my full height. I'm growing tired of this game. "Because there's nothing between me and April."

Nothing but the memory of her skin under my lips. Nothing but the daily kisses I indulge in to keep that memory alive.

Petra shoots me a venomous smirk. "Is that so?"

I don't dignify that with an answer. "Is that all?" I ask instead, moving towards the door. The sooner this nightmare of a conversation ends, the sooner I can get back to things that actually matter.

No such luck. "When's the little *komuk* due anyway?"

"We don't know." I shrug. I went through all of April's medical records from the last nine months: post-term pregnancy, family history, yada yada. Only the sex of the baby was blacked out—at April's request, no doubt. "Apparently, it's comfortable where it is."

She sighs. "Lucky bastard."

"Don't."

Surprised, Petra turns to look at me. "Don't what?"

My fist is balled up on the table, knuckles gone white. I don't make an effort to control the sudden surge of anger rushing through me.

I was clear about this once already. I don't like having to be clear twice.

"Don't call my child a bastard. I told you what would happen if you disrespected either of them."

Petra blinks candidly. "I meant no disrespect, Matvey."

Her tone is astonished. Subdued.

I don't trust it one bit.

"I find that hard to believe."

True to form, Petra circles the table and comes up to me. "What else do you call a child born out of wedlock?" she asks, feigning innocence. "It's not an insult, you know; it's a fact."

"Petra."

"Of course," she continues, refusing to heed my warnings, "if you want a *legitimate* heir…"

Her manicured hand splays over my chest. I can feel my literal skin trying to pull away from her touch, the most unpleasant goosebumps I've ever felt spreading where her palm lays.

And then, just as I'm summoning all of my restraint, she leans up on her tiptoes and whispers, close to my ear, "There's always time to make one."

I shake her off. *Violently.* Then I start walking away before I do something I'll regret.

Like put a bullet between the eyes of my most important ally.

"Oh, come on! What is it?" Petra calls over to me. "What, got someone else on your mind?"

Warm skin. Soft hands. Lips like—

"No."

"Mm. Could've fooled me."

I grab my gun from where I left it. That seems to shock Petra into silence.

"You can go home of your own accord right now," I start, tossing the weapon back and forth between my hands, "or you can go home in a body bag. Your choice."

For a moment, Petra's quiet. Then: "Alright, alright, I get it. God, you really are no fun. I was only joking, you know."

I watch her out of the corner of my eye as she sashays to the door. For all that Vlad's keeping her out of higher management for being a woman, she should count herself fucking lucky right now. If a man had spoken to me like that, I would've put him six feet under.

"Matvey…" she calls from the doorway.

"What?"

A pause. "You're still up for this, right?" she asks, tone suddenly uncertain. It's damn near imperceptible, but it's there. "Us?"

I take my time to reply. "As long as you hold up your end of the deal," I growl, the threat clear in my voice, "I'll hold up mine."

"Alright then," Petra says at last. "Don't forget."

Then, blessedly, she's *finally* out the door.

I sit down heavily on the edge of the bed. Petra has a knack for a lot of things, but the worst is getting under my skin. The conversation keeps playing back in my head, certain sentences sticking out like splinters.

There's nothing between me and April.

Got someone else on your mind?

Mm. Could've fooled me.

"Nothing," I snarl out loud to the empty loft. To myself, willing my own words to fucking sink in. Anything less than that, and this will all become an even worse shitshow than it already is. "There's nothing."

By the time my phone buzzes, I almost believe it.

17

MATVEY

Yuri's text only has four words: ***Up for round two?***

Good. I need to fucking vent.

Fifteen minutes later, I'm back at the warehouse. Gloves on, tools spread out in front of me. Last time, I played nice with the foreigner. This time, I pick a different toy.

"Please," the Russian *mudak* goes as I give him the spa treatment. Specifically, to his right shoulder. "Please, please, *stop—*"

Crack.

"Man," I sigh, rolling my own shoulders with satisfaction. "You're so tense, my friend. When's the last time you had a massage?"

The guy answers with a wail.

Despite being the worst piss-baby I've ever interrogated—and yes, I mean that literally—somehow, he still hasn't cracked. Talk about miracles, huh?

Maybe he's one of my people after all.

"This can all be over in minutes, you know. It's up to you."

I can see he's tempted. The light in a man's eyes when he's struck with sudden hope—nothing shines as bright as that. But then his face shutters with dread. "I c-can't."

"Really?" I drawl, letting my glove snap against my wrist. "I don't get it. What's this guy gonna do to you that I won't?"

I already know the answer to that, of course. If his colleague's intel is genuine, this *mudak*'s got plenty to be scared of. It's still fucking annoying, though.

I far prefer it when they're scared of *me.*

"My..." the piss-baby splutters, whining between words. "My f-family. He'll kill them all."

As expected. I'm the most cold-blooded motherfucker on earth, but even I wouldn't stoop to going after innocents. That's the difference between me and *him*—I draw the line at family.

Not that he even knows the meaning of the word.

However, this guy doesn't need to know that. It doesn't matter what I would or wouldn't do: all that matters is what he *believes*. And I've always been good at playing the monster.

"What makes you think I won't?"

My hostage's eyes go wide. "No."

"Yes." I walk slowly around the chair. Each step echoes in the cold, damp air of the warehouse. "And you know what? I won't just put a bullet in their heads. I'll make it *hurt*."

"You w-wouldn't!"

"Why don't we ask Lefty?"

Snap. Crackle. Pop goes another shoulder.

It's so satisfying—the crunch of bone and resolve. I haven't been here even half an hour, and already, my mood has improved. I can feel my stress melt with every moan of pain.

But every game must be ended at its highest point. So I peel off my gloves, put away my toolbox, and make my way out the door.

"Wait!" the man calls, terrified. "Wait, you can't—"

Clang.

"Actually," I call through the shut metal door, "I can."

I go outside. The crisp morning air hits my face, coaxing me back into the world. On the sunny side of it, where the shadows stick close to the things that cast them.

My world is different. In my world, shadows stretch on forever.

With Yuri still indoors tending to our other houseguest, I'm bored. My hands itch for a cigarette. I quit smoking years ago, but it's a tough habit to break. Especially at times like these.

I fish something else out of my jacket instead. An old, battered pocket watch stares back at me from my palm, its hands long dead. They've been still for decades, a crack in the glass snaking from one side to the other.

I don't know why I keep carrying this. It's a waste of space, really.

You do know, a part of me whispers, the same part that's always hungry. For cracked bone, spilled blood, anything. *It keeps the fire alive.*

It keeps revenge *alive.*

"What was he like?"

Yuri's voice snaps me out of my thoughts. I didn't even hear him approach—that's how off I am today. "He wasn't." I can practically hear my brother's frown. So, sighing, I elaborate. "Absence was his gift to us. Every night, my mother would wait up for him, the dinner table laid out until the midnight toll. Sometimes, way past that."

I don't know what's made me so talkative. Usually, I wouldn't answer a question like this. But then, at the back of my mind, I can hear the echo of April's words: *What about your dad?*

Family dinner. What a stupid expectation to have of a man like him. Back then, it always turned into a family wake. Waiting, as the night grew colder, for someone who might not return.

Until, one night, he didn't.

That's why I keep this, I remind myself, turning over the watch in my hands. *Because of every second he took from me.* When the sickness came—when we needed him—he was nowhere to be found.

And Mama's time ran out.

Are you still up for this? Us?

Of fucking course I am. I won't give up on my revenge. Not for a baby bump in the road. Not for anything.

"Sounds like I didn't miss much," Yuri remarks at last, kicking a piece of debris down the alley.

I feel a nasty smirk pulling at the corner of my lips. "You didn't."

Yuri. He was so small when I found him. Small and scrawny, one gust of wind away from blowing into the Volga River.

"Do you remember when we first met?"

I don't need to ask. The answer's the same every time. "Like it was yesterday," Yuri whispers.

"You were gathering firewood outside," I recall, smiling fondly. "Snow up to your waist. You were practically swimming."

Yuri snorts. "Always calling me short, aren't you?"

At six foot two, no one in their right mind would say that to him anymore. But back then, I felt like he could fit in the palm of my hand.

My little brother. The only family I had left.

It's the one good thing that that monster of man did: gave us each other. And he didn't even do that on purpose.

"You helped," Yuri murmurs after a while. "With my mom."

Of course I did. Who else was going to?

Back then, in rural Russia, the most commonplace illnesses were enough to take a life away. Especially if you didn't have a coin to your name. It's another thing we have in common—watching the ice take everything from us. Our mothers, our homes, our future.

But I refused to bow to that last part. I picked up my grandfather's name, chased after the remnants of his Bratva, and made it anew. Made it *mine.* No one would dare take our futures after that.

"Ready for round three?"

And no one, I think as visions of hazel eyes pass through my mind, *will ever take it again.*

"Lead the way, brother."

18

APRIL

I make my way to the Jupiter Hotel Restaurant with a skip in my step. Usually, I'd have no reason to be in such a good mood while still in my gilded cage—but today's different.

Today, I get to *see them.*

"Over here!"

I'd recognize June's voice anywhere. I rush to the restaurant entrance with the speed of a cracked-out-on-sugar five-year-old at Disneyland. Who knew a pregnant woman with sore feet could run this fast?

Behind me, Grisha chuckles.

I pull June into a crushing hug. Then I turn to the third person in our party and do the same.

"It's been too long, Apes!" Corey says, nearly picking me off the ground. Which, considering the extra Nugget in my body, is no small feat.

"God, I missed you both so much," I squeak, throwing my arms around the two of them.

Truthfully, it hasn't even been a week since I've last hugged June. But that tearful goodbye has us both swallowing back tears now, like a pair of mushy little schoolgirls.

"Ms. Evans," Grisha greets, ever-polite. "Mr. Evans. I'll leave Ms. Flowers in your capable hands."

Corey mock-salutes. June makes a sound that might have been a giggle. I do a double-take. *What the hell? Since when does June giggle?*

"Thank you," I tell Grisha. "I'll meet you back here in an hour."

An hour. That's the most I've been able to negotiate for today's get-together. Apparently, the safety risk is too great to linger on the ground floor for long. The penthouse is isolated, but anyone could walk in here. Anyone skilled enough to evade the security check, that is.

I suppose the people after me definitely qualify.

A waiter leads us to our reserved table, pulling out the chairs for both us girls in turn. June shoots me a look, but I can only shrug.

We sit down and pick up our brunch menus. "So," June says, glancing back at the waiter, "lap of luxury, huh?"

"Pretty much." It will never stop being weird—this sudden role reversal. From berated worker to potentially berating customer.

Which I'd *never*, of course. But the awkwardness stays.

Corey wolf-whistles. "Snazzy place. Reminds me of the old days."

"Right?" June nods. "It's like that time Papa took us to the Four Seasons."

With people like June and Corey, it's easy to forget. A waitress and a publishing intern, respectively, both minimum wage earners counting pennies to make it through the end of the month.

It's easy to forget that they come from money.

Like many wealthy families, the Evanses had everything money could buy. And because of that, they desperately wanted the one thing it couldn't: a child.

After lots of struggle for "a child of their own"—something they never failed to word as painfully as possible—they finally swallowed the hard truth: only a miracle could give them that. Thus, they decided to go down the adoption road. That was how Corey came into the family.

Weighed down by expectations, Corey grew up among the finest things in life… and the coldest. Not a day went by that Mr. and Mrs. Evans would let him forget he wasn't "theirs." That he was the second choice. As such, they claimed, he had to work hard to "repay them." In that loveless house, Corey spent the first five years of his life alone.

And then Mr. Evans packed up.

Of course, Mrs. Evans couldn't let that happen. As a Hamptons socialite, she'd built her reputation around the image of a perfect, happy marriage. Divorce would have been a scandal.

So she made the miracle happen.

Nine months later, June was born. Mrs. Evans presented her to the world as her little miracle—and Mr. Evans was forced to come back from his "business trip."

Problem was, Mr. Evans never believed in miracles. He knew the truth. And so he retreated to his studio and his cognac bottles. After a while, Mrs. Evans gave up trying to save what couldn't be saved. Their rings stayed on their fingers, but it was never more than that.

And June was a miracle no longer.

With a background like that, the Evans siblings should have hated each other. Their parents certainly never lost a chance to pit them against each other, like living pawns in a sick game of chess. That was the *real* miracle: that, instead, they grew up inseparable. The second choice and the glue baby of dubious parentage, together against the world. A family of two.

Then I came along and made three.

"I'm thinking Buddha bowl," June muses, looking up at the waiter who's since come back. "It's cheap enough, and—"

"We're putting everything on Matvey's tab," I announce.

"Lobster hash, please," June rectifies. "And a glass of your finest white."

"Hanger steak and eggs for me," Corey pipes up. "Heavy on the eggs. And an Old Fashioned."

"Waffles and fried chicken," I decide, earning two pairs of disbelieving eyes on me. "And a sparkling water, please."

The waiter bows to us and leaves.

"What?" I ask the two Evanses. "Nugget's got cravings."

"Nugget needs to watch *Eloise at the Plaza*," June remarks. "And step up that palate."

"Bold of you to assume it has a palate," Corey comments. "Need I remind you what its mother eats for breakfast, lunch, and dinner?"

"Hey!" I counter. "There's nothing wrong with mac and cheese."

"Sure thing, Drew Barrymore."

I pout. "I don't remember hearing you complain about my lunch boxes when you were twelve."

"Yeah, because I was *twelve.*"

I blow him a raspberry. June—my cheesy partner in crime —joins in. "*Boo.* You're missing out on the finest thing in life."

"I'm missing out on a coronary attack and an endless case of diarrhea."

Listening to them bicker like this, my heart fills with warmth. It brings back memories of afterschool ice cream and bowling nights. Whenever Corey was around, we felt invincible—no bullies would dare come close to us. He wasn't just June's big brother—he was mine, too.

And we were both his little sisters.

Which is why I'm not surprised when, after our delicious brunch arrives, Corey suddenly turns serious. "Look, Apes," he says, glancing around the restaurant with suspicion. "This all looks very nice, but… you're okay, right?"

June draws close to me, nodding along. "Because, you know, if anything's off…"

I give them both a reassuring smile. "I'm okay," I tell them, taking their hands in mine. "I promise."

I don't feel half as confident as that, but I hope it doesn't show. This whole thing with Matvey is... complicated, for lack of a better term. But I still don't think it's dangerous.

Not in a life-or-death way, at least. As for other types of danger... you'd have to ask my traitorous hormones.

"You're sure?" Corey frowns, picking up on my uncertainty. "'Cause Rob's one hell of a lawyer. I bet he could get you half of everything here, plus full custody. And if he ever lays a hand on you—"

"Oh, no danger of that," I joke bitterly. "He won't touch me with a ten-foot pole. He's made that very clear."

"That's... good?" Corey tries.

"Of course it's good." I frown. "Why wouldn't it be?"

"I don't know," June says evasively. "You did kinda say it like it was a bad thing, babe."

Did I? As if on command, the back of my hand starts tingling with the memory of his lips. His touch. His warmth. His—

"Nope," I splutter, chasing that thought firmly away. "Nope. Absolutely not."

"If you say so," Corey says, clearly skeptical. "But my offer still stands. If he so much as raises his voice..."

I shake my head and smile. "He really cares about this baby," I tell Corey, and I mean it. "He cares about family." *In his own ominous way, but still.* "He wants us to have dinner together every night."

"He wants *what*?" the siblings squawk in unison.

"For the baby!" I cut in quickly. "I'm just saying, he cares. And I know… he'll take good care of us."

The words come out of their own accord. The Evanses blink at me in surprise, and I realize I'm surprised, too. *Since when do I feel this way?*

"Okay," June exhales. "Cool. So when's the wedding?"

I promptly spit out my water.

It takes a good few minutes—and Corey patting me forcefully on the back—for my coughing to subside. "*Jay.*"

"What?" June asks defensively. "You're his baby mama now. Surely a guy like that will put a ring on your finger?"

I shake my head like a wet Labrador. "I *crashed* his wedding, in case you forgot."

"With a mobster chick," Corey adds helpfully.

"Yes, with a *mobster chick*!" I shiver internally at the thought of Petra overhearing anyone calling her that. From what I've seen, that "chick" has claws like a harpy. "So that kind of disqualifies me."

"Does it, though?" June squints. "Plans can change."

Gee, don't I know that? "Not these plans," I mutter. "Trust me."

"Who knows? A smile here, a token of everlasting love there, a bit of lace in the right spot…"

"Jay, please."

"Alright. If you insist. Party pooper."

"Thank you."

"… It's not Mobster Chick he's taking to dinner, though."

I choke again.

Once the waiter's been talked out of calling me an ambulance, we inhale the rest of our food and make a hasty retreat. With my cheeks still filled with fried goodness, I walk my friends to the exit. That's when I notice a familiar face waving to us. "Hey!"

I light up. "Rob!"

Corey bounds up to meet him. "You made it!"

"Of course," Rob says, leaning over to peck him on the lips. "Couldn't miss the chance to say hi, could I?"

He crushes me into a hug. That's the third time today, but I don't mind. After nine months in there, Nugget's a squeeze warrior. "God, I haven't seen you in forever!"

"Guilty as charged," Rob admits. "In my defense, the partners have been riding me like it's the damn Kentucky Derby."

"Price of success, right?" I grin. We all know how hard Rob's been working to become the youngest junior partner at his firm, and we're all one hundred percent behind him. "A little bird told me it's a matter of months 'til you get the corner office."

"Did he, now?" he says with a sly grin, turning to Corey. "Little bird talks too much."

"Little bird's got spousal privilege. He can do it."

"That's the opposite of how it works, Cor," June pipes up, earning an instant hair ruffle from her brother-in-law.

"Well said, June-bug."

Rob. It feels like yesterday that Corey introduced him to us.

Two shy teenagers, holding hands as if that simple gesture took all the courage in the world.

Which I guess it did.

Predictably, Corey's parents didn't take it well. That's when both siblings left the nest—and their nest eggs—behind. They never looked back once.

Last spring, Corey and Rob finally tied the knot. It was so beautiful—I cried like a piglet. But I couldn't help it; not when they looked at each other like there wasn't anybody else in the world.

I remember thinking, *This.* This *is what I want. Nothing less than* that *look.*

Alas, plans change.

"Ms. Flowers," Grisha calls, materializing at my side like the Ghost of Christmas Past. I barely restrain myself from screaming. "Shall we head back?"

It's his way of saying, *It's time to go.* I appreciate the discretion, but a part of me deflates. I wish moments like these could last forever.

I hug everyone goodbye. "Don't be strangers," I joke, trying to hide how much I mean it.

They all see right through me. "Never," they promise in unison.

Before leaving, June presses something into my hand. "Here."

I open my palm. It's a hair ribbon—a new one.

"Since you keep losing them," she explains. "If you miss me too much, hug it three times and sing the lyrics to *Fireworks.* I'll appear like Beetlejuice."

"That's very funny."

"I know. I'm hilarious."

I walk back to the elevator in high spirits. Screw Matvey's idea of family—*this* is my family, and I wouldn't trade it for the world.

Back at the penthouse, my eyes fall on my workspace. On a scrap of fabric dyed a deep blue, almost violet in the light. *A smile here, a token of everlasting love there...*

I shake June's voice from my head. No one is making any tokens of everlasting love. But maybe...

I glance at the hair ribbon. Then I look at the fabric strewn all over my workspace.

Maybe, I think, an idea forming in my head, *I can give him something else.*

19

MATVEY

Ring-ring-ring.

I groan into my pillow. It's the second time today that someone's trying to commit suicide by my gun. You don't fuck with a man's sleep—you just don't.

I pick up my phone like it's committed a capital offense, not even glancing at the name on the display. So much for my afternoon doze.

"*What.*" It is not really a question.

Yuri's voice answers, more solemn than I've ever heard it before. "Motya…"

I immediately sit up, on high alert. Yuri's tone, the tremor in that single word—it's all wrong. "Tell me what happened."

My first thought is April. Cold dread snakes up my spine: did someone break into the penthouse? Did they find her?

Did they *hurt her*?

"You'd better come to the warehouse," is all he says. "We have a situation."

"Yura," I growl into the speaker, *"tell me what happened."*

A beat goes by. Two. Three.

"It's the kidnappers," Yuri exhales finally. "They're…"

Free, a part of me fears he's about to say. *Free to harm her again. Free to take her from me.*

But that's not what Yuri says.

It's worse.

"They're dead, Matvey."

In fifteen minutes, I'm at the warehouse. I storm in like a tornado. "How the fuck did this happen?"

Yuri hangs his head. "It's my fault. I left to get something to eat, and when I came back…"

"You left them alone?!" I roar. Right now, all I see is red.

"No!" Yuri answers quickly. "No, our men were here, but…"

It's only then that my tunnel vision finally clears. The two bodies by the cell doors—I'd thought they belonged to the kidnappers at first, but the clothing's all wrong. They're wearing suits, black and sleek, untainted but for the bloodstain spreading from their backs.

Their *backs.* My men were shot from goddamn behind.

Whatever *mudak* did this has no honor.

I shake my head. I may be furious, but I'm not so far gone that I can't see what's right in front of me. "It's not your fault," I sigh, turning to Yuri. "If you'd been here, they would have gotten you, too."

The thought alone sends chills down my back. Losing my only brother to the same bastards targeting my child?

Not a chance in fucking hell.

Yuri swallows, nodding meekly. The guilt on his face is plain as day, but I can't worry about that right now. I already absolved him—if he knows what's good for him, he'll take it.

I'm not the kind of man to forgive twice.

I stride into the cells. Room A first, then B. The Russian's lying sideways on the ground, still tied to the chair, a bullet hole weeping blood on his forehead. His face is twisted into a horrified expression. Whatever he saw before he died, those last moments must have been a living nightmare.

Good, the vengeful part of me whispers. *At least you suffered.*

The other guy's face is equally disturbing, but for the opposite reason. I kneel in front of the chair, still upright, and tilt up his chin. Same bullet hole, same place, but with one key difference.

He's *smiling*.

I kick the chair over in a fit of rage. Yuri rushes to see what's going on, but I barely hear him. I flip the tool cart, sending scalpels and pliers flying through the air. "*Blyat*!"

This was our only lead. Without the interrogation, we will never find out for certain who our enemies are. I may have my suspicions on the foreigner, but the Russian's still a big, fat mystery.

And now, we'll have to start over.

"Who knew?" I snarl to Yuri.

I don't have to elaborate—Yuri understands immediately. "Our four men on rotation."

And now, two are dead. "Who else?"

"Me and you."

"Who *else?*"

Yuri's lips press into a grim line. "You know who."

I twist around. "That's nonsense and you know it."

"Is it?" Yuri growls. "Because whenever that errand boy's involved, there's trouble."

"I hardly think Grisha qualifies as an 'errand boy.' He's twice your age."

"That doesn't mean—"

"Yura." My imperious tone stuns him into silence. "He hasn't left the hotel in days. It couldn't have been him." I stride out of the cell, all the way to the warehouse door, my brother close on my heel. "I don't care if you can't see eye to eye. Either put your differences aside or hand in your guns, because I do not need squabbling schoolgirls in my ranks; I need *men*. Have I made myself clear?"

Yuri's teeth draw blood on his bottom lip. But he finally stops arguing, and that's the only thing I care about right now. I need my ranks in order. "Yes, *moy pakhan.*"

"Good. Now, call him." I fix my sleeves and wipe the blood off my soles. "You'll handle the clean-up—*together*. Dispose of the bodies and the blood, but do not touch anything else until I return. Got it?"

Yuri blinks. "Where are you going?"

I glance at my watch. "It's late. I need to be at the hotel by seven."

"You can't leave!" Yuri objects, walking a full circle around me. Like a riotous goddamn Pomeranian. "We need you here."

"It's family dinner, Yuri."

"But this is an emergency!"

"I don't give a shit." I whirl around. "Everything is an emergency in our line of work—or have you forgotten that? I can't start putting this shit above family. Especially when my child hasn't even been born yet." I grit my teeth, forcing myself to calm down. "I won't be like *him*, Yuri. I can't."

At the mention of our father, Yuri finally seems to understand. "Alright. Don't worry. We'll handle things here."

I nod grimly. "Question the other men on rotation, too—but be subtle. If there's a rat, we don't want to scare it away just yet."

Yuri straightens up. "Understood."

And with that, I finally stride out.

By the time I reach the hotel, I'm in an even fouler mood.

April seems to catch on to that. She greets me, shows me in, takes the trays off my hands to set the table. All the while, she doesn't speak a word out of place.

I wish Yuri was that smart.

Conversation, to the extent that it exists at all, is stilted even more than usual. Seeing April on edge like this—it makes me feel like shit. Like I'm *him* already.

I still can't force a word past my lips.

After this sad affair dies a merciful death, I head right to the door, expecting that April can't wait to be rid of me. But instead, she turns to me with a tentative smile. "Wanna get a drink?"

With a sigh, I nod.

We step out on the balcony. The city lights spread out like a carpet in front of us, twinkling and shimmering from here to the horizon. You don't really get to see the stars in Manhattan; this is the next best thing. It's why I chose this place.

If you can't see the stars, you should count yourself among them.

April offers me a glass. I take a whiff: bourbon.

"Found it in the cabinet," she explains. "Thought it looked like something you'd drink. Neat, right?"

Speechless, I nod. I never told April my drink of choice, and yet, here she is—offering it up like she's known all her life.

I watch her sip a tall, pink monstrosity. "Mocktail," she explains, catching my gaze. "Don't worry—I know Nugget's not old enough to drink."

I frown even harder. "Nugget?"

April points at her belly. "Can't pick a name until I know if it's a boy or a girl. So, until then…" she shrugs. "It was either that or Cheese Bite."

"Your fondness for fast food concerns me."

"Take it up with management," April chuckles. "It was only mac and cheese for me until this little one came along. Now, I'm craving KFC every other minute."

"Probably trying to make you eat healthier," I mutter.

"Hey!" April protests, but there's a smile playing on her lips. "Cheese isn't that bad for you."

"I'll introduce you to a nutritionist one day."

She pouts. "Killjoy."

Then she leans on the railing with her elbows, looking down at the rest of the world.

In this light, her dark dress is almost invisible. Like she's a part of the night itself, and the only thing covering her are shadows. Is it odd that I'm jealous of them—that they get to touch her and I don't?

I try to tear my gaze away from her body, heavy with the evidence of what we did; from her eyes, filled with artificial stars and happiness. *Warmth.*

I fail miserably.

"Did something happen today?"

I snap back to the present. April spoke, but she isn't looking at me: her gaze is still fixed on Manhattan.

Part of me wants to tell her. That's the most terrifying realization of all: I *want* to tell *her*. This woman, this *stranger*, is prying me open without even trying. A bloodless, effortless interrogation.

But I steel myself. I'm not this weak. If feminine wiles were all it took to crack me, Petra would have the keys to the fucking kingdom by now.

"Nothing unusual."

And then there's the other reason.

April glances at me then, still a bit fearful. Like she's expecting me to blow up at her for simply breathing in the same space as me. It makes me furious—that someone taught her this. That she was raised like this. If I had any less restraint, I'd have gone knocking at her parents' doors and demanded answers by now.

"Nothing?"

This is the other reason—the worry in her eyes. She thinks something's got me in a mood, and that alone is enough to put a look like that on her face. Why the fuck would I tell her that we lost our only lead?

It would be bad for her. Most of all, it would be bad for the baby.

That's what I tell myself over and over. *This is all for the baby.* Not for her.

To me, April Flowers means...

"Nothing," I confirm, and down the last of my drink.

At the door, I take her hand in mine for my customary goodnight, but she quickly slips it out.

"I almost forgot!" she says, rushing over to a corner of the room. A corner brimming with utter chaos, but I've been trying not to think about it. That's for housekeeping to deal with.

When April rushes back to me, there's a small bundle in her hands. "Come closer."

I do. Despite all my intentions, all my instincts, I do exactly as she says.

She frowns in concentration, then rises up on her tiptoes. For a second, I wonder if she's trying to chloroform me. That, or kiss me.

I can't say which one would be worse right now.

But she doesn't do either of those things. Instead, she goes for my breast pocket and carefully stuffs the bundle inside it.

That's when I finally realize what it is.

"It's lucky you're wearing this jacket tonight," she chirps, clearly pleased with herself. "Now, I get to see how it looks."

The color is a deep, vivid indigo. I glance at the rest of my outfit, and it doesn't take long to realize that it fits the ensemble perfectly. The hue, the size—it's all flawless.

"I know you don't think of outsiders as family," April mumbles, wringing her hands. Her voice is barely a whisper. "But we're going to share one. So, if you can't think of me as family…" A tentative smile. "At least let's not be strangers. Okay?"

I'm stunned. For a while, all I can do is stare.

Then I shake myself back to the present and take her hand again. I kiss it. The warmth is overpowering—nearly enough to break me.

But I won't break.

After all, *not strangers* is still a far cry from *family.*

"Goodnight, April."

"Goodnight, Matvey."

~

I drive back to the warehouse.

Once I'm there, I give one simple command: "Out."

Everyone obeys.

I search every nook and cranny of the two interrogation rooms. I search like a man possessed. If there's even a clue that can lead me to whoever wants to harm April—*whoever wants to harm my child*, I correct myself mentally—if there's even a trace of a hint of a scrap of a clue, I will find it.

And I do. It's nearly dawn when a little piece of metal blinks at me from the wall behind the Russian. In the corner, pressed into a crack in the concrete...

A bullet.

I grin like a wolf. "Game on," I snarl out loud, hoping the piece of shit who fired it can hear me, wherever he may be.

I got you, motherfucker.

20

APRIL

I'm woken up at the ass-crack of dawn by knocks on the door. *Insistent* knocks. More like a bongo orchestra, really.

"What the actual…?"

I drag myself out of bed, ready to curse whoever has decided to disturb my beauty sleep. When you're nine months pregnant, you need beauty sleep. Preferably up to twelve hours a day.

I yank the door open with the force of a thousand suns. *If it's housekeeping again, I swear.* "Can I hel—"

It's not housekeeping.

"April," Matvey greets in his sandpaper voice. "The doctor's here."

An old woman in a white coat pushes past me with a curt nod. Her entourage follows—two younger recruits with bright eyes and just as many manners as their team leader. Or just as few, rather.

Then they start to set up shop.

Several questions crowd my head at once: one, what the fuck? Second, what the *fuck*? Third—

"Ms. Flowers, please undress and lay down."

What the fuck?

I'm tempted to ask what happened to good ol' flowers and chocolate as a seduction technique when Matvey strides in last, bringing up the rear. The door is firmly shut behind his back, as final as a death sentence.

Somehow, I feel like any arguments would fall on deaf ears.

So I walk up to the impromptu examination table. I swallow my rage, duck behind the privacy screen with a flaming glare, and do what I do best: as I'm told.

Doesn't mean they won't hear my teeth gritting from the lobby.

The examination begins. Dr. Whatsherface—which is what I'm calling her, since she couldn't be bothered to say hello, let alone introduce herself—pours a generous amount of gel on my belly. And by "generous," I mean enough to drown a damn elephant. It's about as cold as rubbing bellies with a penguin, and a thousand times more uncomfortable. Not that I've ever rubbed bellies with a penguin, but right now, I think I'd prefer it.

"Mm," Dr. Whatsherface hums eloquently, looking at the screen.

What? I want to scream. *"Mm," my kid's still there? "Mm," it pulled a Houdini? "Mm," it's triplets?*

But, throughout it all, only one serious question keeps bubbling up in my head:

How dare *he?*

"Where's Dr. Allan?" I ask out loud to the bustling room.

Crickets.

I try again, thinking maybe my words weren't clear enough. Maybe this privacy screen's actually soundproof. "Where—"

"Please refrain from talking," Dr. *Ass*face scolds me. "I need a clear image."

And I need to punch you in the mouth. "Certainly." I smile broadly, dragging out each syllable.

The doctor and crew keep poking around my body. My baby daddy stays on the other side of the privacy screen, still like a statue. I'm tempted to bounce a stress ball off of him to see if that gets a reaction.

"There," Dr. Assface comments at last. "Sex is clearly visible—"

"And I'd prefer you keep that information to yourself," I cut her off, only remembering to smile at the end. "As *my doctor* well knows, I'd like to find out at birth. If it's not too much trouble."

Dr. Assface scoffs.

I hope one of these fuckfaces is a dentist, because by the end of this, either my teeth will have ground themselves to dust or I'll have knocked a row out of Nameless Bitch's mouth.

"You're past your due date," Dr. Assface points out eventually. I refrain from clapping my hands. *No shit, Sherlock!* "You should induce as soon as possible. Or get a C-section."

The *assistants* take notes. I take a breath and remind myself murder is frowned upon in all fifty states. "No, thank you."

Dr. Assface finally turns to look at me. My *eyes*, not my uterus. "Pardon?"

"Is the child showing signs of fetal distress?" I ask innocently.

Dr. Assface looks taken aback. *What, you thought this peasant couldn't speak your language?* "No."

"Is the child podalic?" I press, pulling out every term I've ever learned from Dr. Allan in the past nine months.

"Well, no—"

"Is the child affected by fetal macrosomia?" I insist, blinking two big doe eyes at Ratched and wishing they could shoot lasers.

"… No," Dr. Assface admits quietly.

"Then I don't see the reason," I conclude with my biggest smile. "With my family history, it's all perfectly normal."

"Your family history?"

"Yes," I say with the fakest surprise I can muster. "Surely you've read my file before coming here, Doctor. Haven't you?"

I hear a snort from beyond the privacy screen, quickly covered up by a cough.

I hop down the examination table and put myself back together without waiting for a dismissal. In fact, *I* dismiss *them.* "Well then!"

My cheerful demeanor leaves no room for argument.

Stunned into silence, the team begins to pack up. Dr. Assface hands Matvey a quickly put-together folder.

Matvey inclines his head. "Thank you, Doctor. I'll be in touch."

That's another clear dismissal. The three leave without a word.

When I see Matvey heading for the door as well, I call, "Wait."

Matvey turns. He's clearly got somewhere to be, tapping his fingers against each other like he's losing a million dollars for every second wasted with me.

I don't care if it's a goddamn billion. He can wait and he can fucking listen.

Once the doctors' steps have faded, I finally speak my mind. "What the hell, Matvey?"

Evidently, Matvey wasn't expecting that. "Come again?"

"Sure," I answer, unfazed. "I said, *What the hell?*"

Matvey's eyebrow shoots up. Like, way up. "I'm not sure I appreciate your tone, April."

"Oh, you're not 'sure' if you 'appreciate' my 'tone'?" I take an aggressive step forward. I'm all up in his face right now, but I don't care. I'm *fuming*. "Well, let me tell you what *I* don't appreciate: being woken up at the ass crack of dawn, being forced to *strip* in front of strangers, being *groped everywhere* by said strangers—"

"They're doctors, April," Matvey growls back, a familiar vein pulsing at his temple. "That's their job."

"I *have* a doctor!" I yell, too far gone for politeness. I used up all my reserve to keep my fists to myself earlier; I don't have any to spare. "A perfectly good doctor whom I trust, who's already scheduled our appointments for the month *with my consent*. A foreign concept to you, I'm sure."

His face goes dark. "I don't remember ever having to force you, Ms. Flowers."

Now, I've done it. He only calls me *Ms. Flowers* when he's mad or teasing. And right now, I think it's safe to guess which one it is.

But again: don't care.

He takes a step towards me, too. Like this, we're close enough to touch. His comment makes the memories spark in my mind: the changing room, the tie.

Everything.

All the sins that brought us here.

I shake it off. This isn't the time to be daydreaming. Not even with his solid body an inch away from mine, warming me by proximity alone. "What do you call this, then?"

"Taking care of our child," he snarls. All his patience is gone.

That's okay, though. Because, newsflash: so is fucking mine.

"*Our* child," I reply painstakingly slowly, jabbing a finger in Matvey's ridiculously broad chest with each syllable, "is still in *my* body, in case you forgot. And as long as that's true, I'll pick my doctor; I'll make my appointments; and I'll decide who gets to touch my body. I don't care if you're a Bratva Pacman—"

"*Pakhan*," he corrects distractedly.

"—or the second coming of Jesus himself," I finish. "My body, my rules. Have I made myself clear?"

Matvey's face shuts off. For a long moment, I can't get a read on him at all: is he mad? Is he furious? Is he gonna start yelling, too?

But then, surprisingly, there's a twitch. Just one, right at the corner of his lips.

And then he picks up my hand.

He unfurls my fingers one by one, watching me intently. He holds it like in the evenings, like the moment before he leans down to kiss it.

But this time, he doesn't.

"Crystal," he says, tone strangely neutral.

Then he walks out the door.

I'm left standing in the middle of the room, staring at the empty space he left behind. My cheeks are flushed crimson; I can feel it by the heat.

In my confusion, only one thought makes its way to the surface.

Was he... laughing?

21

MATVEY

I've never been so hard in my fucking life.

"Quite a temper, your missus," Grisha comments off-handedly as he starts the car. "Dare I say you've finally found your match?"

I'm thinking the same thing, but I don't let it show. After all, there can be no *match*. "Drive," I order Grisha instead, nipping this conversation in the bud.

Not that that's ever deterred him before.

"I'm just saying," Grisha insists, turning the key as he continues talking. It's his specialty: obeying spoken orders while defying unspoken ones. "She may have had a point. Perhaps a nice bouquet to smooth things over might be in order?"

"I won't apologize for caring about my child," I snap. "Now, shut up and drive."

Grisha raises his hands in surrender and replies, ever-cheerful, "Yessir."

April. What a fucking woman. No one, not even Petra, has ever had the guts to speak to me that way. Kitten's got claws, alright—and they're razor-fucking-sharp.

I shouldn't find it funny. Hell, I shouldn't find it hot. Being disobeyed like that? Being *questioned* like that? I've killed people for less.

But April Flowers is something else.

I'll decide who gets to touch my body. The second she said that, I wanted to test her. Wanted to put my hands on her and see how long she could go without begging. Would my baby mama still be so feisty with my fingers dancing between her legs?

I can still remember how it felt: my fingers pumping in and out of her. Her walls, so tight around me. Her voice, breaking with every thrust.

Get a grip. Stop thinking about her.

But it's easier said than done. If I'm not thinking about fucking her, I'm thinking about that goddamn mouth of hers. Even back at the shop, when we first met, she didn't take anything lying down. She was perfectly polite, perfectly courteous—and perfectly infuriating. I don't remember ever being insulted to my face with a smile that bright.

I shouldn't be so forgiving. I should storm back in there and make it clear which one of us sets the rules.

But I've always liked a woman who could hold her own. Someone with character. When your name's Matvey Groza, you get swarmed with brain dead socialites looking for a rich daddy to replace their rich daddy—one with benefits beyond a thick wallet. To get that, they'll turn into anything they think you want: chirpy little birds, clucking hens, temptress harpies. Anything at all.

It takes a real woman to know exactly who she is.

And exactly what she wants, a treacherous part of me whispers.

By the time the car stops by the warehouse, I've gathered myself. It takes more than a pretty face—or a stunning body —to make me lose my cool.

"Status update," I command the second I walk in.

Yuri rushes to meet me. "Here's the autopsy report," he says, handing me a file. "Our usual coroner."

The one we pay off to keep everything to himself, I note mentally. Good. We wouldn't want to get any extra players involved—especially not the boys in blue. "Give me the bullet points."

"Quite literally," Grisha comments from my side, leaning over the pictures in the report. Four men, two of them ours, all shot dead.

Yuri makes a sour face at Grisha's joke. But clearly, our earlier conversation must have made an impression, because for once, he doesn't start anything. "Estimated time of death between 4:00 and 5:00 PM. For the hostages: single shot to the head, point blank."

"No surprises there," Grisha mutters, pointing at the burn mark around the entry wound in both pictures.

"For our men," Yuri resumes, as if he hasn't heard him, "we're looking at a shot through the heart."

"*And you're to blame...*" Grisha hums to the music in his head.

"Excuse me?" Yuri bristles.

"Grisha, no singing," I cut in before another fight—and another headache—can materialize out of this. "Yuri, no taking Bon Jovi lyrics personally. Continue."

"But—"

"*Continue.*"

Yuri's frown deepens, but he obeys. "Both our men were shot in the back, from a distance of approximately thirty feet, at a forty-five degree downward angle."

"That's strange," I mutter. "Our men would have had their backs to the door they were guarding, facing the front door."

"And the distance between the cells and the entrance can't be more than fifteen, twenty feet," Grisha finishes for me.

"Exactly," I agree. Then, turning to Yuri: "What did we find at the scene?"

"Not much," Yuri admits. "Aside from gunpowder residue on the kidnappers' clothes—"

"Which would be inevitable," Grisha says. "Being shot point blank and all."

"—and what's written in this report," Yuri continues, grinding his teeth audibly at the interruption, "we found nothing. No bullets. Just two extra sets of footprints from the cells to the back door. Oh, and a coin."

"Footprints?" Grisha inquires. "What kind?"

"Size twelve," Yuri explains. "Standard issue combat boots. Can be bought anywhere."

"And the coin?"

Both of my subordinates turn to look at me.

"The coin?" Grisha blinks.

"Yes," I reply, impatient. "The coin."

Yuri quickly flips through his notebook. "It was a common quarter. Nothing special, no prints. Likely belonged to one of our men."

"Where was it found?"

Yuri doesn't seem to understand my line of questioning, but he answers promptly anyway. "About halfway between the two cell doors."

"There's a game our men play when they're bored," Grisha adds. "Sometimes, if they're standing guard on opposite doors, they'll toss a coin back and forth between them to pass the time." Like a stage magician, he produces a quarter from his pocket to demonstrate, throwing it at Yuri and nearly hitting him in the eye. My brother catches it at the last second, fuming.

"*My* men don't waste time on stupid games like these," Yuri hisses at Grisha.

"Have you ever seen an employee play around while the manager's clocked in?" Grisha replies evenly. "They wouldn't do it in front of you, Yurochka. Especially not with that feisty little temper of yours."

"Listen, you fu—"

I tune out their argument. Instead, I walk to the center of the warehouse. With slow, deliberate steps, I look around me.

Twenty feet to the front door. Twenty more to the back door. No nooks to hide in at the corners, no holes in the walls to shoot through. Only—

"You two. Come here."

Silence returns.

Trading suspicious looks, Yuri and Grisha make their way over to me. "Did you find anything?" Yuri asks.

Find? No.

Find out, though? "Yuri, give me the coin."

Yuri blinks, but does as he's told. He tosses it lightly and I catch it midair, feeling the cold metal between my fingers. "Go stand at the doors."

Still exchanging glances, the two obey.

Grisha settles in front of Room A. Yuri takes Room B. "What now?"

"Now," I say, feeling a grin tug at the corners of my lips, "pretend you can't see me."

I toss the coin.

While it spins in the air, I take a few steps back. Yuri and Grisha stare at the coin until it lands, the *clink* of metal against concrete ringing out in the empty warehouse.

Nothing happens.

I run a hand through my hair, sighing. "You're still seeing me," I chide. "*Don't* see me. Yuri, pass me the coin again."

Yuri walks to the center, picks it up, and tosses it back at me.

I take back my spot between them. "You're the guards. You're alone. You're facing the door."

The two turn around, their backs to me, and I place the coin on my thumb.

Three, two, one...

The coin flies. I retreat.

Clink.

Grisha turns. So does Yuri.

"Both of you," I call from my position, "go pick it up."

Yuri moves first. He rushes to the center of the room and kneels. Soon enough, Grisha catches up with leisurely steps, crouching down slightly.

Bingo. "Stop."

They freeze. I walk around them—one first, then the other. I settle behind Yuri.

Then I pull out my gun and touch it to his back.

"Motya...?" Yuri calls, distraught.

"Trust me," I say. "The game's almost over."

Through the barrel of my gun, I can feel Yuri swallow.

"Now, look up," I order. "Both of you."

They obey.

Above us, the skylight illuminates the warehouse in six wide squares, their reflection on the ground broken only by a line of beams.

I can see the moment realization dawns on them. "The roof."

"Thirty feet exactly," I confirm. "Now, Yuri. What would it look like if I shot you right now?"

Yuri's transfixed, staring at me with eyes wide in admiration.

And, understandably, a primal fear. "A forty-five degree angle."

I grin. "Precisely."

I put my gun away. Yuri breathes a sigh of relief, the picture finally clear. "They came from above. From the skylights."

"That's why the footprints went from the cell doors to the back door," Grisha adds. "One-way. Nothing near the entrance."

I nod, pleased with the results of this little experiment. "The coin was a distraction. Tossed from above, it caught the attention of our men. But they didn't see it drop—they only heard it. So they turned, walked up to it to examine it…"

"And crouched," Yuri completes for me, in awe.

"And crouched."

"Then the intruders went to kill our guests," Grisha continues. "They fished out the bullets from the bodies. They left through the emergency door in the back. It's the perfect locked-room mystery."

"Not perfect," I point out, tossing the coin back to Grisha. "And they didn't get *all* the bullets."

I pull a small plastic bag from my pocket. Yuri's eyes widen to the size of melons, while Grisha walks up with a curious glint in his. "Where did you find this?"

"Room B," I tell him. "Last night."

"Why didn't you say anything?" Yuri asks, a trace of hurt in his voice.

I pat him on the shoulder. "We still don't know the Russian's identity. Until we do, we keep the clues to ourselves. Our men are on a need-to-know basis. Got it?"

They both nod. *Good.* I can't afford anything less than complete obedience on this. I'm about to hand the bullet to Yuri for testing when, unexpectedly, April pops back into my thoughts.

April. Her fierce determination the day of the wedding, handcuffed and still showing up in front of me, demanding my protection. Her fire today, ready to raze cities to the ground.

Perhaps a nice bouquet to smooth things over?

I'm not one for apologies. I don't owe anyone shit. If people are displeased with me, so be it. It's none of my concern, and I certainly won't lose sleep over it. If I had to send flowers to every person I've ever offended, every garden on the planet would be a wasteland by now.

And yet. And yet, part of me wants to do *something.* Not to grovel—God fucking forbid—but to...

Reward her, a part of me whispers.

It doesn't make sense. Disobedience shouldn't be rewarded; it should be punished.

But how will you punish her? that part goads. *You know exactly what you want to do to her. So why don't you?*

I grit my teeth and change trajectory at the last moment. "Grisha, you test this."

Grisha nods. "Right away."

Yuri notices my split-second decision. "Why not me?" he asks predictably, like a child being denied candy.

I sigh and ruffle his hair. "Oh, Yura. I couldn't possibly waste your time like that. After all, I've got a special mission for you today."

Yuri stares at me. He stares for a very long time, and very, very hard. Then he shudders. "I'm not gonna like this, am I?" he mutters, too cornered to fight back.

My face splits into a grin. "That depends. How do you feel about shopping?"

22

APRIL

When the knocking comes back with a vengeance in the afternoon, I nearly choose violence. In fact, I'm this close to picking up a broom and brandishing it like a katana against whoever's come looking for trouble.

In the end, I don't. Not only because I can't find it, but also because the only people who could reach me here are either Matvey's men or his enemies, and I have a feeling they all come equipped with guns. So, no taking brooms to a gunfight.

"I swear, if someone else's come to feel me up today—"

The words die in my throat.

The first thing I see is toys. A *mountain* of toys. Plushies, rattles, building blocks—everything that would make a child's eyes go wide and shiny while making grabby hands. My eyes aren't any less wide, but it's not exactly wonder.

The second thing I see is Yuri.

His head is poking from a million bags and boxes, barely visible. With his face scrunched up like that, I almost take him for a Furby. "Let me in," he groans, going for commanding and falling way short of the mark. "Please."

I take pity. He looks like he's about to be crushed under the weight of impulse shopping. Yuri stumbles in, toys falling off his shoulders in an avalanche. Luckily, everything's boxed up pretty thoroughly and made entirely of synthetic fibers and/or plastic, which means there are no victims. Other than the environment and Matvey's wallet, that is.

"Did Matvey ask you to rob a toy store?" I ask, closing the door behind him.

Leaning against the back of the couch—and still very much wheezing like he's on his asthmatic death bed—Yuri shakes his head. "You don't do robberies while the sun's up. That's basic common sense."

"Is it?" I blink innocently. "I'm not that familiar with the activity, so I wouldn't know."

I crouch to examine the boxes more closely. There really is everything in here—and *yup*, that's a Furby. I discreetly push that particular box under the couch while Yuri's busy busting a lung.

Taking pity on him, I shuffle to the kitchen and pour him a tall glass of water. "So," I start, watching him drain it all in one go, "toys."

"Toys," Yuri confirms. He licks every single droplet off the glass. "Kids need 'em."

"They sure do," I agree vaguely. "And I mean, who wants a baby shower? They're a nightmare anyway. So, thanks, I guess."

"Thank Matvey," Yuri corrects. "They're from him."

"Wait." I frown. "Is this your brother's way of saying he's *sorry*?"

I glance at the amount of bags once more. This whole scene does have a *"grand gesture"* feel to it. A *"sorry I was a colossal dick"* kind of vibe. Am I dreaming? Is Hugh Grant going to pop up around the corner?

"No," Yuri answers promptly—and, if I'm not mistaken, a bit proudly, too. "Matvey doesn't do apologies."

"Doesn't he, though?" I tilt my head towards Toy Mountain. "'Cause with gifts like these, it's either that or overcompensation."

Not that Matvey has anything below the belt to compensate for, but I'm not gonna say that out loud. Certainly not to his irritating brother, who would use his dying breath to make a joke about it.

Predictably, Yuri grits his teeth. "Matvey does not apologize."

"Fine."

"… But he does occasionally admit when he's wrong."

I bite back a snort. "Does he now?"

Yuri doesn't reply. I keep snickering under my breath. I'm still mad, but how can I stay serious? God, being a macho man must be exhausting. The posturing alone would make me throw out my back.

I shake my head and smile. Then I let my gaze swoop over the toys: beautiful, shiny, new. Every kid's dream.

I never got to have something like this. Until a week ago, I thought Nugget wouldn't, either. We'd be too busy trying to make ends meet.

But Matvey's changed that. And, asshole or not, I can't help but be grateful.

"Well then," I call over to Yuri, scooping up a model train that no kid under eight should ever touch according to its box, "what are you standing there for?"

Yuri blinks like I've spoken in Klingon. "What?"

I gesture towards the toys. "These aren't gonna put themselves away. You wouldn't make a pregnant woman carry all this, would you?"

I can see his throat bobbing up and down, like he's weighing his options. Option A: make up a cat on the stove and bail, but risk Matvey's wrath afterwards. Option B: sacrifice.

"Fine," he gives up eventually. "But I'm not touching those."

I follow his gaze.

From the floor, three more Furbies stare back ominously.

"So," I pipe up after a while, "you and Matvey. What's the story there?"

Yuri cocks his head at me like an offended bird. "Why would there be a story?"

"There's always a story." We've nearly run out of places to stash these toys—which, considering how huge Matvey's penthouse is, is saying something—so I stuff a couple more in the guest wardrobe and shut it before the precarious tower of boxes can fall on me. I almost don't make it out alive. "I have four half-siblings and a story for each one."

Though none with a happy ending, I don't say out loud.

Yuri kicks a fish catching game under the guest bed. I can see the gears turning in his head, calculating just how much he's willing—or able—to share. Finally, he mutters, "It's not much of a story."

"I've been cooped up in here for a week. I'll take a boring story over the sound of the neighbor's garbage disposal."

Yuri snorts. "Suit yourself." He tosses a few more boxes on top of the wardrobe—which he can actually reach, unlike me —and stares at the ceiling for a while, collecting his thoughts. Finally, he says, "We're half-brothers, too."

I don't speak. For some reason, it just doesn't feel like my turn to talk.

After a beat, Yuri continues. "I didn't know I had a brother. For the longest time, it was just me and my mom. Then she got sick."

I feel a pang of sympathy. I don't know if it's the pregnancy that's making me slip into Mom Mode, but I can't help it: I *feel* for him. It's not like Yuri's a kid—at most, he's a couple of years younger than me—but he still feels too young.

Too young to lose so much.

Too young to grieve so much.

Too young to be so Bratva.

"I was seven," Yuri murmurs. "I was out collecting firewood. It was snowing. Had been for a week. I thought it'd never stop." Another beat. "Then I saw him."

I try to picture it: a younger, smaller Yuri, gathering branches in his hands to feed a meager fire and keep his dying mother warm.

"He was standing there," Yuri whispers, his gaze fixed on nothing. "He called me by name. I remember wondering how he knew."

"Your father?" I venture, afraid to step on something delicate. Something that might crack under the weight of too many questions.

Yuri gives a bitter laugh. "In a way. Matvey had been tracking his movements. Somehow, that led him to me."

How old could Matvey have been then? Eleven? Twelve?

Subconsciously, I run my hand over my belly. I think of Nugget, alone in the world. The mere idea makes my heart ache.

"I'm glad he found you," I say sincerely, even though it's not my place.

Yuri gives me an odd look. "Yeah," he says eventually, "I'm glad he found me, too. If he hadn't…"

I don't dare think it. Again, images of the two brothers overlap with Nugget. If I had to leave someone behind like that, if I had no other choice…

I'd want to know they wouldn't be alone.

"That week, my mom died," Yuri confesses in the end. "Matvey helped me care for her until she went. Afterwards, he helped me bury her. And then he took me into his Bratva."

It's so easy, isn't it? Judging a book by its cover. Judging people for living in the shadows. Like it's a choice for everyone.

For so many, it's no choice at all.

That's when I realize: Matvey founded his Bratva as a kid. That, or he took up the mantle from someone else. Either way, he never had a childhood.

Looking at the toys now, I can't help but see them in a different light.

Toys. Family dinner. Everything he never had.

Everything *I* never had, either.

Yuri pushes the last box on top of the wardrobe. Without thinking, I rest a hand on his shoulder.

He freezes. The look he gives me is quizzical, confused. Like what I'm doing is something completely foreign.

Thank God I didn't hug him. He'd have sprinted out the door.

"Hey," I say, leading him out of the guest room. Away from painful conversations and painful memories. "How about a cup of tea?"

23

APRIL

Matvey appears in the doorway just as I'm bidding Yuri goodbye. "You're still here?"

Yuri looks, for all intents and purposes, like a kid caught with his hand in the cookie jar. It doesn't help that there's a literal cookie dangling from his mouth. Chocolate chip, with just a sprinkle of caramel.

"She invited me to tea," he says defensively.

"Just a little thank you," I add, patting Yuri comfortingly on the shoulders. "Now, be careful on the way home. You have my number if you need to reach me."

"Yeah, yeah," Yuri grumbles. His eyes dart toward the exit and his feet shuffle in place, like he can't get out of here fast enough. Honestly, it's kind of adorable. "Thanks for the tea."

"Thanks for the help," I reply, waving as he goes. All throughout the exchange, Matvey keeps looking at me as though I've grown two heads.

"Why are you acting like you're his mother?" he demands as soon as the door's shut behind our backs. It's not unkindly, though. If anything, he sounds... amused?

I shrug and steal the dinner trays from the cart. "He's younger than me."

"By two years."

"Still."

We sit at the table. For some reason, the air's different tonight. Lighter. Maybe it's thanks to Yuri's cameo, or maybe it's the sock monkey watching over from the top of the fridge. Impossible to say, really.

"You didn't have to do all that, you know."

Matvey doesn't so much as shrug. His frozen posture seems to scream, *That's how casual I am about this. See? I didn't even move.* "I know. I wanted to."

"It was a nice gesture."

"Good."

"I'm still gonna need you to vet Dr. Allan."

Matvey glances up from his plate with a glint in his eyes. His lips curve helplessly upwards—something I take as a personal victory. *A-ha!* I nearly shout. *So you* can *laugh!* "I'll put Grisha on it."

"Thank you," I reply graciously.

All throughout dinner, I can't keep a grin off my face. It's stupid, but I can't help it—I'm in a really good mood. A far cry from this morning, surely.

"Is Yuri the reason you hoard chocolate chip cookies?"

"Mhm. His sweet tooth will be the death of him. But I suppose there are worse ways to go."

"It's really sweet," I tell him. "Both the gesture and the cookies."

"Don't eat too many," Matvey warns. "Too much sugar's bad for the baby."

"Says the guy who always brings me dessert," I chirp, undeterred. "Nice pocket square, by the way."

Matvey glances at his jacket. It's a different one, but the indigo pops just as beautifully against the black. "Thank you. A decent tailor made it for me."

"Just decent, huh?"

"Good with the hands, but a bit mouthy for my taste."

I lob a dinner roll at his head and the smile that's been simmering since we sat down finally dawns on Matvey's face. I take it as a win.

All in all, it's a relaxed evening. Fun. It's been a while since I've had that—I'd nearly forgotten what it felt like.

I always knew Matvey had a playful side. Seeing it out in the open like this, however, is different. It makes me feel like I'm in on the joke rather than the butt of it.

Again, that's something I haven't had often in life.

After dinner, as usual, Matvey picks up my hand to kiss it. I steel myself against the familiar rush of warmth, that brief, intense burst of sensation, three seconds at the most.

One, two, three...

Matvey's lips stay.

I freeze. I don't dare say a word. All I can do is shoot a covert glance at my baby daddy's face, the long shadows of the night covering his expression. A curtain I can't peek through.

And then his mouth moves.

One more kiss, just shy of my knuckles. This time, he lingers, brushing against my skin in a slow caress. Indulgent. Like he's savoring the taste of me.

"Matvey...?" I venture, voice small.

He doesn't answer, but he doesn't stop, either. Up, up, all the way to the curve of my wrist, kissing the spot where the bone dips. Then higher still.

I'm quivering from head to toe. This isn't warmth—this is a bonfire. And right now, I'm dangerously close to the flame.

"This is a bad idea," I breathe once those burning lips rise all the way up my arm, my bare shoulder, planting shivers all over. Goosebumps—my skin rising to meet his.

He doesn't deny it. "Mm," is all he says, a growl that I can feel against my throat. He nips at the delicate skin there, dragging a gasp from me, but I force myself to swallow it. Force myself to keep it quiet. If I do, maybe he won't realize how badly I want this. How badly I *need it.*

But it's already too late.

His lips meet mine. It's the barest brush of skin, almost an accident. I exhale raggedly, my breaths coming in short, failing me—

Suddenly, I feel his strong fingers trapping my chin, forcing me to turn my head and look him in the eye. Cerulean eyes, the color of frostbite.

"Good or bad doesn't matter," he whispers against me, his lips a hair's breadth from mine. As he speaks, I can feel them moving. "Do you want this?"

I wish I could say no. I wish I could turn my head away, put one foot in front of the other, leave his kisses behind. I wish that I could make the smart choice, for once.

But I've never been a good liar.

And my heart makes terrible choices.

"Yes," I breathe.

So he kisses me.

He kisses me long and deep. He kisses like he's hungry, like we haven't just had the kind of dinner that could make you sleepy just by glancing at it. He kisses like he's *starving*.

And I'm the only meal worth going for.

We stumble backwards into the ottoman. He catches me by the waist, lowering me down gently. It paints a stark contrast with the way his mouth is devouring me. Bite after bite, like an offering.

"Fuck," he groans into the curve of my neck. "You were made for this."

I shudder. The second his sandpaper voice strokes my ear, I lose it completely. "Matvey..." I breathe, unable to say anything else, anything coherent. It feels so good—to finally have a name.

His teeth scrape all the way down: down my jaw, my neck, my throat. At the same time, I can feel his hands working at my sash, tugging impatiently to pull it free.

Finally, my dress falls open.

I try to fight the impulse to cover myself back up. It's embarrassing—my belly's gigantic right now, stretched full with the evidence of what we did last time we ended up like this. It makes me feel self-conscious, even more than usual. After all, there's no way anyone would find this body—

"Beautiful," Matvey murmurs. "Absolutely fucking beautiful."

He forces my hands back at my sides. Forces me to let him *look*. Even his eyes seem to be devouring me right now, leaving behind nothing but bones. No: I have a feeling he'd crush those under his teeth, too. Anything to swallow me whole, to have more of me.

Then he kneels between my legs, and suddenly, I can't think straight.

"Mat—" I start, but my words are cut short. Swallowed, almost literally. Abruptly, his tongue claims me where I'm most sensitive, sending shocks of pleasure down my spine, and it's all I can do to bite my lips and choke on my own voice.

But he won't have that. "No," he snarls, five fingers pressing into each thigh. Keeping them apart. "Let me hear you fall to pieces for me."

So I do.

I writhe on the ottoman, moaning shamelessly while Matvey ravages me. With his tongue, his teeth, his everything. I can feel the trace of stubble on his chin when he turns to bite into my inner thigh, and that faint scrape drives me to madness.

I feel like a live wire. I've never been so sensitive in my whole damn life. "Matvey," I call again, this time weaker. Wrecked in all the ways that count. "*Matvey.*"

Blindly, I reach for his hair. I make a fist around his roots, not to hurt, but to hold on. Otherwise, I feel like I might drown.

Matvey groans into my flesh, the sensation reverberating all the way inside me. "*Blyat', kalina.*" His efforts redouble, eager to hear more broken moans from me. I'd laugh at the size of his ego, but truthfully, it's the size of something else that's haunting my mind right now.

I want it so bad. I want my baby daddy to flip me over and fuck me like he means it—but I also don't want him to stop. I don't want his mouth to leave me.

His teeth come out to play, rolling my clit between them, and I nearly white out from pleasure. "Matvey, I'm gonna—"

My fist goes tight in his hair. Suddenly, it's all too much: his tongue keeps lapping into me, hot and deep, and I simply can't hold on any longer.

I come with a scream. I've never been a screamer, not once in my life, but apparently, that's another thing Matvey Groza's made me: pregnant, and *loud.*

Loud enough to want to die afterwards, shame curling over me in the wake of pleasure. How far is it to the balcony, I wonder? Maybe I could make it. I was always a fast sprinter.

But Matvey doesn't let me. In fact, Matvey doesn't let me go anywhere. "Hips up, *kalina,*" he commands instead, and all but yanks me to the edge of the ottoman, rising with my legs in his grip. The back of my thighs is flush against his rock-hard chest—and it's not long until I feel a rock-hard something else pressing against me, demanding entrance.

I look up. Matvey's staring at me from above like a vengeful god, ready to take back what's rightfully his.

Do it, a shameful part of me whispers. *I'm yours.*

"April," he rasps, voice dark and serious. It makes me pay attention. "Is it safe?"

It takes me a moment to figure out what it means. *Of course it's safe*, I think hazily, glancing down at my humongous belly. *It's not like you can get me double pregnant, right?*

Then I realize: *Oh.*

He's worried about the baby.

"Yes," I breathe, for once sure of myself.

"Are you certain?"

Unless you don't fuck me right this second. In that case, I'm gonna die, and Nugget's gonna be pissed at you at least until college. "Yes, Matvey, you won't break my water by pounding me into an ottoman. Now, just—"

My voice breaks. It's like all sound has been punched out of me: I can't speak, I can't *breathe.*

All I can do is *feel.*

Matvey's face splits into a grin. A feral one, the kind that's born in the wilderness. "Good."

He's already inside me. It's just the tip, but it's a big tip, and it splits me completely.

"Matvey," I whine, rolling my hips to take him deeper, but he's just as much of a sadist as the first day we met, when he tied up a poor, innocent tailor and had his wicked way with her—well, maybe not that innocent—because he *refuses.*

He doesn't thrust, doesn't move. Only grabs my thighs tighter and keeps me from moving, completely at his mercy.

"Nuh-uh," he tuts, holding me perfectly still. "Not so fast, *kalina.*"

I want to die. Is it okay to want to die?

I can feel tears gathering at the corners of my eyes. Frustration, impatience—and, most of all, pleasure.

Because he's *there.* Inside-but-not-quite, just enough to give me a taste, to make me want to squirm for it. *Beg* for it.

I can tell that's exactly what he wants.

Ego—that's what it comes down to again. Which one of us is the most stubborn? Which one of us can endure the longest, resist temptation to gain the upper hand?

Right now, it's sure as hell not me.

"Please," I break, too far gone for pride. "Please, I can't take it anymore, I need—"

His eyes darken. I can see his pupils blow wide, eating away at the blue like dark water chipping at ice. Slowly, slowly—

"Ah—!" I cry out, fisting the pillows by my head as Matvey finally, *finally* slides home inside me.

He leans over me, blocking out the light. "Hold fast, *kalina*" is all the warning he gives me before he starts pounding in earnest.

He pulls nearly all the way out. I can feel every inch of him sliding away, the friction almost too hard to bear. Reflexively, I clench my thighs around him, locking my ankles at the small of his back to prevent him from leaving, leaving me empty and aching and—

And then he slams back in, giving me no room to breathe.

"Matvey!" I call uselessly, too lost in the pleasure to care. "Matvey," I moan, over and over again as he fucks me into the ottoman without a care for my life.

That's not entirely true, a lucid part of me whispers, small as it is. I can tell, despite everything, that he's holding back; that, if it weren't for the baby, he'd be rearranging my insides mercilessly.

I don't know how I could've taken that. As it stands, I can barely take this: this reckless rhythm of push and pull, driving me damn near crazy.

Matvey doesn't stop. He fucks me exactly the way I asked him to, hard and fast and deep, grinding his cock into that one spot that always brings me to tears. I can feel my orgasm building up again, thrust after thrust, as if I didn't come hard enough to cry just a few short minutes ago.

"Come for me," he growls as if reading my mind, hips stuttering against mine. "Come for me, April. Show me those noises you make."

Mindlessly, I do.

I throw my head back against the pillows and cry out, wracked with pleasure for the second time tonight. It's even more intense than the first. Matvey's cock keeps hitting that spot over and over, choking me to tears as I come helplessly. I shake and shake, and I'm still shaking by the time I feel him grunt, push himself flush against me, and fill me all the way up.

Put a baby in me, I think incoherently, my already pregnant belly jutting out between us. *Put another one inside.*

Dazed, I let myself fall down from the high.

We catch our breath against each other, lips just shy of kissing. I realize that Matvey hasn't pulled off a single article of clothing. He's looming over me in perfect elegance, if a bit disheveled.

Good, I think with satisfaction. *So the ice man can melt, too.*

And *I'm* the one who did it.

He pulls out slowly, carefully. I whine at the feeling, keeping him in place by his tie. "No," I moan.

"No?"

"No." I feel childish, but I don't have the energy to care. "Stay."

At that, Matvey goes oddly rigid. It takes me a moment to fully realize what I've said, the staggering implications of it.

Way to fuck this up, Flowers.

He sits up. So do I. The pocket square's still there, tucked neatly into Matvey's jacket.

"I have to go," he says, tone guarded.

"Yeah. Right." I fix my hair as I tuck my legs behind me. My now very useless legs, if the way they're trembling is any indication. "Yeah, of course. Me, too. It's late. Weeknight, you know. Gotta... gotta rest up for work."

We part like that, me mermaid-posing on the ottoman and him fidgeting with everything his hands can find: cufflinks, collar, buttons.

The pocket square.

He lingers at the doorway, long enough for me to risk a look up. "Goodnight, April," he says, a bit quicker, raspier, more throttled than usual.

"Goodnight, Matvey."

He doesn't kiss my hand this time.

For a second, I wonder if he ever will again.

24

MATVEY

The Jupiter Hotels office building is on the other side of Manhattan. This is intentional: I don't mix business with pleasure. What I do mix business with is *more* business, the kind that can't be conducted in the light of day.

Unless you're me, that is.

I stride into the conference room on the uppermost floor of the office building. As I walk by, secretaries scramble to pick up documents, make themselves look busy. I make a mental note to let one go by the end of the day, so they won't need to pretend any longer.

Yuri and Grisha flank me as I enter, always one step behind. They sit at my sides near the head of the long table.

Around us, the *vory* have already gathered.

Vor. That title is the greatest honor, second only to mine: *pakhan.* Being a *vor* means being one of the heads of the Bratva hydra, with the power to command legions. And, of course, serve the *pakhan* directly.

"Gentlemen," I greet curtly. None of us has time to waste on pleasantries, least of all me. "Let's begin."

It's the usual signal. Around me, everybody straightens. Once I push down the first chip, the others will fall accordingly.

"Araes Inc. has shown a 43.25% quarterly growth," the first voice says. It's Ivan, the highest ranking among them. He's the one who opens the dance: the subsidiary company he's in charge of, Araes, is a leading force in the firearms industry, and as such, brings in the big bucks. All perfectly legal and above board—unless you stumble by the warehouse on the third Friday night of the month, when our friends from the African coast come pay us a visit with presents aplenty.

I like letting Ivan go first. Rank aside, he always knows how to put the fear of God in the others: Araes is the North Star. And everyone, with no exception, will stew with envy at yet another incomparable report.

Competition—that's the key. If you want anything out of these savages other than the bare minimum, there's only one way to get it.

Pit them against each other.

Predictably, the room fills with awkward coughs. A few murmured words of congratulations, a few respectful nods. On the inside, however, everyone's seething.

Good. Stoke that fire. Use it.

Next up, Gora makes his report. To him, I entrusted Ceresial Green: a whole foods and supplements producer that makes us millions. The environment isn't particularly happy with us, but the vegans sure are.

12% growth, as expected.

It goes on like this for a while: M-Nerv, academic publishing, 9%. Hestiana Hosts, real estate, 11.5%. P.L.U.T.O., funeral services franchise, 14%.

After that, I zone out.

It's not that I'm uninterested. This is my empire, my creations. Of course I want to know how much money they're making me. If any heads need to roll, and which ones.

But today, I can't make myself focus.

"Boring," Stanislav says—or at least that's what I hear. "Boring, boring, boring." He's probably talking numbers about Venus Lounges, but I can't make myself give a shit.

There's only one person on my mind.

I look at the long conference room table and I can see her, spread out over the papers, dress undone and legs parted to beckon me in. Her gorgeous belly jutting out, filled with me and only me. A claim for everyone to see—and oh, how I'd claim her again in an instant. Right here, right now, in front of the whole world.

I'd rise from my chair, lifting her ankles to hook over my shoulders. I'd feast on her, every drop of her juices, until she's crying for it. Begging.

Then I'd take my rock-hard cock out and spear her open. I wouldn't care if anyone was watching; better, even. Let there be an audience to testify. Let them see exactly who April Flowers belongs to.

Who her body belongs to, that is.

That's the crux of the matter: I don't care about relationships. I don't want them. Never have, never will. It's why I agreed to a political marriage in the first place—how else would I have done it? Yuri may get all sentimental about it, but I never have. Love isn't for me. *Trust* isn't for me.

Almost everyone I ever trusted has either betrayed me or died.

But this thing with April isn't love. It's *lust*, pure and simple. The most common of all sins. And, unfortunately, I'm not immune to cliché.

My mind flies back to last night. It's like it never left, really. Mentally, I'm still there: my hands over her breasts, my tongue between her thighs.

So what if I'm in lust with her?

Really, she has no one to blame but herself. If she didn't want me to ravage her, she shouldn't have talked back to me. Shouldn't have made herself into the only type of woman I can't say no to: rebellious, drop-dead gorgeous, and made to be fucked into oblivion.

It's no wonder I lost my head. If I hadn't regained my senses, I would've fucked her until dawn.

But then she said, *Stay.*

And that's the one thing I cannot do.

"Matvey?" Yuri calls to me, leaning over slightly. I blink back to the present.

The *vory* are giving me concerned looks from around the table, but no one dares say a word. Good. I'm not in the mood to make up excuses. If anybody asked, I'd tell them the truth here and now: *I haven't heard a single word you said because I was busy picturing the seamstress leaking all over your papers.*

Alas, nobody asks.

"It seems like this quarter went really well," Grisha pipes up from his seat. "All-around growth, no issues. Well done."

"Yes," I quickly agree, clearing my throat. "Good job, everyone."

The looks don't stop, but a few nods come my way, acknowledging the praise. It's a rare gift—better if they make it last.

Finally, a voice rings out. *"Moy pakhan."*

I lift my gaze. Ivan is sitting on the edge of his chair, fingers drumming on the dark glass table the way they always do when he's got a question on his mind. Out of all my *vory*, Ivan is the only one who's never given me problems.

I have a sickening feeling that that's about to change.

"The D.C. acquisition. Should we move forward?" he asks at last, cutting through the chase.

I appreciate how direct he is. I've never been a fan of mental gymnastics, and Ivan never struck me as the type, either. I've never known my grandfather, the original founder of the Groza Bratva, but if he was anything like me, he wouldn't have wanted his men to beat around the bush either.

"Of course," I answer. "I don't see a reason to delay it."

Some of the *vory* exchange uneasy looks. "It's just," Gora tries, "with the wedding…"

"The wedding will proceed as planned."

More whispering. What is this: lunch break at the kindergarten? "We thought, after what happened…"

"You don't need to think. We agreed a long time ago that I'd be the one to do that for the rest of us." I straighten myself, silencing their inquisitive gazes with a single glance. "All you need to do is act."

"It'd be helpful," Stanislav cuts in, "if we knew why we were doing it, sir. This whole acquisition has been shrouded in mystery ever since it began." A few approving nods. "If we knew what you were looking for—"

"*I* know what I'm looking for," I interrupt, rising from my chair. "It's that building. Get it done."

Everybody takes the hint. They stand up, nodding their heads in respect. "Yes, *moy pakhan*."

"Good. I'll see you next month."

They file out. One by one, until it's only me and my inner circle remaining.

It's Yuri who speaks first. "You shouldn't talk to them like that."

"Why not?" I retort. "They're my men."

"They're your *top* men," Grisha corrects gently. "And they matter. If you treat them like they don't, they'll get fed up eventually."

I look from one to the other. "Christ, you're creepy when you gang up. Can't you go back to bickering like an old married couple?"

"He's old enough to marry? I didn't notice," Grisha taunts, earning a scowl from Yuri.

"Don't you have a bullet to test?" Yuri retorts acidly. "Or a bingo game to host?"

Good. World order's restored. "Alright, break it up; I changed my mind. Grisha, you go back to the hotel. Yuri, with me."

Grisha gives a courteous half-bow and leaves, but not before pinching Yuri's cheek, to which Yuri responds by trying to bite his finger off, but that's to be expected.

Afterwards, to my growing surprise, Yuri says, "He's not wrong, you know."

I turn. "Alright, who are you and what have you done with my brother?"

"I'm just saying," Yuri insists. "The *vory* matter."

"The *vory* don't matter," I spit back as we head for the exit. "They're not blood. *That's* what matters. And that's you and me, Yura—no one else."

Yuri falls silent next to me. I get into the elevator and listen to my own words echoing in my head. *No one else.*

For now, anyway.

25

APRIL

"You don't understand!" I freak out over the phone. "I *slept with him.*"

On the other end of the line, June snorts. Because of course she does. My best friend, everyone. My ride-or-die, my soul sister, ruthlessly making fun of me in my time of need. "I mean, that's nothing new, though, is it? Clearly, you've done that before, or else—"

"I know how it works, June!" I stop her before my face can go up in literal flames. "You don't have to give me the talk about the birds and the bees. I think I've got that covered."

"If you saaay sooo," June sing-songs.

"Ugh, I hate you."

"No, you don't."

"Yeah, I don't." I flop on the couch with a sigh. Then I scramble back up, because that's the ottoman where—where we—

"Did you see a bug?" June asks.

"Worse. I saw the death of my dignity."

"Look, what's the big deal?" June asks over the buzz of background conversation. I shouldn't be bothering her while she's on a shift—but then again, she's the one who said, and I quote, *If I have to pay attention to one more teenager counting pennies for a milkshake, I'm gonna put my head in the blender. Please, distract me.* "You guys hit it off once. It'd be stranger if you never fudged again. I don't get what the big deal is."

In any other circumstances, June's feeble attempts at censorship would make me laugh. Especially since those coin-counting teenagers probably know three times the amount of swear words we do.

"The 'big deal,'" I yell, making air quotes as I go for emphasis, "is that he *specifically* told me he wanted none of that!"

"Well, he wanted some last night, that's for sure."

"*Jay.*"

"It's true, though!"

I sigh. "Co-parents—that's all we were supposed to be. What now?"

"You can still co-parent and share a bed. You know, most people do it. It's called 'being a couple.'"

"But we're *not* a couple!" I almost scream. "That's why this was such a bad idea! It'll be confusing!"

"For who, Nugget?" June asks skeptically.

"At the very least!" I retort. "When it's old enough to understand."

"I think it'll eventually figure out it didn't come by stork mail, A."

"Ha. Ha. Ha. Truly comedic genius you're doling out here."

"Besides, I hope you'll keep it down so he doesn't hear you getting all wanton with it, y'know?"

I smash my head against the wall. Kidding. I wish I had the courage. As things stand, all I do is lean against it, flailing my arms uselessly like a crippled jellyfish. "You are so not helping, Jay."

"One order of pancakes with extra bacon on the side, coming right up," June says cheerfully to someone luckier than me. I wish I had pancakes right now. And bacon.

"When did my life go so off-track?" I sigh, heading back for the couch. The *other side* of the couch. The one we didn't taint with unspeakable acts we'd sworn never to commit again. God, that makes me sound like a nun, doesn't it?

"It was on a track before?" June asks, puzzled.

I ignore her. "Oh, I know: when a certain Bratva Pikachu picked *my* store to buy a wedding suit instead of ordering online, like every other person born in the twenty-first century."

"I thought it was *pakhan*," June muses.

I scream into a pillow. The pillow doesn't scream back. It's already more than I deserve, really. "Fuck my life. Like, *fuck* my life."

"Language," June chides. "There are minors here."

"Did you put me on *speaker*?"

"Of course you're not on speaker!" June replies, somewhat offended. "... Now."

I gauge the distance between myself and the balcony. I could make it. I really could.

"Look, it's not the end of the world," June sighs. "So you did the horizontal tango. The spicy salsa."

"Please stop."

"The porny polka."

"June."

"Alright, alright," June acquiesces. "No more bad dance metaphors. Go on."

"You wanna know what the real tragedy is?"

"You know that's why I'm here, babe. Spit it out."

I try to roll over. I fail. Sometimes, I forget the physical limitations of growing a human being inside your body. "It was the best sex I ever had," I confess, defeated.

"Wow. Better than Carter Niles?"

"*Way* better than Carter Niles," I confirm.

"Damn. Now, I'm thinking *I* should find myself a Bratva Pokémon."

I groan into the back of the couch, dignity forgotten. "It was out of this world, Jay. Both times. Did I tell you about the tie?"

"Only over a million breakfasts."

"Well, this time, there was no tie. No nothing. And it still blew my brains out my ears."

"That's graphic. Are you sure he didn't just shoot you?"

"Believe me," I whisper dreamily, letting my mind indulge in the memory of those big hands on me. "I wish he had."

That's the crux of the matter: it was *good.* Not just good, but spectacular. If it'd been like all the other times—a tumble in the dark with a random guy from the club, or a blind fumble under the bleachers—it would have been fine. Just me, a good shower, and maybe a round of vibrator to pick up where anyone other than Carter Niles left off. And even then, it's not like Carter ever put his mouth where his money was.

But *this?*

How am I supposed to forget *this?*

Just the thought's enough to get my body all worked up again. My treacherous, hormonal body and its streak of bad, bad choices.

Granted, I didn't take many dips in the dating pool. Mostly I was just too overworked to do it. The shop, my projects, fixing a leak in the house every other week so that our sticky-fingered landlord wouldn't withhold our deposit—I've been a busy gal. That's not to say I've grown cobwebs. Just that I haven't had much… experience. So maybe that's what's blinding me here.

But man, those *hands.*

I slap myself on both cheeks. "No," I scold my body sternly. "Bad girl. We don't chase after pant hems in this house. Even if they're covering a truly spectacular—"

Someone clears their throat behind me.

I jump. I fall right off the couch and onto the rug—back-first, luckily. Or, well, luckily for Nugget. I can already tell I'm gonna be needing a cane.

Above me, Petra smiles innocently. "Caught you in the middle of something?"

Fantasizing about your future husband, actually. Funny you should ask.

"Not at all." I smile back. "Please, make yourself comfortable."

Which she's clearly already done, if the fact that she *let herself in* is any indication. Did Matvey give her a key? I swear, if he gave his psycho fake girlfriend a key…

Petra perches gracefully on the back of the couch. Way less gracefully, I pull myself up. I look and feel like some sad, floppy sea creature.

"What brings you here?" I ask, using my best customer service voice. The one that means *I can't tell you to fuck off but I'm blinking it in Morse code.*

"Just dropping by to check on your precious cargo," Petra replies amiably. "Which… Is it me or is it getting bigger by the day?"

You-huge-bitch. "Guess it's you!" I chuckle, brimming with rage.

"Hmm, pretty sure it's you!" she sing-songs back, chuckling just as warmly. God, is this what it's like to catfight? Please, somebody give us swords. "That's gonna be rough, isn't it?" Petra adds, mock-wincing. "I hear pregnancy weight never really goes away."

Ha-ha-fuck-you. "I'll manage," I say with a strained smile. It takes more than some snow globe gnome calling me fat to shake my pride. Besides, her fiancé didn't seem to mind the extra pound or two.

I'm shaken out of my high school regression to catty-as-fuck when Petra rises, her cropped cream blazer fluttering with the motion.

"Wait. Is that a tear?"

Petra halts. "What?"

"In your blazer."

Forgetting all self-preservation, I walk around the couch and grab the fabric. I can see Petra flinch like a feral cat, can hear what's most likely the sound of a pocket knife being unsheathed—and like, I know I asked for swords, but I didn't actually mean it—when her eyes find the same spot mine did.

"Oh," she says. "Guess I must've caught a nail or something."

That's clearly a bullet hole. "Take it off."

Petra's face goes scandalized. "Pardon me?"

I sigh. "Take it off so I can mend it. Come on, I don't have all day."

My words only seem to confuse her more. "Why would you—"

"It's a Vuitton!" I cut short. "No Vuitton deserves that. Off now, please."

Shocked, Petra complies.

I take the patient to the table. It's a really nice blazer—Korean neckline, butterfly sleeves. It must've cost as much as my entire deposit, if not more. What do people say: three months' worth of salary for an engagement ring, six for a designer blazer?

Regardless, I can't bring myself to leave it like this.

All throughout the process, I'm painfully aware of Petra staring at my every move, like she's trying to catch me sewing a micro-bomb into her sleeve—which, I mean, should I?

"So," I say for the sake of conversation and not dying of laser eyes, "how'd you end up working with Matvey?"

I can tell Petra's stunned. Honestly, I'm a little stunned myself. Why make the effort?

"We met on a job," she answers evasively. "It was love at first sight."

Yeah, and I've got an island to sell you. "So you were already in the business, then?"

For some reason, that seems to irk her. "I was born into it," she answers proudly, a lioness shaking her mane. "I was Bratva before I could walk. My first word was *pistolet.*"

"That doesn't mean *hug*, I gather."

"It means *gun.*"

That tracks. "So, what'd you do to get kicked out?"

Petra stares at me like I'm the stupidest person on the planet. All things considered, I might be. But I can either work or keep a social filter, and right now, this blazer needs me. So I elaborate. "C'mon. You're a mafia princess. Why would you scheme for a crown if you already had it?"

Something flits over her expression. Outrage, maybe. Admiration, perhaps. "I'm a girl," she answers at last. "Girls don't get the throne. They get a ring on their finger and a smelly ogre to pick up socks for."

"That's a romantic outlook."

"If you ever met my father, you'd know that's a rosy option."

"*Fathers*," I snort back. "I know something about that, alright."

For a moment, Petra doesn't say anything. I don't expect her to speak again at all.

Except she does. "I have the highest body count in the Solovyov Bratva," she huffs like she's complaining her dad won't let her go out wearing a miniskirt. I shudder. Maybe I shouldn't have let my filters go wild after all. "But all my father sees is a little girl to marry off. So I struck a deal with Matvey. He gets our numbers; I get a position."

"Pikmin?" I venture.

"What?" She blinks in confusion until she realizes what word I'm butchering. "No, not *pakhan*. It's still a man's world, after all. But he'll make me *vor*. That's the next best thing." Then, quieter: "No woman has ever been *vor* before. I intend to be the first."

I must be going insane. Because this is *Petra*—harpy-grip, threatens-my-baby-in-Russian Petra—and yet... and yet, I feel for her. If anyone knows what it's like to be overlooked because of the circumstances of your birth, that's me.

And besides—Jesus H. and all his friends, it's the twenty-first century. Would it kill men to stop thinking with their dicks?

Says the gal currently making life-altering decisions based on her uterus, a voice whispers in my mind. *And/or clitoris.*

Goddammit. I hate when the voices are right.

"I hope you get that," I say sincerely, dusting off the mended blazer. "Vore or whatever."

"*Vor.*"

"Right. That."

Petra inspects the blazer. Her expression's guarded, but I can tell she's impressed.

Of course she is. You'd never know it was torn to begin with. That's the mark of a good tailor—making things look new even when they aren't. Giving a second chance to what's been broken.

"You're weird," she decides finally, slipping the blazer back on.

"Right back at you," I say. "Next time, use the doorbell, will you? I'm not gonna leave you in the hallway." She eyes me skeptically, so I add, "Pinky swear."

She does not, thankfully, take my pinky.

On the way out, though, Petra's gaze lingers on something. "That yours?" she asks.

I follow her line of sight. It's a midnight blue maternity dress —slightly sheer, with silver embroidery. "Yeah," I answer. "Why?"

"It's... nice," she says with a grimace, like it's taking her a lot of effort to spit out a word that's not a scathing insult. "You should wear it. It'll look good with your coloring."

I'm speechless. There's no other way to describe it—I have forever lost the ability to form words.

Because there's no way that Petra just paid me a compliment, is there?

"And also it'll hide your fat," she adds, making a quick getaway.

I blink. The door closes.

Still a bitch, then.

26

MATVEY

"Evening, boss."

I return Grisha's greeting with a nod. Standing here again, in front of April's door—*my* door, I remind myself—makes my mouth water. After last night, the wise thing to do would have been to keep my distance. Let this heat simmer down to a smaller flame.

Unfortunately, I made my own bed. I was the one who demanded family dinner every night. What kind of man would I be if I backed out now?

I've never backed out. Of anything.

A pretty face isn't going to change that.

With that grounding thought in mind, I ring the doorbell. Dinner is dinner; it doesn't have to come with dessert. I've steeled myself against the cold of Russian winter, the pain of gunshots, the bitter taste of defeat. I can steel myself against April Flowers.

And then she opens the door, and I change my mind.

She's wearing a dress. Not just *any* dress: a stunning maternity dress, the deepest midnight blue. It looks like it's been poured onto her—a liquid veil to lap gently over her curves, masking them from view.

But not enough.

Nothing could hide that belly from me, swollen with *my* child.

"Grisha…" I clear my throat. "You can go now."

With a flourish of his hand, Grisha obliges.

I wait until his steps have faded into the hallway. I wait until I hear the telltale *ding* of the elevator. I wait for the doors to close.

"Hi," April breathes. "The food's already inside, if you want—"

Then I don't wait any longer.

I grab April by the back of her neck and tilt her head up to meet mine. My mouth is on hers in seconds, claiming those sweet, plump lips without a moment's hesitation.

April is on me just as fast.

I kick the door shut behind me, yanked forward by eager hands pulling on my tie. We stumble inside like a pair of goddamn teenagers, too swept up to even look where we're going. I bump against a chair and secure my arms around April's waist, preventing her from tripping. As long as I'm here, I will never let her fall.

But *fall apart* is something different entirely.

I don't separate from her until I absolutely have to. I feel her gasping for air against me. "The food— Don't you want—" she tries, but I silence her with a finger on her lips.

"I *want*," I growl, dark and commanding, "something else."

Then I dive into her again.

I kiss her until she's moaning. Until she's pushing against my chest with both hands, begging to breathe. I'll decide if she gets that. I'll decide anything she gets tonight.

And I'll decide *when*.

Finally, I let her pull away. She's breathing hard, chest heaving against mine. I want to rip that pretty dress off of her and strip her naked, expose those gorgeous breasts to the air and bite into them. To devour April Flowers whole.

She looks up at me, her hazel eyes now dark and hooded. Her pupils are blown to high heaven, letting only a ring of those forest-green irises survive my assault. If I had my way, there wouldn't be anything left.

I drop my gaze to her lips: kiss-bruised, bitten, red. Shiny and ready to be claimed raw, over and over again.

I want.

I *want*.

But I won't take any more unless she begs me to.

For a long moment, April doesn't speak, just keeps breathing hard against my body, driving me insane. Those quiet little moans of effort… I want to hear them grow louder. I want them to haunt me.

But she must want it, too.

I see her steel herself. For one devastating second, I think she's going to be braver than me. That she's going to push me off and away, shove me at a safe distance once again. As she should.

But neither one of us is doing what they should tonight.

So April looks me dead in the eye and breathes the answer that seals it for both of us: "Then come and get it."

I don't need to be told twice.

I hook my palms under her thighs and hoist her up on the table. With one long swipe of my arm, I sweep everything away, sending it flying on the floor. It's just a teacup and a cookie jar—the food's still safely on the tray—but I wouldn't have cared either way.

With April Flowers in my hands, I don't need anything else to eat.

"Matvey," April sighs against me, wrapping her legs around me, "that was rude."

Laughter bubbles up to my lips. "I pay housekeeping well," I tell her, smothering a chuckle in the curve of April's neck. God, this woman will be the death of me.

"You're such a—*ah!*" April gasps, digging her fingers into my hair as I eat her whole. "Nightmare... customer—"

I lick a wet stripe along her jugular, right up to her soft earlobe. "I've never had any complaints."

"You—liar—!"

April's voice breaks as soon as my teeth come out to play. I nip at the shell of her ear, drinking in the sweet sounds pouring from her lips.

How many times can I make her fall apart? How many ways?

Let's find out.

I kiss and suck at every place I can reach. Bruises, bitemarks—I want her covered in them. I want her covered in *me.*

Her belly juts against me, reminding me, *You've already done that. Look at the proof.*

It's not enough.

I grab her dress on either side of the plunging V-neck, wanting to rip it off of her. April seems to guess my plan, because her hands rush to cover mine. "Oh, don't you *dare.*"

I smirk. "But it'd look so much better on the floor."

That's a lie. It's just that she'd look so much better without it.

"Kill my dress and I'll kill you."

I grab her chin and tilt her to the side, making room for myself to whisper in her ear, "I'd like to see you try, *kalina.*"

Just like that, we're kissing again, open-mouthed and dirty. I decide to spare her dress—I do like it on her, after all—and settle for yanking the cups down, taking her bra with me. I squeeze her breasts in my palms: full, ripe, *mine.* A feast for one.

I duck my head to take one into my mouth, and April keens. "Oh, God—"

"God has nothing to do with this," I snarl. "It's all me. It's my name you should be calling."

I bite down on her nipple, dragging a gasp from April's throat. I suck, circling it with my tongue, taking advantage of these gorgeous breasts for as long as I can have them for myself. *No offense, kid—Daddy can be a little jealous.*

I run my hands up her thighs, prying them apart. April doesn't get the chance to beg for her lingerie: as soon as my fingers find the lacy hem, I tear her panties right off.

"You…!" she gasps, outrage and pleasure mixing together. "You owe me a new pair."

"I'll buy as many as you like."

"Matvey…!"

I plunge my fingers inside, finding her wet and needy. *Fuck.* She's drenched. Ten minutes, and she's already like this.

"Did you miss me this much?" I tease, circling her clit with my thumb. It's the barest hint of pressure, and yet she's already moaning.

"No," April lies, hips fucking back onto my hand.

"Mm. Is that so?"

Suddenly, I pull away. April blinks, dazed and lost, until her gaze meets mine. "What…?"

I tut her. "Naughty *kalina.* Lying to my face. I think you deserve to be punished."

Her eyes go dark and hooded. "Is that so?"

"Mm," I hum, picking up her wrist. "That's right."

Then I cup myself with her hand.

I watch her gasp, clearly trying to repress it. It's the hottest thing in the world. "You want it?" I whisper, leaning in close. "Then *earn* it."

For a second, I wonder if April will refuse. If her pride will triumph over her desire. I know, if it were me, that it would.

But April isn't me.

Trembling, her dainty fingers find my belt. They work it open slowly, embarrassment covering her every gesture. It's clear she isn't used to this—being ordered around. Being *guided.*

Luckily, I'm a patient teacher.

She pops my buttons, then frees me. At the first touch of those delicate fingers on me, I inhale sharply. *"Blyat', kalina."*

It's feather-light. She doesn't grip the base crudely or attack my sensitive spots right away. Instead, she brushes over the full length of it, dragging goosebumps in her wake.

If she wasn't pregnant, I'd take her hard enough to make her scream.

April furrows her brow in concentration. "Like this?" she asks, closing her fingers around me in a too-gentle grip. When her palm drags against the tip, smearing precum in its wake, I groan.

Taking it as an encouragement, April repeats the motion.

I severely underestimated my opponent. That's not a mistake any *pakhan* wants to make. If I didn't know any better, I'd say this little vixen was teasing me on purpose.

Oh, well. Two can play at that game.

I grab both of April's wrists, pinning them behind her back. April gasps, "M-Matvey—!"

"Now," I murmur against her lips, one hand around her wrists and the other on her ass, "time for your punishment."

I plunge into her. I don't give her a second to prepare, to think, to *breathe*. She's so wet it doesn't take any time at all. One good push, and I'm sliding right in.

"Oh, God," April sobs, arms struggling against my grip. "Matvey…!"

I set a quick, shallow pace, not bothering to give April the *real* fuck she's yearning for. If she wants it, she'll beg.

And if she knows what's good for her, she'll do it soon.

I grind my head against her sweet spot, but only for a second. On the next thrust, I avoid it completely.

"Matvey," April whines, high-pitched and keening. "Matvey, *please.*"

"'Please' what, *kalina?*"

A frustrated groan. "I lied, okay?! I missed you, I missed you so much, wanted you to fuck me into the floor last night— Now, will you *please* just—"

Without warning, I slam deep into her. April's voice twists into a scream, her thighs trembling on either side of me.

I breathe into her neck, "As you wish."

I don't stop until she's jelly. Until she's quivering with every thrust, forming words that aren't words, begging me, *Please* and *Yes* and *More.* Too much and not enough.

"Matvey," she moans, fluttering around me, fucking herself back onto me. "Matvey, I'm—!"

"Come," I order. "Now."

April shudders, *hard*.

She arches off the table, but my hands are there, pinning her into place. With a broken whimper, she thrusts back against me, riding the wave of her orgasm with a violence I didn't think she was capable of.

I come so hard I nearly white out.

We stay like that for a while, catching our breath. April whines as I fill her up, clutching her thighs around me to avoid making a mess. *Good*, a savage part of me snarls. *Keep it all in.*

You're mine.

When I finally pull out to look at her, I could come again just from the sight. April is marked. Everywhere I lay eyes on, a fresh bruise is blooming, purple and beautiful, on her skin. Around a few, bitemarks pop out, angry and red. A *claim.*

And now, everybody will see it.

April gazes back at me. Her shiny lips part around a word, but she seems to think better of it, closing them immediately. But I know what that word was.

Stay.

Last night, I didn't. I *couldn't*. If this was allowed to spiral any further, it would've spelled disaster on both our lives.

But now, I realize I'd miscalculated. I'd failed to account for one, fundamental variable in my plans:

I *want* her.

And nothing's gonna change that.

So when she starts scooting back to make room, fixing her dress to send me off, I kiss that goodbye straight off her mouth.

"Did you think," I growl against her lips, "I'd let you off that easy, *kalina*?"

April swallows. I watch her throat bob with the hunger of a predator.

Then she yanks me back to her.

It's hard to think of anything else after that.

27

APRIL

We start having sex everywhere.

And I do mean *everywhere.*

"This," Matvey snarls as he rips—literally, not metaphorically —my clothes off, "means nothing."

"Agreed," I moan back, drawing him close again and locking my legs around his waist.

We do it on the couch. We do it on the kitchen counter. We even do it on the Persian rug. That thing must be worth more than one or both of my kidneys on the black market, but Matvey doesn't hesitate for one instant to make an absolute mess of it. Or of me.

"You're…!" I gasp as he hooks one of my legs around his shoulder, thrusting deep inside me. "Such an asshole…!"

"And you're—" Matvey grunts while he annihilates me, leaving me without a single second to catch my breath, "an insufferable… naughty… tailor."

Family dinner is now always preceded by the kind of aperitif no one else is invited to. The kind that would invite complaints by the neighbors, if we had any.

And if Matvey didn't own the entire building.

The worst part, though?

I've started getting wet just *waiting* for it.

I'm not kidding. Suddenly, I'm Pavlov's goddamn dog: as soon as my stomach starts rumbling for dinner, something *else* starts—

"Ew!" June yelps, cutting me off in disgust. "TMI, April! I did *not* wanna know that!"

I try to roll over on the bed and smother my face into a pillow. Nugget makes that little action much more difficult than it has to be. Also, the couch is no longer an option—if I sit anywhere in that den of sin, I'll just get wetter. Really, it's like Niagara up in here. "What kind of best friend are you?"

"The kind that did not wanna know that!"

"I don't mind," another voice pipes up. A distinctly masculine voice. "In fact, keep going. I'm taking notes."

"Jay," I whine, covering my face with the blankets, "why am I on speaker again?!"

"Because I'm making food," June calls from a distance.

"Because she's making food," Corey confirms. "And also, I'm untouched by hetero drama. It's like watching a nature documentary. But your baby daddy's giving me ideas, so—"

"Goddammit, Corey!" I squeak. "Don't write those down! He'll know!"

"How?" Corey asks, deadpan. "Are there cameras?"

"Probably," June interjects. "HD. With sound."

"I hate you both," I grumble.

"No, you don't," they respond at the same time.

"No, I don't." I sigh, long and deep. "What am I supposed to do, guys?"

"Honestly, if I were you, I'd just keep doing *him.*"

"Corey!" June and I yell in unison.

"Sheesh," Corey says. "Didn't realize I was hanging out at the nunnery."

"I can't just—" I groan in frustration, squeezing my pillow hard. "I can't keep— We're co-parents!"

"So?" the Evans siblings pipe up at once.

"So," I answer impatiently, "this can't keep happening! You guys see the problem, right?"

"Nope."

"Really don't."

"Ugh." I flop on my other side. If I squeeze this pillow any tighter, it's gonna call the cops on me. "He's Bratva, guys. He's engaged. He's gonna get fake-married at some point, and I can't just— I can't be a side-side piece!"

"Now, that depends on how big his *piece*—"

"Corey."

"Alright, alright. Prudes."

From the other end of the line, I hear the telltale sounds of cooking. I picture June moving around our little kitchenette, breaking eggs into the pan and throwing away the shells in the wrong bin. It doesn't matter how often I tell her they're not supposed to go with the plastic—she won't hear it.

I wish I was there. I wish I could smell the eggs and the bacon and the buttery, delicious pancakes I've already traded years off my life for. I wish I could leave this nightmare behind and just go home.

But things have already gotten too complicated for that.

If Corey hears anything in my silence, he doesn't mention it. Instead, he says, "Look. I've had my fair share of guys who didn't want anything serious. It's not impossible to toe the line."

"Thanks," I sniffle. "I was really gunning for 'not impossible' right now."

"'Not impossible' is still a lot of work," Corey warns. "There are rules. More often than not, they're unspoken."

"Like…?"

"Let's see. One: never leave your toothbrush at his place."

I glance to the master bedroom's ensuite, where my toothbrush is most definitely waiting for me.

"Two: never keep a change of clothes there."

I look at the scattered items of clothing around the room. Somehow, a bra has ended up on the chandelier.

"Three: never take up a drawer."

I stare at the giant closet I filled first thing on moving day.

"Four—"

"This is ridiculous, Corey!" I wail. "I'm living at his place. Where else am I supposed to keep my stuff? On Grisha?"

"Is the silver fox still there?" June asks with a touch of interest.

"June, no."

"June, *maybe*," she counters. "That guy wasn't half-bad to look at."

"*Four*," Corey says loudly, drowning out our intermission, "don't talk about feelings."

I let this one sit with me. "So far, we haven't," I say honestly. Unless you count Matvey's sparks of possessiveness, all those *You're mine* here and *This pussy is mine* there, we never exactly had a heart-to-heart. Truth be told, I can hardly see it happening.

After all, it's still up for debate whether Matvey has a heart.

Corey hums like a wise village elder. "Good. Keep it that way. And lastly—"

"There's another rule?"

"Lastly," Corey repeats, "don't ask for more. Don't wish for more. Do not ever, *ever* let yourself think it's okay to want more. That's just asking for trouble."

I stare at the ceiling, lost in thought. What would "more" even look like in our situation? We're having a baby. We're sharing space. We're sharing dinner.

We've also been sharing some *other* things pretty much on the regular.

"What do you mean by 'more'?" I ask eventually.

Corey gives a thoughtful hum. "Well, for starters, don't sleep together."

"Bit late for that, buddy."

"I mean *literal* sleeping together, Apes. Don't stay the night. That's just basic common sense."

I think back to the past few nights. Sure, after that first time, Matvey's been staying after the fact. But that's only been to make more "facts" happen. Once I'm spent and sleepy, he always puts himself back together and heads back to his place. Or rather, his other place. I've still got no idea where that is, by the way.

"He hasn't been staying over," I tell Corey.

"See? That's a win."

I preen a little. So maybe I'm not a complete disaster at keeping things casual. Even if I did get pregnant right off the bat. "What else?"

"Don't do intimate things together," Corey phone-shrugs.

"Again, Corey, bit late here."

"Nine months late, to be exact," June chimes in from the kitchen.

"Ha-ha. Tell me, how long have you been keeping that in?"

"Nine months, actually."

"You're both comedy geniuses," Corey deadpans. "What I mean, Apes, is really intimate things. Couples stuff. Cooking together, cleaning together, picking out furniture…"

"No chance of those happening," I roll my eyes. "Meals get delivered, housekeeping knocks every day at 4:00 P.M., and have you seen the décor here? Let me tell you, it's like living in the Bat Cave."

"Really?" Corey muses. "Huh. Maybe I should come over."

"You'd probably have to swear an oath," June comments. "In Russian. With a gun."

"I could get a gun."

"Rob would divorce you so fast."

"Yeah, he would," Corey sighs. "He's a very militant pacifist. Also, never fuck with a lawyer."

"Never fuck with a lawyer," June and I agree.

"Anybody ever tell you you're like the twins from The Shining? So creepy. I'm gonna go spray myself with holy water."

As Corey's steps fade away from the receiver—presumably to do something other than find the nearest church to rob with a plastic bottle—June's voice grows closer. "Listen up, A. The way I see it, you're thinking too much about this."

"Maybe," I concede. "I don't know, Jay. I've never been in a situationship before!"

"There's always a first time," June quips. "And who knows, maybe it'll lead somewhere else?"

"Did your ears get fried along with the eggs? Your brother was just telling me not to raise my expectations."

"So don't," June says, like it's simple. "Go with the flow. By all means, enjoy the perks of your new lodgings."

"That makes it sound like I'm abusing the gardener."

"Ooh, do you guys have a gardener?" June perks up, suddenly interested.

"Stop binging *Desperate Housewives* while I'm not there. Also, no. We're literally up in the sky."

"*Boooring.*"

"Was there a point somewhere aside from your thirsting after Carlos?"

"One: thirsting after Carlos is always right. Second: relationships evolve. Why not see where this leads?"

"Because it can't lead anywhere, June," I sigh. "That's the whole problem."

"So what? Doesn't mean you can't have fun along the way."

God, I envy her. I wish I could see life like this: take what's offered, shrug at what's not. I was never that kind of person.

For me, every table scrap was a fight.

When June speaks again, her voice is quiet. Softer. "You know you're allowed to enjoy good things, right? You don't have to keep waiting for the other shoe to drop."

Of course she'd hit the nail on the head. She's known me for too long to miss what's actually bothering me.

"I just..." I hesitate, looking for the right words. In this mess, it feels like there aren't any. "I don't want things to get complicated. Again."

June hums in understanding. She knows what "complicated" means for me: the glares, the silence. The awareness of being unwanted. "Then you'll just have to keep them very clear. Think you can do that, A?"

Can I do that?

Matvey's a force of nature. He takes what he wants and is absolutely unapologetic about it. He's strong-willed, mercurial, and unbearable to the extreme.

So can I keep this purely physical?

Put like that, it doesn't sound like much of a challenge. In fact, it doesn't sound like a challenge at all. That's what I tell myself as I huff into my phone and murmur back to my best friend, "Yeah. Yeah, I think so."

"Attagirl," June replies, a smile in her voice. "See? That wasn't so hard now, was it?"

Wasn't it? I ask myself in the silence of Matvey's empty room, on Matvey's empty bed, next to Matvey's empty space.

"Yeah," I tell June, trying to force a smile into my voice, too. "You're right."

28

MATVEY

Not once in my whole fucking life have I failed to sleep when I needed it.

I don't toss and turn restlessly, replaying my regrets. I don't ponder. I don't reflect. I just close my eyes and sleep the sleep of the dead, the sleep of a man who's earned six hours' respite from a world intent on putting him in the dirt.

My men—even Yuri and Grisha—know better than to intrude on my sleep, because my work demands that I am at my best at all times. Most people, when they are a step too slow, a day too late, a dollar too short, accept it and trudge on anyway.

But when I'm off my game, people die.

So all those around me understand it. The one entity that seems not to have gotten the memo?

My dick.

I'm lying awake in the pre-dawn murk with a raging hard-on and sleep nowhere in sight.

I know whose fault it is, of course. The same person who's been haunting my dreams. Ever since we resumed our "changing room activities," I can't seem to close my eyes without the images of it hounding me: April's legs, locked around my waist. April's lips, sealed around my cock. April's—

Suddenly, my phone lights up.

I don't have to check who it is. The only people brave enough to call me at this hour of the day are Yuri and Grisha. And Petra, but I can't imagine she'd do something as pedestrian as call when she can just storm in.

Note to self: change the goddamn locks before she gets any ideas.

However, when I look at the display, my mood changes.

It's April.

For a second, I wonder if something's happened. If this is an emergency call. Even after I promised to be available 24/7, she'd never actually used the burner phone I gave her. If she's using it now…

Without a second's thought, I accept the call.

"April."

"Oh—hi, Matvey." On the other end of the line, April sounds surprised by how quickly I picked up. "Sorry, did I wake you?"

I take in the tone of her voice: frazzled, but not scared. Without realizing I'd stopped, I begin to breathe again. "No. I was already up."

Part of me, anyway.

"Oh, good! Good," April mumbles. "I wouldn't have called so early, but…"

"April," I interrupt, though not unkindly. If anything, there's a small smile playing on my lips now, one I don't let show often. "Just tell me what's wrong."

"Well, nothing's wrong, exactly," she says. "But Dr. Allan had to move up today's appointment. She's been called in for a double this afternoon, so she's coming over in an hour. I know you don't like surprises, so I just wanted to let you know."

"Oh." For once, I'm speechless. It's taken me years to train secretaries to be half as competent as April's being right now: sorting out priorities, anticipating my needs. "Good. You were right to call."

Mindlessly, I begin to stroke my cock over my boxers.

"I'm glad," April sighs. "Again, I really didn't wanna bother you, it's just—"

"It was time-sensitive," I complete for her. "I understand."

"Thank you."

It feels like a natural place to end the call. For a second, I'm sure she'll do just that. I pick up my pace, wanting that velvet-smooth voice to carry me as far along as possible.

But her next words aren't a goodbye. "So… early bird, huh?" April jokes. "I had you pegged for a night owl."

"Definitely a night owl," I correct.

"The plot thickens, then. What could possibly be keeping Your Owlishness awake?"

The little lilt in April's voice is driving me insane. I hook a finger under my waistband, take myself fully in hand. "Feel free to guess, Ms. Flowers."

Maybe I imagined it, but I think I hear her breath hitch. It never fails to rile her up—calling her that. "Let's see... Shootout by the river?"

"Guess again."

April harrumphs. "Fine, then not a shootout. Important Poo-king duties, then?"

"*Pakhan.*"

"Right. That."

I huff a laugh into the darkness. "Wrong."

"Really need to go to the bathroom but don't feel like getting up?"

"That's extremely specific."

"Try being pregnant. I promise you, it's a journey filled with extremely specific experiences."

The image of her pregnant belly sends a spark running down my spine. *Fuck.* "Last guess before you're out of lives."

For a long moment, April's quiet. I can practically hear the gears in her head whirring, her determination to win this game no matter what. With April, everything turns into a race.

"Thoughts?" she hazards finally.

I mull it over. "Mm. 'Thoughts' isn't wrong."

"A-ha! I knew it. It's always thoughts."

"Not so fast," I chide. "You haven't told me what kind of thoughts yet."

"Oh, I see. Someone's playing hard to get."

You don't even know how hard. "Time's ticking, Ms. Flowers."

"Alright, fine! How abouuut…" She lets the last word drag to buy a few extra seconds for herself. "Evil mafia CEO plans to take over the world?"

"Why do you seem to think I'm some cartoonish overlord?"

"Because it's funny?"

"You and I have very different definitions of 'funny.'"

"That's because you're no fun at all."

"Oh?" I say, giving myself a squeeze. "I seem to remember you having your fair share of 'fun' last night."

This time I didn't imagine it: her breath *does* hitch, and for a fair handful of seconds, too.

"In fact…" I drawl, picturing her pretty pink cheeks, blushing just for me. "The *thought* alone would be enough to keep a man up at night."

"Is…" April swallows. "Is that so?"

"Indeed," I confirm. "It'd be madness, really. Trying to go back to sleep like that."

For a moment, I wonder if I haven't overdone it. If April's delicate sensibilities won't have the better of her and force a quick, awkward goodbye out of her lips—lips much better suited to other things.

It'd be natural. In all my life, I haven't once found a woman who could keep up with my appetites. I don't expect it to be the seamstress I randomly knocked up nine months ago in a changing room.

But, as always, April surprises me.

"And, uh… What would these thoughts entail, exactly?"

I feel my face split into a grin. Feral, hungry. "Let's see," I reply, lazily playing with the head of my cock. "First, there wouldn't be any clothes. It takes energy to think things up, you know. Best save it on what matters."

"And what…" April clears her throat. I can tell her voice has gone hoarse, can almost picture her face: cheeks flushed, pupils blown wide, lips parted around half a choked breath. "What does matter?"

Hook, line, sinker.

"Your wet, eager little pussy, for example."

My tone is harsh now, commanding—just how I know she likes it. On the other end of the line, April whines, making my cock jump. "T-That's…"

"I'd start out nice and slow," I tell her, even though it's a lie. If I had her here, right now, I'd be plunging deep into that tight heat without so much as a finger to pave the way. "With my tongue. Taste how slick and ready you are for me."

Her breathing is completely gone. Held captive in her throat. Taut. Desperate.

"Then I'd make you readier. I'd drag my tongue all the way up that sweet clit of yours, enjoying all the little sounds you'd make. Quiet at first, and then louder and louder."

"Matvey…"

"Are you touching yourself?" I demand.

A long pause. "I—"

"Do it," I order. "Touch yourself or I'll hang up."

I can practically see the outrage on her face. It's my favorite look on her: that who-does-he-think-he-is, *how-dare-he* glare that makes her eyes squint like sharp crescents, her lips press tight together. It's a treat unlike any other.

But what I love even more is her surrender. "Ah…"

I let out a hiss. My hand's working faster now. I can feel the slick of precum all over my fingers. Closing my eyes, I pretend it comes from her. "Don't go in yet. If you do, I'll know."

April makes a quiet sound of protest. "I thought that was… the point… of phone sex?"

Already so far gone. I squeeze myself at the base, forcing my excitement to slow down. I want to make this last.

And I want to hear her come first.

"I'll decide what the point is."

Another low whine. "Fuck."

"Language," I chastise. But truthfully, it makes me fucking throb. It's so rare to hear April swear—every instance is a gift. It makes my chest swell with pride.

Well, that and something else.

"Touch your clit," I command, softer now. Lower. "Pretend it's my tongue. Wet your fingers at your entrance, but do *not* go in."

It's an exercise in restraint—not coming from the sounds alone. "You're such an asshole," April whimpers, all the while doing exactly what I ordered her to. I can tell from the wet noises of her fingers, the gentle slide that isn't quite pumping.

Not yet.

"Good girl. Keep going."

A few panting breaths break against my ears. I roll my hips into my grip, bucking up. "You—goddamn—*prick*—"

"You don't even know the half of it."

A moan, long and deep. "Oh, you'll pay for this…!"

"Yeah?" I quip. "I was thinking I'd get a reward."

"Not a chan—ahh…!"

"Here's what I had in mind," I continue, feeding on her stream of insults. With every word, my cock grows harder, impatient. "First, I'll lap up all those sweet juices of yours. Get my appetizer straight from the source. You with me so far?"

"Mhmm…"

Fuck. We haven't been at this five minutes, and she's already moaning like that. This little vixen will be the death of me.

I force myself to focus on the scene. On this little game of ours—one I intend on winning. "Then I'd fill you up nice and easy. My fingers first, then my cock."

"Ahh…!"

"I'd dip the head in. Grind it against that sweet spot of yours, but without relief. If you wanted more, you'd have to beg for it."

"Matvey…"

"Beg, *kalina.* I promise I'm a reasonable man."

That's a lie. Right now, I'm feeling anything but reasonable. I want to grip those full hips of hers until they're bruised in the shape of my hands and sink in, without giving myself a moment to breathe.

Without giving her a moment to breathe.

Eventually, her pride breaks. It always does in the end. "Please," she whispers, barely audible.

"What was that?"

"Please," she blurts out again, frustrated. "Please, Matvey, I need—!"

I grin. "Go on, then. Take what you need."

I can hear it when she does. There's a wet sound of fingers breaching, then a whimper. "Ah—*ahh—*"

"Come for me," I growl, close enough to taste it. "Let me hear it, April."

"Matvey—!"

A high-pitched moan pierces my ears, and then I'm coming, too, following my little vixen over the edge.

Hot cum spills out over my hand and pools in the crevices of my hips. It feels like it's ripped from a deeper source than I've ever tapped before. Like it was meant for her and her alone.

I catch my breath as the mental whiteout fades and reality comes rushing back in. That was… intense. More intense than I'd expected, for sure.

But then again, April Flowers always manages to defy expectations.

Expectations. The word settles heavily in my stomach. There are no expectations between us—no commitments other than the one growing inside her belly. Even if we did break our promise to keep our distance, the most important one still stands: *This means nothing.*

That's the only vow worth keeping.

When I come back to the present, April's still panting softly in my ear. "Need a hand?" I joke.

"Mm. I hate that you weren't even here, but now, I can't stand."

"Consider it part of the service package. In-person or remote —exchange if unsatisfied."

A quiet snort. "You're a real comedian, aren't you?"

"Don't let my men hear you say that. My reputation would never recover."

It's strange, how mellow I get after this. After *her.* With other women, all I felt was the crawling urge to get away.

With April, I keep wanting to make it last just a little longer.

"Well, I'd love to stay for more of your pitch," April yawns, clearly exhausted by our little marathon. "But I'm afraid Dr. Allan's gonna be here in half an hour. So I really need to grab a shower."

For a second, I try to picture it: April, fucked out of her mind, spreading her legs for her lady doctor with my seed still warm between them.

Fuck. I'd better take my shower cold.

"See you tonight," I murmur, letting an unspoken promise fill the air between us.

April doesn't miss it. "See you tonight," she echoes, voice quivering with anticipation.

Then the call disconnects.

Outside, the sun is rising. I consider going back to sleep for a moment. Like this, satisfied and spent, I could easily down another three hours.

But the sooner I get to work, the sooner I can clock out.

And the sooner I can finish what we started.

29

APRIL

Like everything else in the Matvey Groza Bat Cave, the bathtub is big. Like, ridiculously big. Bigger than would make sense for the laws of physics.

"Someone's having fun," Matvey comments dryly, watching me starfish in the tub-slash-indoor pool.

"Mhmm," I hum in agreement. "It's your fault, really. If you didn't want me to have fun, you shouldn't have put a spa in your penthouse."

Rough lips graze the back of my neck. "Who says it wasn't meant for fun?"

"Hand me another?" I try with my best puppy eyes.

Matvey gives me an impressed once-over. "Someone's forgotten her manners."

"Hand me another, pretty please?"

With an amused huff, Matvey presses a cheese cube to my mouth.

As I chew, a moan escapes me. "This is better than sex."

"Careful, *kalina*. I just might let you starve."

A shiver runs down my spine. Whenever Matvey growls his threats into my ear, I always want to push those boundaries. See how far he's willing to take it.

I shake my head and force myself to focus on the food. If I keep thinking like this, it won't be long before yet another part of me starts calling the shots. Again. "You'd never. I'm carrying our child here."

"Which is the only reason I'm entertaining this." His big palm comes to rest over my belly, rubbing circles into the taut skin under the hot water. "So don't get used to it."

Too late. "Yes, sir."

A few minutes go by in silence. It's strange how quickly that's changed: before, Matvey's silence was tense, charged. Now, the atmosphere between us has grown mellower, as relaxed as it could be. If it does get charged again, it's for an entirely different reason.

I let my head loll to the side, nestled against the firmness of Matvey's pecs. God, this man is wasted as a *pakhan*. He'd make such an excellent mattress.

Never let him hear you say that, April.

"Your appointment with Dr. Allan," Matvey brings up after a while. "Tell me about it."

"There's not much to say," I reply, sinking further into hydromassage bliss. "Everything's stable. No signs of fetal distress, no labor."

"'Cozy', was it?"

"Yeah," I groan. "Bit too cozy for my tastes. I'd like my bladder back, thank you."

An amused huff. "So small, and already the boss of you."

"The boss of *us*," I correct. "Don't think you'll be immune. I have it on good authority that babies are excellent brainwashers."

"Is that so?"

"Mhmm. Especially when it comes to their daddies. One look into those big doll eyes, and you'll forget anything else exists in the world."

"That sounds a bit farfetched. Who told you that?"

"My mom."

Silence falls again. This time, I can feel the undercurrent of unspoken questions in it. "She must have loved you very much to say that," Matvey murmurs eventually, breaking the curtain of quiet.

"Yeah, right." I let out a bitter laugh. "She was talking about Charlie, not me."

"Your half-brother?"

"Mm." I shift in the water, pulling up my knees. "It was the same with him, you know. The late birth. I was post-term, too, but Charlie must have broken some kind of record."

"That long?"

"Forty-six weeks. In the end, the doctors convinced my mom to induce. It wasn't…" I shudder at the memory. "Pleasant."

"You talk as if you were there."

"I was," I rasp. "Charlie's dad was nowhere to be found. His friends dragged him out of an alley later, drunk off his ass. And it's not like *my* dad wanted anything to do with his ex after everything, so…" I make finger-guns at myself. "April Flowers, trained doula. At your service."

I throw a glance behind my back, meeting Matvey's skeptical gaze. Something in his eyes gives me pause. If I didn't know any better, I'd say he's… *angry?* "You couldn't have been older than ten."

"Nine," I correct. "And thank you for reminding me you have literal files on my life."

"I'm thorough," Matvey says without a trace of guilt. Then: "Difficult birth, I assume?"

"It was a goddamn battlefield," I exhale. "I remember being in this shitty public clinic, paint flaking off the walls, staff staring off into space like they'd rather eat a scalpel than be there."

"Charming."

"You don't know the half of it."

I take a deep breath. Reliving these memories… It's not easy. Especially considering the circumstances I'm in now. For the longest time, I thought I'd never have kids at all—not if it meant suffering like that.

Goes to show: a lot can change in nine months.

And besides… Matvey's voice in my ear is calm. Grounding. It makes me feel—

Safe.

I shake my head. That's not a thought I should ever be entertaining. Matvey's made it perfectly clear for which one of us he's here, and it's not little ol' me.

Still... it's hard not to let myself be soothed by it. The strong, comforting presence of this man's arms around me.

So, without thinking, I keep telling the story that's been haunting my nightmares for the past seventeen years.

"She was in labor for thirty hours," I whisper, hugging my knees to my belly. "She was losing so much blood, I didn't think she'd make it. It was like one of those scenes from a regency romance—the tragic backstory to some grief-stricken single dad. Only, there was no dad there. Just me."

Suddenly, Matvey's hands come up to my shoulders. The grip is warm, firm. Soon, they start rubbing circles into my back, working the knotted-up muscles loose.

Why? part of me wants to ask. *Why are you taking care of me? Why are you being so kind to me?*

Why do all that, when you're not gonna stay?

I shake off that thought, too. I remember Corey's words: *no expectations.*

"Where's the father now?" Matvey asks, snapping me out of my reverie. There's a note of danger in his voice, one I can't immediately make sense of.

"Tom?" I ask, surprised. "Oh, he's probably passed out on the couch. You know how it is."

"I really don't."

A small smile fights on my lips. "Right. Sometimes, I forget."

"Forget what?"

"That there are fathers who actually want to be a part of their children's lives in this world."

Matvey doesn't say anything to that. For a moment, I wonder if I rendered him speechless. It's a silly thought, one that makes me huff a quiet laugh afterwards.

You think too much of yourself, April Flowers.

"Anyway," I say, reaching for the tray to snatch up another tasty morsel. "Charlie was born healthy. Mom recovered. Tied her tubes. Tom sobered up enough to drive them home. Happily ever after and all that."

"I don't see a little April in this happy ending."

"Little April got driven to school by a really nice nurse." I shrug. "She gave me a lollipop. Most nutritious breakfast I'd had all week." When I see the way Matvey's eyes widen, I give him a playful punch on the shoulder. "Kidding. Though it was a really nice lollipop."

Still staring at me like I've gone halfway crazy, Matvey says, "I assume this is why you're against it. Inducing."

I give a slight nod. "After what happened with Mom... I don't want to go through that. Not if I can avoid it."

I brace myself for the pushback. I've had to defend my choice to every doctor I've spoken to—including Dr. Allan—and I just know Matvey isn't going to be happy with it. Someone with his penchant for control? He'd want to schedule it down to the minute. "Look, I get that—"

"Then don't."

I blink. "Sorry, what?"

"Don't induce," Matvey says, like it's the easiest thing in the world. "There's no point risking both your lives like that. When the baby's ready, it'll come."

My eyes are probably the size of watermelons right now. "Wow."

Matvey frowns. "Did I say something funny?"

"Nope. I just…" I force myself to float back down to Earth. "Honestly, I was expecting a cage fight about this. Who are you and what have you done with Matvey?"

"I think the steam's gone to your head."

"You know what? Me, too," I say, turning around. "Because there's no way you just agreed with me."

Matvey brushes a wet lock of hair behind my ear. "Stranger things have happened."

I can feel heat rising to my cheeks. "Stranger than Matvey Groza telling me I get to be the boss? I don't think so, no."

Suddenly, it strikes me: I'm naked, dripping wet, and straddling Matvey's lap. I didn't end up in this position purposefully, but now that I'm here…

Now, I kind of don't want to leave.

"You can be the boss of some things," Matvey concedes.

"Like my body?" I hazard.

With a wicked smirk, Matvey's hands move down my frame. One of them settles on my hip, while the other…

"Ah…!"

I gasp at the intrusion. I'm still stretched and sensitive from before—it takes nothing at all for his finger to slip right in.

"No," Matvey breathes directly into my ear. "Definitely not that."

His finger starts pumping in and out of me. Slow—maddening—until I'm panting with need.

"You see, Ms. Flowers," Matvey rasps, with that sandpaper tone of his that never fails to set me on fire, "I'm a real stickler for rules. The rules *I* set, specifically."

I grip his shoulders. Without my permission, my hips begin to move, chasing Matvey's touch to make it deeper.

But Matvey doesn't let me. Every time I sink down onto him, he draws back, leaving me with nothing except the exact amount of friction *he* wants to give me. It's enough to drive me wild.

"And we both know..." Matvey breathes against my neck, grazing it with his teeth. "You like following them."

Suddenly, he grabs my hips and turns me around. I reach behind my back to find purchase—something, anything—until I finally find his hair. Nails digging into his scalp, I let out a whine.

I hate how right he is. How easily he's seen through me. When we're like this—lined up, ready to sink into each other —I want nothing more than to stop thinking. About myself, my memories, everything.

And when Matvey fucks my hips down onto himself, impaling me on his throbbing cock, that's exactly what I do.

I stop thinking.

And it feels so, so good.

30

MATVEY

As soon as I climb into the car, Grisha's nose twitches like a hound on a scent.

I watch him sniff the air without even trying to hide his intrigue. I'd remind him of curiosity and all the cats it did in, but honestly, I'm just too goddamn spent.

"Bath salts?" he ventures.

"Yes," I drawl, sliding in my seat. "New brand. It's called *None of Your Fucking Business.*"

Grisha whistles. "Never heard of it."

"Tell me something I don't know."

All I wanted tonight was to stay in that bathtub. Stay until I'd had April in every conceivable position above and below the water. Above and below *me.* Until my fingers pruned beyond repair, until my neck spawned gills. For one more taste of that little siren, I'd have learned to breathe underwater.

Unfortunately, work is a thing.

I gaze out the window as Grisha carries me through Manhattan traffic. It's a nightmare during the day, but at night, it's… not any different. It's the purpose of it that changes: under the sun, people trudge to work, cursing the day they were not born rich. Under the moon, they thrive.

It's not quite the same if you're Bratva.

Being Bratva means standing on top of the world regardless of how you were born. It means biting into life and feasting on the juices, knowing no one can keep you from drinking it dry.

It also means you don't get to keep office hours.

But my mind doesn't seem to care about that. Tonight, my mind has well and truly betrayed me, deciding to stay behind in that tub with the object of my desires.

And, now, my concerns.

"She must have loved you very much to say that."

"Yeah, right. She was talking about Charlie, not me."

It isn't the first time April's mentioned her family. Or rather, that she talks about it like a special kind of hell she's lucky to have escaped from.

It is the first time she's mentioned her mom.

I shouldn't care. The former Mrs. Flowers should be no one to me except my child's future *babushka*. I should pretend she never mentioned anything and move on with my—

"Grisha, what do you know about April's mother?"

Goddammit. I tell myself that practicality is why I'm asking. If this woman is a danger to my child, I need to know.

If this woman was a danger to *hers*—

"Not much," Grisha answers. "We checked the basics. Eleanor Hill, forty-four years old. She has a daughter from her first marriage—that'd be Ms. Flowers—and a son from her second. Currently lives on Staten Island with her husband and kid."

It sounds so utterly mundane. So unlike anything worth investigating.

I don't trust it one bit.

"Run a full background check," I order. "I want to know everything about this woman and her known associates. Don't leave anything out, especially from her past."

Grisha gives me a curious glance from the rear-view mirror. If he has a comment, for once, he's wise enough to keep it to himself. "Yes, sir."

Then we pull up to the venue.

A valet takes the car for us. I unfurl from my seat with a pop of my shoulders. That bone-deep relaxation I was feeling in the bath has evaporated completely. It's a message from my body to my mind: from now on, it's all business.

Which is curious, considering where we are.

Hedoneros Club. The Groza Bratva's newest business venture: an exclusive club with stellar franchise potential, spearheaded by our newest *vor*. A man of excess—and this club reflects that in every detail, starting from the name: the goddess of pleasure and the god of love, joined in a single tacky neologism.

Ipatiy comes to greet me at the entrance. He's a portly man with a sunny disposition and a knack for making friends worth millions. The Muñoz family, for example, who controls shipments for every experimental drug this side of the East Coast and often has him over for dinner. Apparently, César makes a mean empanada.

"Welcome, welcome!" my man bellows, grinning from ear to ear.

"Ipatiy," I greet with a firm handshake. "Opening night seems to be going well."

"Oh, more than well, *moy pakhan*." Ipatiy beams. "Did you see the line out front? Stretches all the way into the street."

I didn't. Men like me don't stand in line, and I don't often pay attention to things that don't concern me. Still, I give a short nod. "Impressive."

"Thank you, sir. That means the world, coming from you."

It damn well should. "I'm assuming there's a table for us somewhere."

"Oh! Of course!" Ipatiy flounders, rubbing his thick hands together. "This way, please."

Ipatiy leads us through the club, giving us the panoramic view. Blue and red lights cast their neon glow over the guests' faces, painting everyone in a double hue that never quite melts into purple. Eros and Hedone—love and pleasure.

If there are two things that *aren't* meant to mesh, it's those two.

A futuristic-looking elevator takes us to the roof. I step out onto a terrace filled with greenery, encased in a glass dome that turns the night sky into the club's starlit ceiling. I hum with approval on the inside, but don't let it show. The worst thing a *vor* can do is get cocky. I won't let Ipatiy think he's already got what he's chasing.

Besides, my approval is fickle.

And a lot can happen in one night.

Ipatiy leads us to a round table at the edge of the dome. Yuri's already there, springing up when he sees me. "Motya."

My lips twitch with a smile I keep to myself. The relief on Yuri's face is impossible to miss. There's only one thing he hates more than socializing, and that's socializing by himself. Even Grisha's presence at my side isn't enough to put him off.

"Enjoy yourself, brother?" I ask, biting back a smirk.

"To death. Hopefully, it comes sooner rather than later."

Next to us, Ipatiy preens, seeming to take it as a compliment. Then he excuses himself to go greet the stragglers.

"Poor Yurochka," Grisha croons to Yuri as soon as Ipatiy's out of earshot. "Up so late past your bedtime. Do you want the car keys? You can take a nap in the backseat."

"I'm shocked the DMV's still letting you drive."

"Down, boys," I chide. "Or else I'll have to order you to kiss and make up, and no one here wants to see that."

They grumble and grouse, but neither one is keyed up enough to keep picking a fight right now. Not when there's business to attend to.

"Champagne?" a smiling waitress asks with exquisite timing as she glides by with a tray.

"Yes," we all say in unison.

I sit at the head of the table, letting myself be swept up in greetings and kiss-assery of every kind. This may be Ipatiy's venture, but I'm the one who gave the green light; *I'm* the one who invested. Therefore, his success is mine.

So would be his failure.

But it doesn't seem like I'll have to be concerned about that. Below, pills were swapping hands like coins, and up here, where the atmosphere is clearly intended to come across as classier, I can still spy little round pick-me-ups wrapped in napkins or sliding between tongues.

Oh, well. Ipatiy can iron out the kinks. As long as the bottom line's promising, I won't look too closely.

"And we're all here!"

Speak of the devil.

Ipatiy walks back to our table with Ivan. He's got an arm lazily draped over Ivan's shoulder, which everyone can tell isn't going over well except for the man himself. My oldest *vor* looks just about ready to crawl out of his skin, pulsing vein and all. Ipatiy tightens his hold in a show of friendship, and I could swear Ivan's eye starts twitching.

"Ivan," I say, "nice of you to join us. Come sit."

Ipatiy's grabby hand finally falls away. I spy a flash of relief on Ivan's face—the slump of aborted carnage. With a stiff nod, he takes his place across from me.

For a while, the night is bearable. I have to give it to Ipatiy: the man knows how to show hospitality. Refined appetizers make their way onto our table, from caviar tarts to crab *tapas*, with a fine selection of cheeses and rare honey dips. I take small sips out of my champagne, wanting to keep sharp, but I can tell from the heat rising to my men's cheeks that the drink list measures up to the food. I pop a cube of brie with orange blossom honey and pistachios into my mouth, and all I can think about is April back home: her ravenous hunger for fine things she never got to try, her quiet little moans of pleasure when a morsel melted into her mouth.

God, I wish I was here with her.

The thought snaps me out of my reverie. Why would I want that? April's no one. Nobody. She's the mother of my child—but to me, she's nothing.

A co-parent, sure. A person to protect for the sake of my kid.

But she's not a *date*.

Events like these, they have rules. Codes, and very strict ones at that. A *pakhan* walking into a business christening with a woman on his arm…

He wouldn't do that unless that woman was important. Unless she was *his.*

April could *be yours*, the most feral, possessive part of me snarls. *She'd be yours if you claimed her.*

But I can't claim her like that.

Then, suddenly, I feel a kick under the table. "Matvey," Yuri hisses, bringing me back to the present.

I realize the *vory* are looking at me. Someone must've been trying to get my attention.

"This is Ipatiy's night, Gora," says Grisha pleasantly. "Certainly, the D.C. acquisition can wait."

So that's what they were asking after. "Grisha's right," I say. "We can talk business in the morning. Tonight, we're celebrating."

Of course, I would rather talk business if I'm to be here. Truthfully, I'd rather not be here at all. But if that's not an option, then I'd gladly make this time count.

Unfortunately, I wasn't listening to a single word that was spoken, so that rules it out.

"That may be true, boss," Stanislav intercepts. "But surely…"

"Surely you can drop the mystery now," another voice cuts in. "*Sir.*"

I look up. Ivan returns my gaze with something unusual in it. Something close to fire.

Has he ever spoken to me like that?

Ivan's lip twitches. Passing his outburst off as a joke, he continues, "It's good to be kept on your toes, but we didn't join the Russian ballet. There's no secrets among brothers. Right?"

A few voices chime in to agree.

Ah. So that's how it is. I got distracted for one minute, and here I am—cornered by my own men, demanding answers. Demanding transparency.

Another reason I can't let April sink any deeper into me: for better or worse, she's a distraction.

And I cannot afford to be distracted.

"You're right."

A hush falls over the table. Everyone's eyes are on me now. Yuri's are bulging most of all, disbelief written into every muscle.

"You did join the Bratva," I continue calmly. "*My* Bratva. The Bratva my grandfather founded. You remember Igor Groza, don't you, Ivan?"

Ivan tenses. I see his hand go tight around a napkin. *Good.* "I could never forget," he mumbles. As expected of my grandfather's most loyal man.

"And yet, you forget yourself. This is still the Groza Bratva, is it not?"

Ivan grits his teeth. "It is."

"And I'm still the *pakhan*, correct?"

"… Correct."

Of course Ivan hasn't forgotten. When I was rebuilding the Groza Bratva from its ruins, *he* sought *me* out. Wanted to see the blood heir of the man he'd followed into the darkness of the underworld. The man he'd failed to protect.

He wanted to make it right.

I don't know if he's still trying to do that. If this is all a misguided attempt at protecting my grandfather's legacy.

But this is *my* Bratva now.

And I'll be damned if I let a single *vor* undermine me in front of the rest.

"Then you've got nothing to worry about," I conclude, draining my glass. "Enjoy the opportunities of this new continent. Enjoy the power, the money, the fame. Enjoy tonight. But don't make the mistake of forgetting who made it all possible."

"How gracious," Ivan replies thinly. "It seems our fearless

leader forgets, too. That he didn't accomplish all of this alone."

A murmur of assent lifts from the table. I nip that shit right in the fucking bud.

"Of course not."

For once, my *vory* are speechless. Not a single one of them was expecting me to agree. Perhaps they were even anticipating an outburst.

On another night, I might've given them that. I might've snarled and put them back into their place by their scruffs.

Tonight, though, I've had a very nice bath.

"After all," I say, rising from my seat, "my *family* was always there by my side. Isn't that right?"

Every single *vor* tenses like a violin. There's no mistaking the meaning of my words—they all know where they stand on family.

And they all know I don't consider them part of mine.

But Bratva means *brotherhood.* Ivan used that very word earlier, referring to us all as brothers. So how could they possibly disagree?

"Enjoy the rest of your night," I murmur. And then I leave.

Two sets of footsteps ring after mine. One of them is faster, hurried. It catches up in seconds. "Motya."

"What?" I snap, my patience used up.

"This—" my brother hesitates, trying to find the words. "This isn't smart," he settles on. "You know that, right? You can't just alienate the *vory*. You need them."

"I really don't."

"Matvey—"

"I never needed them." I shrug, striding through the blue-and-red lights. "I had you. That was always enough for me."

Yuri's step falters. "That's not fair," he bites back eventually. "To them, I mean."

"I don't care what's fair to them," I growl. "They're not blood. They're just glorified attack dogs. They'll take what bones I throw at them and they'll be fucking grateful for my generosity."

Next to me, Yuri falls quiet. We make it outside and wait for Grisha to bring the car around.

"Dogs... they're loyal," Yuri remarks at last. "But even the most loyal dog will bite if backed into a corner."

"Will it?" I ask idly. "Then I'll just have to put it down."

For the entire ride back, Yuri doesn't speak a word.

31

APRIL

For the first time in a long time, I wake up refreshed. Like, *actually* refreshed. I thought it was a myth, but who knew? A good bath, a nice meal, and now, I'm positively glowing.

Of course, it wasn't *just* the bath and meal, but still.

As I walk around the kitchen, humming to myself and picking out a particularly mouthwatering box of Madagascar vanilla cookies, last night's conversation comes back to me. Or rather, last night's monologue.

I still can't believe I did that. Things like that... I'd never said them to anyone. Aside from June and Corey, who know my sad backstory like the back of their hands because they were there for most of it, I'd never felt the urge to tell anybody else. To... confide in anybody else.

But I did. And now, there's this floaty feeling inside of me, this lightness, that makes me want to do things. Things I never did before.

Things like calling my mom.

The kettle whistles. I pour myself a generous cup of who-knows-what million-dollar tea from Japan and munch on a cookie, lost in thought.

It's been a while since I've heard my mother's voice. I tell myself I don't miss it. That the woman gave birth to me and that's just about all she did. I have no reason to expect anything else from this stranger who never even wanted to share my name.

And yet.

And yet... right now, I'm *expecting*. I have a child growing inside me. A child who's going to call me "Mom," and I still don't know what that means.

But Eleanor does. She has a son.

And maybe, just maybe...

With trembling fingers, I pick up my phone and dial.

For a bit, it rings out. I listen to those dull, electronic beeps with a growing sense of relief. She's not going to pick up. She's not. I'll be able to say I did my part and save myself the trouble of this uncomfortable conversation. Scolding at best, indifference at worst.

But what if she's happy for you?

And then, at the last ring—

"What."

No question mark this time, either. "Hi, Mom."

Eleanor's voice is clipped, factual. In the background, I can hear the clattering of pots and pans, the rush of running water. "Get to the point, shortcake. Momma's got dishes."

You've also got a husband with two functioning arms, I think but don't say. Who knows? Maybe Tom's hands fell off the same wagon he did. It's been a while since I last saw him— anything's possible.

"I just wanted to catch up, see how you're doing," I answer as meekly as I can. "If this is a bad time—"

"Every time is a bad time," my mother dismisses. "Out with it. Poker night ain't gonna clean up after itself."

Don't I know it. "I've actually got kind of a big news. We could meet, if that's better."

On the other end of the line, Eleanor scoffs. "Yeah, right. 'Cause I've got that kind of time on my hands."

My smile falters a little more. I shake myself. I'm the one who wanted to do this. If I don't give it my best, then what's the point? "Well, I'm a bit freer right now. I'm on leave from work for a bit, so maybe I could come and see you—"

Eleanor's barking laughter cuts me right off. "Oh, sweetie. Don't you know better than that? If it's about money, I don't have it."

For a second, I have to reboot my brain. "Money?" I repeat stupidly. "No, I wasn't—"

"Why don't you ask your father?" Eleanor suggests, spitting the last word out with ill-concealed contempt. "I'm sure Nella can do without a new Birkin this season."

"Nora," I correct automatically.

"Whatever," Eleanor scoffs. "If that's all—"

"Mom," I cut her off. "It's not about money."

It's a herculean effort to snap my sentence in half there. Because the other half would be a huge, long overdue rant: *I've never asked you for money in my life. I could've—I should've —but I didn't. So why in the everlasting hell would you think that's why I called you now?!*

"Oh," Eleanor breathes. "Well, if that's not it, then—"

"I'm pregnant."

Silence falls over the line. For a second, I think I might've lost signal. I hold my phone away to check—

"HAHAHAHA!"

—and Eleanor bursts into laughter.

"Oh, sweetie," she wheezes, as if she's drying away a tear or something, "you didn't tell me you were going into comedy."

"I'm really not." Nothing about this conversation strikes me even remotely as funny. "Glad you're enjoying yourself, though."

"Honey," she gasps, still between bursts of hilarity, "come on. There's no way you're pregnant."

"I kind of am, though."

"Please. Since when?"

I take a deep breath. Without thinking, I've started rubbing circles into my belly. "Nine months, actually," I exhale at last, fighting to keep my tone even. "The baby's due any day now. And since it's your grandchild, I thought you should know."

There, I huff mentally. *Done.* Whatever Eleanor chooses to do with the information, I don't give a rat's ass. I did my part.

What I don't expect is for her to keep laughing. "Aw, shortcakes. Where'd you leave your math? Either you're pregnant, or it's been nine months. In which case, the little munchkin would already be out and about."

"Seriously? You've been post-term *twice*!"

"And that's already rare enough," Eleanor retorts. "Besides, you'd know the sex by now. But no—you said 'it', 'grandchild'..."

My eyes keep bulging. I can't believe what I'm hearing: is my mother playing detective? Trying to catch me in a lie? I just told her I'm goddamn *pregnant*. And that's what she does with it?

"Mom," I try, "you can't possibly think—"

But she tuts me halfway through. "Please, dear. Let's not insult Mommy's intelligence. This prank is just like you: sloppy."

My heart sinks. All my hopes for this—hopes I should've known better than to nurture—shatter into a million pieces at my feet. All these years...

All these years, and my mom still has no idea who I am.

"Tell you what," Eleanor says with forced benevolence. "You wanted my attention, you got it; we had a nice chat—"

"Attention?" I splutter. "You think I'd make up a pregnancy for *attention*?"

"If the shoe fits, dear."

Hang up, urges my last scrap of self-respect. *Hang up and never call again.*

But I'm not fast enough.

"Besides," Eleanor remarks knowingly, readying her coup-de-grace, "you can't be pregnant. You'd need a man for that."

My mother, ladies and gentlemen. The woman who gave birth to me. Gave *birth*, and nothing else.

"And I couldn't possibly get that, right?" I laugh bitterly, voice shaking. At this point, I don't care anymore. "A man? A partner?"

"You're not blind, shortcake. Surely you can answer that yourself."

"Right," I mutter. "Guess I know where I got my good genes from, then."

I can hear the air freeze on the other end of the line. "Careful, dear," Eleanor warns, fractals in her smiling voice. "Mommy's patience isn't infinite."

Neither is mine, I begin to say but can't. The words get stuck in my throat, somewhere around the huge lump there.

"Alright, good chat," Eleanor says briskly. "Talk soon, bye!"

"Mom, I—"

And she hangs up.

... I need you.

∼

By the time the food cart comes, I've gone from heartbroken to furious.

The poor waiter seems to sense it, because he retreats with a short bow and a quick step. It's not unlike when Matvey's here. Have I turned into a scary mobster, too? Perhaps I should be so lucky.

Then Eleanor wouldn't fucking *dare*.

"Faking my pregnancy," I mutter, disbelief in every word as I pace up and down the living room. "Faking my—the nerve on that woman! Can you believe it, Nugget?"

From its warm nest, Nugget doesn't offer a comment. Probably for the best. I wouldn't want its first memory to be its bitch of a grandmother.

Grandmother. It's insane, how different it is. Eleanor as a grandma, versus…

I shake my head, drying a stray tear. It's no use thinking of *her.* Maia isn't here. *I'm* here.

And I'll protect my child for the both of us.

Just as I'm readying another rant in my head, the doorbell rings. I can practically feel Matvey on the other side: his confident stride, tendrils of his cologne sneaking in through the gap under the door. Everything about him makes me hungry.

You can't be pregnant. You'd need a man for that.

When I answer the door, I don't let Matvey speak. I grab his tie and yank it down, claiming those rough lips with mine. Matvey makes a surprised sound in his throat, but it doesn't take a second before he starts kissing back. Just as passionate, just as hungry.

This man wants *me*, I want to scream through the phone. *This man claimed me in the only way that matters.*

When I finally break away, panting against Matvey's chest, big hands slide down my hips. With a firm pull, they bring us flush together.

Immediately, I feel how hard he is. How badly he desires me. With a gasp, I run my hands everywhere, itching to claw and own and touch.

Usually, that's his role. Right now, though, I don't care who leads this dance. I just want to move until I can't think.

"Someone's impatient tonight," Matvey growls against my ear, making me shiver from head to toe.

"Yes," I breathe. "So come and take me."

We stumble back into the penthouse, every step a hazard. Through our kisses, we can't see anything but each other. The only care we take is not to squish what's between us— the evidence my mother wouldn't believe. Our child.

The child we made just like this.

Once we're at the couch, I push Matvey down on it. I have no illusions: if he wanted to, he could flip me around like a ragdoll. Take me on my back, on my knees.

But he doesn't. Instead, he sits back and lets me climb into his lap, lets my hands roam all over his firm, taut body. Until he's half-naked and so am I.

"Something happened, didn't it?" Matvey asks, eyes dark and hooded. It looks like it's taking everything—every ounce of self-control—just to push the words out.

I don't want them. Tonight, I don't want a single thought to cross my mind. "Just fuck me."

"April."

"Fuck me," I rasp. "Please."

Matvey groans into my neck. A big palm comes to gather my wrists together, pinning them behind my back.

I let out a whine. "Matvey…"

But then I feel his other hand start to work. It slides between us, where it matters, popping buttons and yanking flies, pushing my panties aside so his thick cock can sink—

"You want this?" Matvey snarls, all animal, showing me how it works. Showing me how to move my hips just right, how to ride him. "Then come and get it."

And by God, I do.

32

MATVEY

"And then she said, 'If the shoe fits, dear.' If the shoe fits! Can you believe it?"

April's voice rises in shrilly outrage. She slaps the water and it ripples throughout the pool, as if trying to get away from her fury. I can understand the sentiment. Right now, I wouldn't want to be in the way of April's fury, either.

"That nasty... Ugh!" April slumps back into me, deflated. "Faking my pregnancy. What a joke."

I can't help but agree. I'm doubly glad I asked Grisha for that additional background check: a woman like this isn't safe to have around my child.

Or my child's mother.

Anyone who's known April for more than five minutes could tell her problem isn't lying: it's honesty. Wearing her heart on her sleeve at all times, no matter who's on the other side of it. Getting it broken so often she's taught herself how to mend it back together. How to fix the unfixable.

Eleanor Hill is lucky that I don't know where she lives.

Yet.

"Sorry," April murmurs into the surface, making bubbles as she speaks. "I've been venting ever since you came home."

"To be fair, you've been doing other things to me, too."

"Hey!" April's face flushes a delicious shade of red. I could eat her up like this: naked, warm, skin peppered with droplets. If I had my way, I'd kiss them off until the pool was dry. "Cheater."

"Never." It's an automatic response, one I don't think about. In the seconds that follow, though, I pause. I shouldn't be making these kinds of promises. April hasn't lied to me so far. I don't want to be the one who starts.

But she doesn't seem to have caught my slip. She's still looking ahead, gaze lost far away, no doubt replaying the conversation with her mother in her mind.

I grip the edge of the pool, white-knuckled. It's going to take a lot of restraint not to storm right over to Staten Island and demand a pound of Eleanor's flesh in return for this. "Hey."

April snaps out of her reverie. "Yeah?"

"Look." I point at the other edge of the pool, where the water falls freely off. It's an illusion, of course—it cost me an arm and a leg just to get the permits for this—but that's what my hotels are for: illusions. A dream of infinity.

Here, one night should feel like forever.

I watch as April's gaze softens. Her pupils are wide now, reflecting the dancing lights of the pool. This terrace is the crown jewel of the Manhattan Jupiter Hotel. No other location has it.

"It's beautiful," April breathes.

I agree.

Only, my gaze isn't on the water.

"You could give birth here," I mention.

April looks at me like I've grown two heads. "No way."

"Yes, way."

"I couldn't," she gasps, scandalized. "It's the hotel pool!"

"It's *my* hotel's pool. I decide who gets to use it and how."

April peers up at me, trying to gauge if I'm being serious. Little does she know, I'm always serious. Twenty minutes ago, I had Grisha empty out the place with the excuse of emergency maintenance. Every single guest will be given a generous discount in apology for the inconvenience.

But April doesn't need to know that. "Births are messy, Matvey!" she shudders. "You could clean it a thousand times afterwards, and still no one would ever want to use it again."

"Then we'll just have to use it ourselves," I reply, drawing close.

I tilt up April's chin. Big, hazel eyes look up into mine, shining with a million specks of light. Her lips part, but for a while, no sound comes out. "We can't," April murmurs in the end.

"My pool," I repeat. "My child's mother." I lean in, brushing past her lips at the last second to speak into her ear. "I'll do exactly as I please with both."

A shiver. April's body reacts without a single touch. It's intoxicating—a kind of power unlike any other. Even being *pakhan* doesn't compare. "Is that so?"

"It is. Allow me to prove it."

The next few minutes are a blur of kisses. I rarely kiss my conquests—just enough to be a gentleman—but with April, I could spend the night doing just this: tasting, prying her lips apart, eating her whole, swallowing down moan after moan after moan.

I don't linger on what that means. That's the only thing I can't afford to do.

Instead, I flip us around. April's back hits the pool wall and her thighs wrap around me, ankles locked to trap me. It's a pointless effort—I'm not going anywhere.

My hands roam over her body until they find her belly. It feels even more swollen than yesterday. *Our child's growing here*, I remind myself, getting bigger every day. Getting ready for the cutthroat world that made their father sharp and their mother kind.

Will you be like me?

Like her?

Will you be like both, somehow?

"Matvey," April gasps. "Please."

She's still slick from before, open and wanting, and I waste no time: in one smooth push, I'm inside her again.

"Yes," April breathes, lost in the pleasure. "Yes, like that."

"*Blyat',*" I bite out. "Wish I could show you off like this."

"Yeah?"

"Yeah," I growl, beginning to thrust. "Take you just like this, in front of everyone. My *vory*, my guests, your parents."

"Nghh—!"

"I'd dare them," I snarl, plunging into those tight walls, "to question you again. To question *this.*" I splay a palm over her belly. "Who would still doubt, if they could see you like this?"

"Ahh—"

"Naked, wanting," I rasp, feeling myself grow closer from the image alone. "Filled with my seed and still begging for more."

"Matvey—"

"I'd show everyone," I roar, even as the thought of sharing April in any way brings me to madness, "just how we made this." Both my hands are on her belly now, forcing April to squirm on my cock to get the friction she needs. "And then, if they still weren't convinced…"

"Then what…?"

I smirk. "Then I'd just have to put another one in you."

April screams.

She's so close I can feel it, her pussy fluttering around me like a swarm of butterflies; but I don't want her to come yet. Instead, I drive into her in slow, deep pushes, refusing to give her the frantic rhythm she craves, driving her wild with too much pleasure.

"Matvey, please…!"

"I'm not done putting babies in you, *kalina.* Who said I'd stop at two?"

"Ahh—!"

"I'd pump in another," I groan, punctuating my words with thrusts. "And another, and another—"

"Matvey…"

"Until you're full to bursting. Until no one can doubt exactly who you belong to."

April gives a hard shudder. She tries to slip a hand between our bodies to touch herself, bring herself relief, but I don't let her. Instead, I catch it and pin it to the pool wall.

"We'd—make a mess…" April moans, squirming like crazy.

"Yeah?" I taunt, grinding the head of my cock into her sweet spot once, twice. "Then you'd better keep it all inside."

That does it. April's whole body jolts, hard, and she comes with a choked shout as I pump into her, fulfilling my promise.

33

APRIL

The last time I woke up in a good mood, it didn't last.

Still, I can't bring myself to sour it on my own this morning. Call me a sucker, but I believe in second chances. And right now, I'm giving my luxury tea break a second chance.

"Yesterday, we had vanilla," I say out loud. "Whatcha feeling like today?"

Nugget doesn't reply with words, but it gives a little kick instead.

"What was that?" I call, leaning in with my hand around my ear. "Extra dark chocolate chip from Ecuador?"

Another, gentler kick.

"Alright then!" I clap my hands together. "It's forever on *my* hips after all, not yours. Better enjoy it while it lasts, yeah?"

On second thought, I grab some Greek yogurt from the fridge, too. *Just to have something healthy with it,* I tell myself.

Then, on third thought, I grab the Nutella jar.

"Brunch," I murmur to myself. "Let's call this brunch."

But Mom, I picture the tiny creature in my belly objecting, *we've already had breakfast.*

"I won't tell if you don't," I whisper, holding up a pinky to my belly.

God. This is getting pathetic, isn't it? I'm so lonely I've started talking to the walls. Worse, to an imaginary projection of my future child.

It's clearly out of character, too. Nugget wouldn't chide me for having breakfast twice; instead, it'd kick me around noon for the third. I swear, it's like I'm growing a hobbit up in here.

"Sir, you can't go—"

I'm distracted from my daydreaming by a deep voice by the door. I don't recognize it, but it takes me a couple of seconds to realize it must be one of the bodyguards that stay here when Grisha's busy elsewhere.

That poor man. When does he even sleep?

"She knows me! Please, just let me—"

Another voice—and *this...*

This, I recognize.

I walk to the door as if in a trance. Because there's no way, right?

"Sir, step away from the door."

"I'm telling you, she's my—"

"Charlie."

Big eyes blink up at me. Hazel eyes, just like mine.

"… sister," he finishes.

And then those eyes zero in on my belly.

It takes longer than I'd like to bring the boys to heel.

"Miss," Gorilla #1 insists, "you can't have unannounced visitors."

"Not without permission," Gorilla #2 doubles down.

I cross my arms. "'Permission,'" I echo.

"That's right, Miss."

"No one goes in or out without the boss knowing, Miss."

By my side, Charlie blinks at me like I've gone insane. But before he can say anything, I give him a look. The *let-your-big-sister-handle-this* look.

Then I turn to my guardian angels in Gucci. "Permission from the boss. That's what we need, right?"

"Thank you for understanding, Miss—"

"Luckily, I've got his heir right here." I make a show of leaning down, hand cupped around the shell of my ear. "What was that, young master Nugget?" I ask my belly in front of three pairs of dumbfounded eyes. "Uncle Charlie can come in, you say? That's great. Thank you so much." I look up with a big smile. "Looks like there's no problems on our end."

The bodyguards exchange a look. "Miss, the boss—"

"The boss said it's fine," I interrupt. "If you've got an issue, you can take it up with management."

"M-Management?"

I point to my belly with both thumbs. "Right here."

A few nervous glances fly between the gorillas. I can practically hear the conversation: *I'm not crouching down there. The boss will kill me. You do it. You speak to the fetus.*

"No one?" I ask innocently. "Then we'll be on our way."

"Miss—!"

Then I usher Charlie inside and shut the door. "Phew," I exhale once we're out of earshot. "Sorry about that. They can be a bit…" *Sexist.* "Overprotective."

But Charlie isn't looking at the door anymore. Going by his face, he's not thinking about the bodyguards at all.

Instead, he's staring at my belly.

"Charlie…?"

"So it's true," my brother breathes. "You're really…"

He stretches out a hand, but quickly pulls it back again, as if afraid I'll bite. I can read Tom's influence all over the gesture: *Don't touch the chips, kid. If they get mixed up, you'll pay.*

"Here," I say, reaching out to take his hand. "You can touch if you want."

Then I place it gently on my belly.

Charlie's face lights up. He looks mesmerized, like that time I snuck him out to the aquarium on his tenth birthday. I remember watching him stroke the manta rays' fins in the open tank, reverent and awed. Now, he's wearing the same expression.

Then Nugget gives a kick, and he startles.

"Don't worry," I reassure him. "Nugget's a bit rowdy today. Hasn't had second breakfast yet."

For the first time since he came here, Charlie gives a small smile. "Just like a hobbit."

"Probably takes after you," I tease.

It's so strange, seeing him here. My brother. *Half*-brother, his parents would both chide, but I never cared to tell the difference. We were born from the same womb: what would we be, if not family?

Internally, I roll my eyes. All of Matvey's blood talk must be getting to me after all.

Charlie. He's grown so big since I last saw him: fifteen now, and way taller than me. Not that it's hard, but still.

With my sisters on my father's side, I don't have any relationship to speak of. Nothing that I like to remember, at least. But with Charlie, it's different. It was always different. Even if Eleanor followed the same exact playbook as her ex-husband, trying to pit her new kid against her old one—the purebred heir versus the unfortunate mutt born from a youthful indiscretion—Charlie never bit. He was always too kind, too sweet. A gentle soul, one even Eleanor couldn't ruin.

Neither could Tom, though he tried.

"I overheard the call," Charlie speaks up eventually, still transfixed by the child growing inside me. *His niece or nephew*, he must be realizing. "I asked Mom about it. She kept saying you made it up, that there was no way..." His lips press into a tight, angry line. "I got mad. We had this huge fight."

"I'm sorry." I mean it—I feel horrible. This is exactly why I left: aside from not wanting to be there, I also couldn't afford to be. With Charlie always jumping up to defend me against Eleanor's words—and against Tom's hands—it wasn't safe for me to stay. It wasn't safe for *him.* "I never meant to make trouble for you guys."

Charlie quickly shakes his head. "You didn't," he promises. "Mom shouldn't have said those things. She shouldn't—" A pause. "She shouldn't treat you like that," he mutters at last.

I smile. *My little knight in shining armor.* "Well, as you can see, I'm perfectly fine. And pregnant. Unless this is a very good prop."

"It'd be a very lively prop," Charlie snorts, feeling Nugget squirm against his palm.

"Swiped it from the *Alien* set." We both laugh before that semi-awkward silence creeps back in. "How did you know where to find me?"

"I went to the shop," Charlie confesses. "You weren't there, but Elias was. So I asked, and..."

"Of course. Makes sense. You're too smart for your own good sometimes, kiddo."

When he took me under his wing, Elias didn't mind the little rooster that came along for the ride. Whenever things got bad at home, Charlie would take a ridiculous combination of ferries and buses and trains just to hang around the shop for the day. Afterwards, we'd get ice cream and he'd crash on my couch. June always liked having him over—said he was the perfect test subject for her skincare masks.

"I hope it's not a problem," Charlie blurts out, taking my silence the wrong way. "I didn't mean—"

"No!" I answer immediately. "Not at all. It's…" I pause, looking for the right words. "It's nice to see you again," I tell him, from the bottom of my heart. "And to see a familiar face in general. Don't tell anyone, but I've been going crazy."

"I bet," Charlie laughs, looking around for the first time. "Nice digs, by the way. How'd you end up here?" He glances towards the door again. "With hired guns?"

Just then, my stomach growls. "How about I catch you up over tea?" I suggest. "Otherwise, your nibling just might eat me."

He gives me a warm smile. "Tea it is."

I feel the same smile pulling at my lips. "Okay. Right this way, sir."

34

MATVEY

I haven't even been at the office for five seconds before two folders are slammed onto my desk.

Well, not *slammed* exactly. Grisha's face is as serene as ever, but the stack is just that heavy. Even Yuri does a double-take at the sight.

"Ballistics report," he announces, pointing at the thinner file, "plus a full background check on April's family."

Instinctively, I reach for the first report. I can tell that's what Yuri wants to read, too, his hungry gaze zeroing in on it. Those were his men that got killed. If anyone's going to want justice, it's him.

But Grisha's words stop me. "Family?" I repeat.

"That's right," Grisha confirms. "I took the liberty of researching her father's side as well. Everything's in there from her birth to the day she turned eighteen."

I stare at the second folder. I only asked for details on April's mother, but my subordinate has always been thorough to a fault. Now, April's entire past is at my fingertips.

Veering at the last moment, I snatch the background check instead.

"Christ," I mutter, weighing it in my hands. "What's this, the goddamn Bible?"

Grisha shrugs. "What's the Bible if not a family saga?"

Shaking my head, I open it. The first page is mostly housekeeping: April's date of birth, nationality, blood type. Nothing of particular interest.

Yuri walks around the table, perching behind me to look over my shoulder. "That's a lot of paper," he comments.

"Ever seen a file so thick when we vet our recruits?"

"Negative."

"Yeah. Me neither." I turn to the summary page. A mother, Eleanor Hill, born Fisher. A father, Dominic Flowers. So far, nothing out of the ordinary. They were married seven years before splitting in a drawn-out court battle for alimony.

Money for the ex-wife—that's what mattered to these *mudaks*. Not the kid.

Then, between April's seventh and eighth birthdays, both parents settled down with new people: Eleanor Fisher became Mrs. Hill, marrying one Thomas Hill, and Dominic Flowers took a second wife by the name of Nora Le Blanc.

Grisha whistles. "Not one, but *two* evil step-parents."

"When did you get over here?" Yuri balks, suddenly walled in between me and his nosy colleague. "And why 'evil'?"

"Have you ever been in the company of Ms. Flowers?" Grisha asks rhetorically. "She had me over for tea once. Broke a teacup. For a whole minute, she looked like she was scared I was gonna gun her down for it."

Yuri's face darkens. "Yeah. I smeared the wall while putting the toys away and she spent fifteen minutes scrubbing it clean again."

"Quiet," I bark.

I rub my temples. I couldn't give a rat's ass about some cup and some smeared wall. All I can think of is April's anxious grimace at dinner, those early nights when she didn't know who she was dealing with.

Tense. Ready to bolt.

I want to snatch up whoever did this to her and make them regret ever being born.

But this file doesn't have that. This file has names, information, and sterile words on a sheet. So that's what I'm gonna work with.

For now.

"This says her mother's been to rehab," I note with a frown.

Yuri leans in to look, while Grisha nods. "That's right. Several quick staycations at the expenses of one charitable organization or another."

"Quick" is an understatement. From these records, it looks like Mrs. Hill didn't even get to step three of the program. I can't imagine she ever made it to step nine: making amends.

If that phone call with April is anything to go by, she's not even aware she should.

"What's her poison?"

"Alcohol."

I grimace. April's pregnant, so of course I've never seen her touch even a drop of the stuff, but I can't help remembering that night out on the balcony. The skittish way she handed me my bourbon.

"What about Thomas Hill?"

Grisha helpfully points to the blue tag. "That's his section. Chronically unemployed. Saturday night poker every week, a few debts here and there."

"Average scumbag," I summarize.

"Pretty much," Grisha says. "But there's one thing worth noting, I think."

He turns the page, squishing Yuri against the wall in the process. Yuri makes an offended sound, but I don't pay it any mind. I'm far too busy grinding my teeth into dust.

"This is a police report."

"For domestic violence," Grisha fills in.

"Great," Yuri snarks. "A wife-beater. What a catch."

I scan the page. Luckily, I don't see April's name anywhere on this. Only Eleanor's and a certain Charlie's, plus a couple of pictures of nasty bruises.

Charlie—that must be the brother April mentioned.

I inhale through my nose. Just because something hasn't been reported, it doesn't mean it didn't happen. It doesn't mean April was *safe*.

I snap the section shut. "What about April's biological father?"

Grisha turns to a purple-coded page. "Dominic Flowers, aged fifty-seven. Has three more daughters by his second wife, all teenagers: Anne, Catherine, and Diana Flowers-Le Blanc."

"This says they live in the Upper East Side," Yuri comments, elbowing Grisha away.

That's the first thing I noticed, too. By the looks of these records—bank statements, properties, shares—the Flowers family should be loaded. If April came from money, why would she share a ratty Brooklyn hole-in-the-wall with a friend who worked minimum wage? Why would she stick to a diet of pre-packaged mac and cheese?

Why would she *struggle*?

"Her address," I demand. "Show me her addresses across the years."

Grisha obliges. "Until the age of seven, she lived with her parents in Manhattan. Then—" He points at the next line over. "—here. For the next ten years or so."

A Brooklyn brownstone. "This is registered to Dominic Flowers."

"It is," Grisha confirms. "But Dominic wasn't living there. Instead, this person was."

I glance at the unfamiliar name: *Maia Toussaint.*

"This woman," I say. "Maia. Tell me about her."

Grisha's about to turn the page when Yuri finally manages to slither under his arm. "Maia Toussaint," he reads out loud. "Born in Haiti. Green Card by marriage to one

Augustus Flowers." He frowns. "That's not April's dad, is it?"

"It's not," Grisha answers. He settles his chin obnoxiously on Yuri's head in retribution and continues, "That's April's grandfather. He died shortly after she was born. Maia was his second wife—Dominic's mother had already passed."

"It looks like Maia lived with Dominic throughout most of his first marriage," Yuri says, scanning the page. "Then, when he split, she must've taken April in."

Maia Toussaint. April's grandmother by marriage, not by blood—and yet, from these files, she might have been the only one who truly cared about her.

"There's no record of a custody battle," I observe.

"Not exactly," Grisha clarifies. "The court transcript says there was a brief scuffle between Eleanor and Dominic over who was going to keep the child, but for the opposite reason."

Yuri frowns. "Meaning?"

"Meaning neither one wanted custody."

I clench my fist under the table. No wonder April's so jaded about blood. All her life, she's been betrayed by the ones she came from—and saved by the ones who had no obligation to help her.

"Oh," Yuri mutters. "This says Maia…"

"She died." Grisha nods. "Seven years ago."

Seven years ago. How old was April then? Sixteen? Seventeen?

That's when her address records become a mess, I realize. Staten Island to the Upper East Side, then Staten Island again

—switching schools, switching houses. Every few months, she'd be ping-ponged between her parents. "What the hell?"

"There's your custody battle," Yuri says grimly. "A shadow war of *'You take her; no, YOU take her.'*"

"After Maia's death, the brownstone was sold," Grisha fills in. "It was sudden. She didn't leave a will, or at least none that I could find. Dominic got everything."

"And kept the money," I guess.

"And kept the money. Every last cent."

I need Grisha to keep this file locked away from me. This thing has addresses, workplaces, license plates—everything I need to turn these motherfuckers' lives into hell. If I have to look at this for one more second, I won't be responsible for what comes out of my mouth next. Maybe it'll be a kill order —maybe it'll be worse.

So I snap the folder shut and breathe. "Grisha."

"Yes?"

"Keep this for me. Don't let anyone see it."

Grisha bows. "At your service."

A shitty family. Two shitty parents, two shitty step-parents. A sea of half-siblings who got everything April didn't. And one woman—only one—who took pity on her and raised her as her own: Maia. Her grandmother.

So of course April twitches at every loud noise. Of course she rushes to clean up after herself and others, trembling at the thought of consequences. Of course she was scared to tell me she was pregnant—who knows what I would've done? How could *she* know?

I want to go scorched earth on these fuckers. I want them to pay for every tear they've made her shed, every invisible scar they've given her.

But why do I want that?

April's my co-parent. Knowing about this is enough for my purposes: keeping my child safe. Everything in these pages has already happened. I can't turn back time for April to grow up safe, loved, wanted—and I shouldn't even care.

So why do I?

Suddenly, I feel like a kid again. I'm back in that shed-turned-house, buried in the snow, a weak fire flickering over ashes. My mother, coughing her life away; her child, powerless to do anything.

It's been a while since I've felt that: powerlessness.

I shake myself. I shouldn't be thinking like this. April's *nothing* to me.

The thought scrapes like nails on a chalkboard, but I swiftly bury the noise.

There's one last problem, too: April hasn't told me any of this. I can't possibly bring it up. She's already scared shitless of every shadow—what am I even going to say?

Good evening, co-parent. I went down the rabbit hole of your past and found out your parents are horrible and the one woman who ever loved you is dead. Wanna fuck your troubles away?

I rise from my chair. "Let's go."

Yuri frowns. "Go where?"

"Out," I say, impatient. "We have work to do. Don't make me say it again."

"But—"

"*Yura.*"

Yuri swallows his words. "Yes, *pakhan.*"

Then he's at my heels, Grisha in tow, and we're out of the office and into the city, thinking no more of April Flowers.

And then, several hours later, I see the bodyguards' calls.

35

MATVEY

I rush to the penthouse with my heart in my throat. I didn't think I had one, but there's nothing else this lump could be—this wild hammering in my veins.

A strange man came to the penthouse, my men told me. *He's with Ms. Flowers right now.*

I've been an idiot. I've been so focused on keeping April out of my mind that I forgot the thing that matters most: our child.

If something happened to them because of me…

He said he was family. That was my soldiers' excuse for letting him through: *He's family.* They know what that means to me.

They have no idea what it means to April, though.

I storm out of the elevator. The bodyguards try to intercept me, already spouting more excuses, but don't spare those bumbling buffoons a single glance. They're either fired or dead. It all depends on what I find behind that door.

My blood is roaring in my ears. I can smell ash under the gap, can hear the mad beeping from the smoke detectors.

My child. My woman.

I whip out my keycard. I almost never use it—I promised April this would be *her* place for the time being—but this counts as an emergency.

So I swipe it, yank the handle down, and swoop in.

"April!" I call at the top of my lungs, gun in hand. "Are you—"

And then Charlie Hill turns to stare at me.

"Matvey!" April jolts. "No guns at the dinner table. That was a rule."

I give myself a moment to breathe—to calm my racing heart. *In, out.*

Then I take in the sight before me.

April, wearing an apron from the kitchens. A pot, bubbling wildly on the stove. Dark smoke, rushing out of the open window.

And a fifteen-year-old boy with hazel eyes, hands raised in surrender, a pack of mac and cheese clutched tight between them.

"You…" I grimace. "You're *cooking*."

April crosses her arms. "You could be less shocked."

"You set off the smoke detectors."

"It's part of my process."

I glance towards the pot, now bubbling over. "To burn and flood my hotel?"

"Okay, fine, you got me!" April throws her hands up in surrender as well. "So maybe dinner got away from us." An awkward blush spreads over her cheeks. "Just a little bit."

"'Us' being...?"

In a flash, April turns off the stove and pushes the trembling boy in front of me. "Matvey," she begins, "this is Charlie, my brother. Charlie, this is Matvey, my..."

April fumbles for a word to describe us. "Matvey Groza," I cut in, holding out my hand.

Then I realize my gun's still in it.

I quickly put it away and try again. "Pleasure to meet you."

"Uhh, um..." Charlie mumbles, his handshake a bit unsteady. "P-pleasure's all mine. I'm Charlie—Charlie Hill."

"I know who you are," I tell him. "I make it my business to keep informed."

"Oh," Charlie says. "That's—good. Always... nice to know things."

My lip twitches with the urge to smile. This kid's got April all over: same eyes, same freckles, same foot-in-mouth syndrome. I can't help the fondness that comes over me. Minutes ago, I was ready to lay waste on the world. But now...

Consider me charmed. Must be a family superpower.

"I assume there's a reason you were trying to destroy my kitchen." When the siblings keep throwing guilty glances between each other, neither one quite sure how to navigate my whiplash wrath, I beckon April with my finger. "A word."

Charlie trudges off to the balcony. April approaches me with small steps, as if waiting for the guillotine to come down. "I'm sorry," she murmurs. "I broke a rule."

"So you're aware."

She fidgets with the hem of her maternity shirt. I don't think for a second that she's forgotten about our conversation at the beginning of all this. I was clear back then: no visitors. "It just happened so fast. I swear, I didn't tell him to come."

And yet he knew where to find you. Part of me wants to throw those words at her like daggers, sharp and precise. To hit her where it hurts, call her out on her lie. I don't appreciate being toyed with.

Instead, I hear myself demand, "Why is he here?"

April bites her lip. "It's… complicated."

"Make it simple for me."

"Look," she sighs, "I'm really sorry. I'll accept whatever punishment you think is fair. But right now…" She gives me a pleading look. "He needs me."

Whatever punishment you think is fair. For a moment, I wonder if this little vixen's trying to play me. To appeal to the most primal part of me to get off scot-free. I'm even tempted to let her—or at least pretend to. In the last thirty seconds, I've already come up with half a dozen *"punishments"* I'm itching to try on her.

And then I realize she's being serious.

Something dark stirs within me. Not for the first time today, I'm glad I gave Grisha the file to keep. If I had it on hand right now, nothing—*nothing*—would keep me from exacting a swift, painful revenge.

Because here April is, twenty-four and counting, still thinking she's going to be *punished.*

I don't even think. I turn and call the boy's name. "Charlie." Charlie rushes in from the balcony, straightening up like a little soldier. "Y-Yes?"

"Would you like to stay for dinner?"

Brother and sister both gawk at me.

"Matvey...?" April whispers, low enough that only I can hear. She's asking me with her eyes: *Are you sure this is okay?*

"I—I'd love to," Charlie splutters. "That is, if it isn't too much trouble..."

"Nonsense," I cut in. "Family's always welcome. Though..." The siblings follow my line of sight to the disaster on the stove. "I hope no one minds if we order in."

Two heads start shaking in sync. "Not at all," April blurts out.

"Definitely," Charlie agrees. "By all means."

Again, I bite back the urge to smile. "Pizza it is, then."

When Charlie pads away to rummage through my stack of takeout menus, April inches closer to me. "Thank you," she mouths.

I give her an impassive look. "Oh, you'll pay me back."

She blinks. "For the pizzas? Sure—"

I catch her chin in my fingers. When I speak next, it's directly into her ear. "You promised me a punishment," I stroke her bottom lip. "I intend to take you up on that offer, *kalina.*"

April shivers against me.

This time, it's the right kind of shiver.

Despite the convenience of pizza boxes, the mess at the stove must be addressed eventually. For obvious reasons—namely a tall, lanky redheaded teenager sitting on our couch—I can't claim my *punishment* just yet, no matter how much I'd like to.

That's how we end up at the sink—April washing, me drying. It's... unsettlingly domestic.

Feeling the tension between us, she clears her throat. "About Charlie..."

"You don't need to explain," I interrupt, surprising myself in the process. When have I ever said those words to anyone? "He's your brother."

April bites her lip. "He had a fight with our mom," she says quietly. "Because of me."

Out of the corner of my eye, I watch her. April's face is a slideshow of conflicted expressions—guilt, compassion, hesitation, each giving way to the next.

You broke a rule, I should be saying. *You brought a stranger into my home and you didn't tell me. I don't give a fuck* why *you did it.*

Instead, I say, "I'm glad."

April frowns at me. "What?"

"He took your side," I elaborate. "He stood up for you. That's nothing to be ashamed of."

"It is for me," she replies softly. "I never meant to be a burden. To him, or..."

I clutch the plate in my hands. A little tighter, and it will crack straight down the middle. "If people didn't want to be 'burdened,'" I growl, "they shouldn't have kids."

April blinks up at me. Her hazel eyes are shiny, two beacons of pure light. Not for the first time, I find myself wondering how she does it—clinging to hope like that.

After everything she's been through, she should want the world to burn.

"Hey, Matvey..."

"Yes," I say immediately. "The answer is yes."

April's head tilts. "You don't even know what I was going to ask."

"You were going to ask if he can stay the night." April's not the only one who's shocked—tonight, I keep shocking myself as well. *Where'd this version of me come from?* "The answer's yes," I repeat. "He can stay as long as he needs."

She blinks slowly as she processes. "You're... sure?" she asks uncertainly. "You don't mind?"

"Not at all," I say—and I mean it. "He's a good kid. Very polite."

I don't doubt for a second that that's April's doing—everything good about Charlie seems to be. Seeing them stand side by side, you'd never guess they were siblings except for their eyes. Charlie's tall, lanky, a head full of carrot-red hair. That spray of freckles on their cheeks could be chalked up to coincidence.

It's when you hear them talk that the resemblance becomes uncanny.

So what? the *pakhan* in me growls. *Who cares that they're alike? Who cares if he reminds you of April?*

Why should anyone get special treatment because of that?

I feel torn in half. Like I'm stuck in the middle of a fight between two sides of me, one of which I didn't even know existed.

But right now, I don't want to deal with it.

So I turn back to our conversation. "Certainly more polite than his sister," I add in a teasing tone. "I bet he's never cursed out a customer before."

"Hey!" April elbows me with a smile. "Neither have I."

"But you've thought it."

"No body, no crime." Then, finally, April's posture softens. "Thank you."

The sheer gratitude on her face unnerves me. I don't know what to do with it. In my line of work, you don't get to hear those two words often. Even less so when you're me.

Luckily, I'm saved by the man of the hour. "Hey," Charlie calls to us both, "if you guys aren't too tired, would you maybe... wanna watch a movie?"

He gets those last four words out all in one breath— *wannawatchamovie?*—like a schoolboy confessing to his crush. Honestly, it's kind of adorable. Reminds me of Yuri at his age.

"If the boss is up for it," I joke dryly with a glance toward April's belly.

April rolls her eyes. "You're never gonna let this one go, are you?"

"You scarred two of my toughest men."

"Then maybe they're not so tough."

And maybe, I think to myself, *neither am I.*

That's how we end up on the couch, all three—*four*—of us. It's… strange. A quiet night in, but with company. Only it doesn't feel forced—the atmosphere is as relaxed as it could be. Like we're just an ordinary couple, having April's brother over for pizza and a movie.

I glance over at April, curled up next to me, snuggled in a blanket. She's laughing so freely. I've never seen her this lighthearted.

Next time, we'll have to do things properly. Invite Yuri along. We could cook. April can't be trusted with a stove, but I still remember the recipe of my mother's goulash. It'd be fun. It'd be worth it.

And then, once the baby's born…

We could celebrate together, I find myself thinking idly. *Right here, just like this.*

I don't feel my eyelids growing heavy until it's too late. Lulled by the movie, and the darkness, and the warm weight of April leaning against my arm, I do something I haven't done in a long time.

I let down my guard.

I sleep.

36

MATVEY

A crackling fireplace. The scent of sweet smoke. Snow, just outside, rattling the windows.

It doesn't matter, the snow. Even if the wind sneaks in from the cracks, chilling and biting, there is warmth. Warmth like fire. Warmth like a hug.

A mother. A child. Another endless night.

"Go to sleep," the mother laughs softly. "If Daddy comes home, I'll wake you."

I don't give a crap about Dad, *the child wants to say.* He can sleep in the snow for all I care.

But his eyelids are heavy, and his mother's voice is warm, and her embrace is warmer, warmer, warmer still.

So the child cuddles closer, burrows into his mother's arms, and sleeps.

∾

I blink awake slowly. It takes me a moment to put my surroundings into focus: the couch, the television, the freshly cleaned kitchen. Morning light streams from the curtains, illuminating an empty living room.

Empty but for two people.

Or maybe I should say three. Inside April's curled-up form, our child sleeps, tucked close against my chest.

When did we fall asleep? I wonder, sluggish. *Why did we fall asleep like this?*

And, lastly, *What was I dreaming about again?*

As my senses slowly come back to me, I realize there's one person missing from this equation: Charlie.

"Guest room," April mumbles sleepily from under the blanket. "Didn't wanna wake you."

I look down at her mess of curls, made messier by the position she slept in. I'd never seen April with bedhead. It suits her. Goofy, but endearing. Like pretty much the rest of her. "And what's your excuse?" I ask lightly.

April just burrows deeper into me. "Comfy," she mutters, not bothering to uncurl from the embrace.

It sparks unfamiliar warmth at the center of my chest, which I do my damnedest to fight off. It's been a while since this has happened—waking up with another person by my side.

How strange.

I should be aching in a million different places. I should be crawling out of my skin, itching to get away. Instead, all I want to do is follow April's example and go back to sleep.

Stay. The first time April suggested that, sex-addled and dazed, I bolted. It was instinct; it was self-preservation.

But now...

Get it together, I snarl at myself. *This isn't like back then.*

This isn't your family.

Except that it is. At least in part—the part April's cradling inside herself. My blood. My child.

Perhaps that's what's driving me crazy here, making me see things that aren't there. Because, even though it's been years since I've had this, I can't help but remember what it felt like.

Family.

Not like the family I've grown used to—a family on the run. Just me and Yuri against the cold, hard world. This feels different; a woman and a child, a blanket and a fireplace. The kind of family that comes without a fight.

The kind that makes you want to...

"What are you thinking about?" April murmurs into my side, lifting her messy head towards me.

You, part of me wants to tell her. *Us.*

Staying.

For so long, I've been telling myself I can't have that: an *us.* Not with anyone. If family's the only thing that can be trusted, who's left to make one with?

I'm not going to leave myself open to betrayal. I'm not going to let anyone close enough to try. Not after my own blood turned its back on me.

And yet, when April looks up at me with those warm, hazel eyes, the color of forest floors and riverbeds...

When she looks at me like that, I almost want to risk it all again.

It's a foolish thought. It's the haze of sleep, I tell myself, making me cling to stupid dreams. Childish dreams. Dreams I haven't entertained in forever.

But why not dream a little longer?

Without thinking, I draw close. April draws closer still. Our breaths are brushing against each other, lips nearly touching. This isn't going to be like all our other kisses, I realize. This isn't going to be hungry, desperate, passionate. This isn't going to be *physical.*

It's a terrifying thought.

And then, just as I'm tilting up her chin, just as her lips are parting to meet mine—

For the second time in as many days, all hell breaks loose outside my door.

"I told you to let me through, you oversized excuse for a chimpanzee!"

April's pupils shrink. From the guestroom, a lanky figure emerges, just as sleep-mussed as his sister. The siblings lock eyes.

"Mom's here," they whisper in unison.

It's a day of firsts. Before I've had a chance to assess the situation, April jumps up, ready to assume her battle position. "Charlie," she calls firmly. "Hide."

But Charlie shakes his head. "It's me she wants," he rasps, like some tragic hero from a comic book, ready to face his demons.

I decide I've had enough of the dramatics.

No demons are getting through my door today.

I stand, grab my jacket, fix my tie. Then, once I've made myself presentable again, I cross the distance between the couch and the door with swift steps.

But, just as I'm about to throw the door open, April rushes over, stilling my hand.

"No!" she pleads. "Let me handle this."

I don't want to let her handle this. I don't want to let her handle anything. Worse, part of me wants to bundle her up and turn back time a few precious minutes, bring her back to that couch, pick up exactly where we left off.

But I'm way too familiar with that look. It's the look my men get in their eyes when they cross paths with an old foe, finding a score to settle.

Right now, April needs to be the one to settle this score.

So I give her a nod, step away, and let her handle this.

The second April pulls the door open, a woman-shaped hurricane storms into the penthouse. "You!" Eleanor Hill barks, jabbing a trembling finger at her daughter.

And there's truly no mistaking it. Her eyes, her freckles, her height: everything about her screams *April's mother*. If not for the disdain on her face, they could almost pass for half-siblings themselves.

Almost.

"Hi, Mom."

April's voice is calm, clear. But Eleanor isn't so easily pacified —wagging her finger like a weapon, she starts yelling at everybody in the room, starting with her wayward daughter. "How dare you steal my son?"

April's taken aback. She gives Eleanor her trademark customer service blink, the one that seems to say, *I beg your fucking pardon?* but doesn't actually spell it out. What was her phrase of choice? *"No body, no crime"?*

"Mrs. Hill," I greet impassively.

Eleanor gives me a cursory scowl. "And who the fuck are you?"

"Mom!" Charlie scolds. He sounds every bit the embarrassed teenager whose mother is making a scene in front of everyone—which, considering the situation, really isn't far off the mark. Even the bodyguards are leaning in close to eavesdrop, those lazy fuckers.

"Oh, don't you 'Mom' me!" Eleanor snaps, whirling around to face her son. "You think this is funny, don't you? Disappearing on me, yelling all those mean things—"

"I wasn't yelling; you were—"

"Quiet!" she hisses. "You are in a sea of trouble, young man. Go pack up your things right this second. We're going home."

"Mom," April interrupts, her tone still placating, "let him explain."

"Don't think I'm done with *you*," Eleanor snarls, not even looking at her daughter. "You're lucky I could track Charlie's phone. Otherwise, you know who would've shown up at your snazzy door? That's right: the fucking *cops!*"

"You tracked my phone?!" Charlie shouts.

"Pack. Your. Bags," Eleanor cries back. "Now. Or else, I'll make your dad come get you."

That gets a reaction out of both siblings. I watch them freeze and, not for the first time, I'm hit with the urge to reach for my gun.

Let him come, I want to snarl. *Let's see how he likes the taste of lead.*

But it's not my fight.

"Mom," April pleads, "can we please just talk about this?"

Fucking hell, it's taking every ounce of my willpower not to step in. Especially when Eleanor whirls around again like a harpy, staring daggers at April right in front of me. "Oh, so now you wanna 'talk,' huh?"

"That's *all* I've ever wanted!"

I notice Charlie's still standing in the middle of the room, conflicted. On one hand, he clearly doesn't want to upset his mother even more—or worse, risk his dad's wrath. On the other...

On the other, his sister's still in the line of fire.

Last night's conversation comes back to mind. It plays back in my head like a recording, word for goddamn word.

"He took your side. He stood up for you. That's nothing to be ashamed of."

"It is for me."

Taking advantage of the chaos, I inch closer to Charlie. "Go," I mutter to him. "I've got this."

Only then does he finally shake himself. With a quick "Thanks," he disappears into the guest room.

I turn my attention back to the conversation between April and her mother. Though it isn't much of a conversation to begin with: it's a one-sided assault, with Eleanor tearing into her with sharp, vicious words.

At my sides, my fists clench tighter.

"'That's all you've ever wanted?'" Eleanor mocks, throwing April's honesty right back into her face. "Hah! Could've fooled me. And here I thought you were just trying to snatch yourself an *actual* kid." Her glare turns to April's belly. "What's that, by the way? A prop?"

Without ceremony, she lifts April's shirt.

I nearly whip out my gun.

Don't you dare touch my child.

Don't you dare touch their mother.

But Eleanor doesn't go any further. All she does is gawk at the very real belly before her and sneer, "Well, well, look at that! Seems like someone was brave enough after all."

"Mom…" April's voice wavers, mortified.

"I guess everybody gets lonely sometimes," Eleanor dismisses, letting the shirt drop. "Even desperate."

"Mom, please. I'm—"

"Is this why you tried to kidnap *my* child?" Eleanor continues, oblivious to the murderous rage mounting inside me. If this woman wasn't my child's biological grandmother, she would already be six feet under. In several pieces. "Because you know you can never do better?

Charlie's always been a good kid, after all. Nothing like you."

"Leave Charlie out of this!"

"You've always been jealous," Eleanor spits, full of scorn. "And now, you're trying to poison him against me. All so you can ruin him!"

"I never wanted…!" April tries to cut in, but her voice is too unsteady. It breaks before she can finish her sentence.

Smelling blood in the water, Eleanor jumps right on it. "Oh, *you, you, you*. It's always the same song with you. Don't you know you have to be selfless to raise kids?" A mocking laugh. "Some mother you're shaping up to be."

April's eyes dim.

It's the most sickening feeling, watching the light go out of her gaze. April, who always has a kind word for everyone. April, who always sees the bright side. April, who never takes shit lying down. Sun or fire, her eyes always hold a spark.

Until now.

React, I want to scream. *React! Didn't you ask me to let you handle this?*

But she doesn't.

She dims.

"It's my fault for never teaching you a lesson." Eleanor is lost in her delirium, spit flecking her painted lips as she sneers and jabs that spindly finger here and there in the air. "I always let Tom take up that burden. But you couldn't even be grateful for that."

"I'm s-sorry," April chokes.

"Not yet." Eleanor raises her hand. "But you will be."

April flinches back; Eleanor's hand draws an arc in the air; and just when the sharp *crack!* of a slap should echo—

"*Ow!*"

My fingers close around her wrist, freezing it midair.

Eleanor recovers quickly. Her fury zeroes in on me. "How *dare—*"

"You asked me who I am." The witch tries to talk, but her words fizzle out when I squeeze her wrist harder. I don't intend to give her a chance to open her damn mouth again. "No—you asked me 'who the fuck' I am, to be exact."

I tighten my grip more. Not quite enough to cause damage, but enough to make her stop trying to yank her wrist away.

Enough to make her *listen.*

"My name is Matvey Groza," I continue icily. "I'm the owner of this hotel. I'm the father of your daughter's child. And, unless your hand goes right back into your pocket, I'm gonna be the man who ripped it clean off your body for daring to touch someone like that in my presence."

I whisper that last part, careful not to let Charlie catch it.

But I make sure Eleanor hears every word.

"You're threatening me?" she squeaks. Her earlier bravado has already started to leak out of her voice. Through my fingers, I can feel the clear tremor of her wrist.

It reminds me of an old Chinese saying: *The mantis stalks the cicada, unaware of the oriole behind it.*

Meet the fucking oriole, bitch.

"Mrs. Hill," I say with a hint of amusement, "the only reason you're getting a choice at all is because your children are here. And because, unlike your deadbeat husband, I don't enjoy hitting women and kids."

I catch a flash of surprise across April's face. Eleanor's off-handed mention of Tom shouldn't have meant anything to me—so how do I know? I can practically read the question written across her face.

But April's too smart not to put two and two together. In a second, her expression changes again, this time to something more complicated. Something I don't have the time to decipher.

"In the interest of unsolicited advice—" I turn back to Eleanor. "—you should think twice before hitching yourself to a known felon. But then again, you probably weren't thinking much, what with all the drinking."

Eleanor bristles. "Keep your filthy implications—"

"As long as you keep your filthy hands to yourself," I cut in "and your filthy, alcoholic breath out of my face."

Then, abruptly, I let her wrist go.

Eleanor stumbles off-balance. She tries to catch herself on April's shoulder, but April flinches away again, this time with purpose. It's only the open door behind her back that prevents Eleanor from falling face-first on the floor.

"Next time you want to criticize the mother of *my* child, you might want to consider looking into a mirror." I take an instinctive step closer to April. "Then you'll see what a failure of a parent really looks like."

In that moment, Charlie comes back with his overnight bag. He watches the scene with a confused expression, which confirms for me that he's caught nothing of the last few exchanges. *Good.* If Eleanor's grown any wiser in the last three minutes, she'll keep the details to herself.

If not, I doubt Charlie will mind.

"I don't have to stand here and take this." Eleanor quivers, face red with rage. "Do whatever the fuck you want. I'm out of this shithole."

And she storms right out.

"What happened?" Charlie rushes over.

"Just made a couple of things clear," I answer. "As for you…"

Charlie straightens up, as if expecting a blow of some kind. *Some mother*, I find myself thinking bitterly. *Her kids flinch and cringe whenever she's close enough to touch them.*

"Feel free to stay as long as you need," I finish.

April finally snaps back to reality. "Yes!" she agrees wholeheartedly. "If you don't want to go back—"

"No." Charlie shakes his head, smiling faintly. "I… Thank you. But I'd better go after her. You know how she gets."

April gives an understanding nod.

The look on their faces is one I recognize. I've seen it often enough on Yuri as a kid—chopping wood, making dinner. I've seen it even longer in my own mirror. It's the look of a child forced to grow up too soon.

Though, in our cases, our mothers didn't have the choice to spare us.

"Thank you for everything," Charlie says again, holding out a hand to me.

I give it a firm shake. "If you change your mind, call."

He nods. "I will."

Then it's April's turn. He looks at her with a hangdog frown. "Sorry for making a mess," Charlie adds sheepishly.

She crushes him into a hug. "Promise you'll visit."

"Okay," he swears. "Lemme know when the little one's popped, yeah?"

"Deal."

Then Charlie's out, too, chasing after his harpy of a mother, who's still screaming bloody murder in the hallway.

Just like that, we're alone again.

Shit. That's my first thought. Did I really just threaten April's mother? Right in front of her? After she asked me to *let her handle it*?

I search my mind for regret. I find none. If I had to do it all over again, I wouldn't change a goddamn thing.

That woman was going to strike her.

And no one touches what's mine.

But I can't imagine April's thrilled with me right now. "I should go, too." I clear my throat. "Work. People to see."

It's the flimsiest excuse I've ever used—it's not even 8:00 A.M.—but I figure I should give her space. To… process. Or whatever it is normal people do.

I'm almost out the door when—

"Wait."

Two fingers catch my sleeve, butterfly-light.

I turn. "Yes?"

April's eyes are shining again. It's not the sun-bright glow she usually has, but it's still a spark. It's still more than she had with Eleanor in the room.

"Thank you," she breathes, stunning me.

For once in my life, I don't know what to say.

Luckily, it seems that April does. "See you at dinner?" she asks, all hopeful.

I should tell her no. I should nip whatever the fuck this is in the bud—this *warmth* that has nothing to do with the fire of sex and passion. Instead, I tilt my head in acknowledgement. "See you at dinner."

Only then does April let me go.

When I climb into the car, I practically slam the door off its hinges.

Fuck.

This shit is getting out of control.

37

APRIL

I wasn't looking to find myself in this situation again so soon: legs spread, eyes fixed on the ceiling, someone moving about between my thighs.

Correction: someone who isn't Matvey.

"A little wider, please." Dr. Allan taps my knee.

With an inner sigh, I obey.

It really couldn't be helped, though. After my mom's class act this morning—a memory I wish I could scrub from my brain—Matvey made an executive decision: an emergency check-up for my baby.

This time, I didn't put up a fight.

Luckily, Dr. Allan was available and dropped everything to come. After hearing the gist of my mom's antics, she spent the first five minutes of the check-up muttering "Unbelievable" under her breath. She's been extra gentle with me, too.

It still feels a bit surreal, being treated like this. Like I've just been through something awful. That was a regular Tuesday night back home. Sure, I wasn't pregnant back then, but Dr. Allan hasn't only been asking pregnancy-related questions; she's been asking about *me*. How *I* feel.

Like I said: surreal.

And Matvey...

I still can't wrap my head around it. How he defended me. For over half the conversation, I was terrified Matvey would hold me responsible for making a scene, terrified he'd act on it. He's never raised a hand on me before—he never struck me as the guy who would—but there's a first time for everything.

In the beginning, Tom never hit me, either.

But Matvey stepped in without hesitation. Even after I begged him not to, after I failed, he still took my side.

No one has ever defended me like that before.

"Ew," Petra gags from the couch. "Keep your gushing to yourself."

I roll my eyes. "Emergency check-up" also meant an assigned Bratva babysitter. And since both of my bodyguards were taken away by Matvey for "urgent business," someone had to cover the shift.

Unfortunately, that someone turned out to be none other than my baby daddy's fiancée.

"I wasn't even talking to you," I grumble.

"Don't care." Petra shrugs, flipping her magazine. "No drooling over Matvey where I can hear. It's disgusting."

How about you make like a tree and leave then? "Bold words for his future wife."

"Ugh, don't remind me. You don't know how good you have it."

For some reason, her remark makes me bristle a little. But I quickly push it down—pissing off Illegally Blonde isn't on my bucket list. When it comes to Petra, I get the feeling the *find out* part never comes much later than the *fuck around* part.

"And I wasn't 'gushing', by the way."

"Right—and I'm not wanted in fifteen countries."

"Okay, first: *not* a flex." I list off on my fingers. "Second: I'm just…" God, why are words so hard? "… grateful."

"Grateful," Petra deadpans.

"Yeah. Grateful. Matvey didn't have to do that."

Petra bursts into laughter. "Yeah, right." Then she notices I'm not laughing. "Oh. You're serious." With a sigh, she shuts her magazine. "Of course he had to, *durak.* Matvey's an alpha."

"I literally have no idea what any of those words mean."

"God, you're so dumb." I'm tempted to steal Dr. Allan's ultrasound wand and chuck it at her head, but my mother taught me better than that. Namely, that you don't do these things in front of witnesses. "He's territorial. The little *komuk*'s part of his pack now. That means you are, too."

For a second, I wonder if I've really gone dumb. Hit my head or something. "Are we talking about the same Matvey here?"

"No, we're talking about his good twin. He has the exact same name and face, only he's not a complete asshole."

That sounds boring as hell.

I scold whatever part of me came up with that thought. *Bad, bad brain cell! Who told you to unsubscribe from feminism?*

"Ha-ha," I fake-laugh. "I still think you've got the wrong guy." Without my permission, my voice turns bitter. "Believe me, Matvey's been crystal clear about where we stand."

"That's because he's an idiot," Petra retorts. "Just because he hasn't noticed yet, it doesn't mean he isn't feeling it."

"B-but…" I stammer. "But I'm not blood."

Petra's eyes roll all the way back into her skull. "Please tell me you're not taking that fixation of his seriously. It's all a pile of horseshit."

I'm stunned. I never expected to hear anyone speak of Matvey's philosophy like this, let alone so openly. "I don't think he sees it that way."

"No shit, Sherlock. That would imply he's willing to question himself." With a graceful leap, Petra hops off the couch and glides towards me. She keeps on the other side of the ultrasound machine, face scrunched up in disgust at everything going on around me—including poor Dr. Allan, who's just trying to do her job and landed herself into a Bratva gossip session instead. "Listen up, *koshka*: if blood were really that important, everybody would be marrying their siblings, and the world would be filled with hemophilic Habsburgs."

"That's really gross."

"Glad we agree on something."

"I meant the fact that you're a history buff. Seriously wrong with your character."

With a fake smile, Petra flips me off.

"Alright!" Dr. Allan announces. "Everything looks good, but I'd like to review the images to be certain. Is there anywhere I can plug my laptop?"

I point her towards the studio and she hustles off gratefully.

Once she's gone, I put my clothes back on, feeling slightly more dignified. Being in Petra's presence makes you feel naked on your best days, let alone when you're actually naked.

I expect her to leap at the chance to clock out, but she doesn't. Instead, she prowls around the room like a lioness staking out uncharted territory.

And then, out of the blue, she says, "Your mom must be a real piece of work."

I blink. "Beg your pardon?"

It's not like she's wrong, but still. Would it kill her to use a little tact once in a while?

On second thought… it might.

Petra purses her perfect lips. "Matvey isn't known for going nuclear on women," she muses. "Believe me, I've pushed every button there is."

"Ew! I did not want to know what!"

"Pot, kettle, whatever."

I'm tempted to slam my palms over my ears and go *la-la-la* until my unwanted babysitter finally gets the memo. Unfortunately, that stops being an option the second you turn twelve. Being twice that age, I really can't indulge. So instead, I say, "Isn't that the case with most moms?"

Petra's silent for a while. "I wouldn't know," she admits eventually. "I never had one. She died in childbirth."

The words are an ice bucket on my head.

I must have gone pale, because the next words out of Petra's mouth are, "Oh, don't worry. Medical science has improved by leaps and bounds since then." She waves it off like it's nothing. "And if I'm the reason you're making that face, don't. I don't need anyone's pity."

I'm sorry for your loss. The words are already in my throat. But I force myself to swallow them back. Instead, I say something else. A question. "Your father… He never remarried?"

I don't know where it came from. Maybe I was just thinking about mine: how he was married again before his divorce's first anniversary.

Hopefully, Petra's father didn't find another Nora, but someone else. Someone who actually wanted to take care of her.

But all Petra does is shake her head. "He's much too hung up on honor," she explains. "To a traditional man like him, marriage is for life. Though that does mean he didn't get any male heirs," she adds with a bitter smile. "He's stuck with a princess instead. That's why he's looking to put his crown on Matvey's head. He's traditional that way, too."

Traditional. I never knew Petra to mince words, but for her father, she makes an exception. Otherwise, she'd be calling it like it is: sexism, pure and simple.

This is ridiculous. I *hate* Petra's guts. If nothing else, she certainly hates mine.

So why am I feeling bad for her?

Then she walks up to me. Her eyes find my belly, for once without the vitriol she usually reserves for it. "For your sake, April, I hope your little one is a boy," she murmurs. "In this world, boys get everything."

Her gaze is intense. I find myself squirming under it, huddling on myself as if fighting cold winds. This must be the cold she grew up with—the ice she learned to make into a weapon.

"I wouldn't know," I reply in the end. "I asked Dr. Allan not to tell me."

Petra's eyebrow rises. "A romantic. Color me surprised."

For some reason, that drags a laugh out of me. "Not exactly. I just... There's so many expectations, you know? Once you're born, everybody expects something from you. Especially your parents. So, even if it's just for a bit... I wanted this baby to be free."

I brace myself for Petra's sarcasm, but it doesn't come. "Maybe that's why it doesn't want out, then," she says softly. "Freedom's nice. Gotta enjoy it while it lasts."

I must be wrong. That can't be a smile, can it? A genuine one? On *Petra*?

"Anyway," she exhales, "it's not a problem I'm ever gonna have. Kids, expectations, any of it."

"You don't want kids?" I ask, forgetting that there's another possibility out there. That maybe, aside from not being able to *have* a mother—

She might not be able to *be* one, either.

But Petra just laughs. "I can't even make *vor* like this. How's a pregnant candidate gonna go over?"

Wow. I had no idea the Bratva was this similar to the job market. Maybe going into crime isn't easier after all. For girls, at least.

"What about after?" I try. "Let's say you're *vor*. You have Manhattan wrapped around your little finger. Would kids be on the table then?"

Petra seems to entertain the thought. She looks amused by the tale I've spun, world domination and all. "Me? A mother?" she laughs. "That's rich. Can you imagine?"

"Actually, I can."

Petra's face colors with surprise. Crap, did I say the wrong thing? Is this how my big mouth finally gets me killed?

But she doesn't whip out her gun, only her phone. Then she starts checking the time, tapping her foot, fidgeting with the case. Almost like she's embarrassed.

"*Blyat*,'" she mutters, glancing impatiently towards the studio Dr. Allan's disappeared into. "Did your damn doctor fall asleep or what?"

I bite the inside of my cheek.

So even an assassin can blush.

38

MATVEY

Baby's safe, April texts me later that afternoon.

I immediately let out a sigh of relief. On the inside, though, because Grisha and Yuri are here in the office with me and I'm in no mood for follow-up questions. But it's still a weight off my chest.

After a bit, another text bubble pops up. ***Still cozy, though.***

"Motya?"

My amusement must show on my face, because Yuri's staring at me like I've suddenly suffered a stroke.

"Yurochka's idea isn't half-bad," Grisha summarizes for my benefit. Lately, my third has been able to tell at a glance when I've missed an entire chunk out of a conversation. With how distracted I've been in the past few weeks, it's a miracle I've been able to make it through meetings at all. "Expanding in the Middle East would certainly build a reputation for the Jupiter Hotels' name."

I hum in approval. "It would be quite an investment."

Under the table, I type a reply: **Good.** I press send. Then, on a whim, I add, ***I trust Petra's been behaving.***

My screen lights up with April's answer moments later. It's a picture, blurry and clearly snatched against the subject's will. Petra's arm is outstretched towards the phone, her face scrunched up in annoyance, while April's grinning in the corner and making a peace sign.

Caption: ***Hasn't knifed me yet!***

"—making it a medium-term investment with guaranteed returns," Yuri wraps up.

Shit. I spaced out again. What a fucking hassle. "Mm."

"It would also give the *vory* an alternate project to focus on," Yuri adds. "To take their minds off of…"

He doesn't need to say it. The words *"The D.C. Acquisition"* are seared on everybody's mind.

"The *vory* will focus on what I tell them to," I half-snarl. "I don't intend to babysit them with side quests."

That said, when I finally glance at the report in my hands, I realize the numbers look good. More than good, in fact.

Besides, Yuri showed initiative. That's something to be encouraged, not punished. Every *pakhan* worth their salt knows this much.

"Make it three years."

"What?"

"Make our money back in three years," I repeat, rising from my chair, "and you can move forward with this."

Yuri looks over the moon. "Yes, *pakhan.*"

"Cut it out." I give a light slap to the back of his head. "I swear, it's like you think I'll hit you."

"You *did* hit me," Yuri points out. "Just now."

"Trust me: if I'd hit you, you'd know."

Pushing Yuri's strange behavior aside, I check my phone again. A new picture has popped up: Petra's bodyguards, raiding *my* pantry.

Also, we're out of food, the caption reads.

I'm itching to walk out the door. Christ, it's not even *five*. Am I really so keyed up that I can't wait a couple of hours to give April the punishment I promised her?

I'm this close to ordering Grisha to drive me back. Take an early leave and kick Petra's goddamn locusts out, kick *everybody* out, until it's just me and April. Until I can finish what I never got a chance to start this morning.

And then the door bursts open.

My hands fly to my gun. So do my men's. But it's only for an instant: the second I see who it is, I lower mine. But I don't tell them to lower theirs.

"Vlad," I greet coldly.

"You!" Vlad splutters, followed by two brainless gorillas that roughly resemble the ones I fired earlier. Seriously, does the vacant stare come with the job or do they give them a complimentary lobotomy? "Do not 'Vlad' me. You know why I'm here."

"I'll assume this is a social call." The threat in my tone is clear enough: *Do not test me.*

Unfortunately, Vlad's not much brighter than the company he keeps. "What are your intentions with my daughter?" he demands, spittle flying everywhere. Grisha looks tempted to hold out an umbrella for me. Really, I wouldn't say no.

"Marriage," I deadpan. "You've known this for a while, if I'm not mistaken."

"Marriage! You've got some nerve, young man."

"A necessary quality for any *pakhan* worth their salt, you'll agree."

Clearly losing the battle with his own nerves, Vlad pushes on. "You think we're all idiots, huh?" I don't answer that. It wouldn't be diplomatic. "You think I don't know what you're up to?"

"Enlighten me."

He slams a dried-up palm on my desk. "Where's the DNA test?!" he screeches, frantically looking around the office like he thinks he's going to find it pinned under a paperweight. "And don't even think of lying to me. I want a straight answer: Is that *curva*'s brat yours or not?!"

My gaze turns to ice. *Don't kill him*, I chant over and over in my head. *He's your future father-in-law.*

If I didn't need his daughter's godforsaken dowry, he'd have bigger concerns than even my hands around his throat.

But somehow, I manage to rein myself in. Unlike Vlad, I know how to play this game. And I'm not about to lose to a geriatric idiot's idle threats.

"*Ms. Flowers's* child," I correct icily with a firm step forward, "is none of your concern."

"None of my concern!" Vlad balks. "You've been *dishonoring* my daughter! And you won't even take responsibility—"

"The DNA test has already been run."

That seems to douse Vlad's flames, if only a bit. "Well, then?" he demands. "Is it yours or not?"

Without a word, I hand him a sheet of paper. One I've had on my person for quite a while. One that Grisha personally prepared.

I watch Vlad's beady eyes scan the document. When they get to the bottom of the page, I already know what they'll read:

INCONCLUSIVE.

In his grip, the paper crumples. "What is the meaning of this?!"

"It means we'll have to wait," I answer, clipped. "Until the baby's born."

"Until it's *born*?!" Vlad's eyes damn near bulge out of their sunken sockets. "This is a travesty!"

"This is biology," I correct. "I'm afraid even the Bratva's powerless against that."

At first, I wonder if Vlad's too far gone to listen to reason. My excuse is ironclad, but will it be enough?

An annoying part of me reminds me that Petra warned me about this. *My father isn't a patient man.*

Luckily, I'm even less patient.

So when Vlad starts spluttering again to the tune of, "This is a trick! This is—" I stomp my foot down.

Hard.

"This," I growl, taking yet another step forward, "is how it is. So either get with the program or get the fuck out my office. I can find another bride, but I can guarantee you'll never find another heir."

Vlad's face goes up in flames. "You...!"

"Me," I agree. "Me, who's going to save your dying Bratva. Me, who's going to double your numbers. Me, who's going to marry your precious daughter. *Me.* So if I were you, I'd start showing a little respect."

I don't bother disguising my threat. I want it to be crystal clear: if he pisses me off, I can find a million ways to make him pay for it. Including making his daughter pay for him.

Of course, I'd never fucking do that. I'm not the kind of scum that goes after women and kids, regardless of whether the woman in question can or cannot kill you with a toothpick.

But Vlad doesn't need to know that.

"That said, we've both invested a lot in this union." I relax and unclench my fists. "I'm certain neither one of us wants to go back to square one for such a pointless reason. Right?"

It's a question in name only. But Vlad's a businessman, too, and it doesn't take long for him to remember that. "Right," he agrees uneasily. "I admit... I may have let myself get carried away."

It's as much of an apology as I'm going to get. Not that I give a fuck about Vladimir Solovyov's regrets. "No matter. I'm glad we could clear this up."

Vlad looks like he's just swallowed a lemon. "Likewise."

"Well then," I say, grabbing my suitcase, "if there isn't anything else—"

"Actually, there is."

I stop halfway to the door. Yuri and Grisha exchange a long look. "Speak," I force out.

"We should bury the hatchet properly," Vlad says. "Man to man."

"We just did that."

"Did we?" Vlad remarks. "I don't see a drink."

I roll my eyes inwardly. Of course—Vlad's old school. To him, everything from a minor business deal to a shootout with a rival organization demands to be made official through alcohol.

"We haven't shared a bottle since you asked for my daughter's hand." Vlad taps his foot lightly. "It's long overdue. A man should drink with his future son."

I nearly punch him then. *I'm no one's son. My mother's dead and my father saw to it.*

But I force myself to calm down. This close to the finish line, I can't afford to slip up. Vlad's goodwill is a better outcome than I hoped for—I shouldn't let it go to waste.

But if you go, you won't make it to family dinner.

The thought makes me beyond furious. When has April become more important than my business? My dream?

"Fine," I accept at last. "But you're paying."

Vlad's face breaks into a sly grin. "I wouldn't have it any other way, *syn.*"

On my way down, I type a quick text to April. ***Can't make it tonight. Something came up.***

Hopefully, Petra can hold down the fort a little longer.

39

APRIL

I stare down at the text that just made my phone light up.

Can't make it tonight. Something came up.

Huh. That's weird. Ever since I came here, Matvey hasn't missed a single family dinner. It's that important to him. If he's missing it now, he must have a good reason.

I try to swallow down the tiny lump in my throat. Why am I disappointed? Dear God, why am I *sad*? When did I turn into a dog with separation anxiety?

Shaking off the sensation, I type a quick reply. **Hope everything's okay! No problem for dinner.** Then, feeling a little bold, I add: **You'll just have to make it up to me.**

I nearly tag on a heart emoji, then slap myself mentally. *Girl, what the hell? Play it cool for once in your life.*

"Why are you having a stroke?"

I jump. While I wasn't paying attention, Petra snuck up all the way behind me. *Jeez, wear a bell!*

Before I can gather my wits, she peers over my shoulder. Her face scrunches up. "'Something came up'?" she parrots.

"I'm sure it's nothing," I reassure her. I get the feeling it's as much for my benefit as it is for hers, but I quickly swat at that crumb of self-awareness.

She scoffs. "It's overtime, is what it is. That *mudak.*"

Not for the first time, I wonder if the Russian language's completely made up of swear words. "You guys don't have to stay," I offer. "If you're busy…"

"Of course I'm busy."

Busy raiding my pantry? I throw a glance at Lena and Julia. I still haven't managed to figure out which of Petra's bodyguards is which—nametags would be a wonderful addition to the uniform—but if there's another way they're completely alike aside from their appearances, it's their eating habits.

Which seem to include *everything.*

Hey, I'm not one to judge. All that muscle can't come for free. It's just that I was actually planning to eat, too.

Thank God for room service. And Matvey's bottomless wallet.

Next to me, Petra's still tapping her foot, but she also isn't leaving. Which I take as a sign that either she's not as busy as she claims, or that she can't. Matvey probably swore her to babysitting duty. All of a sudden, I'm feeling like a kid whose parents' date night is stretching out longer than they've paid for.

So I blurt out, "Wanna stay for dinner?"

Petra looks at me like I've gone mad. "Excuse me?"

"I mean—" I gesture towards the twins. "—they've already started. We could order room service?"

"Dinner," Petra repeats flatly. "With you."

Damn. This is going to be a harder sell than I thought. "Matvey's paying?" I try to sweeten the deal. "We can get lobster thermidor or whatever it is rich people eat?"

The twins perk up at that. "I could eat," says Lena.

"Be rude to say no," agrees Julia.

Which leaves only one holdout. "C'mon," I whip out my best puppy eyes. "We can have a girls' night. Paint each other's rifle guns and all."

I watch Petra falter. "You're seriously inviting me?" she asks, squinting suspiciously around the room like there are prank show cameras hidden in the crown molding.

"I seriously am."

"To dinner?"

"To dinner. On Matvey's card."

Her eyes narrow. "Which one?"

"I don't know." I shrug. "The black one? Aren't they all bottomless anyway?"

Petra's mouth opens and closes like a goldfish. I can taste victory already. What's that saying? *If you can't beat them, aggressively befriend them?*

And then, just as Petra's about to give me an answer—

BOOM!

I watch the door fly clean off its hinges.

The twins leap into action. Before I can even understand what's going on, they've made a human wall before us, shielding me and Petra. Their guns are already raised.

A figure stumbles into the apartment. In the next second, it's shot full of holes.

Then I scream.

It's not an intruder. It's a waiter—one I've seen often enough in the evenings. The one who always brings our cart.

But, judging by how little blood pools under his body...

He was already dead, I realize. "It's a decoy!" I yell.

Just then, more bullets fly in from the doorway. If the twins had taken just one more step towards the body, they'd have been shot full of holes, too.

Then an army of masked men swarms in.

Bullets start raining down in all directions. I grab blindly for something, anything, to use as a weapon. I've almost got my hands on a frying pan—if it's good enough for Rapunzel, it's good enough for me—when Petra suddenly grabs my wrist.

With near superhuman strength, she drags me behind the kitchen counter. "Stay down," she snarls.

Then she's off, too.

Okay. I force myself to breathe. *This is fine. Still not worse than Carolina Torres's quinceañera. You can handle this, right?*

I most definitely can't, but I'm not about to admit that.

I peer from behind the counter. The action's exploded everywhere: couches have been overturned, walls have been decorated with smoking polka dots, the air's been filled with eau de gunpowder. Just another Bratva Tuesday. Right?

I take stock of the bodies on the floor. One, two, three—five bodies. When I realize that none of them seem to belong to women, I breathe a sigh of relief.

But there are still five more men on their feet, shooting everything in sight.

I whip out my phone. It's the burner Matvey gave me—the one to reach him at all times.

Pick up, pick up, pick up...

Tears prickle at the corners of my eyes. I keep making a single, desperate wish: *If only Matvey was here.*

But he isn't, and the call rings out.

"It's okay," I whisper to my baby. "I'll keep you safe for both of us."

It's an empty promise. Right now, I have no power to keep anybody safe—least of all myself. Is this how it starts? Lying to your kids?

Suddenly, I hear steps close by. I clutch my pan tighter and peer out again—

And I find myself face-to-face with a masked man's gun.

This is it, I realize with an odd sort of calm. *I'm going to die.*

And then: *But fuck it, I'm not going to make it easy.*

I yell out a battle cry. I swing my pan wildly, kicking the man's gun God-knows-where. I can't see the intruder's face beyond the mask, but I can tell he wasn't expecting resistance. That a heavily pregnant woman with no battle training *wouldn't* go gently into that goodnight.

Think again, bitch.

But my triumph is short-lived. The man yanks my frying pan away single-handedly and mutters something in Russian. Call me a skeptic, but it doesn't sound like anything good.

And then, just as I've wrapped both my arms around my belly in a desperate attempt to shield my baby—

The man drops to the ground, a stiletto heel sticking out of his skull.

"I thought I told you to stay down."

Never in my life have I been so glad to hear Petra's voice. "Wasn't working for me," I croak, a half-assed attempt at joking the tension away.

Petra makes a haughty sound in her throat. "Is that so?" she throws her remaining shoe away. "Then watch."

With a leap, she lands on the counter. There's a gun in her right hand and a set of throwing knives in her right.

I couldn't look away if I tried.

She flies back into the fray—literally. I watch her do a flip mid-air, landing on the back of whichever poor bastard was unlucky enough to be closest. Without hesitation, she shoots his brains out.

I should be disgusted. I should be crying and screaming and throwing up everything I've ever eaten.

But honestly?

It looks badass as *fuck.*

Petra doesn't stop to admire her kill. Instead, she flies off the guy's shoulders before he starts to drop and lands squarely on the second. Her thighs wrap around the man's neck and *squeeze.*

"Wanted in fifteen countries," was it?

I think a few more ought to add her to their no-fly lists.

The second guy drops as dead as the first. Only then do Petra's feet finally touch the ground. She lands with unearthly grace, a cat or a ghost.

Or—

Solovyova. I remember looking it up. After our first meeting, I wanted to know who I was dealing with.

I couldn't find anything. Petra really *was* a ghost. All I came up with was that Instagram account I managed to find before the wedding, and a word from an automatic translator.

Nightingale.

That's exactly what Petra looks like as she fights: a bird, flying weightlessly through the air, swooping down at the last second to paint the snow red.

And her father still refuses to make her into a *vor*? Fuck that. If it were up to me, I'd let her run the whole damn show.

Just as I'm thinking that, Petra whirls around to the third guy and throws a knife straight through his eye.

It's the last body to drop. Lena and Julia have already taken care of the remaining two, sent to join their comrades on the floor. Ten assassins—all dispatched in less than five minutes.

Petra turns to me, slightly out of breath. "You okay there, *koshka?*"

I give a stunned nod. "Yeah, I'm okay."

"Everybody else?"

Lena and Julia shrug in unison. "Good workout."

"Bit hungry."

"Great," Petra says. "Get this mess cleaned up. We can get pizza later."

The promise of food seems to be a powerful motivator. Just like that, the twins roll up their sleeves and get to work.

"Yura," Petra says into her phone. I can't make out anything else she says—it's all in Russian.

Is she calling Yuri? I wonder. *Why not Matvey?*

But then I remember that I tried to call Matvey, too—and he didn't pick up.

Bitterness wells up in my mouth. Wasn't this a rule? That no matter when I called, he was going to answer me?

I turn away from the scene. Petra's kills had a kind of glamor to them, but the twins stuffing bodies into trash bags is something I'd rather not have nightmares about.

"I'll go make some coffins—*coffee*," I blurt out. "Anybody want coffee?"

Three bloodied hands rise.

I start to prepare for three. Then I figure we're gonna have company soon. *Yuri. Grisha. Matvey.*

I say fuck it and make a whole pot.

40

MATVEY

Vlad's company is to die for.

Literally. I'm considering asking Grisha to just shoot me in the head to end my misery. When I saw the first bottle run out, I almost couldn't help a sigh of relief.

Then Vlad ordered another.

And another.

And another.

Needless to say, the old man isn't looking so sharp right now.

I can't say the same for me. I've been throwing my drinks into a potted plant all night. If it's still alive in the morning, it'll be the most hungover ficus on the face of the earth.

"I'm so happy we did this, *syn*," Vlad practically burps in my face. "Men should drink together. It strengthens their bond."

For me, this bond's already feeling too fucking tight. The old bastard wouldn't even let me take calls—switched off both my phones himself. *It's a matter of respect*, he grumbled.

I was tempted to cut his hand off in return, but this is my future father-in-law. If I can't pick my battles now, I can't imagine what my marriage will look like.

A shitshow, my mind supplies. *You already know that.*

Fuck me, I do.

As if summoned by the word "*marriage*," April's face pops up in my thoughts. Which is ridiculous, because that's not even remotely on the table. For me or her.

I have my dreams. It'd be foolish to think she doesn't have hers, too.

"Yes," I reply through gritted teeth. "We should do this more often." *Anything to hasten your entry into the afterlife.*

Just as I'm thinking up an excuse to leave, I watch Yuri take a call and pale. "Motya," he whispers, "something happened at the penthouse."

I freeze. Then I spring to my feet. "Excuse me," I tell Vlad. "Duty calls."

"Duty?" Vlad blinks. "No, no—we're drinking now. Duty can wait."

"I'm afraid it can't."

It's taking everything I have to keep calm. Vlad tries to get up to stop me, but the alcohol in his system finally seems to be taking effect. He drops right back onto his chair, steadied by his bodyguards.

"Drinks are on me." I hand my card to a waitress and don't stick around to get it back. I'll send Grisha later—if I remember.

Right now, I've got only one thing on my mind.

As soon as we're out, I turn to Yuri. "Tell me what happened," I bark.

And Yuri does.

I've never forced Grisha to drive this fast. I feel like a heartless cowboy digging my heels into a horse, spurring it to death.

But right now, I don't give a fuck about anybody else. Grisha can deal.

Only one person matters.

Every second in the elevator is a nightmare. As soon as the doors open, I rush out and stride into the penthouse.

I'm greeted by a bloody sight.

The place is trashed. There's no other word for it: carpets stained, couches gutted, furnishings overturned. It looks like someone put a hit on the apartment specifically.

But they didn't.

They put a hit on *April.*

I find her in the kitchen. She's serving coffee, of all things. Her hair's a mess, dress stained red around her neckline. The left side of her face is sprayed with blood, too.

I charge to her side. "Are you hurt?"

April shakes her head. Without thinking, I move to brush the bloodstain off her cheek, but the mess only seems to get worse. I want to cart her out to the bathtub and scrub her clean from this—want to make her forget. But I already know she won't forget this as long as she lives.

April isn't Bratva. To her, a hit isn't just another Tuesday.

"You didn't pick up," she croaks. "I called you, and you didn't pick up."

Not for the first time tonight, I wish I could kill Vlad with my bare hands. "I'm sorry," I say. I'm not used to these two words; they feel strange, foreign. "Bastard made me switch my phones off."

"You promised," April chokes, tears blinking from the corners of her eyes. "You promised you'd always answer—"

"I know. I'm sorry."

"You lied to me. You broke a rule."

"I'm sorry."

I pull her close. As she sobs into my chest, I check her from head to toe. She wasn't lying—she really isn't hurt.

She's safe. The baby's safe, too.

So I turn to the person responsible for this. The person who protected her when I couldn't. "Petra."

She stops her conversation with Yuri and glances over at me. "Yes?"

"I… *Blyat'.* Thank you."

Petra stares at me like I've gone insane. Like she just ate a lemon and it had cayenne peppers in it. I've never seen my fiancé flustered, but there's nothing else this could be.

Leave it to April to melt the Snow Queen.

"I'm going," Petra blurts out. "Since you're back and all."

I nod. "I'll take it from here."

April peeks out from my chest. "You're leaving?"

She's sniffling like a little kid. Just what happened between these two while I was away?

"Yeah." Petra shifts from foot to foot, unsure what to say. "Let's... get a raincheck. On girls' night."

That seems to brighten April up. "Okay," she hiccups. "I'll stock the pantry."

"Please do," Julia pipes up.

"More of those chocolate chip ones," Lena suggests.

"Alright." April smiles. "It's a date."

Then Petra turns on her heels and practically runs out the door, face red.

"I'll see them out," Yuri adds in a rush.

I nod. "Grisha, you go, too. Check the perimeter. Make sure no one's loitering."

With a bow, Grisha obeys.

Then it's just the two of us.

My thoughts are a mess. I feel like I'm being torn apart. The *pakhan* in me is roaring at the idea of his territory being invaded. And the man—

The man can't stop looking at April.

"I never should have missed dinner," I tell her. "I should have been here."

She shakes her head. "You couldn't have known."

"I should have answered you."

"Yes." April quivers. "You should have." But then her arms are around me, wrapping me in an embrace. "Next time, don't forget."

Next time. Just like that, she's already forgiven me. After I made such a big deal of her breaking our rules with Charlie—

After all that, she still can't hold a grudge.

I don't deserve her. The thought's already out before I can push it back where it came from. *She's too good for me.*

And then: *This isn't just about the baby anymore.*

It's a terrifying realization. When did I let myself get in so deep? Where's the Matvey Groza I've always been? The iceman, the *pakhan*, the ruthless killer?

The one who doesn't give a fuck about some woman?

But that's the worst part. The *pakhan* in me is right here, howling at the thought of somebody else touching what's his. His child. His *queen.*

I need to nip this shit in the bud. I need to go scorched earth. I've seen what feelings get you; I don't want any part in it.

I won't end up with a knife in my back.

I won't end up like my mother.

"Besides," April laughs through the tears, "I could've conked out one or two."

I feel my lips twitch. "Oh, yeah?"

"Yeah. I had a frying pan."

"Wish I could've seen that."

April shrugs. "Next time."

This would be so much easier if she yelled at me. If she started cursing my name, throwing stuff, hitting me. But this hasn't been easy from the start. Why would that change now?

"There won't be a next time," I tell her.

April blinks up at me. "What do you mean?"

As *pakhan*, I've had to make countless hard decisions. Long-term, split-second, life-or-death; everything comes down to me.

But none have been harder than the two decisions I'm about to make right now.

One: I will never touch April again.

Two…

"I mean that I'll be here." I look April in the eye. "I'm moving back in."

41

MATVEY

It's agony.

I didn't sleep a wink all night, but that's not the agonizing part. It was holding April through it, watching her chest rise and fall, brushing the dried salt off her cheeks.

And knowing, all the while, it would be the last time.

"I'll have my men bring my things," I inform her that morning at the breakfast table.

"Oh," April says. "Good. What time are they coming by? I'll make some room in the closet—"

"I've instructed them to put everything in the guest room."

April's face falls. "I… I see." She tries to force a smile. It's painful to watch. "Makes sense. So much space in here. Be a pity if we didn't use it."

"Mm." The guest room is just across the living area, near the kitchen. It's also closer to the door. If anybody were to break in, I could neutralize them before they crept any further in.

But I don't tell April any of that. It's no longer her business to know my reasoning.

It never was in the first place.

That's what I tell myself as I watch her pick at her breakfast. April's appetite is her dashboard light: if she's eating, that means she's happy. If she's not…

Ignore it, I growl at the part of me that's grown soft. *It's none of your concern anymore.*

But it's easier said than done.

This is ridiculous. I'm a Bratva *pakhan.* I've killed countless men in cold blood. So why does this fucking hurt so much?

When I leave for work, April walks me to the door. Her hand twitches, as if expecting I'll pick it up and kiss it. Like I've always done.

This time, I don't.

"I doubled your guard," I tell her instead. "If you need anything from downstairs, just ask them."

April frowns. "Why? Can't I just go grab it?"

"No."

She almost flinches at that. *Like she flinched away from her mother*, a masochistic part of me points out.

"Until further notice, you're confined to your quarters," I force myself to say. "No walks, no visits."

"But June was supposed to—"

"No. Visits." I channel all my authority into those two words. I don't care if she doesn't understand—I can't go through it again. Last night, the aftermath. The blood on her dress. "Have I made myself clear?"

Steeling herself, April swallows. "Crystal."

It's better this way, I tell myself as I climb into my car. April and I had already crossed too many boundaries. I need to be firm about this. Decisive. I can't afford to falter.

I need to bury the man and embrace the *pakhan*.

So that's exactly what I do. I go to work. I attend to my duties. I re-read Yuri's proposal from scratch and go over the quarterly reports I've been ignoring from my *vory*.

All throughout the day, I push April far from my mind. *She's safe*, I tell myself. Her guards have been replaced and doubled. My best men are on the job, like they should've been from the start.

Well, my second-best men.

On either side of me, Grisha and Yuri are sorting documents from the unstable piles they'd become on my desk. With Grisha's organizational skills and Yuri's competitiveness, everything quickly finds its way back where it's supposed to be.

And then I glimpse a file under Yuri's arm.

Ballistics Exam Report.

I rise from my chair and snatch it away. "M-Matvey?" Yuri balks, but I don't pay him any mind. I'm too busy cursing myself.

See? the *pakhan* inside of me hisses. *This is why April's bad for you. She's an obsession. A distraction.*

For once, I'm inclined to agree. Because I slipped up on the job. I *never* slip up on the job.

This isn't just any random oversight, either. This report is the key to finding out what happened at the warehouse that night: who killed our men, who executed the hostages. Who sent the kidnappers after April.

Most likely, it's the same person who sent those assassins at the penthouse.

How could I just fucking *forget* about it?

This is all my fault. It's not a thought I have often, but now, I can't shake it. If I'd only been more careful, more focused—

Maybe those men would've been long dead before they could even think to touch April.

Or my child.

But… no. Back when this landed on my desk, something else landed there, too: April's background check. All the dirt and the scars that her shitty family inflicted on her. Once I saw that, I didn't have eyes for anything else.

A mistake.

I give this report my full attention now. I scan the pages like my life depends on it, because in a way, it does. My child's life, laid out on the line because of my carelessness.

Never again will I put April Flowers before my own blood.

"*Parni.* Come take a look at this."

Yuri's already peering over my shoulder. Grisha catches up swiftly, peering over Yuri's. "Any matches?" he asks.

"Get off of me!" Yuri snarls. "Christ, you're heavy."

"It's not my fault you're pint-sized."

"I'll show you—"

"Quiet!"

Silence falls in the office. I catch Yuri and Grisha throwing quizzical glances between themselves, but I don't have time to spare it any thought. My eyes are glued to the page.

Specifically, to one line.

"The bullet was traced to D.C.," I exhale. "An underground arms dealer."

"D.C.?" Yuri asks, suddenly nervous. "Why would…?"

"Why indeed?" Grisha echoes. He's using that tone again, the one that lets you know he's caught on more than he lets on. "It appears your interest in D.C. isn't one-sided, boss."

You want D.C., Grisha's undertone seems to say. *And now, D.C. wants you.*

The words from Hostage #2 play back in my mind: *My boss sends his regards.*

I already knew then. I didn't want to rush to judgment, but I fucking *knew*.

"Pressure the *vory*," I order. "This acquisition needs to happen now."

Yuri straightens up. So does Grisha. In unison, they reply, "Yes, *moy pakhan*."

42

APRIL

If I felt like a hamster in a cage on my first day here, now, I feel like the freaking wheel.

I mean it. I'm stuck in place, thoughts whirring with nowhere to go, my feet striking the same four tiles over and over again. And for what?

My co-parent won't even look at me.

Okay, that's unfair. I know why I've been confined. After almost eating a bullet, anyone would get a little overboard with the safety measures.

And if it's Matvey, he'll definitely go full Azkaban.

"I can't believe I'm about to say this, but I agree with Mr. Wrong: you cannot go strolling about on your own."

I sigh into my phone. "Great, now, you're ganging up on me. My best friend and my baby-daddy-without-benefits, all out to get me."

"We're out to protect you, babe," June coos from the other end of the line. "Wait. What do you mean 'without benefits'? I thought you guys were going at it like rabbits."

"We were!" I blurt out before I can realize what June actually said. "I mean—"

"No need to be shy, sweetcheeks. I've seen everything there is to see down there."

"That's because you're allergic to knocking," I pout. "Anyway… I don't know. Something's different."

"Different how?"

I throw myself down on the couch. Correction: the *carcass* of a couch. Matvey's men are supposed to stop by with new furniture later in the day, but for now, it's foam-on-skin action. "You're gonna laugh," I whine.

"I promise I won't."

"Liar."

"April. Spit it out."

I capitulate. There's no point in telling June "no": she can't physically understand the meaning of the word. "He didn't kiss my hand."

I get it out all in one breath—*hedidn'tkissmyhand*—but of course, June catches every word. When she wants to, her ears can be as sharp as a bat's. "I'm sorry—*kissed your hand*? Is that Russian slang for something kinky or…?"

"It's not!" I burst out. "He… Before he leaves, he always kisses my hand. And today, he didn't."

"Uh-huh…" June hums. Why can I suddenly picture a bucket

of popcorn in her lap? "Tell me again how you're not together."

"We're not! It's just... something he does. Did." Dammit, why am I blushing all over? I'm not a schoolgirl anymore. I shouldn't be this flustered over *kissing*. On the hand! "And now, he doesn't and I'm wondering if I did something wrong—"

"Besides nearly getting yourself killed?" June ventures.

"I didn't exactly invite those hitmen for tea!"

"Oh, babe, babe, babe," June sighs. "You can't expect your man to be logical about this. From what you've told me, he rarely ever is."

"That's..." I try to object. "... not wrong."

"I mean, *I'm* freaking out, and I didn't even get to do you."

"Jay!"

"It's true! Do you know how hard it is not to march over there and hug you until you can't breathe?"

I curl up on myself. "I'm sorry. I wish Matvey wouldn't be such a hard-ass about visits."

"Honestly? I'm kind of glad he is," June says, surprising me. "Of course, I should get infinite passes, because I'm cool and amazing and your bestest friend forever—"

"Is this going anywhere?" I mutter.

"*But*," June tuts, "I get where he's coming from. Truly, I do."

"Really? Because I don't."

There's a noise on the other end of the line, like an old mattress creaking. I wonder if June's thrown herself down on the bed. Without thinking, I lie down, too. It's how we used to gossip and cry over our woes: knees to chest, face to feet, the yin to each other's yang.

Not for the first time, I'm struck by how much I miss her. *Us.* Our life before this.

But then I think of Matvey—his strong hands, his warmth— and I can't bring myself to regret it. Not all of it.

And certainly not this *part of it,* I think as I stroke Nugget.

"Loving someone isn't a walk in the park," June murmurs, quiet for once. "It's like having your heart beating outside of your body. And here's the kicker: you can't do a goddamn thing about it. You can try to shield it, keep it in a gilded cage, but you'll never be able to protect it from everything. And that's scary as all hell."

I try to picture it: the golden bars and the bloody thing inside. Beating, bare. Vulnerable. "Yeah," I find myself murmuring back. "It's scary." Then I shake myself back to reality. "But Matvey doesn't love me. Not… that way. That's not how it is between us."

"Yeah?" June breathes back. "Then why does it sound like you're about to cry?"

I touch my cheek. Sure enough, there's wetness there—tears pooled at the corner of my eye, spilling at first touch. "I…"

I feel like someone plucked me from a field. Like someone's tearing my petals off one by one.

I love him.

I don't love him.

He loves me.

He doesn't...

And then, suddenly, the doorbell rings.

"I have to go," I blurt into my phone. "Bye, June."

I don't wait for her to say it back. I drag the red button down the screen and shut the call. I'm too raw right now— if she said anything else to me, I really might burst out crying.

Instead, I pick myself up. I dry my tears. I dust off the pieces of foam. Then I stride towards the door.

At the last second, I stop.

I'm not expecting anyone, I realize. *Matvey's men shouldn't come around until later. What if...?*

I try to swallow my anxiety. Surely an assassin wouldn't bother to ring the freaking doorbell.

Right?

"Who is it?" I call faintly, my fingers already scrolling for Matvey's number.

If I call him, he'll be here. If...

"*Moči perhoti*, who do you think?!"

I throw the door open.

Petra's tapping her foot, arms crossed, glaring at me like I've committed some deadly sin. Making her wait, most likely. "Hi...?"

"Hi," Petra all but spits. "Get out of the way. Girls!"

With a gesture of her manicured hand, two hulking figures emerge from the hallway. I stare at their arms. Specifically, what they're holding: takeout bags. Heaps of them. "Uhh, are we having someone over for lunch...?"

Petra's nose twitches like a haughty bunny's. "I moved up girls' night." Just like that, she pushes past me.

The twins follow. They set the bags on the table. I peer at the logos: Chinese, Indian, Greek... "Just how many girls are coming...?"

Petra shrugs. "Didn't know what pregnant women ate. It was a hassle to ask, so we just got one of everything."

"We'll eat the rest," Lena reassures me.

"Won't leave a crumb," Julia agrees.

I let myself take in the scene before me: Petra, turning pointedly away with a blush on her cheeks. The twins, unpacking delicious-smelling food on the kitchen counter.

"Shit," Petra startles. "What's wrong with her?"

Belatedly, I realize I'm crying.

"Are there onions in those?!" she bellows.

"It's okay! I'm not... I just..." Finally, I turn to Petra. "Thank you," I say sincerely. "I kinda... needed this."

Petra's looking at me like I've grown horns and a pair of leathery wings. "Alright," she says briskly. "Here, take a tissue —no, you know what, take the whole pack. I don't... Goddammit, how do I make you stop?"

But the twins, having already begun stuffing their faces, simply shrug.

I hear myself laugh. "I'm fine!" I tell her. I blow my nose, dry my eyes, fix myself as best I can. "See? Good as new."

"Really?" Petra leans in suspiciously. "Because Matvey's gonna kill me if you're not."

I wonder if he's the one who sent her. Maybe not. Maybe Petra's just catching the friendship bug.

And you know what? That's okay. I don't need Matvey to make every single one of my days. I've got other options.

"What's that, Nugget? You're hungry?" I pat my belly. "Then we'd better set the table. Come on."

I drag Petra by the hand and head for the kitchen.

Against all odds, Petra doesn't let go.

43

APRIL

When I hear the keycard beep, I tense.

Matvey's back. Once, the thought would've made me light up like a Christmas tree. But now...

Now, I don't even know if he'll look at me.

He strides in. Of course—he lives here now. He's not going to ring the doorbell anymore. No need for me to let him in. That little ritual hasn't been gone a day, and I already miss it like hell.

"Good evening," he greets impassively, putting down his briefcase.

I force a smile. "Evening."

Then his gaze sweeps over the table.

I wince. I already know what he's frowning at: a spread of takeout foods with no rhyme or reason, from pizza to noodles to sushi rolls. "Do I need to call Dr. Allan back?" he asks, but there's an amused lilt to it. "Get you checked for tapeworms?"

Finally, my smile turns real. "Petra," I explain simply.

Matvey nods. "Yeah. That tracks."

"It does?"

"She's got weird ways to show she cares." He hangs his jacket and loosens his tie. "Like a cat."

"Do I need to worry?" I joke. "Is she gonna leave dead things on my pillow for me to find?"

"She hasn't already?"

I bite my cheek. Now, *this*—this is what family dinner's supposed to be all about. Bantering, messing around. Sharing secret smiles over stupid jokes.

I take a few steps towards Matvey. My hands find his tie, slipping it free. "She's not the only one, you know."

Matvey's throat bobs. "The only one?"

"Who's got weird ways to show they care."

Kiss me, I tell him with my eyes. *Show me you care.*

But he doesn't.

"We should eat." He clears his throat. "Food's gonna go cold."

I let my hands fall. "Yeah. Let's."

For the first time since this little ritual began, we spend it in silence. There's the clinking sound of cutlery and chopsticks, the bubbling of water and wine. But nothing else. No jokes, no laughter, no glances.

Look at me, I beg the whole time inside my mind. *Stop pretending I'm not here. Just tell me what I did wrong. I'll fix it, I promise. I'll do my best.*

Just look at me!

But he doesn't.

I've been staring at the ceiling for the past two hours.

"What's wrong, Nugget?" I mutter into the darkness, a hand on my belly. "Why can't you sleep?"

Of course, it's not Nugget. My baby's curled up and cozy, and I bet it wants nothing more than for its mommy to stop tossing and turning so we can both get some quality rest.

But no matter what I do, I just can't close my eyes. The silence. The loneliness. It all feels too familiar.

Snap out of it, I order myself. *This isn't like back then. I'm not...*

Not what? A guest? A nuisance?

Unwanted?

Then, suddenly, there's a noise in the kitchen.

I stretch my ears. For a second, I'm terrified. *Are the masked men back?*

Reflexively, I pat the space next to me. The space Matvey slept in last night, holding me close until morning.

Now, it's empty.

I slip out of bed. I grab something from the nightstand. Silently, I pad out of my room.

And then I hear a familiar voice curse. "*Blyat!*"

I slump. "Couldn't sleep?"

From the kitchen sink, Matvey turns to me. In the semi-darkness of the room, all I can see are the shadows on his face. "April." Then: "Is that a frying pan?"

"Judge all you like," I shrug. "This baby's been christened in battle." I glimpse a few shards of broken glass in the sink. "Are you hurt?" I ask immediately, taking his hand without thinking.

Matvey shakes his head. "It's just a cut."

"That's what Khal Drogo said, and look what happened to him." I grab the first-aid kit under the sink. Then I swipe two intact glasses from the cabinet and fill them with water. "Sit."

"I'm fine."

"And after a little disinfectant, you'll be even finer." My lips twitch, but it doesn't reach my eyes. "Or are you afraid I'll put a spell on you?"

Without another word, Matvey complies.

To his credit, he wasn't lying: it really is just a tiny cut. A couple of dabs of soaked cotton, a little bandage, and it'll be good as new.

"Where did you learn how to do this?" Matvey asks as I work, breaking the silence.

"I was a total klutz as a kid," I answer. "Got my fair share of bumps and scrapes. Figured it'd be quicker if I learned how to take care of them myself."

I don't say the quiet part out loud: *Because no one else would.*

But Matvey seems to hear it anyway. "You're good at it."

"Thanks."

I don't tell him that it's just another way for me to fix things. Tailoring, nursing—all of it's just more of the same. Taking what's broken and giving it a second chance, a third, a fourth.

Then maybe it won't have to be thrown away.

Silence falls between us again. But this time, it doesn't feel as tense as before. Maybe it's the night; maybe it's the city lights dancing in from the balcony. When it's late like this, everything takes on a different hue.

Even loneliness.

"You know," I venture, "when I was a kid, I used to have all sorts of nightmares."

Matvey's face tells me I hit the nail on the head. Not that the big bad Bratva Puckman would ever admit to having nightmares. Clearly, it's nightmares who have him. "Is that so?"

"Mhmm. Sometimes, it was just your run-of-the-mill jump scare: monsters under the bed, ghosts behind the curtains, creepy dolls coming alive."

"Can't relate." Matvey shrugs. "I didn't really dream as a kid."

We all dream, I think but don't say. *We just can't always remember.*

Sometimes, it's too painful to remember.

"It wasn't those dreams I was afraid about, though," I continue. While I talk, I start wrapping gauze around the shallow cut on his palm. "After those, I could usually go right back to sleep. But when the real nightmares came, then I'd just stare at the ceiling until dawn."

A beat goes by. Two.

"What nightmares were those?" Matvey asks eventually.

I shouldn't be telling him this. I shouldn't be telling anyone this. Old wounds should fester in silence, at least when it comes to someone like me. Someone who's too weak to fix herself.

But the night's making me bolder. For some reason, right now, I can't find my fears anywhere.

"Sometimes, it was my parents," I confess. "Throwing me out, sending me away. Or, God forbid, getting married to each other again."

"Sounds like a nightmare alright," Matvey scoffs.

I snort. *Can't disagree with that.* "Other times, it was just... me. Alone, somewhere I couldn't recognize. I'd scream myself hoarse for someone—*anyone*—to come get me. But no one would."

It's strange. For the past few days, all I've wanted was for Matvey to look at me.

But now, I'm the one who can't bring myself to look at him.

"What would you do?" I hear his deep voice ask. "When that happened?"

"Burst out crying," I tell him frankly. "The one who actually knew what to do was my grandmother. She'd give me a tall glass of water, just like this—" I shake my glass for emphasis, "—and make me drink it all. 'Water purifies,' she used to say. 'Water heals.' And then..." I smile. "Then she'd sing to me."

"Sing?"

"Yeah. Sometimes in French, sometimes in Creole. They were the lullabies she grew up with in Haiti." A sudden memory makes me laugh. "There was one about a crab. If you didn't sleep, it would eat you."

"How comforting," he drawls sarcastically. "Must've put you out like a light."

"Eh." I shrug and grin. "It's like German fairytales: it's the thought that counts. Besides, the crab didn't actually eat you in the end." I try to remember how that song went. "'*Dodo ti pitit manman*,'" I sing quietly under my breath. "'*Dodo ti pitit papa...*'"

Suddenly, I realize Matvey's staring. "What?" I laugh, embarrassed.

"Nothing," he replies a little too quickly. "You are..." He clears his throat. "Your grandmother must've been quite a person."

I smile. "She was definitely that. Her life alone... You could've written a book about it. She was my grandfather's second wife. When it happened, remarriages weren't all that common, and mixed marriages even less. She had a rough go of it, especially with my dad."

"Your father didn't like her?" Matvey ventures.

"Not one bit." It's still painful to think about—how rejected she must've felt. By society, by her husband's own son, by everyone. "But she didn't mind me. She took me in and raised me as her own, in her home. For that, I'm forever grateful."

I don't mention what happened to that home. It feels dirty, somehow—the thought of bringing money into this. Under the cover of darkness, everything feels more honest. Sacred. Raw.

Suddenly, I realize I can't take it.

"Well then." I clap to put a bookend on that morbid detour in the conversation as I rise to my feet. "Drink it all. Keep those bandages dry."

"Or the crab will eat me?" Matvey teases.

It's too much. The night, the lights, *us*. The way Matvey's looking at me—finally looking at me—with an intensity I can't bear.

"Or the crab will swallow you whole, yes."

Matvey rises with me. Then, surprisingly, he takes my hand.

He doesn't kiss it, but his thumb comes up to stroke my knuckles. Somehow, it feels even more intimate like this. More raw.

"Goodnight, April."

Twenty-three steps between our rooms. I know, because I counted them. Soon, there will be twenty-three steps between us. A distance so short—and yet, it feels like an ocean.

"Goodnight, Matvey," I whisper, and cross back to my side of the dark, churning waters.

44

APRIL

"Ow!" Petra winces under my pins.

I don't pay it any mind. Right now, I'm focused on one thing only: the dress coming to life around her. "Stay still."

"Christ, fine!" Petra pouts. "And I thought *I* was bossy."

It's not completely unfair, as far as accusations go. When I'm like this, I can't see anything else. "Put yourself in my shoes: I've got two gowns to deliver and my mannequin quit on me—"

"Can't imagine why," she mutters under her breath. Her eyes fix pointedly on the plastic carcass in the corner. I'm aware of how it looks: riddled with holes, one arm missing and the other dangling at the wrong angle—wait, was that a *shiver*?

Either way, I choose to ignore her. "Would you be calm in a situation like this?"

"I'm always calm," she retorts. "You can't exterminate a rival Bratva if you're busy fretting about how long it's taking."

"And you can't be a good mannequin if you keep moving, Petra."

"You know, if you weren't pregnant, I'd have killed you already."

"Can't be the first time you've thought that," I mumble distractedly. God, would it kill this hem to just work? It's being as difficult as she is.

"No," Petra admits. "But you should at least pale a little."

"Sorry. I'll do my best to act terrified."

She quirks an eyebrow. "Your Work Mode is scary."

"Thanks. Means a lot coming from you."

I can feel Petra's urge to fidget under my hands. She's just not the type to sit still: tapping her foot, cracking her knuckles, huffing and puffing like the big, bad wolf in heels. Now that I've stuffed her into a ballgown, I feel like she's finally experiencing what it's like to be on the other side of the throwing knife.

Whatever. I'll bake her an apology cake. After I finish this dress, that is.

Like clockwork, Petra starts moving again. I'm about to scold her when I hear, "This is really beautiful."

"Oh," I say intelligently. "That's... Thank you?"

Petra's hand travels over the fabric, caressing the short tulle butterfly sleeves, lingering on the place they meet the bodice. "It's true. The stitching's flawless." She says it with a shrug, like it doesn't matter in the slightest. Like she's just stating the obvious. "Are you having a stroke?"

I shake my head. "You wish."

"I mean, yeah. Then at least I'd be free."

I'm terrible at taking compliments. Really, seriously terrible. I'd rather face a thousand throwing knives than this.

But also, I can't help preening a little. "Would you wear it?" I try to sound casual. "You know, if I wasn't forcing you at pinpoint?"

"Probably," Petra concedes. "It's not exactly my style, but if I had to go for the *Beauty and the Beast* vibe, I'd definitely pick something like this. The design's very elegant, too."

Preening Points: +50%. "Thanks. That's... actually one of mine."

"Yours?" Petra frowns. "As in, you drew this?"

I give a sheepish nod. "It's a bit of a hobby," I confess. "Sketching out models and whatnot. Sometimes, Elias will let me take lead on commissions."

"I bet. This is easily worth four figures."

My head starts spinning. "Alright, that's enough. You don't have to say that."

But Petra only arches an eyebrow. "*Cyka*, do I look like I need to suck up to you? No? Didn't think so. So take the goddamn compliment. I don't say shit I don't mean."

That's a very aggressive way to praise someone. "I just... I'm not used to it. When I started out, I was just mending my own clothes."

"You guys couldn't afford new ones?" she ventures. I'd expect the words to be snobbish, but they come out without a trace of judgment.

"Yes and no," I reply. "Mostly, my parents were too busy arguing to notice. I didn't want them to fight about that, too, so I picked up a needle and thread and just did it myself. Grandma taught me a few stitches. After a while, I got pretty decent at it: altering my clothes, making new ones, all that jazz."

"God, you're so infuriating," Petra mutters. "'Pretty decent.' I can't tell if you're fishing or you're serious."

"Well, I am a pro now," I amend. "But I wasn't always. And besides, I'm a tailor. Designing's a whole other bag of candies."

"But it's what you want to do?" Petra guesses.

I don't deny it. All kids have dreams—and kids from broken homes? They need to dream twice as hard. "It doesn't matter," I brush it off. "Fashion's all about connections. And money."

"You realize you're currently pregnant by a billionaire, right?"

I shake my head with a smile. "I couldn't possibly ask Matvey for that. I don't want to. I… I want to get there on my own. If I can't, then it wasn't meant to be."

If I can't, then I wasn't good enough in the first place.

"Dreams…" Petra's voice shakes me out of my reverie. "They don't listen to reason. So, if you're going to pursue one… *blyat'*, you shouldn't listen to reason, either."

I blink. "I'm sorry—did you just comfort me?"

"Don't get used to it."

"I'm totally gonna. I'm gonna call you up at 3:00 A.M. and vent my woes into your ear."

"Try it. I'll cut out your tongue."

"I'll show up at your place with nail polish and face masks," I continue as if she hadn't spoken. "We can watch *Mean Girls* and gossip about tall, criminally-inclined Russian men."

"You don't know where I live."

"I'll bribe it out of Julia."

"I'll fire her."

"You'd never."

"Then I'll just kill you with a safety pin right now."

I grin. Now, *that's* the Petra we all know and fear. "Can I at least finish this dress first?"

"Please do," she begs. "How much longer anyway?"

"Not long."

"Oh, good—"

"Just one more gown and we're good to go."

Petra's eyes grow to the size of melons. "I'm sorry. One more *gown?*"

"Well, yeah. Client's asked for two."

"You've got to be kidding me."

"*And* you're just her size! How lucky is that?"

While Petra's muttering, "God, please kill me now" into the ceiling, I whip up my phone and snatch a selfie of the two of us—me beaming, her scowling.

Then, before I can think twice about it, I press *Send.*

45

MATVEY

"What's wrong?" Yuri asks, leaning over my right shoulder.

"Is it Ms. Flowers?" Grisha chimes in, leaning over my left.

Merry fucking wives, the both of you. But I don't have it in me to scold them right now. Because what I'm staring at is... concerning.

A selfie with my fiancée and my baby mama, playing dress-up in my penthouse.

"They're... *bonding*," I grimace.

Petra's face is the worst of it. She always looks like an angry chipmunk: cheeks puffed up in outrage, front teeth biting into her bottom lip like she can't wait to tear someone's throat out with them.

And yet, in this one, she's also... happy?

Behind me, Grisha whistles. "That's some talent on Ms. Flowers's part."

"The dress?"

Even I have to agree with that. I'm not the type to notice what women are wearing. If I'm interested, I'll just tear it right off—April can testify to that. But when it comes to April's work... then, even a heathen like me has to recognize talent when he sees it.

But Grisha shakes his head. "The gown's impressive, but I was talking about the taming of the shrew."

Ah, right. Petra. "Tamer than I've ever seen her," I agree.

"She hasn't killed April yet. That's an accomplishment in and of itself."

I notice that Yuri seems to be boiling over next to me. "You alright, brother?" I ask him.

"Just thinking that someone here has got guts, insulting an ally like that," he mutters, glaring daggers in Grisha's direction.

Here they go again. I swear, whenever these two are in a room together, my Bratva turns into a goddamn kindergarten.

I follow Yuri's gaze back to the picture. I don't think the man has blinked. "Should I send you a copy, brother?"

"What?" Yuri shakes himself. "No, I was just... the dress," he blurts out. "Grisha's right. April's good at what she does."

My third and I share a look. We don't speak, but we're both thinking the same thing: *Did Yuri just say the words "Grisha's right"?*

"Yurochka?" Grisha asks carefully. "You aren't running a fever, are you?"

"You are looking a bit flushed," I agree. "If you're not feeling up to this…"

"What? No," Yuri scoffs. "Fuck all the way off, both of you."

"Oh, good, he's come to his senses," Grisha deadpans.

"Shut up."

"Both of you shut up," I cut in. "It's time. Let's go."

Even as I say that, I throw the picture one last glance. I can see why Yuri was so mesmerized: April's work is astonishing. Seeing a dress like this in a boutique's window display is one thing, but watching it come to life under someone's hands?

That's something else entirely.

I wonder, briefly, if this was Maia's doing, too. If April's grandmother taught her to sew, just like she taught her how to love the world and everyone in it. Even the ones who don't deserve it.

Right now, I suspect I can count myself among them.

It's a shitty feeling: keeping April at arm's length, rebuking her attempts at closeness—it's all so wrong. The other night, every part of me was screaming against it: *Don't let her go. Don't push her away.*

Don't you leave her alone, too.

But I don't have a choice.

I pocket my phone and stride into the Venus Lounge. "Welcome!" Stanislav greets me with a warm handshake. "It's an honor to have you here, *moy pakhan.*"

I'd rather have stayed home, I think but don't say. "The honor's all mine," I reply instead. "Your numbers speak for themselves."

The thing is, they do. After his mediocre performance last quarter, Stanislav took it upon himself to crush the competition. When I heard he was planning to open a new location in Little Italy, I thought he'd finally lost it. You don't put a restaurant here if you can't back it up with skill; the locals will eat you alive.

But in the end, the gamble paid off. Thanks to this location alone, Stanislav might come up on top in next quarter's earnings meeting. Not above Araes, of course, but definitely above everybody else.

Maybe that's why, for once, he's smiling. A rare sight indeed. "Thank you, *moy pakhan.* I hope you'll enjoy our cooking tonight."

"I'm looking forward to it."

A waitress leads us to the VIP table. I can see the other patrons gawking at her as she walks. Is she pretty? I can't tell. Lately, I've lost all interest in going on the hunt.

Once, I would've noticed. I would've followed her into the pantry and made her scream until she couldn't breathe. Until there wasn't one patron left who didn't know exactly what we were doing.

Now, all I can think of is a tailor shop's changing room.

Get it together, I snarl at myself. *Especially here.*

As if following my train of thought, Yuri asks, "Is it true that the food here...?"

Grisha snorts. "Puberty finally catching up with you, Yurochka?"

"How about I stick a baguette up your ass and watch it wave out of your mouth?"

"It's not," I cut in before Yuri can get any more graphic. "It's all advertising."

There's a reason Venus Lounge is called that: every food item on the menu is, without exception, made up of aphrodisiac ingredients.

Well, *alleged* aphrodisiacs. If a chocolate-dipped fig's enough to get your blood flowing, you probably didn't need it to begin with. But the theme has made the lounges very popular with couples wanting to try something new. Young adults come here on a dare, couples book a table for their anniversary, and slimy bosses take their secretaries here to hint at what they're really looking for in their working relationship. Mostly, they just manage to make them uncomfortable as all hell.

Either way, the Venus Lounges make a boatload of money.

At the table, the *vory* greet me. It wasn't long ago that we were meeting just like this, around good food and celebration.

That time, it didn't end well.

Our aperitifs are laid out before us. I watch Yuri pick suspiciously at an avocado and salmon tart, probably waiting to hear the crunch of a hidden Viagra pill under his teeth. "Isn't this nice?" Ipatiy beams from my left. "Celebrating success—now, that's what being Bratva's all about."

"*Vashe zdarovye!*" Gora cheers. "I'll drink to that!"

For some reason, everything about this conversation irks me. No, that's not right—it pisses me the fuck off. Being filthy rich off restaurants and clubs? *That's* what being Bratva's all about?

The mother of my child was almost killed twice, and they're drinking to our *success*?

Blyat', my men have gone soft. Worse, they've gone native. Forgotten what it's like to have to be one step ahead of frostbite at all times. Forgotten what it's like to fight.

Well, I'm about to goddamn remind them.

I slam my glass down. The cheer at the table dies. Silence fills the space where laughter reigned not five seconds ago.

"Is something the matter, *pakhan*?" Ivan asks quietly.

I draw myself up in my seat. "While we're here celebrating, our most important project still lies unfinished. Or does anybody here have more good news to share?"

The *vory* exchange glances. "*Moy pakhan...* the acquisition is proceeding," Gora blurts out. "It's nearly in the bag."

"'Nearly' isn't good enough."

"It's just..." Ipatiy's voice cuts in. "It'd be easier for all of us if we knew what we were doing. In D.C., I mean."

"You don't need to know what you're doing," I snarl. "You need to do it. Or have I not made myself clear enough?"

"Matvey."

I turn. Ivan's gaze is a piercing shade of blue—almost white. Icy, like the rivers back home. If there's one of us who hasn't forgotten what we came here for, that should be him.

But lately, Ivan's been leading the resistance. He's been pushing back against me more than anybody else. And yet, it still manages to surprise me when he asks, cold and factual, "Do we need to prepare for war?"

War. That's a word you don't throw out lightly at a Bratva table. These men, who had just been celebrating their success —with that one word, they're done boasting about what they've gained. Now, all they can think about is how quickly they could lose it all.

I rise. Grisha and Yuri follow suit. I catch Yuri's worried gaze, the same he'd been wearing at the Hedoneros inauguration, but I don't let it shake me. Right now, I can't afford to be shaken.

So I stare Ivan dead in the eye and I tell him the truth. "Always be ready for war."

Then I do what I've been wanting to do ever since I got here.

I grab my jacket and fucking leave.

46

MATVEY

When I get back to the penthouse, I'm in a foul mood.

My men. My fucking men, and this is what they've become: a bunch of spoiled millionaires.

And Yuri's concerned I'm not treating them well enough? Clearly, it's the opposite. I've been treating them too goddamn well. Lulled them into a false sense of security by creating an empire too powerful to take down.

Blyat! We've been on top for so long, they've forgotten what it was like to claw our way there. They've forgotten what it was like to work for it.

And now, they've gone too goddamn soft.

On the elevator ride up, I rub my temples and sigh. I want nothing more than to switch off my brain and sink into April's voice, the easy chatter of her words over dinner. I want to sink into far more than that, but I have to remind myself of all the reasons I can't. Unlike my men, I still have a goddamn grip on reality.

Though I start to doubt that the second I walk into the penthouse.

My first impulse is to reach for my gun, because only a break-in could justify this mess. Right?

Wrong. For starters, there's no blood. The furniture's intact, the couches ungutted. Last time, it looked like someone had taken out a hit on everything in the apartment.

Now, it looks like a bomb's gone off at a Gucci factory.

As I look closer, my suspicions are confirmed: everything at the scene screams "April."

There are fabrics scattered everywhere, a million different varieties I couldn't identify with a gun to my head. Needles and pins are strewn across the carpet, the perfect trap if someone did get the idea to try and break in again—barefoot, that is. I clock about a dozen OSHA violations just while making it from the door to the balcony.

Something rustles in my peripheral vision. I whirl around, still on alert, and I'm treated to a unique sight: April Flowers, emerging from a pile of tulle.

Her bloodshot eyes zero in on me. I don't like how bright they get—like I'm a three-course meal on legs. Fucking Christ, I'm usually the predator here. So why do I feel like the tables are about to turn?

"Oh, good, you're here!"

In seconds, she's inches from me.

So much for keeping our distance.

"Care to explain what happened?" I demand, trying to ignore the warmth radiating off her body.

"Work," April says simply. Which explains fuck-all, but I don't get the chance to tell her that.

Because, suddenly, her hands are on me.

For a second, I'm too surprised to even react. April's been daring before, but this? This is too far, even for her. I'm about to snap at her, demand to know exactly what the fuck she thinks she's doing—

And then she manhandles me to the center of the room.

"Off," she commands, pulling at my jacket. "All of this—off."

"Give me one good reason why I should do that," I growl.

Part of me wants to comply. A *specific* part of me, to be exact. Wants to flip April around and teach her exactly who's in charge.

No, I snarl at myself. *We can't do that anymore.*

But April just blinks. "How else are you gonna put this on?"

And then she holds up another jacket.

Oh. Right. Work. She mentioned that, didn't she?

I force myself to relax. This is still inappropriate as hell—in any other context, I would've given her a piece of my mind—but one look at April's face tells me she's on a different planet right now.

"C'mon." She yanks my jacket all the way off. "We don't have all day."

"It's night," I point out.

"No, it's not." She works the other jacket onto my shoulders. "Wait, is it?"

I jerk my head eloquently towards the window.

April pales. "Where's the sun?"

I hang on the last thread of my patience. "As much as I'd love to explain basic astronomy to you—"

"Shh." She puts a finger to my lips. "Don't breathe. Your chest's gonna move."

I'm honestly speechless. No one has ever shushed me. *Me*. Matvey fucking Groza.

But before I can teach April a lesson, her face breaks into a grin. "I knew it! Client's got your same measurements."

"You kept your notes from when we met?"

"No need," April shrugs. "I remember yours by heart."

I inhale sharply. *By heart.* All this time, and April's had my fucking measurements floating around in her head? She memorized them?

It's been nearly ten months. Ten months—and she *remembers*.

The urge from before comes back with a vengeance: to flip her around, rip her pretty dress clean off, and show her exactly what *I* remember, too. All her sensitive spots, all her weaknesses.

I want to plunge my fingers inside her. I want to hear her scream as I torture her sweetness over and over. I want to make her come with my hands, my mouth, my cock. Feel her tight little pussy squeeze me dry as she moans, and moans, and *moans*.

My name. No one else's.

"Matvey...?" she asks. "You okay?"

I snap back to the present. "Why wouldn't I be?"

"I don't know," April ventures. "You're just... looking a little flushed, that's all."

It's a miracle she hasn't noticed my raging hard-on. I'm tempted to blame the food at Venus Lounge, but I know no amount of gourmet jalapeños are gonna get me like this.

Only April.

But that can't happen anymore. I need to get a grip on myself: April is off-limits. It can't be otherwise. That night, I nearly lost her, and it almost tore me apart. I can't let her wield that kind of power over me.

She's a stranger.

She's not *family*.

And she's never going to be.

I need to maintain a safe distance between us. It's the only way this works. The only way I can stay fucking sane. Distance—of mind *and* body.

Which would be a hell of a lot easier without her hands all over me.

Without a moment's hesitation, I throw the jacket off. "Hey!" April protests. "I wasn't done."

"Yes, you are."

"No, I'm—"

I grab her wrists. "April."

Her breath catches. "Y-Yes?"

"Tell me how long you've been working today."

"I…" She pauses. "How long's the sun been down again?"

I'm taking that as an answer. "We're going to eat."

"But I—"

"We're going to eat," I repeat, firm. "Because, frankly, I'm fucking starving."

It's not a lie, but it's not exactly the truth, either. I pecked enough at the Venus Lounge to tide myself over until later. But one look at April tells me it's a miracle if she's had breakfast, let alone lunch.

It should make me furious: my child's in there, for fuck's sake. How can she be so irresponsible? Skipping meals, losing track of time?

And yet, the *pakhan* in me is… appeased. Proud, even.

After the huge disappointment my *vory* have proven themselves to be, it's refreshing to see someone working her ass off. Someone who still knows the meaning of the word. If half of my men worked as hard as April, we'd have conquered the world by now.

The biggest irony of all is, she doesn't have to do that. If she asked me to provide, I would.

For fuck's sake, she's *pregnant*. Soon enough, she's going to have a whole kid to care for. Even I'm not enough of an asshole to ignore that. Distance or not—if she asked, I'd say yes.

But she hasn't.

"Okay." April nods eventually.

Only then do I let her wrists go.

The loss of warmth nearly gives me whiplash. I'm overcome with the urge to yank her back, to press myself flush against her and never fucking let her go.

But I won't.

"Okay," I reply. "So let's eat."

Distance. That's what I need to focus on right now. I can't let myself go soft like my *vory*—I won't. I have to stay sharp. Most importantly, I have to stay the fuck away.

This little vixen's thrown my life in disarray enough already.

After the enemy's been dealt with, I promise myself. *Once that's done, I'll move back out. I'll visit the kid. I'll be here for dinner.*

And I won't stay a minute more.

Until then…

Until then, I'll have to get a goddamn grip.

47

APRIL

Elias stares at the packed clothes in front of him. "This is all of them?"

"Yep, that's all." I feel like a little soldier reporting for duty—all that's missing is the salute. "I hope my blood, sweat, and tears didn't leak on them."

Elias lets out a booming laugh. "Oh, child. You're really something else."

We sit down for tea. That's a good idea, seeing as how the living room's started to spin again. Lately, it's been doing that a lot.

Elias shoots me a fond smile. "Is there really nothing I can do to convince you to take it easy?" he asks, concern seeping into his voice.

I shake my head. "Actually, I was going to ask you for more work."

My boss nearly drops his cup. "*More* work? April, you've cleaned me out for the month."

"I could get started on next month's tasks?" I venture. "Early bird gets the worm and all that?"

"If you've got all that time on your hands, you should spend it on your baby," Elias playfully scolds me. "Knitting tiny socks. Making onesies."

Wordlessly, I show him a picture of Nugget's wardrobe.

Elias's eyes bulge. "You made all that?"

"Almost. Some of it's from Matvey. And, well, the aunts and uncles," I add, which is code for Yuri and Petra. Who both separately went on shopping sprees, apparently. I don't know which one was wearing the sourest face when they dropped the gifts into my lap.

As for Charlie, well—he's still on house arrest. But he's been texting me pictures of Minecraft-themed baby shoes all week.

All in all, I could've slacked off.

Except that I didn't. And there's a very good reason for that. "I just…" I put on my best puppy eyes. "I want to keep busy. I'm going crazy in here, Elias. Please?"

The reason I'm going crazy?

Matvey.

To say he's been acting weird is an understatement. He's late to dinner, leaves at the crack of dawn, and doesn't speak a word to me if he doesn't absolutely have to. I went to pick a piece of lint off his shoulder the other day and I could swear he almost lunged for his gun.

But I can't let myself think about it. I can't let myself obsess over it; I'm gonna go insane. Frankly, I feel like I've already started.

So I'm going to do what I do best: deep-dive into my work. The more grueling, the better.

"Alright, alright," Elias relents. "I can see I'm not going to change your mind. I admit defeat."

"You're a saint amongst men, Elias. Thank you."

After getting my assignments, I hug my boss goodbye at the door.

"Oh!" Elias says. "Almost forgot." He hands me a pamphlet.

I take it with a frown. I recognize the location printed on the front: the Mallard Expo Hall. At the center, a beautiful blue gown with a matching tiara, all diamond-studded from head to toe. "Last year's winner?" I guess.

My boss nods. "The designer called it *Opulence.* A fitting name."

"Yeah, no wonder," I mutter bitterly. "This piece is probably worth more than all my organs combined."

"And mine," Elias agrees.

The Mallard Fashion Expo: the impossible dream of every designer out there. Every year, they hold a fashion contest for new talent. Technically, anyone's free to join.

Realistically? The winning pieces usually look like *this.*

In a word: *expensive.*

"What's the grand prize this year?" I ask anyway. Because, apparently, I enjoy torturing myself. "Tour of European fashion museums? Internship at Versace? Interview with Vivienne Westwood via Ouija board?"

"A scholarship for the Mallard Institute."

I stop snarking on the spot. "You can't be serious."

"Oh, dead serious," Elias assures me. "Three years, full ride."

The living room starts spinning again. This time, I have to hold myself up against the back of the couch.

A full ride. To the *Mallard Fashion Institute.* The single most prestigious fashion academy in New York City.

"That's... nice," I croak at last. "Whatever rich kid wins that is going to make their parents really happy. Let them buy the fourth mansion of their dreams."

If I sound salty, it's because I am. No one ever wins these contests who couldn't buy their way into the prizes in the first place. Touring Europe? That's the Upper East Side's run-of-the-mill summer vacation. Interning at Versace? With the right connections, you'd get a job there before you even graduate. And now, attending Mallard?

If it's a joke, it's a really poor one. Pun intended.

But Elias doesn't seem to agree. With a soft smile, he puts his hand on my shoulder. "Oh, April. Why do you never give yourself a chance?"

I swallow. Elias's words hit deeper than I'd like. "I just..." *Don't want to get my hopes up. Not again.* "I just have so much on my plate. You know, with the baby and all."

"Promise me you'll consider it," Elias says with a squeeze of my shoulder.

I give a small nod. "Alright. I promise."

It's a lie. But sometimes, lies are easier. Lies make everybody happier.

Elias hugs me goodbye once more. "Your grandmother would be proud, you know. Of the woman you've become."

I don't answer. I don't think I can.

As soon as Elias is in the elevator, Petra rounds the corner. "Who's that?"

"Good morning to you, too."

She drops her bag unceremoniously on the table. "And why are your eyes red?"

I rub them off with the back of my hand. "New shampoo. Wanted to test if that 'No Tears' thing was real."

"It's a scam," Petra huffs. "It means 'No Tearing.' As in, no tangles and whatnot."

"That's not very nice."

"No, it's not." She snatches a Greek yogurt from the fridge. "So who was that?"

"My boss." I shrug. "Clothes hand-off. Nothing exciting."

"*That* looks exciting," she comments, giving the crumpled pamphlet in my hand a pointed look. "Since you're trying to hide it and all."

Crap. Should've known better than to play this game with Mrs. Bond here. "It's just something Elias brought over."

"Something secret?"

I sigh. "Something ridiculous."

"Gimme." She motions for me to hand it over.

"You know, you're almost as controlling as your fiancé."

"'Almost'? You insult me." She gives the pamphlet a quick scan. "This doesn't look ridiculous."

"It does if you're broke," I reply. "It does if you're me."

"Why?"

"Because."

"Oh, right, thanks," she drawls. "I completely understand now."

I roll my eyes. "It's the Mallard! No one from public school goes to the Mallard."

"This doesn't say anything about entry requirements."

"It's implied." I throw myself down on a chair. "Like with any other fashion school, really."

Petra puts the pamphlet down and stares me in the eye. "I think you're full of shit."

That shuts me up.

"Humor me," she presses. "What happens if you compete? What happens if you win this?"

"Well..." I try to find the words. "The Mallard Fashion Expo's like an audition. If you win the contest, you pass. If you pass, you've got your foot in the door of the fashion world."

"Doesn't sound like a total waste of time to me."

"Well, it is," I insist. "It's a cutthroat environment. The competition's insane. And everyone's filthy rich, so they've got access to the best materials: silk, cashmere, freaking *diamonds*. Like I said, there's no point."

"Like *I* said: you're full of shit. If it's so rigged, then why hold a contest at all?" Petra retorts.

I hesitate. "I guess… money doesn't always guarantee you'll make it. You also have to prove what you're worth. That's why there's an audition—lots of people want this. Lots of rich people, even. But the spots are limited. You still have to earn yours."

I watch Petra listen intently. "So if you want it, you have to take it," she summarizes.

I'm reminded of Matvey's words when we met: *You saw something you liked. You took it.*

And then—

What do you want?

I sigh. "It's complicated."

For once, Petra doesn't press. "This dress," she says instead, pointing at the diamond gown. "It's impressive. Must be worth a fortune."

"They'll put it on display at the expo," I say. "Last year's winner. They'll be announcing this year's at the same event."

"So this pamphlet's for next year?"

"Mhmm. Submissions close in a few months."

Petra's eyes fix on the tiara. "Can't imagine what security's like at events like these. That alone would feed a small country."

I'm inclined to agree. "It's probably the safest place to hang out."

"Safe enough that Matvey would let you go?"

I blink. I hadn't thought of that. "Probably? I'd still need a personal guard, I think. Unless you'd like to come," I joke.

"Sure."

"Right, didn't think s—Sorry, what?"

"I said I'll come," she repeats. "That should be enough, right?"

For a second, I wonder if I've misheard. But no—Petra's actually offering to take me somewhere. *Without* a gun to her head. Are pigs going to start flying? Do I have to check outside for airborne pork?

"Unless you've got better places to be...?" she adds.

I quickly shake my head. This is a golden opportunity. I shouldn't look the gift horse in the mouth. "Nope," I reply. "Nowhere at all."

This should make for a good conversation with Matvey, I think to myself. I'm shivering already.

48

APRIL

In the end, I don't manage to ask. Not that night. Not any of the others that follow.

I keep telling myself I should find the right time. Catch him in a good mood, maximize my chances of success.

But Matvey's never in a good mood anymore.

When he comes home, he's as silent as the grave. If I try to coax him out of his shell with a joke, he'll only give me the ghost of a smile. A twitch of his lips at best, and then it's gone just as quickly as it came.

While we're eating, he doesn't look at me. He doesn't speak to me, doesn't ask about my day. Even after Dr. Allan's visits, I'm the one who volunteers the information. I've started to suspect he's got someone looking into her files just to avoid having to bring it up with me. Having to bring *anything* up with me.

Except at night.

"Couldn't sleep?" I yawn from my room's doorway.

Matvey's head turns to me. "Just getting some water."

"Any chance I can get some, too?"

It's a new routine of sorts. When the moon is high and we're both losing our battle with sleep, we'll meet here, in the kitchen. It's always well past midnight, and there's never a single light on.

But at least, while we're here, Matvey will look at me.

I don't know why the night's different. Maybe it's the dark that makes it easier. Maybe we're both just really thirsty. Either way, I've begun to look forward to these quiet, honest moments. With family dinners having turned into grim staring contests between us and our plates, it's the only chance I get to truly *see* him again.

"Thanks." I accept the full glass from his hands. "Is work giving you trouble?"

Matvey shrugs. "Something like that."

"The tough life of a Peking."

"*Pakhan.*"

"One day, I'll remember how to say that."

I can't be sure in the dark, but I think I glimpse a smile pulling at the corner of his lips. "I'll believe it when I see it."

It makes my heart ache.

"Your work seems to be going well," Matvey comments. "A little too well, even."

"Oh, don't start growling now," I laugh. "I asked Elias for the extra load."

For once, Matvey doesn't press. Maybe a part of him is aware of the *why*. Maybe he'd rather keep the pretense alive.

Sounds like we've been doing that a lot lately: *pretending*.

"You like it," Matvey says in the end. "Sewing."

"I do, yeah," I reply. "It's the only thing I've ever known how to do. The only thing that's ever felt good."

"So you always wanted to be a tailor?"

"A designer." The word's out before I can stop myself. It seems to be another mystical power of these nights: stripping us bare. No disguises. No pretty little lies. "I love tailoring, don't get me wrong. But I always wanted to sew my own ideas. Even had a school lined up and everything."

"But you never went."

I nod. "But I never went."

"Was it about money?" Matvey asks after a moment.

I shake my head. "No. I mean, yes, but—it shouldn't have been. My grandma, she had savings. She was going to help me out. Then…"

Fortunately, Matvey doesn't make me finish that sentence. "I'm sorry, April."

I give him a grateful smile. "Yeah. Me, too."

Then I gather the strength to continue.

"What happened after was…" I hesitate. It's hard, putting certain things into words. All these ugly feelings. "All I ever wanted was to mourn, but my dad had other plans. He cleaned out the bank account, sold the house…"

"And you were left with nothing."

"Pretty much, yeah."

I curse myself for ruining our one moment together. For dragging bitterness into it. But now that I've opened the floodgates, they just won't close again. Not until everything's come rushing out. "The worst thing, to me, isn't even the money. It's that my grandma's will was ignored so blatantly. Everybody knew what she would've wanted—they just decided to pretend otherwise. It was the worst kind of betrayal."

Matvey nods gravely. "Blood should never betray blood."

"Mhmm. You've said that before."

I leave my question unspoken: *Why? What happened to you? Who betrayed you so badly you couldn't ever forget?*

I have an inkling of who that might be. After that talk with Yuri, and after seeing how Matvey reacts whenever a certain person is mentioned, it'd be hard not to guess.

But I still want him to tell me.

At first, I think he won't. That his answer will stay unspoken, too. The silence stretches for so long that, in the end, I almost lose hope. I get ready to stand up, to leave our little haven behind.

And then he speaks.

"When I was seven, my mother got sick."

I don't say anything to that. This moment feels fragile—like it could shatter with a single word out of place.

"Winters weren't like the ones here," he rasps. "You think Times Square at New Year's is cold? Try Karelian spring. It'll make January here feel like beach fucking weather."

"Is that where you're from?" I whisper. "Karelia?"

Matvey gives a curt nod. "Everybody dreaded the winter there. The coast was warmer, but we weren't on the coast. We were smack in the middle of nowhere. Nothing but snow for miles every which way."

It must've been terrible. I choke back the words. Matvey wouldn't want that: pity.

"I didn't dread it, though," he adds with a twitch of his lips. "Because she was there. My mother."

Unconsciously, I put a hand on my belly. Matvey doesn't miss the motion. "What was she like?" I ask.

"Warm."

He doesn't say it, but I try to picture it: Matvey and his mom, huddled up in front of a flickering fireplace. Finding strength in each other to get through the night.

I wonder if that's why night's easier for him. If the memories are good enough to sweeten it, even now.

"It sounds like she truly cared about you."

"She did." Then his face darkens. "She was the only one."

Here we are, I tell myself. "So your father...?"

"My father was a scumbag," he growls. "Always disappearing to God knows where. For days on end, he wouldn't show. My mother used to wait up for him all night. It was freezing cold, but she refused to go to bed. Then he'd come back with an excuse and everything would be forgiven. But every time that happened, she grew paler."

I can't even begin to imagine how that must've felt. My parents gave up on each other right away. But if one of them had made the other suffer like this…? I'd have carried that with me for the rest of my life.

"One night, she passed out. She was feverish in the morning. I did what I could, but I wasn't really any help."

I reach for his hand. "You were just a kid," I murmur. "You couldn't have done anything."

"I should've," Matvey snarls. His face twists into something vicious. Something animal. "Instead, I went out like a fucking idiot. To search for *him*."

Of course you did, I want to say but don't, because Matvey would hate it. *He was your dad.*

"By the time I came back…"

I shudder. "I'm so sorry."

"Don't be." His grip grows tighter, tighter. "He'll pay. With his fucking blood, he'll pay. Until the last goddamn drop."

He's hurting me a little bit with how hard he's squeezing my fingers, but I don't say anything. Right now, I want to feel this. Want to share in his pain in any way I can.

Wordlessly, I start rubbing circles into the back of his hand. My thumb presses into the tense muscles until, eventually, it manages to pry them loose again.

"That's why you became Bratva?" I ask. "To make him pay?"

"Yes," Matvey answers without hesitation. "But not only that. My grandfather used to be Bratva. He'd founded his own organization when he was orphaned. By doing that, he survived." He pauses. "I needed to survive, too."

"And then you met Yuri."

"Yes. He's the only family I have left."

I thought it'd hurt less to hear him cut me out like that. Now that I know where the venom comes from, I shouldn't fall to it so easily.

So why do I?

"Thank you," I breathe in the end. "For telling me this."

Matvey doesn't say anything, but I don't need him to.

And then, as I'm heading back into my room, suddenly, I stop. I turn. Matvey's still there, looking at my retreating back. Our eyes meet over the table between us.

I should go back to my side of these dark waters. I shouldn't make this messier than it needs to be—messier than it already is.

I'm not family. I'll *never* be family. But when has that ever stopped me before?

I linger on my doorway. Twenty-three steps between us, and they feel like an ocean. But my grandmother taught me that oceans can be crossed. And someone else taught me that, if you really want something—

Take it.

"Are you going to make me sleep alone?" I ask.

And, for once, Matvey doesn't.

49

MATVEY

In my life, I've never lost a battle.

I couldn't afford to. I still can't. In my world, it's eat or be eaten; kill or be fucking obliterated.

And yet, a few nights ago, April handed me my first defeat.

I've stopped sleeping in the guest bedroom. I can't bring myself to. It doesn't matter how much I harden my heart of stone—because, after dinner, April will stand up and look at me. Just *look* at me, her hazel eyes wide and filled with hope.

That's all it takes.

It's pathetic. I'm supposed to be heartless, hardened. A beast in the skin of a man. A killing fucking machine, ready to gun down whoever's in my path without the slightest hesitation.

So why can't I say no to her?

Worse, I've *told* her things. Things I'd never shared with anyone. Even Yuri doesn't know the extent of it—what my life was like before I found him. Only that our father will pay for what he's taken from me.

But I told April all of it.

Why?

Even now, it's more of the same. I should be getting ready for work, but for some reason, I'm still in bed with her. Watching the rise and fall of her pregnant belly as she sleeps, wrapped in sheets and nothing else.

As if sensing my eyes on her, April stirs. "Mmph'nning."

I quirk an eyebrow. "Am I supposed to know what that means?"

She finally drags her face away from the pillow. "G'morning."

I push my thoughts from my mind. "If you want to be convincing, you should try that with your eyes open."

Big mistake. As soon as those hazel irises are on me, I remember exactly how I lost the battle in the first place. "Top o' the mornin' to ya," she salutes. As she straightens up, the sheets drop off of her entirely. "Better?"

"Much," I answer with a pointed look.

She tries to snatch the sheets back, but I yank them to my side. "Hey!"

"Bit late to get shy on me, Ms. Flowers."

"I'm not shy; I'm cold."

It's a bold-faced lie: her cheeks are so red you could cook eggs on them.

It's the wrong thought to have. Because now, I'm picturing

eating breakfast right off her skin, and it's making me fucking ravenous.

But not for food.

"Where do you think you're going?" I ask, my tone commanding.

"Uhh, to shower?"

I wall her in with my body. "Not until I say so, you're not."

I dip my head into the crook of her neck and bite. Her reaction is instant—she chokes out a gasp, hands flying to dig into my back.

I press one finger into her, find her slick and willing. Still fucked open from last night, streaks of dried cum between her thighs. "Matvey…!"

I want to mark her everywhere. Want my scent on every inch of her. Until there couldn't possibly be any doubt who she belongs to.

I'm not anyone's. I'm Matvey Groza; I belong to myself alone.

But April Flowers is *mine*.

How? asks the last scrap of my reason. *Why? What is she to you?*

I don't answer. I don't feel like bothering with semantics right now. Or at least, that's what I tell myself.

"Matvey," April whines under me. "Matvey, *please*."

I line up my cock against her wet pussy. I'm nearly inside, the tip already pressing into tight walls, April's moans echoing in my ears—

And then my goddamn phone rings.

I'm tempted to ignore it. So, so fucking tempted.

But then I remember all my missteps these past few weeks: the lack of attention at meetings, the forgotten report on my desk—

Cursing, I whisk up my phone. "*What.*"

"Motya, it's me."

"Now is not a good time, brother."

"Is that Yuri?" April mouths below me.

I stick two fingers into her mouth to shut her up. I don't miss the way her eyes go dark and hooded at that—*blyat'*, I'm even harder now.

"It's urgent," Yuri pants. By the sound of it, he's been running. "It's better if we speak in person. Can you meet me at the loft in fifteen?"

The loft. Yuri knows I've been staying at the penthouse. If he's asking to meet there, it can only mean one thing: whatever this is must stay between us. "I'll be there in ten."

April gives a muffled groan.

I shut the call and slip my fingers out. "Next time, I'll have to gag you."

"Do you really have to go?" she blinks up at me with her doe eyes. "I know you're the Batman and everything—"

"*Pakhan.*"

"—but can't you call in sick or something?"

"It's not a government job," I deadpan, pulling away from her warm, willing body. *Someone better be ready to die for this.* "Besides, it's Yuri. If he's calling me this early…"

April's face immediately shifts to concern. "Is he okay?"

"Relax. He just sounded winded."

"Okay, good," she exhales. "You'll tell me if anything's wrong, though?"

I move my lips to say yes, then I stop. Why should I promise that? My Bratva's my business. *Mine.* No one else's.

"I'll call you," I say without elaborating. I was already planning to do that anyway. Ever since the break-in, I've sometimes been dropping surprise calls or texts. Nothing too long, just random pulse checks.

For the baby, of course.

"Okay." April beams. "Good luck."

She pecks me on the lips. That's a new part of the routine: morning goodbyes. The first time she did that, I felt like a fucking deer in the headlights. It's not the kind of goodbye I'm used to.

"Call me if there's any trouble," I say.

Then I grab a few clothes and text Grisha.

We get to the loft with a minute to spare. But Yuri's already there. "Something happened." Then he clocks Grisha and snarls, "What's he doing here?"

"He's here because I told him to be," I snap back. I'm in no mood for games, especially not now. "So are you gonna talk or not?"

Yuri swallows. He looks between us, then seems to make a decision. Good. I wasn't going to wait much longer. "It's about the D.C. plan."

That gets my attention. "What happened?"

I'm expecting news of a delay. I'm expecting to hear the *vory* are being difficult, that they're still demanding to be looped in. I'm even expecting to see an extra zero tacked on the price last minute.

What I'm not expecting is for Yuri to say, "It's over, Matvey."

"Come fucking again?"

"It's over," Yuri repeats. "The deal… it fell through."

50

MATVEY

"*Blyat'*," Petra curses after Yuri's filled her in.

My thoughts exactly. This could bust everything wide open: the operation, our dreams, all of it. That's the only reason I had Yuri call her in. Unbearable or not, she's still my business partner. If I lose, she loses.

And neither of us can afford to lose.

"Grisha, call the *vory*," I order him. "Yuri, help him."

Yuri looks like he's on the verge of arguing again, but Grisha puts a firm hand on his shoulder. "We're on it." Then he steers my brother out of the room.

"I don't get it." Petra stops pacing. "Can't we just buy somewhere else?"

"No."

"Why?"

"Because we can't."

"But *why?*"

"Because I fucking said so!" I snap.

Petra stares at me. "Matvey Groza, I swear to God, if you don't tell me what's going on right now, I'm going to marry the next guy that comes through that fucking door and take my army with me."

I ball up my fists. "I don't enjoy being threatened, Petra."

"And I don't enjoy going in blind, so how about we cut the shit and start being honest with each other?"

I take a deep breath. As much as it pains me to admit it, Yuri hasn't been completely wrong all this time. Clearly, keeping people in the dark hasn't been working as well as I'd hoped.

So I swallow my pride and spit out the truth. "It's because of the Bonaccorsi family."

Petra blinks. "The what now?"

"Bonaccorsi," I repeat, my patience thinning. "Italian mafia. Their HQ is in the building right across from the one we've been trying to buy." I unfold my plans in my mind: the maps, the schemes, all of it. "With it, we could've brought the war to them before they even realized what was happening. It would've been an absolute victory. Now, we've got nothing."

"Right," Petra mutters. "That makes perfect sense. Just one thing: why in the living hell are we picking a fight with *the D.C. Italian mafia?*"

"Because their boss took something from me," I snarl. "Something important. And now, he has to pay."

"So this... all of this..." she says. "It was for a personal vendetta all along?"

Her words rub me the wrong way. "Is there a problem?"

"Oh, I don't know," Petra snarks. "How about… *you could've fucking told me?!*"

"And if I had?" I retort. "Would that have changed the fact that your goals were just as fucking personal? Let's not be hypocrites—we were both in this for ourselves. So get off your high horse and start thinking about how to save this."

"'Save'?! There's no saving—"

"Because make no mistake," I roar over her protests, "if I go down, so do you. And don't you ever fucking forget that."

That finally shuts her up.

For a long moment, silence reigns in the room. Then: "What's the first thing that needs fixing?"

"The *vory*," I answer immediately. "They've been pushing back against me all this time. Now, my blood's in the water."

"So we can't let them smell weakness," Petra completes for me.

This is the Petra Solovyova I struck an alliance with: cunning, vicious, straight to the point. Above all, practical.

I don't need the screaming fiancé—I need the fierce fucking warrior.

"We should go ahead with the wedding."

I do a double-take. "Come fucking again?"

"Think," Petra urges, calculations all but running in her eyes. "A wedding's a show of strength. Unity. Most of all, it will double your ranks. With that kind of power at your fingertips, the *vory* won't dare question you. It won't just be about fear—it'll be about respect. You're going to give them the biggest win they've ever seen; why would anyone move against you then?"

I thought she was speaking nonsense. But the more she explains, the more her plan makes sense. Right now, what matters most is buying time. Time to regroup, rethink, react. And our wedding would buy that in spades.

So why do I feel like it's the last thing I want to do?

"It won't work," I hear myself saying. "It's not enough. Besides, we need to actually solve the D.C. problem first."

"No, not enough—but you just said the priority were the *vory*," Petra argues. "Isn't D.C. the long game? So why—" Then she stops. "Oh. *Oh.* You just don't want to do it."

"I don't want to what, Petra?"

"You don't want to get married," she says, stunned. "You've changed your mind, haven't you?"

I open my mouth to deny it. To reject the insinuation with every fiber of my being. I'm a goddamn machine; there is nothing I won't do to achieve my goals.

So why can't I say it?

My mind fills with images: April, rubbing the sleep from her face. April, smiling at me from the kitchen. April, looking up from her plate with a different kind of hunger in her eyes.

April, moaning my name in bed this morning.

I've been telling myself it was about the kid. All along, I've been telling myself that.

And, all along, I've been lying.

Because it stopped being about the kid a long time ago. That child is my family, my *blood*, but April—

April's something, too. And I'm tired of pretending she's not.

As if reading my mind, Petra's expression turns horrified. "*Blyat'*, it's because of her."

"That's nonsense."

"No, it's not. It's the only thing that makes sense. You were perfectly willing to go through with this before, and now, you're not—so what changed?"

"Petra, I'm warning you—"

"Warn me all you like," she says, still sounding dazed. "She's the only thing that's changed. She changed *you*."

I grit my teeth. "Like fuck she did."

"Like fuck she didn't!" Petra yells at last. "Look at you!"

"Petra—"

"You still *smell like her*!"

"Will you just SHUT THE FUCK UP?!"

Petra reels back as if slapped. It's not the first time I've yelled at her, but it's the first time I've raised my voice like this. The first time I *meant* it.

And then I follow her gaze towards the door—and I see Yuri and Grisha staring at us.

How long have they been here? I ask myself. *How much did they hear?*

"Fine," Petra grits, humiliated. "You know what? Fine. Go marry your fucking whore or whatever. I'll do it myself."

"Petra."

"I've always done it on my own!" she bursts out, too far gone for a dignified exit. "I've always had to pave my own way, so what's new? I'll make *vor* on my terms. I'll do it all by my own damn self."

And she storms out.

I know I should try to stop her. It would be the smart thing to do. But those words—*go marry your fucking whore*—are still ringing in my ears, making my hand twitch for my gun.

So I don't stop her.

I watch my last hope go charging out the door... and I don't say a thing.

51

APRIL

"You don't understand, June—I *completely* forgot to tell him!"

This is a disaster. Total, utter chaos.

Because the day of the Mallard Expo has come, and I still haven't managed to tell Matvey.

It's not that I didn't want to. It's just that there was all that awkwardness before. All those silences. And after...

Well, after, I just kind of lost track of time. And space. And anything that wasn't Matvey's hands, or his voice, or his—

On the other end of the line, June clicks her tongue. "So what? He's not your keeper or anything, is he?"

I wince. "He... kind of is."

Not only am I wracked with guilt about this, I'm also in a complete panic. I grabbed the first dress I could find—the *first dress!* For a fashion expo!—and now, I'm turning the closet inside out to find the shoes that go with it. Why is it that, as soon as you're in a hurry, everything you need is suddenly located in another dimension?

"Besides, we'll have Pyotra with us—"

"Petra," I correct distractedly as I throw yet another pair of wrong shoes behind my shoulder.

Great. Not only have I lied to him, but now, I'm also trashing his place.

"Whatever. She's got hired muscle, no?"

I bite my lip. "Well, yeah, but I've been trying to reach her all morning and she hasn't replied to a single one of my texts. Maybe something came up and she can't make it?" I give up on finding a pair of coordinated shoes and just go with the black ones. When in a pinch, always go with black.

"Maybe she's driving there as we speak."

"Please," I snort. "Petra? Driving herself? Pigs will fly sooner."

"Now, I'm even more curious to meet this mystery woman."

Not only did I forget to tell Matvey about today, I also forgot to tell Petra that June was coming. It was a spur-of-the-moment invite. I really hope she won't mind.

I fumble with a pair of black pearl earrings. This way, at least my shoes will match something. Except that even the earrings are refusing to cooperate.

I throw my hands up in despair. "Forget it. We should just cancel."

"Absolutely not!" June thunders. "This is our first outing since you got jailed!"

"Put under protection," I correct gently.

"To-may-to, po-tah-to."

One earring goes in. *Small victories.* "That's not how it goes, Jay."

She blows me a raspberry in response. "I'm walking down to the car. If you're not in the lobby in twenty minutes, I'm coming up to get you. And yes, that's a threat."

I prick my finger on my other earring. "Goddammit! Why won't you just—"

And then the doorbell rings.

"Coming!" I yell. "June, I think Petra's here."

"And I'm almost at the car," June replies. "C'mon, don't leave me hanging. You know I hate going down these creepy stairs alone."

"It's not the stairs that are creepy," I point out. "It's the neighbors."

"Po-tay-to, to-mah-to."

I throw the door open. "Again, that's not how it—"

The first thing I see is Petra's face: red, tear-streaked, as if she's been crying herself stupid.

The next thing I see is her gun...

And it's pointed right at me.

∾

"Hang up," she orders. "Now."

"Petra, what's going on?"

"Hang. Up." She shoves her gun into my face, silencer and all. "I'm not gonna ask twice."

Automatically, I glance towards the spots my bodyguards usually are. I've long given up learning their names—lately I've just been calling them Big Guy and Tall Guy.

But now, I wish I'd bothered.

Both of them are on the ground. I can only catch a glimpse of their bodies, face-down on the hallway floor. Are they dead? I can't tell.

Finally, my brain catches up to what's happening.

Finally, it remembers to be afraid.

I obey Petra's order. I hang up while June's still talking, asking me something I didn't catch.

I hope she didn't recognize her. As far as I know, Petra's never heard June's voice before. Suddenly, I'm glad I forgot to mention her.

"Lena, Julia," Petra calls over her shoulder. "Take care of the mess."

Without a word, the twins drag the bodyguards away.

"You," she barks at me. "In. Now."

Swallowing, I comply.

This is wrong, a part of me insists. *This can't be happening. This is Petra we're talking about.*

She wouldn't hurt *me.*

"What's going on?" I croak. "Why are you...?"

"You should be asking your boyfriend that."

The words strike me dumb. "Matvey's not my boyfriend."

"No?" Petra's face is a mask of ice and fury. "Then I guess he won't mind me borrowing you."

The twins reappear behind Petra's back. They look torn—like they'd rather be literally anywhere else but here.

"Restrain her," Petra orders.

The twins obey. "Sorry, April," Lena murmurs in my ear as she twists my hands behind my back.

"We really don't have a choice," Julia adds with her palms on my shoulders.

I realize that I should be struggling. Should be screaming, kicking, begging for mercy.

But Petra said *borrow*. However much this may look like an execution—

She still needs me.

I try to calm myself. To *think*. What would she need me for? A hostage?

Then I notice the way she's dressed. Even though her face is a mess, her clothes aren't. In fact, everything on her body screams upper class. She's not normally this elegant. Tasteful, yes, but never overdressed.

Also, her dress is pure white. Call me old-fashioned, but if I was going to blow someone's brains out, I'd at least wear black. It goes with everything, remember?

Even blood.

"Where are we going?" I ask with a trembling voice.

Petra's lips curve into a smirk. "Clever *koshka*. If only Matvey was half as clever as that."

"What did he do?" I stammer, trying to connect with her. Trying to understand.

"He broke our deal," Petra hisses. "So now, I'm honoring mine."

Her gun slides down my cheek like an unwanted kiss. The silencer feels cold against my skin. I try to suppress a shiver, but I fail.

She looks pleased by that: my fear of her. "I told him I wouldn't harm a petal on his pretty little flower's crown... as long as he held up his end of the bargain. But he didn't. He went back on his word. So I have no reason to keep my promise, either."

"This isn't you," I blurt out. It's pathetic—that even with a literal gun to my head, part of me still believes in her. *Wants* to believe in her. "We're friends... aren't we?"

Petra bursts out laughing. There isn't a trace of humor in it: instead, it's a dark and bitter sound. Cold, like the ice in her eyes. "Friends? *Us?*"

Her mask falters. The ice cracks. For a single moment, I can see the conflict on her face. I can see a sliver of hope.

And then her expression shutters again. "We were never friends, April."

Her gun starts trailing downwards: throat, heart, guts. "Petra..."

"Quiet," she snaps. "Or I'll find another way to get what I want."

Finally, the silencer reaches my belly.

For the first time since this nightmare began, I feel a flash of fury. "Don't you dare touch—"

"Then be fucking quiet."

I shut my mouth. With Nugget's life on the line, nothing else matters.

"Good." Petra smiles sweetly. "Now, listen closely. I have no interest in crushing Matvey's toys. He may be an oath-breaker, but I still have honor."

"That's a relief," I mutter sarcastically.

"So keep being good," she warns, pressing the gun harder into my abdomen, "and, after this, I'll let you go. I just need you to do one thing for me."

I set my jaw. So many emotions are warring inside me: rage, fear, heartbreak. If I don't keep myself in check, I'm terrified I'll overflow.

So I do what I do best: I assess the situation. I calculate risk and reward. Most of all, I keep my cool.

"What do you need?"

With her free hand, Petra whips out a pamphlet. It's the same crumpled one I'd shown her that day—I had no idea that she'd kept it. Had she been planning this all along?

Or did she hold on to it for a different reason entirely?

I chase that thought out of my head. It doesn't matter anymore; Petra made her position perfectly clear.

We were never friends.

"Since your boyfriend won't help me anymore, you will." She throws the pamphlet on the table and points. "You're going to help me audition. You're going to help me make *vor*."

I stare at the spot under her manicured finger. "'Audition'?"

"Do you know what *vor* means in Russian, *koshka?*"

"Weirdly, it never came up on my Duolingo lessons."

I glance at the pamphlet again. Her long nail taps against the paper, making a dent into her mark.

A tiara. A diamond-studded tiara worth millions.

Petra grins, baring her teeth. Like this, she looks every bit the predator. The killing nightingale. "It means '*thief.*'"

52

MATVEY

She's not at her place. The twins aren't picking up, either.

I toss my phone aside without replying. Yuri's texts are doing nothing to improve my mood—in fact, it's the opposite.

I don't care where Petra is or what she's doing. I never asked to be kept in the loop. And I definitely never told Yuri to go after her in the first place.

So why the hell is he still out there?

"Just called Vlad with an excuse," Grisha suggests, stepping back into the room. Thank fuck someone is aware we're in crisis mode right now. "He was perfectly polite. Didn't seem like a man who's been told his daughter was just scorned."

"Good."

"I still wasn't able to get a read on the D.C. fall-through."

That's our biggest concern. After all this shit hit the fan, we're still completely in the dark about what fucked us over to begin with. "Show me the system logs."

Every time our *vory* work on acquisitions, they're obligated to log into the Groza Group company system and report their progress. When Grisha first suggested it, I thought it was a bunch of useless extra steps and almost stomped out the idea. I only ended up agreeing because it would let us keep an eye over the *vory*'s activities.

Now, we'll see if it was worth it.

"I have them right here. But..." Grisha hesitates. "I checked in with Ivan and the others. Since everyone was working on this, it appears they haven't been consistent with the logging. If two or more people handled a certain step, they'd just log it under the name of whoever was nearer to his computer. So I'm afraid these won't necessarily show us the person who took point on each passage."

I slam my fists on the table. "You're telling me they've been fucking sloppy on this? On the one thing that mattered?"

"Basically, yes."

I grit my teeth so hard I wouldn't be surprised to hear them crack. "Goddamn *mudaki.* Somebody's head will roll for this."

I yank the documents out of Grisha's hands. I'm about to scan them with red-veined eyes, ready to punish whoever dropped the ball on this, when my phone rings.

I pick up without looking and snarl, "If you're calling me about her again, Yuri, I swear—"

"So you know where she is?!"

I blink. The voice that came out the other end right now certainly isn't Yuri's.

That's when I glance at the display. "You shouldn't have this number," I growl.

"Clearly, you have mine," June Evans replies. "So I guess we can skip introductions. But still, nice to meet you or whatever, Mr. Baby Daddy."

"You have exactly five seconds to tell me why you're calling. After that, I'm hanging up and sending my men to find out."

Turns out, she only needs one. "It's about April."

My senses go on high alert. "Explain yourself."

June seems to hesitate. Then, all in one breath: "I was supposed to meet her at the hotel today. We were on the phone earlier and suddenly, the call cut off, so I thought maybe her phone died, but then I got to the hotel and she wasn't there and the gorillas weren't there, either—"

I filter out the panic and zero in on the one piece of information that really matters.

April's gone.

It's fifteen minutes by car from my apartment to the hotel.

I make Grisha get me there in five.

"Oh, good, you're here!" June rushes over to us as we step out of the elevator. "Also, wow, she wasn't kidding. You're *tall*."

"Ms. Evans," I greet curtly, "I'm not a patient man. If you have anything else to add, now would be a good time to get to the point. If not, I'd suggest you go home." Then I turn to Grisha. "Check the cameras. Also, get a hold of Yuri. I don't care where Petra's fucked off to—I need him *here*. Now."

"Wait, Petra's missing, too?"

June's words make both our heads turn. "How do you know Petra?" I demand.

"Well, I don't exactly *know* her," June rambles. "Of course, I know *of* her—"

"Ms. Evans. To the point. Now."

June purses her lips, arms crossed. "Jeez, she wasn't kidding about this, either. You're, like, super bossy."

I'm seconds away from resorting to enhanced interrogation techniques when Grisha clears his throat. "Ahem. You mentioned you and Ms. Flowers had some kind of engagement. Is that correct?"

"That's right," June says. "We were supposed to go to the Mallard."

"That's impossible," I bark. "If April had any plans to go out, I would know."

"Riiiight." June cringes. "She might have kinda, sorta, totally forgotten to tell you?" I feel a vein popping on my forehead. June must see it, because she starts rambling again. "But she was feeling really bad about it! Like, super guilty! She even wanted to cancel but couldn't reach Petra at all—"

"Petra was supposed to come with you?" Grisha butts in.

"I mean, yeah. She had hired muscle and all. April figured it'd be safe to go if she was protected, and Petra volunteered. She was planning to ask if it was okay but then he wouldn't talk to her and he wouldn't kiss her hand or something anymore? Anyway—"

Those words strike the anger clean off me. I was ready to go off—April had broken the rules *again*, kept something from me *again*—but as soon as June says that, I freeze.

She felt like she couldn't tell me because...?

I stride into the penthouse. My fury redirects towards a single target: *Petra.*

I take in the state of the room. There are no signs of struggle, none that would jump to the eye. The only thing that's clearly out of place is the cracked phone on the ground, one I immediately recognize as April's.

"You said your call cut off," I tell June. "How long ago was that?"

"About half an hour."

The rest of the living room's exactly as I left it.

The bedroom, on the other hand, is not.

There are clothes strewn everywhere: dresses, shoes, you name it. It looks like a bomb went off in the closet. But unless someone was interrupted halfway through robbing April's wardrobe, I'm inclined to guess this was her own doing. As if she really had forgotten she was supposed to go out.

And then, as soon as I step inside, I hear something crunch under my foot.

I bend to pick it up and look it over.

An earring. A single, black pearl earring.

Something happened, I realize. *She was interrupted while she was getting ready.*

"You," I bark. "Come here."

June obliges, her face still scrunched up in displeasure. "Here I am, charmer."

"You said you were on the phone with her. Walk me through what happened."

"First, she was trying to find clothes," June explains, stepping towards the mess at the center of the room. "She was in a panic. Hadn't prepared an outfit—which, if you know her, you know it's a tragedy."

"And then?"

"Then she was putting on her earrings." June walks over to the mirror. "She was struggling with them, though. Cursed like a sailor—for her standards, I mean. Then the doorbell rang."

That's it. She went to answer the door.

If it was Petra, she wouldn't have hesitated to open. If it was Petra…

I stride back to the kitchen and punch the counter with all my strength. "Fuck!"

Right then, Yuri rushes in. "Matvey, is it true? April's missing?"

"Yes." I glare. "And if you hadn't been out chasing butterflies, I wouldn't have to fucking loop you in!"

Yuri's face looks stricken. But right now, I don't have the bandwidth to care. He fucked up. He prioritized the wrong thing.

And so did I.

"Security footage shows April walking out with Petra and the twins," Grisha says, rushing back. "Found our men knocked out in the broom closet."

"*Blyat'*," Yuri curses. "You don't think Petra…?"

"There's nothing else to think," I grit. "It was Petra. She took April."

Everything inside me is raging: the man, the *pakhan*, all of me. Right now, that separation is gone. All that's left is bottomless fury and the urge to scorch the earth.

And something else, too, that I don't dare name.

April's in danger. My child is in danger.

If I can't find them—

That's when I feel something under my bleeding hand: a pamphlet.

I pick it up and turn it over. It's the Mallard Expo, the fashion event June was going on about earlier. On the front, a diamond-studded dress with a sparkling tiara.

The winning piece will be on display from 9:00 am to 11:00 pm on the day of the exhibition.

Then I remember something else. Something Petra said before storming out this morning.

"'I'll make *vor* on my terms,'" I whisper, pieces finally falling into place.

Yuri frowns. "What was that?"

"I know where April is. I know where they both are." Everyone in the room turns to me. "Grisha, stay on damage control. Keep the *vory* occupied and unaware. Yuri, with me."

"Yes, *moy pakhan*," they both reply in unison.

As I'm striding out, I hear someone call out to me. "Wait!"

June rushes up to join us. "You'll bring her back safe, won't you? You'll bring them both back safe?"

I don't even give myself time to think about it. "I give you my word."

And this time, I won't break it.

53

APRIL

The car ride to the expo is… awkward, to put it lightly.

I'm squeezed between Petra and one of the twins. I can't tell which one it is, only that her face is a mask of guilt and shame. Her loose grip on me feels like a constant apology.

When we get there, Petra barks, "Julia, you're on camera duty. Loop the footage, then scrub us out. Lena, you're on getaway."

They both nod. The twin at the wheel—Lena, I assume—stays put, while Julia escorts me out of the car. She's incredibly careful, watching my belly all through my climb out, as if to make sure I don't bump it by accident.

But there's no such care in Petra's grip. Her hand locks like a vise around my arm, almost trembling with rage.

She's not herself. The awareness sinks into me more and more with every step she forces me to take. She's not just furious—she's *hurt*. Lashing out like a wounded animal.

I wonder, not for the first time, what the hell happened with Matvey. Why would he break off their deal? After everything they've been through, why would he suddenly refuse to marry her?

Aren't you glad? a selfish voice chortles inside my mind. *Isn't a part of you secretly happy about this?*

Feeling guilty, I chase those thoughts away. Then I turn to my captor. "What's my role in this?" I finally ask. "What are you expecting me to do?"

Petra's poison smile is as sweet as ever. "You're a woman of many talents, April. I'm sure you'll figure it out."

That stops me dead in my tracks. "Wait. You don't have a plan?"

"I don't need one. I have you." With that, she yanks me forward again. "Didn't you forge Matvey's signature? Didn't you steal his hair for that DNA test? Didn't you escape two armed kidnappers with only your wits and pretty face?" Her smile turns sharp, cruel. "You'll think of something. If not for yourself, then for that tiny life inside you."

The threat to my child makes me bristle, but I force myself to keep my cool—because something else just dawned on me.

This is wrong. This is all kinds of wrong. Petra's a stone-cold assassin: calculating, clever, always one step ahead of everyone else. It's unthinkable she'd come all this way without an inkling of a strategy.

But then again, wasn't it unthinkable that she'd threaten you at gunpoint, too?

Wasn't it unthinkable that she'd threaten your child?

As angry and hurt as I am, too, I can't let those emotions cloud my judgment. Because I just realized what my mission is here. My *real* mission.

One: to save Nugget.

Two: to save my own skin.

Three: to save Petra from herself.

So I take a deep breath, count back from ten, and say, "We're going to need a map."

Apparently, luck hasn't forsaken me forever.

We find our maps right at the entrance. Petra swipes one from the neat pile of trifold brochures and holds it open in front of us with a single hand. The other one is, of course, still threatening to snap my arm at the first wrong move. Definitely not the most charming date I've been on.

"Pen," I request.

Petra frowns at my commanding tone, but I don't have time to be polite. This is a job. Work Mode is the only way I'll get through it.

Correction: the only way I'll get both of us through it.

"Let's take a turn around the room."

"I didn't realize we were two Victorian maidens," Petra mutters.

"You want to keep sassing me out or you'd rather keep your freedom?"

Glowering, she obliges.

We walk around the exhibition a couple of times. In any other situation, I'd have a blast here: the gowns dripping in jewels, the stunning accessories, the artists' commentaries underneath. I could spend hours staring at each piece, each detailed explanation of how it came to be. I could be here with a friend by each side.

But that's not how it happened. And crying over it won't put the spilled milk back in the bottle.

As I jot the final notes down on the map, the grip on my arm tightens. "Are you playing me for a fool, *koshka?*"

"I'm sorry, what?"

"You're buying time," she says icily. "You're hoping *he'll* come save you."

I can't deny it's crossed my mind. Petra still doesn't know about June, so with any luck, she'll have reached out to Matvey by now.

But I know better than to put all my eggs in one basket. "You're wrong."

After all, last time I called, Matvey didn't answer.

"Don't fuck with me, April," Petra hisses into my ear. "You haven't seen me angry yet."

I sincerely doubt that. "And you haven't seen *me* angry," I hiss right back, frustration finally bubbling up to the surface. "So don't you fuck with me, either."

Then I shove the map in her hand.

The expression on her face is like cracking ice—a frozen lake thawing out beneath your feet. But as her eyes scan the map, I can see the realization slowly dawning. "This is…"

"The position of every security guard in here," I fill in with a touch of acid. "You're welcome."

"How do you know this is all of them?" Her eyes narrow. "We haven't been to this side yet."

I shrug. "By all means, lead the way."

Suspicious, Petra drags me to the north side of the exhibit. I watch as her gaze flits between the map and the guards—all positioned exactly like I drew them.

Is it bad that I'm enjoying the dumbfounded look on her face?

Eventually, I take pity on her. "I've been here with Elias last year," I confess. "A friend of his was in the competition. He invited him to the runway show. I came as Elias's assistant, so we both got backstage passes."

"So you've been here before."

More like I memorized the entire layout running around on errands. "The guards are in the same places they were last year. I don't think they switch it up that much. There's just more of them because of the diamond piece."

"Which reminds me: where *is* the piece?"

"Attention!" a voice calls from the loudspeakers. "The fashion show is about to begin. Please make your way to the runway."

The crowd starts to shift. Like a body of water, they all converge towards a single direction: a set of double doors.

"You want your piece?" I whisper into Petra's ear. "There's your piece."

I watch her eyes go wide with realization.

"They're going to show it off," she murmurs. "On the runway."

I nod. "Afterwards, it'll end up in a case just like all the other ones. It'll become untouchable."

I see her face go from pale to red: fear, doubt, rage—the whole spectrum. "So how do we take it?"

"We don't." I turn to face Petra and, for the first time since this nightmare began, I allow myself to smile. "They're gonna *give* it to us."

54

APRIL

Admittedly, it's easier to be smug when it's all theoretical.

It takes a few tries to sneak into the staff area. When we do, I push Petra into the locker room and shove a uniform in her arms. "Put this on," I tell her. "Quickly. Before anyone comes in."

It's the museum guide uniform, the one with the green blazer. I curse mentally: the blue blazer of the runway hostesses would have sped things up tremendously. With that, we could've strutted into the backstage like we owned the place.

But this is the only spare lying around, so we'll have to make do.

Petra glares daggers at me. "And let you go? No way."

"We don't have time to argue."

"If you think for one second—"

I lose my patience then. I even forget to be terrified as I yell in the face of the most dangerous assassin I've ever met, "You wanna hold hands or you wanna make *vor*?!"

Then I realize what I've done.

For a moment, Petra's mouth opens and closes like a goldfish. I wonder how she's gonna do it: single bullet to the head? Knives? How long do I get to pray for my immortal soul?

But, surprisingly, she doesn't snuff me out. Not yet, at least. She just up a finger and growls, "One wrong move—"

"And I'm sleeping with the fishes," I rush to finish. "Understood."

Still narrowing her eyes at me, Petra finally lets go. "No funny business," she reiterates. "And turn around while I change!"

I face the door and exhale, forcing my heart to slow. *Calm down. Keep your cool, April. This is all for Nugget.*

I listen in for any sign of someone coming in. But with the guests all converging towards the runway, I doubt the staff's got time to powder their faces. If this is anything like the time I assisted Elias here, the hostesses for both sides of the event must be running around like headless chickens.

That's when it finally dawns on me: *Holy shit, I'm pulling a heist.*

I glance at the clock on the wall. Somewhere, a part of me is still holding out hope. Hope that Matvey will come for me.

"I'm done."

I turn. The uniform fits her nicely enough—bit tight around the waist, maybe, which is odd, since Petra's figure is nothing to scoff at. But then again, this is the fashion industry we're talking about. Size eight means two sizes too big.

"Why did *I* have to do this?" she complains. "Why not you?"

"I mean…" I point at my gigantic pregnant belly. "Do you see a uniform lying around that can cover up *this*?"

Begrudgingly, Petra concedes. "Fine. But if you try anything—"

"Fishes, sleep—I know."

When she grabs my arm again, I don't make a move. No matter how much I want to run, it would be pointless to even try.

If only Matvey were here. I shake that thought away. Matvey *isn't* here. I can't rely on him to save me over and over again.

This time, I'm gonna have to save myself.

Petra side-eyes me. "What next?"

"Now, you escort me to the bathroom."

"Excuse me?"

I sigh, exasperated. "You're staff. I'm pregnant. You're escorting me to a bathroom—that's our cover story. Unless you'd rather broadcast our status as thieves?"

"Jeez, fine." She rolls her eyes. "No need to be such a bitch about it."

"Say that again when you're kidnapped," I mutter, unable to stop myself. "We'll see how you like it then."

Something flashes across her face then—something like guilt. But it's gone as fast as it came. "Let's get on with it."

Silently, we leave the locker room behind.

It takes less than two minutes for a burly man to come charging at us. "You!" he barks. "What are you doing here?"

Out of the corner of my eye, I see Petra twitch for her knives. I don't have time to think about self-preservation. So I do the only thing I can think of: I elbow her in the ribs, *hard*.

"Sorry!" I yelp at the newcomer. "I wasn't feeling well. She was just—escorting me."

For a second, I wonder if Petra's going to kill two birds with one stone. Like, literally.

Then I feel her grip relax just a little.

"… to the bathroom," she adds through gritted teeth.

"My feet are killing me today." I nod along and put on my best puppy dog eyes. "I went searching on my own and got totally lost. Plus, the baby's been kicking like crazy."

The man in front of us seems to mellow a bit. I glance at his nametag—*Bobby, Assistant Manager*. "Fine," he says gruffly. "Help our guest, then get your ass to the ticket booth. Fashion show starts in ten."

"Will do." Petra smiles, all sweet and poisonous.

I send a mental prayer out for this guy's soul. Petra's perfectly capable of settling matters here, then finding out where Bobby lives and making him eat his words. Possibly with a side of knives.

"And put your nametag on!" he calls after us.

By my side, I hear her mutter, "I'll put my nametag up your—"

I drag Petra out of earshot. As soon as we're around the corner, I hiss, "Are you insane? Were you actually going to kill that guy?"

She seems shocked that I'd dare cross her like this. In my predicament, it's certainly not the smartest thing to do. But I can't let other people get hurt because of me.

"What?" she snaps. "It's not like anyone would miss him."

"I didn't come here to kill, Petra," I hiss. "I came here to help. So let me help."

Something in my words must get through to her, because I watch her mask of ice crack just a little deeper. "And how are you planning on doing that?"

"Do you trust me?"

It's a stupid question: of course Petra doesn't trust me. She kidnapped me. She held me at gunpoint. She forced me to come up with a plan to steal millions in diamonds, risking my freedom in the process.

She threatened *my child.*

So why is a part of me still hoping she'll say yes?

Petra's expression shutters. The cold seeps back in, turning everything to frost. "I trust you to do whatever it takes to keep yourself alive."

I nod, swallowing my disappointment. "Good enough. Then follow me."

Wordlessly, she does.

Getting backstage is a nightmare. Everywhere we turn, there seems to be someone just around the corner: staff, guards, angry businesspeople yelling into their phones.

But somehow, we manage.

The second we sneak into the changing room, I push Petra behind a privacy screen. "Alright, clothes off. Now."

"I beg your pardon?"

I glance around and see the first models starting to line up for the show. "We don't have time to argue," I say. "Do you want your tiara or not?"

Without waiting for a reply, I swipe a black trench coat from the coat rack. Then, rummaging through the pockets, I find a pair of sunglasses and put them on. "I'm gonna need your dress, too."

I'm expecting resistance, but Petra simply hands me her bag. "Watch your hands," she warns.

I frown at her words, but immediately grasp what they're about as soon as I start going through her things. "Oh, wow. That's a lot of knives."

Then a lightbulb goes off in my head.

I get to work without a moment to spare: I grab a knife, pull the fabric taut, and start tearing the dress to pieces.

"*Blyat'*, what the hell are you doing?!" Petra screeches.

"Making you look high-fashion," I answer without glancing up. "If you're gonna strut out there, you need to look the part."

"I'm sorry—if I'm going to *what?*"

"Hey!" a blue-blazered hostess strides towards us. "You can't be here!"

"Put this on," I whisper. "Now." Then I turn and spit, "Ex-*fucking*-scuse me?"

Both Petra and the hostess in front of me seem taken aback.

"Um... this room is models-only," the hostess tries, a bit less flippant now. "You're not..."

I adjust my sunglasses and channel my inner Solovyova. "Of course I'm not a goddamn model. Do I look like I'm gonna go strutting anywhere?" I spit, pushing out my belly. "I'm an *agent*, kiddo."

I'm sorry, Nugget. Mama's gonna make you an accessory to grand larceny after all.

"T-Then you sh-shouldn't be—"

"*She's* the model."

I drag Petra out from behind the privacy screen. She stumbles for a moment before catching herself, glaring daggers at the poor hostess in front of us. Her pristine white dress, once smooth like silk, hangs in tatters from her figure.

The hostess blinks a few times, like she's trying to remember Petra from the lineup. Which, of course, she can't.

But we can use that.

"Don't tell me you don't know who she is?" I pretend to be outraged. "You work in *fashion*, for God's sake. And you don't know of...!"

Crap. I should've come up with an alias earlier. My mind draws a complete blank, every Russian name I've ever known slipping out like water.

All except—

"You don't know Anna Kareni…shka?!" I correct myself at the last second.

By my side, Petra makes a sound in her throat that could be choking.

On the bright side, the hostess looks properly terrified now. "I'm sorry, ma'am, I wasn't briefed—"

"Briefed!" I scoff. "Like anyone needs to be briefed about Belarus's runway superstar! Are you hearing this, *koshka*?!"

I have no idea what that word means, but for the first time in my life, I pray it's not an insult. The last thing I need is for Petra to turn on me in anger and slaughter everyone in sight, myself included.

Luckily, she doesn't knife me. "Unbelievable," she *tsks* instead in the thickest accent she can muster. Then she sticks up her nose and looks away, the picture of a scorned, spoiled diva.

Guess it must come naturally to her.

"Thirty seconds!" a guy yells from behind the scenes.

I give the hostess my best glare. "Well? Are you going to explain to your bosses why their surprise guest star couldn't make her appearance or shall I?"

The hostess's face pales. "M-My apologies! Please, forgive my ignorance. I'll do anything, just…!"

"Anything?" I echo. "Then go fetch me a glass of sparkling water. *Stat.*"

The poor thing runs off. I make a mental note to stop by a church to cleanse my soul after this, assuming I survive. I feel icky from head to toe.

"Nice job," Petra whistles next to me. I can't tell if she's being sarcastic or not. "You should consider joining the Bratva as a spy. I might put in a good word for you when I'm *vor.*"

"Thanks, but I'd rather eat glass."

We approach the line of models. Some are still putting on the finishing touches, even now. Others are standing in front of the curtains, posing for the camera flashes to come.

At the end of the row, I glimpse the model with the tiara.

So does Petra.

Her eyes bulge. The prize in sight, right there for the taking. If she just reaches out…

"Five seconds!"

"Don't," I whisper to her before she can try something rash. "Do your part. I'll do mine."

Then the curtains lift.

55

APRIL

One after the other, the models begin to strut out. It's a slow affair: only one at a time, to better showcase the pieces. The audience oohs and aahs, praising the dresses as they're shown off.

"Here!" a breathless voice squeaks behind me. "S-Sparkling water. I didn't know if you wanted room temperature or not, so I got you both—"

It takes almost no effort on my part. The hostess is so nervous to be near me that her hands are shaking on her own. So, when I reach out for a glass...

Splash!

"Oh, dear!" I gasp.

The hostess, now drenched from head to toe, looks like she's about to cry. "I'm s-so sorry! I'll get you another! I'll—"

"Nonsense," I tut, feeling horrible on the inside. Mass and confession won't be enough; after this, I'll have to tour every church, mosque, and synagogue in the city. A redemption tour to any version of God merciful enough to listen and take pity on me. "Go change, and quickly. Here, I'll take that."

Without letting her protest, I slip the blazer off her shoulders. "B-But—"

"You don't want to meet Giorgio like this, do you?"

"Giorgio?" She blinks. "As in, Armani...?"

"Who else?" I snap. "Hurry up and change before he comes. You've got a spare, don't you?"

"M-Maybe in the staff room..." she sniffles.

"Good idea," I lie. "Now, go. Chop chop!"

The hostess hurries out again. "Sorry, Ami," I murmur, glancing at the name tag. "Once this is over, I'll send you the most expensive chocolates Matvey's credit card can buy."

Just then, I hear the crowd gasp. The chatter amps up and I peek out to see which dress has them in such a frenzy.

And then I choke.

"Incredible!"

"The fashion sense of this piece..."

"It's a metaphor. No matter how pristine we can pretend we are, in the end, we're still broken on the inside."

"So high-concept!"

I cough into my hand. Part of me wants to laugh; the other wants to cry. *I literally just ripped it up. What's high-concept about that?*

Still, heat rises to my cheeks. No matter what, it's still nice to be praised.

Then Petra returns backstage, glaring daggers. "That was humiliating!"

"That was necessary," I quip back. "What's that thing you said? I'd 'do anything to save my life'?"

"You…!"

"Oh, quit growling. All your bits were covered." I herd her behind the privacy screen again. "Put the uniform back on, then wear this."

For once, Petra doesn't argue. She slips back into the hostess uniform and puts on the blue blazer I just pilfered. "'Ami'?"

"That's you. For the next five minutes, at least."

"Enough," Petra snarls, pushing me against the wall. "Tell me what's going on. Where's my tiara?!"

Just then, the crowd roars.

The diamond-studded model struts like she owns the place. The ebony tone of her skin stands out against the pale blue of the dress, each complementing the other flawlessly. On her shaved head, the tiara sparkles with a thousand tiny teardrops.

"Listen to me," I urge. "In about sixty seconds, your tiara's gonna waltz back in here. That's when you're gonna grab it."

"Me?" Petra balks. "But you said…!"

"I said I'd do my part," I cut her off. "I never said I'd commit a crime for you."

I watch her face go up in flames. "You tricked me!"

"Then I guess we're even."

I snatch a pair of glasses from the makeup station. Then I undo my bun and push the hair tie into Petra's hands.

"Wear these," I tell her. "Play assistant. As soon as that model walks back in here, you help her out of her clothes. That's how you pass your audition. After that, you're on your own."

"That wasn't the deal," Petra fumes.

"*Deal*?" I scoff. "You kidnapped me, Petra! You held me hostage. You threatened *my child.* What part of that sounds like a 'deal' to you?"

"But Matvey...!"

"I'm not Matvey," I croak. "But you know what I was? I was your *friend.* And if that ever meant anything to you, you'll let me go."

I watch Petra's mask of ice fall apart. "April..."

But it's too little, too late. "I'm walking out that door," I tell her. "So either kill me or don't. It's your choice."

I stride out of the changing room. My heart is hammering wildly in my chest, from adrenaline and fear. But no knives come flying my way. No bullet whistles past my ear or into my skull.

I walk and walk and walk.

And Petra doesn't stop me.

≈

Melting back into the audience is easy. When we were sneaking in, there were eyes everywhere. Now, with the fashion show in full swing, no one's paying attention to anything but the runway.

I should go, I tell myself. *I should find a phone and call Matvey. I should...*

But then I hear it: commotion.

It's not the kind of sound anyone would pay any special attention to—just a bunch of things falling over, something metallic clattering to the ground, hurried footsteps. A behind-the-scenes mishap.

But I know what it really means.

It's gone south.

From the corner of my eye, I see a pair of guards rushing over.

It's a split-second decision. I don't owe Petra anything—not after what she did to me. To Nugget.

I almost hear Matvey's voice in my mind: *She's the one who came here without a plan. Who was in over her head. Who let emotions cloud her judgment. If she fails because of that, then so be it.*

But it's like I told Petra after all: I'm not Matvey.

"AHH!"

I let out a bloodcurdling scream. The audience turns to me as one; even the guards halt and about face.

I scream louder and clutch my belly.

"Miss?!" One of the guards rushes over. "Are you alright?"

"The baby..." I groan. "I think the baby's—"

At the edge of my vision, I see Petra behind the scenes: mussed-up, empty-handed, ready to run.

But then she hesitates.

For a second, I'm terrified she won't go. That she'll go back in for the tiara, kill everyone in her way. Or that she'll let herself get caught.

That's when she sees me, too.

Go, I mouth to her. *Run.*

Then I double down on my charade. I keep screaming myself hoarse, falling to the floor. The guards are on me now, clearly itching to go but unable, because the crowd is walling us all in.

And then, little by little, it becomes easier. Little by little, I don't have to force myself as much. I roll and wail like a banshee and, for the first time in the whole night, I don't have to worry about lying.

Because now, the pain is real.

56

MATVEY

The first thing I hear is sirens.

I hurl myself out of the car while it's still moving.

Yuri slows down, calling after me. "Matvey!"

But I don't hear him. I can't hear a goddamn thing. Only a sharp ringing in my ears… and those sirens.

When I see the police on the scene, the ringing gets louder. The building's being evacuated—*why*?

I'm a *pakhan*. Fear is a privilege that people like me don't have. Ever since I left that little boy I used to be behind in the Russian snow, ever since I donned the mantle of leader, I never allowed myself to feel fear again.

But when I see April heaving on the steps, I remember what it's like to be afraid.

"April!" I jump the police cordon, oblivious to the officers shouting after me.

They want to stop me?

Let them fucking *try*.

April lifts her head. When her eyes lock with mine, a wave of relief crashes over her pained face. "Matvey!" She tries to stand, but she sways.

The medic by her side holds her still. "Ma'am, you shouldn't be upright. Take deep breaths and relax, alright? The ambulance will be here soon."

I stop dead in my tracks. *Ambulance?*

"Okay." April sits back down. Even with all the pain she's clearly in, she still manages to offer the medic a polite smile. "Thank you."

The medic squeezes her shoulder in reassurance. The familiarity of that gesture almost makes me snarl in jealousy, but I force myself to calm down. This isn't the time to mark my territory.

After all, I wasn't here for her, was I?

The medic's gaze flits to me, then back to April. "I have to check up on the other guests. Can I leave you with your boyfriend?"

"Oh, he's not—"

"Yes," I cut in. "I'll take it from here."

I don't look at her then, or think about the words I just said. The weight of them. The implications.

All this time, I've been lying to myself. Telling myself that there was nothing between us, that she was nothing to *me*. That she was only mine in a way that wouldn't make me hers.

But nothing opens your eyes to what's yours like almost losing it forever.

"Alright," the medic says to me. Then, turning briefly back to April: "Keep breathing like we've been doing. In through your nose, out through your mouth. Got it?"

"Got it," she whispers. "Thank you."

With that, we're alone.

Well, not *alone*, exactly. The place is packed with people, all voicing their panic and/or outrage loudly. Whatever went down here, it's left many guests unhappy.

But I couldn't care less.

All that matters is in front of me.

If only it hadn't taken me this long to fucking *see* it.

"Are you alright?"

April hesitates. "I think... I don't know. I was fine, and then it just started to hurt." She circles her belly with both hands and breathes, hard and deep, like the doctor said to do.

I'm powerless. All this strength, this money, this influence, and I couldn't do anything to prevent this. "Does it still hurt?"

She gives a small, pained nod. "I'm scared, Matvey."

Wordlessly, I take her hand in mine.

Yuri catches up to us. "What happened? Where's Petra?"

Just hearing her name is enough to make me boil over with rage. "Nowhere near here, if she knows what's good for her."

But apparently, Petra doesn't know what's good for her. Because as soon as I say those words, the woman who put my child and its mother in danger rounds the corner in a rush with her bodyguard at her heel.

When she sees April, she speeds up.

Then she sees *me*, and she stops dead in her tracks. "Matvey."

I rise to my feet, ignoring April's tug on my hand. "You."

Petra opens her mouth, hesitates. Then she croaks, "Is she okay?"

"Is she *okay*?" I snarl, pressing up into her space. Julia tenses at her side, but I don't give her the time of day. If she so much as thinks about drawing her gun, I'll put a bullet in her eye before she can fucking blink. Her first, then her mistress. "You think you have any right to ask that? After all you've fucking done?"

"Motya..." Yuri puts a hand on my shoulder. "Maybe we should—"

I shake it off, hard. "There's only one thing we should do," I grit. "Only one thing traitors deserve."

If we weren't in public right now, I would've done it already. The second I saw her, I would've put a bullet in her head. No last words. No excuses. Just death, swift and merciless.

She tries to go around me. "April—"

"Do not fucking talk to her!"

I almost push her, but Yuri gets between us. "Matvey, let's not be rash. Think about the consequences—"

"Consequences?" I snap. "She should've thought about the consequences when she *kidnapped my woman*!"

"You broke our deal." Petra trembles. "What did you expect?"

"I expected you to be an adult." No matter how badly I want to keep yelling in her face, I'm aware people have already started to stare. So I lower my voice and spit, full of barely-concealed fury, "I expected you to keep your shit together. Most of all, I expected you not to abduct a pregnant woman and force her into a goddamn heist."

Her eyes widen at my words. "That's right," I say, twisting the knife. "She didn't even have to tell me anything. It took me five minutes in my penthouse to figure out your plan. Only, you didn't actually have one, did you?"

"Matvey…" April tries to interject.

I steamroll right over her, never taking my eyes off Petra for a second. "You thought you could ride the coattails of someone better than you, again. You thought you could make *vor* on somebody else's dime. So much for doing it yourself, right?"

"Matvey."

"And for what?" I roar in Petra's trembling face. "All this, and you haven't got a thing to show for it. No diamonds, no title, no nothing. And not a single person willing to help you out of it." I look down on her in disgust. "So congratulations, Petra Solovyova: you're finally on your own."

"Matvey, enough!"

That's when I finally turn to the source of those words.

I find April standing, struggling to stay upright. "Don't," I warn, rushing to help her back down.

But she grips my arm and refuses to sit again. "No one's

innocent in this," she breathes through the waves of pain. "Not you, not Petra—and not even me. So please, just… stop."

"She kidnapped you," I growl back. "She endangered our child."

"And I haven't forgiven her for that," April retorts. "But haven't we suffered enough?" Her eyes fill with tears. "Hasn't our baby suffered enough?"

That's when I hear it: sirens, again. An ambulance.

The *pakhan* in me is screaming with bloodthirst, clamoring for revenge with every breath. But I can't be another reason April gets hurt today.

I pull her close, then turn to Petra. "The Groza Bratva is done with you. I'm done with you. And if I ever see you again near me and mine, I will kill you. So don't even fucking try."

I can't read Petra's face at all. If I didn't know better, I'd say she's holding back tears. *Real* tears, of pain and regret.

But this is Petra Solovyova we're talking about. If she ever had a heart, it's been frozen over long ago.

She straightens herself up. Even now, she tries to make herself look dignified. "I'm sorry," she says to April and April alone.

April doesn't reply.

Then she leaves.

"Wait!" Yuri calls after her retreating back. "*Blyat!*" Then he goes after her.

I have no idea what the hell he's thinking. Is he trying to salvage the alliance? Did he not fucking hear me?

The ambulance pulls up. "Ms. Flowers?" a paramedic asks.

April nods. "That's me."

I help them load her up into the back. But when I make to get on, the same paramedic stops me.

"Are you family? Because if not, I'm afraid I have to ask you to leave."

I don't know if he's being brave or stupid. Every single one of his colleagues has already taken a step back, sensing the danger in my aura.

"It's okay." April tries to smile. "I'll be fi—*Matvey!*"

"Sir!" the paramedic insists as I push past him. "If you're not family—"

"That's exactly what I am."

April looks shocked. I suppose a part of me should be as well. Shocked that I've allowed a stranger into my sacred circle. Shocked that I declared it to the world.

But the truth is, I'm just shocked it's taken me this long.

"You want to keep me out?" I snarl. "By all means, go ahead and try."

Then I take my place at April's side.

57

APRIL

By the time we get to the hospital, I've already run through every possible worst case scenario in my head. And I mean *every* scenario.

What if I stressed the baby out too much? What if this is the fetal distress Dr. Allan's been talking about? Worse, what if she was *right*?

What was I thinking, keeping my baby inside me for so long?

The only thing keeping me from a full-blown panic attack is Matvey, his grip tight on my hand the whole way.

When the doctors finally whisk me away for tests, I feel Matvey's hand give mine one last squeeze, as if reluctant to let go. "I'll be right here."

Boyfriend. That's what the on-site medic called him earlier. *My* boyfriend.

And Matvey didn't say no.

I tell myself it was just a matter of convenience. As the doctors poke and prod at me, I repeat it in my head like a mantra: *Matvey didn't mean it.*

But then why did he call me "family," too?

There's a lot of things I could picture Matvey bending the truth about: his business, our relationship or the feelings he pretends he doesn't have.

But family's sacred to him. He'd never lie about that.

So does that mean…?

I distract myself with those thoughts for as long as I can. But when the pain in my abdomen finally subsides, my fears roar back to life, amplified tenfold.

When I find Matvey again in the waiting room, I can't hold it back anymore: I bury my face in his chest and break down.

"What if it's too late?" I sob, fat tears rolling down my cheeks. "What if it's all my fault?"

"It's not," Matvey rasps into my ear. "It'll never be your fault, April."

The way he says it, it's almost like he's claiming that responsibility for himself.

But I don't want that. If this is where it ends for the three of us, I don't want Matvey to carry that guilt. I don't want him to do it alone.

"Why did you call off the wedding…?" I mumble out, unable to keep it in any longer. "Why didn't you marry Petra?"

Matvey's breath halts. His chest stills under my cheek. In response, my heart starts hammering, as if beating for the both of us.

And then, just as Matvey's lips are parting around an answer, Dr. Allan walks in.

"Good news," she says briskly. "Your baby's perfectly healthy. What you just experienced was Braxton-Hicks. It's a common false alarm."

It's like the weight of the world has fallen off my shoulders. Dr. Allan is still talking, but my head's ringing, a single sentence playing in a loop:

My baby's okay. My baby's okay. My baby's okay.

I don't realize I'm falling until Matvey catches me. "Are you alright, April?"

"Sorry," I breathe. His hands are strong around me, warm and firm. *Safe.* "I just… got dizzy for a second there."

Matvey nods. "Dr. Allan, please continue."

Dr. Allan taps her clipboard with her pen. "As I was saying, the pregnancy has gone on beyond what it's considered safe. I try to respect the mother's wishes as much as possible, but in this case, I'm afraid that's no longer advisable."

I swallow. "So you're saying…?"

"We have to induce," Dr. Allan cuts short. "By the end of the week."

I let that word sink in. *Induce.* It's enough to make a chill go through me.

Images crowd my head: my mother, lying in a pool of blood. Charlie, his newborn skin nearly purple as he was dragged into the world with barely a breath left in him. Me, small and powerless and alone.

But it's different now. I'm not that terrified kid anymore. I'm not powerless.

And I'm not alone anymore, either.

"April was very clear, Doctor," I hear Matvey argue on my behalf. "Inducing is out of the question. If there really is nothing wrong with the baby—"

"It's okay."

Matvey turns to me. "You don't have to go along with this."

"I do," I reply. "Dr. Allan's right. It's time."

Then I give Matvey's hand a reassuring squeeze. "It'll be fine," I tell him, or maybe I'm talking to myself. Maybe, all along, it wasn't Nugget who wasn't ready. It was *me*. "By the end of the week, we'll get to meet our baby. Isn't that amazing?"

Matvey's expression softens. "Then we have a lot to prepare."

"I'll call to set the date." Dr. Allan smiles. "For now, go home and rest, April. No more unnecessary efforts."

"No more," I promise.

In the parking lot, we find Grisha waiting for us. "Ms. Flowers," he greets.

Then I realize he isn't alone.

"April!"

June comes hurtling out of the car like a bullet. She crashes into me, but gently, without once touching my belly. "Jesus Christ, Apes, you almost killed me with worry!"

"Sorry," I mumble. "If it helps, you didn't miss much. This year's pieces were very boring."

Cashmere Cruelty 475

"Missed your *Ocean's 8* moment, by the sound of it," June sniffles in my hair.

I can't believe it. I just finished crying. And yet, with June here in my arms, trembling with fear at the thought of something happening to me and Nugget...

It's useless. The floodgates burst open again, and I can't do a thing to stop them. "I'm sorry," I mumble again, holding my best friend tight.

"I bet you are. Don't ever scare me like that again. I mean it." Then she turns to Matvey. "You kept your promise, Baby Daddy."

Matvey clears his throat, somewhat uncomfortable. "I always keep my promises."

Something warm spreads into my chest then. Because I realize, with sudden clarity, the one thing that truly matters:

This time, Matvey came for me.

We drop June off at the Brooklyn apartment and head back to the penthouse. All the way there, Matvey treats me as if I'm made of glass. It's... new. Endearing, in a way.

But when he goes so far as to try to help me out of my shoes, I shake my head and laugh. "It's okay, Matvey. I can do that."

Matvey levels me with a look. "You heard Dr. Allan. No unnecessary efforts."

Then he slips off my kitten heels.

His movements are careful. Gentle. Once again, I'm stunned at the sight of this man—this powerful man with thousands of men and billions of dollars at his command—treating me like I'm something precious. Something that shouldn't be so far as nicked, let alone broken.

It's the first time anyone's treated me like that.

A yawn escapes me. After this hellish day, my exhaustion is finally catching up.

"Lie down," Matvey barks. From his mouth, everything sounds like an order. "I'll get you some water."

"No," I whine, catching the edge of his sleeve. "Stay."

Suddenly, I remember what happened the last time I did this. How quickly Matvey left the room the second that word slipped out of my mouth.

"Sorry," I hurry to say. "I—"

"Alright."

Without another word, Matvey lies down next to me.

For a long time, we just lie there, facing each other. Me, Matvey, and our baby in between. Matvey's fingers come up to my hair, stroking in slow drags. Before long, my eyelids grow heavy again.

As I drift off to sleep, I wonder to myself where this Matvey has been all this time.

And I think, heartbeat slowing to a crawl, that I wouldn't mind if he really did stay.

Forever.

58

MATVEY

Dawn comes far too quickly. I haven't closed my eyes all night, but that's fine.

I had something else to look at.

April stirs against the morning light. "Hi there."

"Hi."

She blinks all the way awake and gives me a cheeky grin. "What's with that face? What are you thinking about?"

"Everything."

It's the truth. All night, I've done nothing but think: about April, our child… and us.

We're going to be parents soon. It's taken a while to sink in, but finally, it has: in a week's time, we're going to meet our baby. In a week's time, April will be a mother.

And I'll be a father.

"That's a lot of thoughts," she teases. "Couldn't be me. It's far too early."

"Is it?" I rasp. "Because I've been thinking the opposite."

"What's that?"

"That I've gotten here far too late."

I've never been this liberal with my words. If I can avoid speaking at all, I do. I've trained my men to respond to one glance, one gesture from me.

But with April, I want to say it all.

As I let my hand trail over her belly, I want to say she doesn't have to do this alone. That I don't *want* her to do this alone. Not anymore.

I don't want to just be there for dinner. Instead, I want to be *there* for her. For *them.* The family we're about to become.

Ever since that cursed break-in, I've been swallowing my words. My fear. The one thing a *pakhan* should never allow himself to feel.

But I can admit it now: I was terrified.

When it comes to April—when it comes to *our child*—I remember what it's like to fear. I remember what it's like to hold something so dear, you'd do anything to protect it. Anything at all.

And I remember something else, too.

"Matvey?" April asks, her hand finding my face.

I grasp it in mine. Then, of all the words I want to say to her, I pick three.

"I love you."

It comes out naturally. Like I never thought it would again.

"Don't say that," April whispers, eyes shining and smile wavering. "Don't say it if you don't mean it."

"I mean it."

I flip her on her back. Like this, spread out under me, hair fanned around her head and cheeks flushed pink, she looks every bit like a flower.

"You asked me why I called off the wedding. This is why."

"But your dream—"

"Revenge isn't a dream. It's a goal."

It's still my goal, I think but don't say, because it feels wrong to stain this moment with that. The blood I still thirst for. Where April's concerned, I don't want anything to taint her.

"But you still want that," she says for me.

"Yes," I admit. "I want that. And I want everything else, too."

That's always been at my core—this insatiable fucking greed. As *pakhan*, I want the world at my feet. As a son, I want revenge.

And as a man...

"I want *you*."

April's hazel eyes fill with tears. I watch them cling to her eyelashes, a thousand tiny pearls. "Matvey..."

"I want you," I repeat, cupping her cheek, "and no one else. Not even if it's fake."

Then I kiss her.

I kiss her softly. Sweetly. Like I've never kissed her before. There is hunger inside me, but for once, it isn't looking to consume.

For once, it's content with *this*.

Her.

Us.

"You mean it?" April breathes against my lips when we pull apart. "You really mean it? This isn't a dream?"

"I can pinch you, if you like."

She laughs. "Why do I have a feeling you'll do it anyway?"

I grab the tender skin of her hips between my index and thumb. "Because, April Flowers, you're mine. And I get to do whatever I want with you."

Her eyes go dark and hooded. "Is that so?"

"That is so."

"And what does Matvey Groza want to do with me now?"

"I want to move in with you. Permanently."

April blinks in surprise. No doubt, she'd been expecting something else.

It's not that I don't *want* that something else. It's like I said: I want everything. But first, I want April to know I'm not going anywhere.

"I mean…" she stammers, flushed from head to toe. "This *is* technically your place…"

"Mm. And everything in it, too," I whisper against her ear. "All mine."

Before I can be tempted, I rise. I don't have many things—I'll just grab the essentials from my loft. The files I keep there, too. This week, I want to work from home as much as possible.

Home. That word still tastes foreign on my tongue.

So I take April's hand and replace that taste with hers.

I kiss it like so many times before. But this isn't like those other times; those were goodbyes. Endings.

This is a beginning.

"I'll be back soon," I promise.

April smiles up at me. "I'll be waiting."

To get to the loft, I hail a cab. After yesterday's scare, I'd rather have Grisha keeping watch outside April's door. If anything were to happen while I'm gone, he can drive her to the hospital.

I'd have Yuri come get me, but he isn't picking up.

When I get to my apartment, I find the door unlocked. *Must be Yuri*, I tell myself, but still reach for my gun on the off-chance.

Then I walk in and see *her.*

"Matvey."

I can't believe it. I truly cannot fucking believe it. "You have five seconds to get out of my sight."

I take in her appearance: she looks like she hasn't slept a wink, either. Hair messed up, makeup smeared. Her eyes are vacant, terrified, her face as pale as a ghost's. Even for me, it's a jarring fucking sight. Enough to almost make me put away my gun.

Then she has the gall to ask, "Is April okay?"

"Yes," I growl. "No thanks to you. Three seconds."

"Matvey, we need to talk."

"Was I not clear yesterday?" I raise my gun to make my point. "Two seconds."

If this is a desperate attempt to talk me into reconsidering our deal, it's far too late. She put April in danger. She put my child in danger.

What could she possibly say to change my mind now?

"Matvey—"

"One."

"I'm pregnant!"

I pull my finger away from the trigger. The words ring in my head like a gunshot. "What did you just say?"

"I'm pregnant," she repeats, voice shaking. "And it's yours."

59

APRIL

All morning, I'm on cloud nine.

"Here comes the bride..." I find myself humming, laundry in hand. Then I smack myself mentally. *It's way too early to think about that, idiot!*

Or is it?

"Well, it's not like Matvey proposed," I say out loud. "Right?"

Inside my belly, Nugget keeps snoozing.

"Not in so many words, at least," I keep rambling to my baby. "But he said he didn't want to marry anyone else, even if it's for show! And then he told me..."

I love you.

I grab a pillow and scream inside it. I'm so giddy, I feel like I'm fifteen again. Like I'm falling in love for the first time over and over.

Love. After so long without it, I thought I'd never get to feel it again. To be warmed by it.

That's when I realize... "I didn't say it back!"

Gosh, talk about being scatterbrained. The man you're head over heels for—the same man who'd rather chew on concrete than admit he has feelings at all—finally confesses to me, and what do I do?

I forget to say it back.

Great job, April. Not even married, and already, you're wife of the year.

"Wife," I breathe. "Can you imagine that, Nugget?"

I most certainly can. Before I'm able to stop myself, I'm picturing it: me, walking down the aisle in a long white dress, the bridal march playing in the background. And on the other side, waiting for me...

God, I'm itching to call June. I want to tell the world about this. I want to shout it from the freaking rooftops.

But I also want to preserve this little bubble of ours. Every second I spend like this, safe in the knowledge that Matvey loves me back—that he wants me and no one else—makes me feel like I'm walking on air.

"He'll be there for us," I whisper to Nugget. "For you. For me. For our family."

Because that's what he said, isn't it? Back at the Mallard, and in the ambulance, too. He called himself my boyfriend. He called us *family*.

That thought alone is enough to get me squeaking all over again.

"I wonder if he'll propose soon. Matvey isn't the type to wait once he knows what he wants. Do we think he'll do it formally? Fancy dinner, ring in a champagne flute, all that shebang?"

I twirl and giggle, the dress in my hands twirling with me. If this keeps up, it's going to take me hours just to put away this one load of laundry. Matvey might as well find me here, dancing with my wardrobe, and rethink his proposal.

Which, it bears repeating, hasn't actually come yet.

"But once it does, how long do we think we'll have to plan the wedding?" I can't stop myself from gushing to Nugget. "Will he want something grand? Or will an intimate gathering do? God, what about the *dress?*"

Once that thought is in my head, I'm gone. I've sewn wedding gowns for so many brides, it'd be impossible for me to have never entertained the thought.

"But there are just so many options," I mutter, pacing with excitement. "Mermaid? Empire? A ball gown or tea-length? Do I go for classy or embrace the fairytale format? And do I want lace or tulle? Organza, maybe?"

Nugget gives a polite kick. I decide to take it as a sign that it's listening. "Crepe would look really nice on a fit-and-flare, though…"

I fold and unfold the same blouse three times, digging a hole into the floor with my slippered feet. "Can't forget about the color, either," I mumble on. "Pure white has its charm, but what about champagne? Ivory? Rose petal?"

I'm still lost in dreamy fantasies when I hear the door open.

"Matvey!" I bound up to him.

I absolutely have to say it back now, before I forget again.

Before I get so swept up in bliss that it doesn't even cross my mind to voice it. The reason I'm so happy.

"There's something I—"

And then I stop.

One look at his face says it all: something's wrong.

His complexion is ashen, paler than I've ever seen. He looks like he just saw a ghost. Like a specter sucked every ounce of happiness out of him.

It's enough to make me terrified.

"What happened?" I ask, a thousand worries crowding my mind all at once. "Is it Yuri? Did something happen on the job?"

"We need to talk."

My stomach plummets. Still, I put on a trembling smile and try to reach out, to comfort him any way I can. "Of course. You can tell me any—"

"Petra's pregnant."

I blink. My voice fizzles out. For a second, I forget to even breathe. "What?"

"Petra's pregnant," he repeats, his words as cold as ice. "And I'm going to marry her."

It feels like a nightmare inside of a nightmare. Like thinking you've woken up, only to be plunged right back into the maw of the monster under your bed. For the longest time, it's all I can do to gape. I replay the words in my mind, and they still don't make any sense.

"You said you didn't want her," I whisper, voice shaking. "You said it was a business arrangement. You said…"

And then it dawns on me: the cold, harsh truth.

"You lied to me."

Matvey remains silent.

It all makes perfect sense now: why Petra lost her head like that. Why Matvey never outright denied they'd been together. He just let me think that.

And I was stupid enough to believe him.

And now, Petra's pregnant with his baby.

"Was everything else a lie, too?" I demand, words cracking at the edges. "Yesterday? This morning?" Finally, my voice drops to a devastated whisper. "Were *we* a lie?"

Matvey's face is unreadable. Even back when we first met, it was never like this: utterly shuttered. Annoyance, interest, even disgust—I could always find it in glimpses. Tiny things, like the muscles twitching at the corners of his lips.

Now, everything is as still as death.

Somehow, that's worse.

"Aren't you going to say anything?"

The worst part is, I still can't bring myself to believe it. Things were fine just hours ago. Better yet, they were perfect.

And now, everything's ruined.

For a long time, Matvey only looks at me. I can sense something moving under the surface of his impassive face. An undercurrent. Is it pain? Rage?

Or is he finally done with me?

"I'm sorry," he forces out eventually. Two words. All this, and he's only got two words for me.

Words that no longer mean anything.

Well, I've got two of my own.

"Get out."

When Matvey's hand twitches towards me, I raise my voice to an inhuman scream. "GET OUT!"

It's the howl of a wounded animal. Even now, a part of me hopes Matvey won't listen to what I'm saying. That he'll hear what I'm feeling. That he'll crush me in his arms and comfort me, explain himself to me. Tell me it was all a mistake.

Tell me he still *wants* me.

Instead, he turns his back on me.

I watch him walk out the door through a veil of stubborn tears. They cling to my eyelashes, but I keep them there. I refuse to let them fall.

I refuse to be vulnerable in front of Matvey Groza ever again.

Only when the door clicks behind his back do I let it happen: I fall. I fall with everything I have. Knees to the floor, tears streaming down my face, dreams shattered around me.

And my heart, somewhere among the wreckage, broken beyond repair.

That's when the phone rings.

60

MATVEY

When I walk out of the penthouse, I don't turn. I just put one foot in front of the other and keep going.

I take the elevator. I cross the lobby. Someone from the concierge tries to get my attention, but I ignore them. I make my way out into the streets.

I duck into an alley.

Then I punch the wall with all my might.

"*Blyat'!*" I curse without restraint. "*V rot yebis, pizdets—*"

I let my rage fly out of my mouth and pulse through my fist. The pain is searing, but I welcome it. If I can punch hard enough to break my bones, that's all I'll have to feel.

Not *this*.

The pain of losing her.

~

"Come fucking again?" I snarl at the woman in front of me.

"You heard me," Petra replies in a whisper.

"You know perfectly well that can't be."

"It has to be."

My finger twitches on the trigger. "I have never touched you, Petra. Nor have I ever wanted to." I spit those last words with venom. With disgust. For this woman, I can feel nothing else.

"You're not listening," Petra babbles.

"And you're not making any fucking sense!"

"I'm not saying it is your baby!" she all but screams. "I'm saying that it has to be!"

The look on her face is crazed. Deranged. At this moment, I can't sense a single scrap of reason within her.

I almost lower my gun out of pity. She's lost it. She's finally lost it.

Then I hear Yuri's voice behind me.

I punch the wall again. And again, and again, and again. Blood is trickling down my fingers now, but I only clench them harder. "Fuck!"

I hit the wall over and over. Soon, the spot in front of me starts filling with red. In the darkness, it looks black as sin.

"Fuck," I spit again, gritting my teeth against the pulsing pain. Not the one in my hand—that's nothing to me.

The one in my *chest*.

The one in the organ at the center of it. In that part of me I deluded myself into thinking I didn't have.

What a cruel way to find out I do.

"Fucking—fuck, *fuck*—"

"*Motya!*"

I feel Yuri's hand around my wrist. His fingers are trembling; trying to keep me from hurting myself further—and failing. "Matvey, look at me."

"Get lost."

"*Look at me.*"

I do. If only to snarl at him again to get the fuck out of my sight—I do.

But then the words don't come.

Because this is Yuri we're talking about.

My brother.

My *family*.

The only family I will ever have.

❧

"Is that true?" Yuri rushes forward.

I open my mouth to speak, convinced that I'm the reason he came.

And then I watch him run right past me and into Petra's arms.

"Yura…" Petra's voice cracks. "You weren't supposed to find out this way."

"I'm glad I did." He cradles her head with one hand. The other, he moves from her hip to her belly. *"So you're really…?"*

"What are you looking so happy for?" Petra scoffs, but it's weak. Undermined by the blush on her cheeks. *"This isn't good news, you know."*

"It's a baby," my brother replies, like it's simple. Like it's the easiest thing in the world. *"How can it be bad?"*

I watch the scene with my jaw on the floor.

"Yuri," I growl in warning, gun tight between my fingers, *"get away from her."*

Yuri turns. Then, for the first time in his life, he looks me in the eye and says, "No."

I raise my gun high as it all hits me at once. "Blyat', Yuri! You can't be serious!"

Of all people. Of all the fucking people on this earth…

But there's no mistaking it. It's in the way he looks at her. The way his hand curls protectively around her womb.

The way he stands between us.

With a roar, I throw my gun to the floor. "God fucking dammit!"

Was it always this obvious? Like dominoes, the pieces start falling into place. Everything's making sense now: every suspicious disappearance, every worried glance. Every time Yuri ran after her, or protected her from my wrath.

It wasn't for my sake.

It was for hers.

"Explain yourselves," I grit, barely keeping my rage at bay. *"Now."*

But when Yuri turns to me again, that flame flickers. I've never seen an expression like this on my brother's face before: smiling, yet sad at the same time. All at once, he looks ten years older.

"What's there to explain?" he whispers. "I love her."

Love. *Before, I would have mocked the very idea. I would have spit in my brother's face that "love" is a bedtime story. Something we tell our kids to balance out the terror of the monster under the bed. Something to give them* hope.

But, just an hour ago, I spoke that very same word to someone else.

And now, as furious as I want to be—

I can't do it.

I can't pull the trigger on this.

"So it's yours?" I rasp. "She's pregnant with your baby?"

Yuri nods.

"No."

We both turn at the sound of Petra's voice.

"It can't *be," she starts babbling again, nearly incoherent. "Yuri, you don't understand. If my father finds out, he'll kill us. He'll kill both of us."*

"He wouldn't." Yuri shakes his head. "You're his daughter. You're—"

"I'm nothing!" Petra spits. "I'm not his heir. I'm a prize mare to auction off to the highest bidder. I'm supposed to get him *an heir!" Her voice drops to a whisper. "Instead, I've dishonored him* and the *family. There's only one fate for people who do that."*

"Then I'll marry you," Yuri says immediately. "We'll tell him together. We'll explain—"

"Explain what?!" she shrieks. "It's Matvey he wants, Yura! He wants the power of the pakhan! And he knows you'll never turn on him to take it!"

For a split second, I wonder if that's still true. All this time, Yuri's been deceiving me: sneaking around, meeting my fiancée behind my back.

Even if we were engaged in name only, he should've known better than to go for her. Should've known better than to lie to me for her.

So who's to say he won't betray me for her, too?

But then I shake myself: this is Yuri we're talking about. No matter what, he's family. We're family. If I can't trust that, then—

"There has to be another way," Yuri stammers, refusing to so much as entertain the thought. "Anything but that, Petra."

Good brother.

"There is," she confirms. "One way to save both our lives. The only way."

And then she looks back at me.

"You did the right thing," Yuri says, clutching my fist tight to his chest. Preventing me from slamming it back into the concrete, back where I can feel it hurt. "You saved us. You saved *me*."

"Of course I did," I growl back. "Of course I fucking did."

Family comes first. I will always protect it; I will always make that choice. And it will always be the right one. *That's* my creed.

So why does this feel like the opposite of right?

"No," I snap. "No way."

"Matvey..." Yuri starts, looking conflicted. "I don't like this, either, but—"

"Then don't ask me to do it!" I pound my fist on the table.

"Do you think this is easy for me?!" my brother cries back. "Asking you to marry the woman I love? Knowing I can't keep her safe, but you can? That I can't keep my child safe, but you can?"

We're inches from each other. Seconds, really, from letting our fists do the talking for us.

But then Yuri's fury breaks. "Matvey," he murmurs, "I can't lose her. I can't."

The ridiculous thing is, he doesn't even realize: he's in danger, too. Petra said it loud and clear. And, for once, I believe her. I've spent too long with Vlad to not know what kind of man he is.

He can't lose Petra, he says?

Well, I can't fucking lose him.

I'm not scared of Vlad. If he wants to come at us, let him: let the Solovyovs taste the lead of the entire Groza Bratva.

But I can't possibly justify taking Petra in.

I can't order my vory to risk their lives, their men, for an outsider.

And Yuri wouldn't listen. He'd follow that siren to the ends of the earth. Follow her into his own goddamn grave.

And I can't have that.

But I also—

I also have somebody else I can't lose.

"Motya," Yuri begs, oblivious to my hell. To how fucking close I am to being torn apart. "Help us."

"I can't."

"Please."

"I—"

"Brother."

That's the final straw.

Like the camel's back, my resistance breaks. Because this is my brother we're talking about. This is my brother, and he's asking me for help.

"No one else can know," Petra says, panic still flooding her words. "No one else can know it's not yours."

"You shut the fuck up," I snarl.

"She's right," Yuri cuts in, pleading. "One wrong word and we're done for, Motya. We can't risk that. She's..."

She's carrying my child. *He doesn't need to finish that sentence. I can read it in his eyes, plain as day.*

"No one," he repeats. "Promise me."

April deserves to know. *The words are halfway up my throat when—*

Do you trust her?

It's that voice at the back of my mind. The voice of the pakhan *in me. The one that's been telling me, over and over—*

She's not family.

She's not *blood*.

But Yuri is.

"Promise me, Motya," he says again, quieter this time. Hopeful. "Please."

And, God help me, I do.

~

"Thank you," Yuri says to me. "Thank you for saving us. For not telling anyone."

I think of April, back at the penthouse. How overjoyed she was when she greeted me at the door, waiting on a happily-ever-after.

But there's no such thing as "happily-ever-after."

"Come," I force out, walking back towards the mouth of the alley. "We have work to do."

I leave my blood on the bricks.

And I leave April Flowers behind for good.

61

MATVEY

I haven't been at the office for one hour before the doors burst open.

"You mangy fucking dog!" Vladimir strides in, waving his fist in the air. "You *mudak*! You dare dishonor my daughter?!"

Great. Just fucking great. One would think Petra would at least give me the morning before tattling to dear ol' Daddy. No such luck, apparently.

Grisha and Yuri come rushing in after Vlad, guns drawn, but I motion for both of them to stand by. "Hello, Vladimir. We really must stop meeting like this."

"How fucking dare you!" Vlad roars. He raises his fist to strike. "I'll wipe that smile off your face, you *govnyuk*—"

Without any effort, I catch his punch midair.

With my *injured* hand.

"I don't believe I was smiling," I growl.

Then I tighten my grip.

I watch Vlad's face drain of all color as my fist clenches around his, making the bones pop. His bodyguards balk, but not one of them has the guts to raise his gun at me. After all, I've still got one free hand. "Matvey—"

"Let's get one thing straight here," I hiss, my grip now steel. "If you have grievances with me, I won't expect you to keep silent. I'm not that much of a tyrant. But you will mind your tongue, and you will remember your fucking self." Vlad's face scrunches up in pain, but I still don't let go. "After all, I'm going to be your *pakhan* soon. So why don't we keep things civil?"

"*Blyat'*, fine! Fine! I apologize!"

Only then do I release him.

"In that case, you have my regrets as well," I add. "Believe me when I say I never intended for any of this to happen."

It's not an apology: it's the truth. If there's one thing I regret, it's this goddamn mess. Had it been up to me, Petra could've lived and died a virgin.

But it wasn't up to me.

And I've already made my choice in the matter.

Vlad is still fuming, but he seems to have calmed down enough to remember his English. "I'm glad to hear that. People may call me old-fashioned, but even I don't expect a young couple to keep their hands to themselves until marriage. I understand a man has needs."

And a woman doesn't? I briefly wonder what it must be like to be married to someone like Vlad. Suddenly, I feel a flash of sympathy for his late wife.

"But a child is another matter entirely," he continues. "My family's honor is at stake here."

"As is mine."

He offers me his hand. Swallowing back my disgust, I give it a firm, hard shake.

"Which is why the wedding has to be celebrated within the week," Vlad concludes.

For a second, I'm sure I must have misheard. "The week," I echo.

"Of course! We want to put this matter behind us as soon as possible. I trust you agree?"

"Yes," I concede. "But this week won't work. April's baby is due."

Those two words—*April's baby*—are enough to turn Vlad's face back to cherry red. "Fuck that *suka*," he spits. "Fuck her *ubljudok.* They can disappear for all I ca—AHHH!"

"I thought," I snarl into his ear, my grip suddenly steel again, "we agreed to be civil."

"Alright, *blyat'*, alright!" Vlad hisses out in pain. "But this has gone on long enough, sonny. It's time you think about your *real* family."

Sonny. I should rip his fingers out just for calling me that. But I force myself to remember the situation—what's at stake here.

My brother. His family.

"So?" Vlad demands. "Are you a man of honor or not?"

"If you doubt that, then you shouldn't be in business with me at all," I growl back.

And then, before my eyes, Vlad's expression transforms.

"Perhaps not," he replies with a newfound calm. "Perhaps I should just cut my losses. Withdraw my support *and* my numbers. Then I'll have to make new friends. Do you want to know what I've heard?"

It's like watching someone rip off a mask. Vlad's voice grows calmer, his demeanor colder. For once, he looks every bit the *pakhan* the streets used to whisper about. The feared Solovyov patriarch, famous for gutting his enemies like pigs, first with his words and then with his knives. It was the reason I sought him out in the first place.

Still, all this time, I never thought I'd see his fangs in person. After age shortened his temper and dulled his mind, every single *pakhan* in New York believed that version of Vlad to be gone—myself included.

If I didn't despise the man, I'd almost have to respect him.

Since I don't bother answering his question, he answers it himself. "I've heard that the feds are in the market for new friends, too," he says. "I bet they'd be very, very interested in the famous Matvey Groza."

"Careful," I warn.

"And you are famous, aren't you? As CEO and *pakhan*. It's not like you've gone to great lengths to keep your cover. In fact, you're the topic of conversation at every table within two miles of the courthouse. State attorneys everywhere are dying to find something that will finally stick."

"I won't repeat myself, Vlad."

"You don't need to. After all, we're still friends. Family, really. But if we weren't, I'm afraid I'd have no other choice."

I can't believe my ears: this *mudak* is threatening me. *Me.* Plain as day, in my own office, in front of my men.

And yet, as much as I hate to admit it, he's found the one chink in my armor: I *haven't* been careful with my cover. This city whispers my name like I'm the goddamn boogeyman— every kill, every catch, I made without paying any mind to the tracks I left. I didn't care about being clean; I just needed to stay a free man long enough to exact my revenge.

I never thought I'd have something to live for afterwards.

"Do you really think you could do that?" I sneer regardless. "Ruin me before I can ruin you?"

"People say my Bratva is dying," Vlad remarks. "I suppose it isn't far from the truth. It's why I need an heir in the first place: a strong man who can lead us into the future. And make no mistake, son—no one would like you to be that man more than me. But if you couldn't be that…" For a second, his eyes flash as cold as Petra's. "Then I'd show you just how dangerous a beast on its dying breath can be."

Kill him, my instincts scream at me. *Kill him now and be done with it. Be done with him.*

But where would that push my revenge?

"But of course, this is all just hypothetical." Vlad backs off, hands raised, voice pleasant again. "Like I said, we're still friends. All that's left to settle is a date."

I clench my fists so tight my knuckles start bleeding again.

If all I did was call things off with Petra after the baby's birth, it would have still been salvageable. If I'd spun Vlad a tale of duty and honor, maybe an alliance would have still been possible. Maybe he would have even taken Yuri as a replacement. As long as I named him my heir, it would have been acceptable.

And I would have. God, I would have.

But now, there's a baby.

And if I risk Vlad's wrath, there's no telling what would happen to mine.

I could protect them, the man in me insists. I could protect my child and April both. Get them out of the city, out of the country. As much as it would tear my heart from my chest, I'd do it.

But no one can keep somebody else safe twenty-four-seven. Not even the strongest *pakhan* in the world.

As it stands, there is only one thing I can do. Only one choice left to make.

"Sunday."

Vlad blinks. "I beg your pardon?"

"The wedding will be celebrated on Sunday," I force out. "I trust this settles the matter to everyone's satisfaction."

For a moment, Vlad looks like he wants to object. I wait for him to do it. Wait for him to give me the last excuse I need to whip out my gun and make a mess of my carpets.

But all he does is nod. "Very well," he agrees. "Sunday it is."

When he offers me his hand this time, I don't shake it.

The second he's out the door, I hear Yuri heave a sigh of relief.

Then Grisha steps in front of me. "What the hell is going on, man?"

It's the first time I've heard him speak like that. Insubordinate. "Remember your place, Grisha," I growl.

"Apologies," he amends. "I'll rephrase. What the hell is going on, *boss?*"

"What's going on is that I'm getting married," I snarl. "As we all knew I would eventually. And I don't owe you a fucking explanation."

"You certainly don't," Grisha says flatly. "But I'd very much appreciate one. And so, I suspect, would April."

"Do *not* say her name!" I slam my injured hand on the table. Red spreads to the papers underneath.

Blood in the water.

"Gather the *vory*," I command. "And do not ever question me again. It'll be the last time I let you."

"Grisha…" Yuri puts a hand on his shoulder. "It's fine. Just… leave it at that. Please."

Grisha looks between me and Yuri. His eyes are filled with suspicion—he can tell something happened while he was elsewhere, and he can tell Yuri knows, too. After all, he isn't my third for nothing.

But whatever he finds on our faces, it's clearly not enough to insist.

So he takes a step back and bows. "Yes, *moy pakhan.*"

Then he goes to gather the *vory* for the announcement.

62

APRIL

The night after he breaks up with me, Matvey doesn't show up for family dinner.

I suppose I should be glad. Honestly, I don't think I could've stomached it. "Family" dinner. What a joke.

It was just another lie, wasn't it? All that sad violin music about how important it was for him, and it was probably nothing but a tool all along. A compromise. A couple of hours for me, and then free run to fool around with Petra for the rest of the day.

God, Petra...

I can't believe I fell for her act. The scorned business partner, the reluctant friend, the dashing defender. I wouldn't be surprised to find out she staged that break-in herself, just to gain my trust once and for all.

"Sisterhood," my ass.

All day I've been rolling in bed with only these thoughts to keep me company. It's like I can't stop my mind whirring.

How many laughs did they have at my expense? How many secret glances did they share behind my back when I was in the room?

How many lies did they make me swallow?

"I love you."

And those three words—they were the cruelest deception of all. Why even lie about something like that? Why lie about that to *me*?

I'd already resigned myself. I didn't expect anything. All I wanted was a happy life for my child, a loving home for them to grow up in. A serene atmosphere for the three of us, one that wasn't dominated by silence and wars of pinching, sneering cruelty waged in the shadows.

I never asked for *love.*

So why pretend to give it to me?

"I love you."

The worst part is, I can still hear his words in my head. Because maybe it wasn't a lie. Maybe, out of all the lies, it was the one thing that was real.

Not that I'll ever know.

And then there was that phone call.

"April? This is Dr. Allan..."

I'm distracted from my thoughts by a now-unfamiliar sound: the doorbell ringing.

I drag myself out of bed exactly as I am. Because fuck it, you know? My hair's a mess, my clothes all over the place. I didn't have the strength to wear anything that required effort, just a pair of shorts and a stained, oversized t-shirt.

Too late, I remember who it belongs to.

"April."

There he is: Matvey Groza, the root cause of my misery.

"What are you doing here?" I ask. I don't even have the energy to sound righteously furious, like I ought to. Just broken. Just a shell of a person.

Matvey's face is the same impassive mask it was yesterday. No matter how hard I try, I can't see what's underneath it.

And then I notice the bloody bandage around his hand. "What happened to your—"

"Dinner."

I blink. "Sorry, what?"

"That's why I'm here," he says curtly. "Dinner."

"Dinner," I echo.

"Yes."

I'm speechless. Honest-to-God *speechless.* "I don't want to have dinner with you. I don't even want to *see* you, Matvey. After what you did, you still think I'd…?"

"What I think is that we had a deal," Matvey says flatly. "And it involves dinner."

I can't believe what I'm hearing. Can't believe this man would have the gall to…

"Get out," I seethe. "Get out of my sight now, before I slam the door in your face."

"You'll find that I have a key."

"Then I'll just barricade you out."

"I'll call the concierge and have them break it down."

"You can't do that."

"Yes, I can," Matvey all but snarls. "Because this is still *my* hotel. *My* penthouse. Whether you're in it or not."

I let the words sink in. Not just them, but the way they were said. The way he said them. As cold as ice itself.

Then I step aside.

It's the hardest thing in the world, to make myself do that. To force my feet to move. But Matvey's right. No matter how angry I am, this is still his place. His home.

I was the fool for thinking it could ever be *ours*.

"Then by all means," I say, putting my customer service voice back on. "Make yourself at home, Mr. Groza."

Something flashes in his eyes then. Something like—

Exhaustion.

It throws me more than any part of this conversation.

All throughout dinner, I don't take a single bite. No matter how mouth-watering the dishes, how sweet the scents, I never once touch my plate.

"Eat," Matvey grits out eventually. "You need the strength."

"I'm not hungry."

"I don't care. The baby needs it."

Right, of course. The baby. God forbid there's anything else to me but that.

... I have news. It's about the induction...

I push Dr. Allan's voice out of my mind. "I'm not feeling well right now, Matvey."

It's not a lie. Even if I wanted to eat, my stomach is utterly closed for business. If I took a single bite right now, I'd just throw it up on the spot.

"April..."

"I'll heat it up later," I concede. "There. Happy?"

But Matvey doesn't look happy. He doesn't look happy in the slightest. And yet, there's no trace of anger on his face. Instead, he seems... weary. Spent.

Defeated.

Which doesn't make any sense. This is Matvey we're talking about: he doesn't give up. He doesn't take no for an answer. He doesn't lose, not to anyone.

Certainly not to me.

So what am I looking at here? Is this for real? Was Matvey so convinced he'd get to have his cake and eat it, too? Was it such a shock when reality finally caught up to him?

... We decided on a date...

I don't know if it's the jarring sight in front of me or Dr. Allan's phone call echoing in my ears. Regardless, for the first time all night, I open my mouth to speak.

And then Matvey cuts me off.

"You should know... a date has been set. For the wedding."

My tongue turns to lead. Still, I manage to croak, "When?"

"This Sunday."

I freeze.

There are a million things I want to say. A million questions, crowding my mind all at once.

But in the end, I only manage to ask one. "So soon?"

Matvey's jaw sets. "We couldn't wait."

That's what finally turns me to stone. *We couldn't wait.* As if they simply loved each other too much to delay. As if that's all I've been all along: a delay. A temporary setback. One that was never meant to last.

I rise from the table. Matvey does the same. "Congratulations," I whisper.

And Dr. Allan's phone call remains locked inside my mind.

"Hello, April. This is Dr. Allan."

I walk him to the door.

"I have news. It's about your induction."

I open it for him.

"We decided on a due date."

I watch him walk out.

"This Sunday."

And I don't say a thing.

63

APRIL

Things don't change much over the next few days.

I wake up late. I keep the blinds drawn. When I do bother getting up, I just wander around the penthouse like a ghost. Restless. Numb.

Silent.

That's the constant of my life now: silence. So many times, I thought I'd rid myself of it for good. First, with my found family, and then with Matvey.

But it follows me everywhere.

When Matvey comes by for dinner, the silence becomes deafening. It's astounding how quickly we've gone back to being strangers.

The worst kind of strangers. Strangers who once said, "I love you."

And then there's the baby. The due date is floating around in my mind every minute of every day.

The first night we eat together, I keep telling myself that, if he will only speak to me, then I'll come clean. If he will only say one word to me—ask about my day, ask about anything—then I'll tell him.

But he never does.

So the second night, I tell myself just one look will do. If he glances up from his plate, if he keeps his gaze on mine for a single, full second, then I'll take it as a sign and spill it all.

But he never does that, either.

Then, by the third day, I'm determined to tell him anyway. He's still the baby's father, isn't he? No matter how badly he scorned me—how broken he left me—he still has a right to know. Doesn't he?

But there's another baby coming.

It's a small, hateful voice spewing poison at the back of my mind. I try my hardest to suppress it, but it keeps coming back stronger, louder: *Soon, he'll have another child. A better one. A legitimate one. One he actually chose to have. And once that happens, he'll forget about the one he never wanted in the first place.*

Just like your parents did.

By the fourth day, I'm determined to snuff out that voice for good. So I tell myself: if he answers me.

If he answers me, I'll tell him.

"Do you love her?"

The sound of cutlery stops. Matvey's hands still. Just like that, the silence grows louder than ever.

A part of me is hoping he'll say, *Yes*. Because if he truly loves her—if all of this was the last trial on the way to his happily ever after—then I'll be able to accept it. I'll be able to put my restless soul at ease.

Not right away. Not for a long time, maybe.

But eventually.

Or at least I'll be able to pretend.

I'll be happy for them. I'll smile and nod and say all the right words. After all, haven't I done this all my life? Live off the crumbs of other people's happiness? Getting out of the way so it could happen?

It wouldn't be my home full of laughter, but it would be *a* home. A home for my child.

I have a half-brother that I love; maybe Nugget could have the same. They could grow to care for each other, like Matvey and Yuri did. Better yet, they could grow up together from the start.

It wouldn't be *my* happiness, but it'd still be happiness.

And yet, another part of me is still hoping he'll say, *No. No, I don't love her. I love you, April Flowers. It's only ever been you.*

But what I'm wholly unprepared for is the answer that actually comes my way.

"It's none of your business."

I look up. Matvey's eyes are finally on me, but they have never felt so cold. His words, too—words that I've begged for in my mind for the whole week. The silence is broken now, but at what cost?

"Matvey…" I try again, gripping my napkin tight. "Just tell me. I promise, I can handle it. I just need to know—"

"You don't need to know anything."

"That's not fair," I rasp around the lump in my throat.

I watch Matvey's fist clench and unclench on the table. Like it does when he's about to lose his patience. "Drop it, April."

I shake my head. "No. You owe me this much. You owe me—"

"I owe you *nothing*!"

The harshness of those words makes me jump. For a second, I'm frozen: I can't blink, I can't speak, I can't breathe.

Matvey's chair screeches. Through a veil of tears, I watch him stand. "I owe you nothing," he repeats, quieter. "And you don't owe me anything, either. So do what you want."

"What… I want?" I stammer.

He gives me a curt nod. "After the birth, I'll arrange for you to be moved to another apartment. It'll be yours in every way that matters. You'll have round-the-clock security and a bank account for your needs."

"And you think that's what I want?" I ask with a trembling voice. "A bigger cage?"

"I will provide for you," he goes on as if he hasn't heard me. "And for our child. You'll be free to have your friends over. If you want June to move back in, I won't stand in your way. And if you…"

"And if I want somebody else to move in, you won't stand in my way, either?"

I can't get through the whole sentence without my voice wobbling. A few days ago, it would have been unthinkable: Matvey Groza, giving me up to someone else?

But now…

Now, what else could he have meant?

"I want you and no one else. Not even if it's fake."

I still want to believe those words. I want it with all my heart.

But then again, I also wanted to believe in *"I love you."*

And look how that turned out.

"No."

I blink. "'No?'"

For the first time since this whole affair started, I allow myself to hope.

"You can't have someone else," he growls. "Not now, not ever. You are mine."

Then kiss me, I beg. *Kiss me now and call me yours. Call off the wedding, take me away, make me forget this ever happened.*

Kiss me and give me my happily ever after.

"And if I can't have you, then no one can."

No one.

My last hope shatters. I can feel the shards sink into my feet as I stand.

No one. Those two words keep repeating in my head like a slap on loop. Not Matvey, and not anyone else, either. *No one.*

"You want me to be alone?" I croak. "You don't want me, but you want me to be alone—forever?"

I'm barely holding back tears. Of all the things I knew Matvey to be—possessive, mercurial, jealous—I just never...

I never thought he'd be this cruel, too.

When his lips remain sealed, I whisper, "You want our child to be alone?"

"I'd be there," he retaliates. "I'd visit."

"For dinner. Without saying a word."

He grimaces. "It's better than nothing."

That's what I deserve—slightly more than nothing. That's what *our child* deserves, according to its father.

Silence.

And no one.

"I want you and no one else. Not even if it's fake."

How quickly they end, fairytales. I can almost glimpse the last paragraph of mine. As I stand shell-shocked in the middle of the living room, listening to the sound of the door closing behind Matvey's back, I try to picture it: the grain of the paper, the black lines of ink. And then, just before the final, empty page...

"Happily never after," I murmur into the silence.

64

MATVEY

It's fucking torture.

All week, I can't bring myself to look at her. I can't bring myself to speak. And for what? What would I even say? What could I say, after all this mess?

The truth, a new, unfamiliar part of me suggests. *Tell her the truth. Tell her everything that happened—Petra's baby, Yuri, all of it.*

It's tempting. So, so fucking tempting.

But if I could trust April with the truth, then we wouldn't be here to begin with.

"I saw April again today," Grisha informs me on the drive to the office. "Her eyes were red."

"Then buy her some eye drops."

"She hasn't been sleeping. I could hear her sobbing from the hallway."

I turn my head to the window and ignore him.

"It's every night, Matvey. This has to stop."

"Then buy yourself some earplugs, too," I snap.

"Are you really going to be so dense?" Grisha snaps right back. "This isn't about me, man. This is about her. This isn't good for her."

"We all do things that aren't good for us."

"How about this, then? It's not good for the baby, either. Assuming you still care about that?"

I pound my fist against the car door. "Pull over."

"Can't. We're in the middle of traffic."

"I said *pull the fuck over.*"

With an irritated huff, Grisha obeys.

A chorus of horns explodes behind us, but I don't care. I step out of the car and wait for my driver to do the same.

When he does, I slam him hard against the closest wall.

"Let's get one thing straight here," I growl. "You don't make the decisions around here—I do. So stay in your goddamn lane."

"And what decision have you made, exactly?" Grisha pushes back, utterly unconcerned about my hands around his throat. "Because from where I'm standing, it doesn't look like this was your call."

"Shut up."

"In fact, if I had to guess, I'd say it was your bro—"

"I SAID SHUT THE *FUCK* UP!"

For an instant, Grisha does.

All around me, people start whispering. *Shit. They're staring.* I'm still a public figure—someone might recognize me. As Vlad so kindly pointed out, I need to take better care with my cover.

"I am your man to the death," Grisha spells out quietly. "You are my *pakhan*. But I didn't sign up to trot along to anybody else's orders."

"Then it's a good thing these orders come from me."

"You were happy with April," he insists. "For the first time since I met you, you were actually fucking happy."

I don't deny it. After so many lies, I don't have the strength. "Things change."

"Then tell me why they changed."

"I don't owe you an explanation," I snarl.

"Is that the issue?" Grisha asks. "Or are you keeping me in the dark for the same reason you're keeping April in the dark—because this is a family matter?"

Fucking Grisha. Always too sharp for his own good.

"I've been by your side for a long time, Matvey," he insists. "I've seen you grow into the *pakhan* you are. Even then, I know you'll never think of me as family because I'm not your blood. And I can live with that."

"Then stop fucking—"

"But April can't."

I release my grip.

Grisha briskly puts himself back together. "Shall we go before the boys in blue show up?"

I'm tempted to let them. Right now, all I want is a good fight.

But people are still staring.

"Let's go," I command.

For the rest of the way, all I can think of is April's red-rimmed eyes. The sound of her sobs through a closed door. Forks scraping over empty plates.

Silence.

Silence.

Silence.

Every night, I come back for dinner.

That's my own brand of torture for myself: I can't be honest with her, but I can't stay away from her, either.

So I pull rank and make her sit with me.

It's the worst thing in the world. I feel like the goddamn Beast. Like I plunged April into a fairytale gone wrong.

But then again, ours was never that kind of story. We never promised each other anything. *I* never promised her anything. Only—

I love you.

"Do you love her?"

Her voice overlaps with the memory of mine. It takes me a moment to untangle my words from hers—to figure out what she's actually saying.

When I do, I want to fucking *scream*.

Love her? *Petra?* I'd sooner chew on glass. What my brother sees in her, I'll never understand. She's moody, unpredictable, always trying to claw her way to the top, incapable of giving a shit about anybody else who might find themselves in the way.

She's—

Too much like me, my mind whispers.

And April...

April is everything I'm not.

Warm. Kind. Always walking on her tiptoes, afraid to break the eggshells under her feet. Her whole life, she's been taught that that was the only way to survive.

But I wanted to show her more.

I wanted to show her that family doesn't have to mean misery. That it can be happiness, too. Me, her, our child—we could make a home. We could *be* a home.

And now, she's asking me if I love *Petra?*

No, I want to scream. *I don't fucking love Petra: I love* you, *April Flowers. It's always been you.*

But then she'd have questions.

And I could never give her an answer.

Why?! A part of me goddamn howls. *Why can't you give her answers? Why can't you come clean? Why can't you trust her?*

"It's none of your business."

It's like a sick game of back-and-forth. Every time I come close to telling her—to spilling my guts and then begging her for forgiveness—that other, older part of me whispers back, *She's not family.*

She's the mother of your child, the newer me argues. *She's your partner.*

And again, that voice: *She's not family.*

She's not blood.

But Yuri is.

"No one. Promise me, Motya."

And I'll be damned if I turn into a fucking blood traitor, too.

I won't turn on my family.

I won't be my father.

So I rise from my chair and I tear April to pieces.

It feels like the worst thing I've ever done: pushing her away. Ripping her love for me out of her chest with my bare hands. Being *cruel.*

But if it'll help make her fall out of love with me, then so be it.

"I owe you nothing. And you don't owe me anything, either."

Her life will continue after me. It *has* to continue after me.

So let me be the monster of her story.

"If you want June to move back in, I won't stand in your way. And if you..."

Say it. Say it, you coward.

Set her fucking free.

"And if I want somebody else to move in, you won't stand in my way, either?"

As soon as I hear her say those words, I fucking lose it. *"No."*

"'No?'"

"You can't have someone else," I growl, too far gone to realize the way her eyes shine with hope. Hope that I'll take her back; that I'll finally claim her. *"Not now, not ever. You are mine."*

But I can't.

I can't claim her. I can't have her.

And if *I* can't...

"If I can't have you, no one can."

Watching her shatter is like taking a knife to the heart.

"No one?" she asks me with a broken voice, all restraint gone. *"You want me to be alone?"*

I want you to be with me. *I want to own you so completely you'll never think about another man again.* Never.

It's so fucking selfish. I wanted to set her free, didn't I? I was tearing her apart to push her away from me, wasn't I?

So why did it end up like *this*?

"You don't want me, but you want me to be alone—forever?"

Because I can't give her up, that's why.

I can never give up April Flowers.

I can never give up on us.

So why don't you tell her?

I feel like my head is going to explode. I barely hear the words she says to me after, or the words I say to her. Everything's wrapped up in a fog.

Anger. Fear. Jealousy. Need.

All I register is her face as she cries.

I shut the door behind my back and bite my knuckles bloody. *"Tomorrow,"* I rasp.

If she's still like this tomorrow...

"I'll tell her. Trust or no trust."

Blood or no blood.

65

APRIL

"If I can't have you, no one can."

After the initial shock has passed, I can only feel one thing: rage.

How dare he? Who does he think he is? Discarding me like a broken toy, then claiming no one else can have me? Condemning me to a life of loneliness because—

Because what?

He *loves* me?

As if.

As. Fucking. If.

That night, I'm a statue of salt. I endure dinner like I'm enduring stitches. I set my jaw, bite down on my lip, and I don't say a damn thing.

Silence—but on my terms.

"April…"

Of course—now, he speaks. The silence isn't working now that he isn't its master any longer. "About this wedding... there's something you should—"

"No."

I watch him blink. "'No'?"

It's a sick parody of last night's exchange. "No," I repeat, putting down my napkin with enough force to make the plates tremble. "I don't want to hear it."

"You have to."

"Oh, I 'have to'?" I hear myself laugh, but there isn't a single trace of joy in it. It's a broken, howling sound. Like the wind through an abandoned house. "Yesterday, you made it abundantly clear it was none of my business. And now, I have to listen to you?"

"Sit down," Matvey growls.

"Or what?" I challenge him, though in truth, I didn't even realize I'd stood. "You'll find a smaller cage to lock me into?"

"Don't test me."

I can't believe I ever fell for his act. Can't believe I let this man fool me for as long as I did. Right now, every word out of his mouth is confirmation: all he wants is power over me.

All he wants is control.

That's not true, a quiet part of me whispers at the back of my mind. It's the part I buried, the part that's still licking her wounds, bleeding from the gash in her heart. *He cared for you once. Maybe he cares still.*

I silence that voice and fix my stare on Matvey. "Test you?" I echo. "Why? What can you possibly do to me that you haven't already? You put a target on my back from day one. Thanks to you, I got kidnapped, cut off from everything I've ever loved, assaulted in my own home. I stared down the barrel of an assassin's gun, challenged the whole mob in handcuffs, and even had to pull a freaking heist. For your fiancée, might I add."

"April, the wedding with Petra—"

"Do *not* say her name!"

The scream surprises me. I didn't think I was capable of this: this unbridled anger. The fury of a broken thing.

But broken things have to take on new forms to survive.

"Don't say her name," I repeat, this time in a whisper. "Don't talk to me about your wedding. Don't talk to me about 'family' when all you've ever done is scorn ours."

"April—"

"You never wanted me. You never wanted our child. You took us in out of sick jealousy, just so no one else could have the toys you didn't care to keep. Because, even broken, they were *yours*."

"You *are* mine," he snarls, rising to meet my eyes from above. "Both of you are mine. That will never change."

"And that scares me half to death."

Matvey reels back as if slapped, but I can't stop now, not even if I wanted to. With the floodgates finally open, everything has to come rushing out. Even the dirt at the very bottom. All the black and rotten and bloody things I always kept to myself, hoping no one would ever see. *My* darkness.

"You ruined me, Matvey Groza. You ruined my life—and now, you want to ruin my child's."

"April, I would never—"

"But you already have!" I half-laugh, half-sob. "Look at what happened the other day. I was in a hospital, Matvey, not knowing whether my baby was still alive inside me. All because of your Bratva. Because of you."

Matvey clenches his jaw. His lips press into a tight line, but he doesn't say a thing. Doesn't seem to have a single argument to defend himself.

Once again, he chooses silence.

So I speak for the both of us. "Ever since we met, you've done nothing but force me into a life I didn't want."

"I never once forced you, April."

"Maybe not," I concede. "Maybe I was so lonely that I just let you." I take a step forward. "But I won't let you anymore. Not if you want me to be even more alone. Not if you want our child to grow up alone like I did. Like *you* did. Not if you intend to turn into…"

The words get stuck in my throat. I've said a lot of horrible things today, but this—this is too sharp. Too evil.

And yet, it's also true.

"Say it," Matvey growls, as if reading my mind. "Say what you're thinking."

I hesitate. "Into…"

"*Say* it, April."

It's his tone that gives me the final push: aggressive, scary, cruel.

"Your father," I breathe.

I can see the exact moment Matvey shuts down. Whatever he'd been intending to say, it sinks back into his depths, sealed under a mountain of grief.

Good, the vindictive part of me rejoices. *Let him feel the pain you felt.*

But why doesn't it feel good? Isn't this the thing Matvey has been after all along—revenge? Shouldn't it feel good?

So why do I just want to cry harder?

Without a word, Matvey turns his back on me. As he walks away, every step echoes like the crack of something broken. Something irreparable.

Something even I can't fix.

∼

I lie awake in bed until morning.

When the doorbell rings, I don't even think: I gather myself and get the door.

"Matvey."

He's wearing the suit I made him. Han blue, like his eyes in the dark.

On the front, folded neatly in his jacket, is the pocket square I gifted him. He looks dreamy. But the bags under his eyes tell a different story: a man trapped in a nightmare.

I don't get it. This is his *wedding day.* He's marrying the woman he loves—the one he actually wants.

So why does he look so wretched?

"You should be getting married," I tell him in a rasping monotone.

Truth be told, it's still early. I didn't ask for details, but if this is anything like his previous wedding, he isn't supposed to be at the venue for at least another hour.

The venue. I wonder if they changed it. If they'll get married in some blooming garden across town, or if they picked the terrace again. *This* terrace. Just one floor above me.

If I stood at the balcony, would I hear it? The music, the march—their *I do*'s?

If I just kept the windows open, would the sounds of my world shattering drift inside?

"I have something to discuss with you first."

"Is this about whatever you were trying to say last night?" I ask.

Matvey's expression turns bitter. "No. Clearly, I can't trust you with that information."

The words cut deep. I think back to my own remarks: the jab about his father. As hurt as I still am, I can't help but regret it.

"Then what…?"

"I know about the induction."

I stare up at him. "Since when?"

"Since Dr. Allan called you," he replies. "You can't keep secrets from me, April. It won't work."

"But you can keep them from me?"

Something flashes across Matvey's face. Something like pain. "I don't have a choice."

"There's always a choice," I retort. "Always, Matvey."

"Not for me. Not about this."

It feels like we're on two different railways in this conversation. Like we're following two different threads, both leading nowhere. "I didn't think you cared anymore," I whisper. "About our baby."

"Whether I care or not is no longer your concern," he spits at me, venomous. "This is my child, too. And I'll do with it as I see fit."

Once, I would have taken this as a claim. Aggressive, misguided—but born out of love nonetheless. Now, all I can do is shiver.

"After the wedding, I'll take you to the hospital myself," he adds, dark and final.

I swallow hard. "What if I don't want you to?"

"Then that's no concern of mine."

His words leave me reeling. Since when has Matvey gone back to being this iceman? Since when has he gone back to threatening me?

When Matvey turns to leave, someone else takes his place in my eyes. Someone just as tall, imposing, and scary.

My father.

It's uncanny, the resemblance. Their taut backs, their disdain.

Suddenly, I'm seven years old again, watching Dominic walk out on me. Rejecting me for a *better* family.

I can't even muster the strength to close the door. I just collapse with my back against it, heart in my throat, the beats too frantic to keep track.

And then, in the worst cosmic joke of all—

"My water," I stammer into the empty room.

I watch the liquid pool under my legs, staining my dress.

The baby's ready.

My baby's ready—and it's coming.

66

MATVEY

From the second I leave April behind, everything turns into a daze.

Grisha corners me in front of the elevator. "Are you really okay with this? There's no going back, you know. After you marry her."

Goddamn Grisha. Even right at the end, he has to find a way to get on my nerves.

When he tries to get on the elevator with me, I bark, "You stay here. Guard her. Make sure she doesn't leave."

After a moment's hesitation, Grisha bows. "As you wish, *moy pakhan.*"

I have Yuri drive me to the Hedoneros Club instead.

When we get there, I notice the place has been classed up from head to toe. Good. It wasn't exactly wedding-appropriate before. It was just the first venue available on such short notice—the only one that wasn't the hotel, at least. And I wasn't going to do this at the hotel.

Not with April just one floor below.

My mind swims as I head to the rooftop. Yuri tries to talk to me, "Motya—"

"Don't," I snarl. "Whatever you're going to say, don't say it."

He obediently shuts up.

My brother. I've never felt so conflicted about him in my life. I love him and I hate him. Why did he have to make me do this? Why did he have to go and fall for the only person he shouldn't?

Why did he have to make me *promise*?

Would it have mattered? a disillusioned voice whispers at the back of my head. *Even if he didn't force you into a promise, would you have told her?*

… No.

It's as clear as day now: I wouldn't have. I shouldn't have.

Because, all along, I was right. April isn't family. She isn't *blood.* And she isn't someone I can trust.

I opened my heart to her once. *Once.* I told her about my past, about my scars—and what did she do with it?

She threw it all back in my face.

Clenching my fists, I walk up to the aisle. Every guest I pass looks uncomfortable. There is tension on everyone's faces… everyone but Vlad. *He* looks overjoyed. Pleased as punch, really. We're so close now. So close to getting what we've always wanted. Me, my Bratva—and that viper Petra, too.

Petra. A sadder-looking bride, I have never seen. Not even when she ran away the first time around, or when she was binging tarts in the kitchen with mascara tracks all over her face.

If possible, Yuri looks even sadder.

It's a wretched affair, all of it. As the priest goes through his spiel, I feel like my head is underwater. When it comes to repeating after him, Petra has to kick me awake.

And when it comes to saying, "I do," we both hesitate.

But it's just two words. Two words and a death sentence.

I say them.

Petra says them, too.

Then the crowd erupts in cheers.

"Not drinking?" Petra asks me, following my gaze to the open bar.

Have I been that obvious in my staring? "Neither are you," I point out.

"If I could, we wouldn't be here."

Right. The baby.

"Didn't figure you for the maternal type," I jab. "Observing the rules, taking care of another being."

"The child's innocent," she mutters. "We are the guilty ones."

"Speak for yourself," I spit. "I didn't do anything to land myself in this mess."

"Last I heard, you had a kid on the way, too."

I grit my teeth. As always, Petra's never more unnerving than when she's right. It's the only reason I haven't followed Vlad's example in downing the entire open bar—the only reason I'm here, enduring her, instead of methodically killing my liver and my clarity.

Because today, I have a child on the way.

My child. It's the one thing that's been keeping me going through all of this mess. The thought that I'm finally going to meet them.

Tonight. In a few short hours.

But it's still too goddamn long.

Yuri joins us. He hands Petra a mocktail and then turns to me. "Your phone's ringing," he points out.

I glance at the display. A spark of annoyance flashes through me at the sight of Grisha's name. "Jesus Christ, doesn't he know when to fucking quit?"

Irritated, I refuse the call and pocket my phone again.

"What are you going to do now?" I snark then at the unhappy couple. "I saved your ass, but it won't last."

"Motya," Yuri pleads.

"Is the child going to grow up calling me 'Dad'?" I taunt. "Are you going to be 'Uncle Yuri' for the rest of your life, brother?"

"Stop."

"Or are you planning to wait until the old man croaks to finally step up?"

Someone grabs my tie.

I expect it to be Yuri. I expect him to yank my collar and punch me in the face, give me an excuse to finally vent my anger. With my fists, the only way I know how.

But it's not Yuri.

"Thank you," Petra whispers against my lips, making it look as if we're about to kiss. "For all you've done. I'm not just saying that, Matvey. I truly mean it."

"I sense there's a 'but' coming."

"But," she hisses, "I'll have to ask you to hold yourself to the same standard you've held me to."

"Which is?" I growl.

"To not disrespect what's mine."

I almost want to laugh. I could snap Petra's wrist with two fingers if I wished to. And yet, here she is—defending her territory tooth and nail. Fangs and claws.

Yuri pales. "Petya, stop—"

"A toast!" Vlad yells, drawing all eyes to us. "To the newlyweds!"

Quickly, Petra releases her grip.

"I should kill you for what you've just done," I whisper into her ear. "You know that, right?"

She goes as white as my brother.

"But I won't."

All along, something else had been spinning in my head—the suspicion that Petra orchestrated this whole thing. That she fucked my brother over just so she could fuck *me* over afterwards.

That she was going to break his heart.

But no matter how good she is, she could never fake this. This consuming urge to protect.

I know—because I've felt it, too.

Petra exhales with relief. By her side, I watch Yuri do the same.

"This time, at least," I add, low and dangerous.

The couple seems to heed my warning. With two quick nods, they disperse.

Who'd have thought? In this whole mess, someone's found a crumb of happiness after all. Sure as fuck wasn't me, though.

I almost give in and head to the bar when my phone rings again. "Goddamn Grisha," I mutter. I shut it off.

The induction isn't for a while. If it's truly life-and-death, someone will risk their neck to come get me at my own wedding.

If it's not, I don't want to hear it. Not today.

I have my own crumb of happiness waiting for me.

After I meet my kid, I tell myself. *After I meet my kid for the first time, I'll handle anything that comes my way.*

Whatever it is, it can wait until then.

Right?

67

APRIL

What is it with me and cabs? I swear, every time I've needed one in the past few weeks, it's been with my hair unkempt, dress soiled to high heaven, and a life-or-death situation on my hands.

At least this time there's no handcuffs.

For now.

Next to me, Grisha's as pale as a sheet. What with being stationed at my door and all, he was the one who found me wailing with pain on the floor.

Not my finest moment.

"You're sure you don't have a spare car?" I joke, gritting my teeth against the throb in my belly.

"Afraid they're all elsewhere occupied today," he replies, scanning the street for our taxi. Then he goes back to tapping frantically away at his phone, like he's been doing for the past five minutes. "You're sure you don't want an ambulance?"

It's uncanny, seeing Grisha like this. So ruffled. If anything, it's a good distraction. Though not quite good enough to drown out the pain.

I shake my head. "They would just take me to the closest hospital."

"That might be wise."

"My doctor isn't there," I insist. "I'm not doing this without her. I'm not doing this without…"

I don't finish my sentence.

But apparently, I don't have to—Grisha's always been quick on the uptake. He curses quietly under his breath in Russian and tries his phone again. His face growing darker by the second, I watch him make call after call after call.

But no one ever picks up.

I don't have to ask who he's calling. I don't have to ask who isn't picking up. I may not be that smart, but even I am not *that* slow. Or at least, not anymore.

"Bad reception at the wedding of the year?" I try to joke.

He spares me a quick, sad smile. "I'm sure that's all it is."

Then my cab finally arrives.

Grisha goes to exchange a few words with the driver. I see him pull out a fat wad of cash and what looks like a particularly nasty threat, at least going by the way his eyes narrow. I swear, mobsters can't do anything normally.

After that, he helps me into the cab.

"I will get Matvey," he assures me.

This time, I'm the one who gives him a sympathetic smile. "Right."

As the cab speeds away with sweaty old me in the backseat, a weak part of my heart keeps holding on to hope. Hope that Matvey will drop his blushing bride and come running, that he will be there for me. For *us*.

Because, despite it all, my heart still hasn't stopped clinging to "happily ever after."

By the time I get out of the cab, I'm barely standing. The pain has gotten unbearable—with every step, I'm terrified I'll fall over. I don't know if the cabbie was paid to walk me in, but he only gets me as far as the front gate before absconding with Grisha's wad of cash. The rest of the way, I'm on my own.

I keep reaching out for someone to hold on to, but no one's there.

The second Dr. Allan lays eyes on me, I'm rushed to the E.R. The hospital hive comes alive around me, a flurry of activity that I can't keep track of. It's all too fast, too soon.

Is this how my mom felt? With Charlie?

That's when it finally sinks in: *I'm about to give birth.*

I'm about to become a mother.

"It's going to be okay, April," Dr. Allan soothes me. It's somewhat undermined by the way she whirls around right after, yelling at some poor resident, "Where's the epidural?!"

I still appreciate the attempt.

"Breathe," she coaches. "In through your nose, out through your mouth."

I try to follow her instructions and calm down; I really, really do. But there's no mistaking the panic in her voice, or the urgent way she rushes off with the rest of her team.

Then I'm left alone.

I'm assaulted by a wave of regret. I should've called June on the ride over—I should've called someone. I still could. My phone is right here, just a few inches away.

But I refuse.

I don't *want* June right now. I don't *want* someone else.

I want Matvey.

I want my baby's *father*.

And if I can't have him…

If I can't have him, I won't have anyone.

It's a fruitless thought. Stubborn and bitter and every other ugly thing I've got locked up inside of me. It's pathetic, all of it.

But right now, I don't have the strength to be anything else.

How ironic. I always believed self-inflicted misery was Matvey's poison, but clearly, we aren't so different. God save our baby if that's the case.

Our baby. "Couldn't wait to meet me, could you?" I joke through the waves of pain. "Hold tight, Nugget. Mommy can't wait to meet you, either."

In a sea of bitterness, that's the one sweet drop that keeps me going.

As the doctors rush me to the birthing room, I cling to that thought like a lifeline. I cling to it as they tell me all sorts of things: that the labor is progressing too quickly, that it's already too late for an epidural. That I'm gonna have to *push, ma'am, push.*

As I call Matvey's name, and no one answers.

As the agony of bringing a new life into the world tears through me, I cling to that one thought with all I have.

I'm going to meet my baby.

And then...

I do.

~

It's everything I've ever dreamed of.

I'm spent, stitched up, bloodied from head to toe—*that* part's nothing like my childhood dreams. No one ever tells you about that in bedtime stories: how bloody the whole affair is.

But there's one thing they got right.

In the end, it's all worth it.

The second they put my child into my arms, I know. "You're perfect," I whisper to the bundle. "God, you're so perfect."

That's when I know something else, too: I won't let history repeat itself.

"You deserve better," I murmur, lips pressed to my baby's head. "You deserve so much better than what I've had."

All my life, I've been living with one foot out the door, ready to bolt. Not because I didn't want to be there—but because I never knew when the people around me would be finally done with me.

I've grown up unwanted. But I won't let my child suffer the same fate. Walking on eggshells, stomach in knots, the constant feeling of not being good enough always in the room with you.

A divided family.

A divided life.

A divided father.

My child deserves better than that.

So, with my sleeping baby wrapped up in my arms, I pick up my phone and make a call to give my baby what I never had.

Even if it breaks my heart to do it.

68

MATVEY

April's giving birth.

That's the first text I see when I turn my phone back on. Along with a sea of missed calls.

Suddenly, it's like the world is spinning. Giving birth? No, that can't be—she was supposed to be induced. She was supposed to…

Idiot, I kick myself. *Did you really think it would be that simple? That having a child would be so neat and easy?*

I'm the biggest fucking moron to ever walk the earth. Of course things wouldn't be that simple; of course they wouldn't follow a goddamn script, especially with a child in the mix.

Some father I'm shaping up to be.

The rest of the texts are more of the same.

Her water broke. She's being rushed to the hospital.

She insisted on a cab. I wasn't sure you'd approve, but then again, you did take all the cars.

Matvey, pick up. She's in labor right now.

Pick up, goddammit.

And then, the last text:

I'm coming there.

"I see your phone isn't broken after all," Grisha quips, appearing at my side with uncanny timing.

I'm flooded with shame—with rage. At the world, but more specifically at the man in front of me. Why didn't he come sooner? Why didn't he send for me? Why didn't he call Yuri if it was so fucking important?!

But I know I'm just making excuses.

Because, most of all, I'm angry at myself.

Once again, I didn't answer. April needed me—*and I didn't fucking answer.*

"Take me to her," I bark. "Now."

As we move towards the parking lot, someone yanks me by the arm. "Where ya going, son?"

"Let go, Vlad."

"Nonsense," my shitfaced father-in-law spits. His breath smells like something crawled into his mouth and died horribly. It takes all my willpower not to vomit. "It's yer wedding, son."

"I'm wed. Wedding's over."

"The guests are going to talk."

"Then let them."

"Son—"

"Call me 'son' one more time," I snarl in his face. "See what fucking happens."

Hands up in defeat, Vlad lets go of me.

"That wasn't wise," Grisha comments dryly. "Vlad's a spiteful man. And he's got a long memory."

"Ask me if I give a fuck," I bite out. *"Blyat'*, where the hell is my brother?"

All the way to the car, I keep trying to call him, but it goes straight to voicemail. *Serves you right*, the bitter part of me snarks.

"Can we really afford to wait for him?" Grisha frowns.

I don't appreciate how clear he's making his disapproval. Once this thing is over, I'm gonna need to have a long, hard talk with him about insubordination and its consequences.

"No," I say. "Drive."

"Alright."

"Like the fucking wind, Grisha."

"Yes, *pakhan.*"

All the way there, a single thought keeps me from punching the car door off its hinges: *I'm going to meet my child.*

When I get to the hospital, I don't stop to look where I'm

going. I don't stop as the nurses yell at me, as security tries to stop me from going up to the maternity ward.

I only stop to roar one question.

"Where is April Flowers?!"

Thankfully, Dr. Allan recognizes me. "Nice of you to show up at last, Mr. Groza."

I have no bandwidth for her sarcasm, for the contempt I can so clearly hear in her words. A year ago, I would've made her pay for the insolence.

Now, I only care about one thing.

"Show me where she is."

As we walk towards her room, a thousand things flood my mind. A thousand things I want to say to her.

I'm sorry.

I should've been here.

I don't love Petra. I never have.

I don't want Petra. I never have.

I don't want anyone else—I meant it then, and I mean it now. It's you I want. It's you I—

"What...?"

Dr. Allan's voice shakes me out of my head. I look up to the source of her confusion—

And I see it.

April's bed: empty.

"She signed herself out," Dr. Allan murmurs, staring dumbly at the discharge papers on the bedside table. "Who the hell let my patient sign herself out?!" Residents scatter like flies at the sound of her screech.

But I barely see any of that.

All I can see is the blood on the sheets.

"Where is she?" I mutter. Then, louder: "Where is *my child*?!"

But one look at Dr. Allan's face tells me all I need to know.

April's gone—and my child is gone, too.

I rush to the penthouse without a second thought.

Maybe she went home, I tell myself as I mash the elevator buttons into a pulp. *Maybe she didn't want to be among strangers. Maybe—*

When I throw the door open, my heart sinks.

April's stuff is gone. Not everything—but a few changes of clothes, toiletries, the essentials. Our child's belongings.

Everything she'd need to run.

Missing clothes, missing items. A missing partner, a missing child.

It's my worst nightmare and I didn't even know it. And now, I'm living it.

"Fuck," I snarl, clenching my fists until my knuckles are see-through. "Fuck, fuck, *fuck*!"

Then I see the envelope on the table.

A letter.

A letter from April.

And it's addressed to me.

With shaking hands, I tear the envelope open and start to read.

Dear Matvey,

I've been staring at this page for five minutes, trying to figure out what to write. I figured I owed it to you to at least say goodbye. To explain why I'm saying it.

But in the end, all I can say is: I'm sorry.

I'm sorry I wasn't good enough for you. I'm sorry that what we had wasn't good enough. That it wasn't as strong for you as it was for me.

I'm sorry I couldn't give you what you wanted.

"*Blyat'*," I swear out loud.

She couldn't give me what I wanted? Is that what she thinks?

"No," I mutter into the silence. "You didn't give me what I wanted. You gave me more. You gave me—"

What I needed.

Grinding my teeth into dust, I keep reading.

I hope you'll be happy with Petra. I know you will. I've seen you at your best, Matvey: how kind, warm, and amazing you can be. I've seen her at her best, too. (I think.) I'm still not sure how much of it was an act, but I'm choosing to believe that part was genuine: the best of both of you.

I hope you'll give each other that.

And I hope you'll give it to your child, too.

There is no child, I want to scream. *The only child I have is the child I have with* you.

But even if I did, April couldn't hear me. I could shout it from the rooftops and still, April wouldn't hear me.

So I curse myself and keep reading.

But you see, I have a child, too. A child who's going to need lots of love to brave this world.

And they'll need to feel accepted.

You have no idea how much this is tearing me apart, Matvey. Even as I write, I keep hoping you'll come in through that door. That you'll see your child and fall in love just like I did.

But you're not coming.

You weren't there for the birth, either. You weren't there when our baby needed you most—when I needed you most. And I'm afraid that, as time passes, you'll barely be there at all.

I don't want my kid to grow up like that, Matvey. I've had enough of it for a lifetime. Being second choice, being second-best... you have no idea how painful it can be. How badly it can scar you.

Our baby deserves better than that. Better than a divided heart.

So now, I'm going to do the hardest thing I've ever done. The hardest thing any mother can do, really.

I'm going to do what's best for my daughter.

I'm going to leave, and I'm not going to come back.

Goodbye,

April

Unblinking, I stare at the letter in my hands. I can't tell for how long—seconds, minutes, hours. It could be days for all I know.

She was wrong about at least one thing, though: My heart isn't "divided."

It's shattered.

"FUCKING HELL!"

I punch the table so hard it breaks.

But the pain isn't enough to ground me. Not the splinters in my hand, not the ache of the scene in front of me: the table where we ate so many family dinners, now lying in pieces at my feet. "I fucked up," I rasp to the only person I haven't alienated yet: myself. "I fucked it all up."

I'm furious. I'm heartbroken. I'm a wounded animal and a raging monster, howling out of grief and anger both.

Because April is gone.

And now, my daughter is gone, too.

TO BE CONTINUED

Matvey and April's story continues in Book 2 of the Groza Bratva Duet, *CASHMERE RUIN*.

ALSO BY NICOLE FOX

Kuznetsov Bratva

Emerald Malice

Emerald Vices

Novikov Bratva

Ivory Ashes

Ivory Oath

Egorov Bratva

Tangled Innocence

Tangled Decadence

Zakrevsky Bratva

Requiem of Sin

Sonata of Lies

Rhapsody of Pain

Bugrov Bratva

Midnight Purgatory

Midnight Sanctuary

Oryolov Bratva

Cruel Paradise

Cruel Promise

Pushkin Bratva

Cognac Villain

Cognac Vixen

Viktorov Bratva

Whiskey Poison

Whiskey Pain

Orlov Bratva

Champagne Venom

Champagne Wrath

Uvarov Bratva

Sapphire Scars

Sapphire Tears

Vlasov Bratva

Arrogant Monster

Arrogant Mistake

Zhukova Bratva

Tarnished Tyrant

Tarnished Queen

Stepanov Bratva

Satin Sinner

Satin Princess

Makarova Bratva

Shattered Altar

Shattered Cradle

Solovev Bratva

Ravaged Crown

Ravaged Throne

Vorobev Bratva

Velvet Devil

Velvet Angel

Romanoff Bratva

Immaculate Deception

Immaculate Corruption

Kovalyov Bratva

Gilded Cage

Gilded Tears

Jaded Soul

Jaded Devil

Ripped Veil

Ripped Lace

Mazzeo Mafia Duet

Liar's Lullaby (Book 1)

Sinner's Lullaby (Book 2)

Bratva Crime Syndicate

Can be read in any order!

Lies He Told Me

Scars He Gave Me

Sins He Taught Me

Belluci Mafia Trilogy

Corrupted Angel (Book 1)

Corrupted Queen (Book 2)

Corrupted Empire (Book 3)

De Maggio Mafia Duet

Devil in a Suit (Book 1)

Devil at the Altar (Book 2)

Kornilov Bratva Duet

Married to the Don (Book 1)

Til Death Do Us Part (Book 2)

Heirs to the Bratva Empire

Can be read in any order!

Kostya

Maksim

Andrei

Princes of Ravenlake Academy (Bully Romance)

Can be read as standalones!

Cruel Prep

Cruel Academy

Cruel Elite

Tsezar Bratva

Nightfall (Book 1)

Daybreak (Book 2)

Russian Crime Brotherhood

Can be read in any order!

Owned by the Mob Boss

Unprotected with the Mob Boss

Knocked Up by the Mob Boss

Sold to the Mob Boss

Stolen by the Mob Boss

Trapped with the Mob Boss

Volkov Bratva

Broken Vows (Book 1)

Broken Hope (Book 2)

Broken Sins *(standalone)*

Other Standalones

Vin: A Mafia Romance

Box Sets

Bratva Mob Bosses (Russian Crime Brotherhood Books 1-6)

Tsezar Bratva (Tsezar Bratva Duet Books 1-2)

Heirs to the Bratva Empire

The Mafia Dons Collection

The Don's Corruption